# BREATHE
# YOUR
# LAST

## BOOKS BY LISA REGAN

# BREATHE YOUR LAST

## LISA REGAN

bookouture

Published by Bookouture in 2020

An imprint of Storyfire Ltd.
Carmelite House
50 Victoria Embankment
London EC4Y 0DZ

www.bookouture.com

ISBN: 978-1-80019-136-5
eBook ISBN: 978-1-80019-1-358

*For Maureen Downey, who has made my life infinitely better.*

# PROLOGUE

I don't always get to see their faces when they breathe their last breath. I wonder, when their time comes, do they know they're about to die? Do they realize what's happened? Are they afraid? Do any of them think about me? Do any of them suspect me? It's kind of a letdown, never getting to be there in those final moments, but what comes after more than makes up for it. The satisfying part isn't in the killing. It's in the aftermath. The real thrill is in watching families and friends stumble around in a haze of grief and shock, as if they really expected nothing bad to happen to them in their lives. I've seen it all, from tear-filled eyes to full-blown breakdowns. My favorite mourners are the ones who are so overcome with their loss that they can't even stand under the weight of it. Their bodies fail them. They collapse and shake, sob and howl. There is one thing common among all mourners, however. Each and every one of them is plagued with this universal question:

What happened?

Sometimes, I want to look right into their eyes and say, "They got what they deserved, that's what happened."

But I can't. If they knew what I'd done, I'd probably go to prison. If I went to prison, I wouldn't be able to play my little game.

Where would be the fun in that?

# CHAPTER ONE

The city of Denton flashed past as Josie drove her friend Misty and Misty's four-year-old son, Harris, into the mountains on the northern side of the city. Sunlight filtered through the canopy of trees over the winding mountain road, making the Denton Police Department polo shirt she wore appear more hot pink than salmon-colored. The shirt—all of her work shirts—used to be white. Under her breath, she cursed her younger brother, Patrick, a sophomore at Denton University. The campus was close enough to Josie's house that he often dropped by to eat or do his laundry.

Misty said, "What was that?"

"Nothing," Josie muttered.

"You're still upset about the shirt?" Misty said.

Josie glanced down at herself again, resisting the urge to curse out loud. "Not just this shirt," she explained. "All my work shirts. I'm going to have to buy new ones!"

Misty reached for the dash and toggled the knob for the air conditioner, turning it up. The weather was still hot for September, even early in the morning, and Josie's Ford Escape wasn't cooling down as quickly as Misty would have liked, evidently. She said, "What was he washing?"

"Every item of clothing he owns," Josie answered, "including a bright red T-shirt his boss just gave him to wear to work. He washed it separately and forgot it was in there."

"Is he working on campus?"

"Yeah, he got a job with the university's towel service—"

"Towel service?"

"Yeah," Josie said. "Basically he is assigned to one of the athletics buildings to monitor towel use. He gives out clean towels, collects dirty ones, and makes sure no one takes any towels out of the building with them. Anyway, they just started wearing red T-shirts. He left in a hurry last night to go see his girlfriend and left it in the washer. Then when I washed my work shirts for the week, this happened."

She motioned to her chest.

Misty eyed the shirt. "You didn't check the washer before you put your own stuff in to make sure it was empty?"

Josie shot her a glare fierce enough to end the conversation. Misty turned away to look out the passenger's side window but not before Josie saw the small grin on her lips. Josie thought about the offending shirt, balled up into a plastic bag in the back of the car. Patrick had called her just before she left to pick up Misty and Harris and asked if she could bring it to him on her way to the station. He was due at work by eight thirty. Josie would be cutting it close, but she fully intended to lecture him on the importance of not leaving any more bleeding garments in her washer. Showing up in her ruined police shirt would surely drive the point home. In the meantime, she had texted her colleague on the police force, Detective Gretchen Palmer, and asked her to bring one of her extra shirts for Josie to borrow. It would be a little big, but at least it wouldn't be faded flamingo pink.

Josie's foot pressed harder onto the gas pedal. The further up the mountain they got, the more discomfort tugged at her, causing a strange feeling in the pit of her stomach.

"I don't like this," she told Misty, changing the subject. "This place is too far out of town. What if there's an emergency? It would take first responders at least ten minutes to get out here, probably longer."

Misty rolled her eyes. "Josie, this school has the best Pre-K program in the entire city. I researched this."

"What kind of 'mergency?" Harris asked from his booster seat in the back. Josie glanced in the rearview mirror and smiled at him. He grinned right back at her and she was struck dumb by his resemblance to her late husband, Ray Quinn, with his dimples and his spiked blond hair. After Josie and Ray had separated, Ray started dating Misty. Harris had been born after Ray's death and, in spite of the initial tension between the two women, their love of Ray's only son had united them in a friendship that Josie now treasured.

"Like the kinds we talked about, remember?" she told Harris.

Misty blew out a breath, her blonde bangs flying up and then landing neatly on her forehead. "Please don't start with this again."

Harris said, "Like what to do in a fire?"

"Yes," Josie said. "Exactly. What do you do in a fire?"

"If I catch on fire, I stop, drop, and roll like a roly-poly bug, only a crazy one cause I want the fire to go out," Harris said.

"Right! What else? What if you're in the classroom and there's a fire?"

Misty said, "Josie, seriously. I want him to have a normal Pre-K experience."

Josie frowned at her. "And I want him to be prepared for anything that might happen."

"Did you go to Pre-K?"

"No. Did you?"

"Well, no, but how many fires are there at Pre-K facilities in this city each year?"

Josie stayed quiet, chewing the inside of her lip. None, that was how many. She knew because she'd looked it up. She'd also talked to the city's fire chief. As a detective with the city's police department she had access to more information than the average citizen.

Harris said, "First thing is, I have to find all the exits when we get there."

"That's right," Josie encouraged. "Now what if you're in the classroom and a stranger comes in and you think that stranger might hurt someone? What do you do?"

"Josie!"

"I go to the closest door and get out and I press my alarm and then you come with Uncle Noah and make the bad stranger go to jail."

Noah Fraley was Josie's live-in boyfriend and a lieutenant with the Denton PD. His polo shirts had escaped the pink massacre.

Harris held up one of his feet and shook it, the shoelaces on his sneaker wiggling. A small, gray device about the size of a quarter but in the shape of a guitar pick had been clipped to one of the grommets. Josie couldn't see it from her quick glance in the rearview mirror, but she knew the tiny orange button was tucked away along one side of the device. It was called a Geobit. It was a GPS tracker for children. Josie had researched about a half dozen of them when Misty told her she was enrolling Harris in school, but Geobit was the only one with an alarm that alerted Josie's phone directly should Harris need to use it.

"Not all strangers are bad, you know," Misty said.

"He knows that," Josie scoffed. "I talked to him about strangers."

"I know. I know you also talked to him about sex offenders and bad secrets and bad touch/good touch. I know you talked to him about abductions, and I also know that you showed him how to get into the trunk of a car to disable and knock out a taillight so he can slip his hand out and signal someone."

"That was cool!" Harris exclaimed. "Can we do that again?"

"No," Misty said.

"It's always good to practice," Josie said at the same time.

"Josie," Misty scolded again.

Josie opened her mouth to apologize but then clamped it shut. She wouldn't apologize for overreacting because she wasn't sorry. When Harris was a baby, he'd been abducted. They'd been lucky to get him back alive. He had nearly died. Between that and all the terrible things that Josie saw in her work as a detective, it was hard not to be paranoid.

# CHAPTER TWO

I was exhausted, even by Monday-morning standards. It had been a long night waiting for her, putting my plan in place, and making sure to leave no trace of myself. I considered staying home and sleeping the day away, but I knew that wasn't smart. I couldn't call attention to myself in any way. Just like all the other times, everything had to appear perfectly normal. This time, that meant going on almost no sleep, showing up when and where I was supposed to, and putting a smile on my face. Besides, I wouldn't really know if my plan had worked until much later. I wouldn't be there when she took her last breath. I rarely was. I had to be patient.

It would be worth it. I imagined the phone call, visualized exactly how I would react, how I would modulate my voice so that people would think I was both shocked and horrified. This one would make the local news for sure. It might even go national, I thought with glee. Of course, there would be a great outpouring of sympathy for her. Everyone thought she was so perfect, which was exactly why she had to die. I knew it was going to annoy me in the coming weeks having to hear about her shocking death again and again—in the news and pretty much anywhere I went because people were going to call her things like "special" and "amazing," and her death would be touted as a "tragic loss." But then the news stories would fade, and I wouldn't have to hear about her supposed greatness any longer. No one should be so universally adored.

She wasn't the only person who was special or amazing. With her around, it was like no one else existed. I couldn't take it anymore. Especially since I knew how she lied. She hid things from everyone.

Vile things. Secrets that made her just as contemptible as anyone else. So I did what I did, and now I waited for the news to hit. I checked my phone. No news yet, but my plan was underway. The magnificent wave of grief was about to hit Denton in all of its glory.

It was only a matter of time.

# CHAPTER THREE

They pulled into the parking lot of Tiny Tykes Gardens Pre-K and Daycare Center. It was an old brick two-story home surrounded by roughly four acres of beautifully kept land. An asphalt parking lot sat in front of the building. To the right, Josie could see a gated playground. To the left was a large garden area with tables, chairs, and a small greenhouse in the center. Just like Misty, Josie had researched the place the moment she heard that Misty was thinking of sending Harris there. She, too, had been impressed by all the different programs they offered, including gardening, raising baby chicks, keeping a small koi pond, and generally learning how the environment worked. Josie hadn't learned so much about the environment in sixteen years of formal schooling. She knew without having to look that behind the large building were more green areas including a small outdoor theater where the children could perform plays for each other and their parents, and a mini petting zoo that was maintained in conjunction with the Denton City Wildlife Rescue Association so that the children could learn about animals.

Josie also knew that the Tiny Tykes Gardens Pre-K and Daycare Center was in full compliance with their legal obligation to conduct background checks on their employees, so she knew none had criminal records. Also, no known sex offenders lived within ten miles of the place. Still, that did little to quell her uneasiness as Harris hopped out of the Escape and hoisted his green dinosaur backpack onto his shoulders. Josie took one of his hands and Misty took the other. He had a nervous habit, just like his father had, of squeezing her hand in rhythmic fashion when he was feeling anxious. If she hadn't been holding his hand, she knew he would have been clenching and unclenching his little fist. Ray had done the same as long as she'd known him and now, even though Harris had never met his father, he did it as well.

Josie felt the pulse of his gentle squeezes quicken as they walked up the ramp to the front door of the school together. She mustered a bright smile for him and said, "This is going to be fun."

He didn't answer. Inside the double doors, the lobby was brightly colored with decorations that mostly seemed to center around learning the alphabet and counting. A few cardboard cutouts of animals stood along the walls. Parents and their small children crowded into the center of the area. Josie looked around, noting that opposite the front doors were two more sets of doors, each one leading down a separate, well-lit hallway. To their left was a wide set of steps leading to the second floor. To their right was a long, wooden desk, presently empty, and behind that, two more doors.

Squeeze, squeeze, squeeze.

Misty said, "Honey, you're squeezing my hand."

Josie compressed and released Harris's hand back in a similar rhythm, and he smiled up at her. She knelt down and smoothed the straps of his backpack over his shoulders. "This is an adventure, remember? You're going to meet lots of new people and learn lots of new things."

Misty knelt as well, still holding his hand in hers. "You'll get to meet all the animals in the petting zoo. You were looking forward to that, remember?"

Another smile lit his face. "I really want to see the goat."

There was a commotion around them as a woman emerged from one of the doors behind the desk. She was in her forties, thick around the middle with an ample bosom, and dark brown hair pulled up into a bun on the back of her head. She wore a bright green T-shirt that said: *Tiny Tykes Are All Right*. She maneuvered through the crowd of parents and children until she was standing between the sets of doors leading down the hallways. She waved her arms like a flagger directing a plane to the gate. "Good morning, everyone," she called. "Please form two lines. Two lines."

Josie and Misty flanked Harris as they joined one of the lines. The woman introduced herself as Mrs. D. "My name is Eileen D'Angelo, but it's easier for the children if everyone just calls me Mrs. D. I'm the director here." Another woman emerged from the same doors Mrs. D had come from and took a seat behind the desk. Mrs. D pointed to her. "This is Miss K. She's the school secretary. Anything you need, either Miss K or I will be happy to help." Miss K looked a bit younger than her boss, but not by much. Josie put her in her early to mid-forties. Blonde hair, graying slightly at the roots, fell to her shoulders. She, too, was slightly overweight. Her T-shirt bore the same slogan as Mrs. D's, but hers was a pale blue. She gave the crowd a wave and a bright smile.

Mrs. D went on for several minutes while the restive children tapped their feet against the wooden floor, tugged on their parents' arms, and occasionally whined—the usual litany from children Harris's age: they were thirsty, they had to use the potty, they were hungry, they wanted to go home. For his part, Harris stood still and silent, observing.

Squeeze, squeeze, squeeze.

Finally, Mrs. D said, "It's time to go to your classrooms and meet your teachers. If you'll just follow me."

But when it came Harris's turn to pass through the doors into the hall, he froze. Misty and Josie tried to gently pull him forward, but he wasn't having it. Three other families waited behind them.

"I'm so sorry," Misty told them. She managed to tug Harris off to the side. She and Josie both knelt again and looked into his face. "Honey, what's wrong?"

"I don't want to go," he muttered.

Josie tried to keep her face neutral. She didn't want him to go either. Since his birth, he'd only ever been in the care of four people: his mother; his mother's best friend, Brittney; Josie; and his grandmother, Ray's mother. She couldn't imagine how scary it must be for him to one day just be thrown into a room full of strange children and left there with no trusted adults nearby. Josie's own heart gave a quick double tap as Harris clutched her hand, squeezing it again rhythmically.

Misty must have seen the look on Josie's face because she elbowed Josie in the ribs and grinned at Harris. "Who is the bravest boy I know?"

"Me?"

"Yes, you!" Misty replied. "You're also the smartest boy I know, with the biggest heart. You are going to make so many friends. It's going to be so much more fun than hanging around with us boring old adults all day."

He looked at Josie, who managed a nod of agreement.

A gentle hand closed over one of Harris's shoulders. They all looked up to see Miss K smiling down at him. "What's your name, young man?"

"Harris," he said, barely audible.

"I'm Miss K. It's good to meet you, Harris. Do you want to walk with me to the classrooms?"

He shook his head. Squeeze, squeeze.

Miss K smiled and lifted her hand. She walked behind Josie and Misty and leaned in between them so they could both hear her lowered voice. "If I can get him to go with me, you two can sneak out. He'll never know you're gone."

Josie stood quickly and turned on the woman, pulling Harris slightly off balance. His hand tightened around hers as he got his footing. "I'm sorry, Miss K, is it? We're not doing that."

"Josie," Misty said, straightening up and giving Josie a look that said, "Back down."

Josie worked to make her tone less snappy. "What I mean is that we don't believe in doing that sort of thing. All that teaches him is that the rug can be pulled out from under him at any moment. We told him we'd be here with him through every step, so if we suddenly disappear all he learns is that he can't trust us. Also, how is he not going to notice? He's four!"

"Josie!" Misty exclaimed, signaling that she had done a piss-poor job of keeping her tone in check.

"I'm sorry, Miss K," Misty said sweetly. "We appreciate your trying to help, and I know that works well for some children, but we prefer not to handle drop-off that way."

Miss K gave Josie the side-eye before smiling brightly at Misty. "Of course. That's all you had to say." Turning her gaze back to Josie, she frowned. "You're that detective, aren't you? The one who's always on the news. Or are you the other one? You've got a twin sister, right? She's a famous reporter?"

"Yes," Josie answered. "My sister, Trinity Payne, used to be a network anchor. She lives in New York City. I'm Detective Josie Quinn, Denton PD."

Miss K was unimpressed. Without a word to Josie, she moved around to address Harris once more, kneeling down so that she was face to face with him. "Harris, did you know that this is the first day of Pre-K for all the students in the whole school today?"

"No," he said, voice barely audible. Squeeze, squeeze.

"That's right," she said. "And guess what? All of them are kind of scared because they're going to be here with us and not with their families. You know what else?"

Again, he shook his head.

"It's okay to be scared."

Josie felt the vibration of her cell phone ringing in her back pocket and ignored it.

Harris didn't look convinced. Squeeze, squeeze, squeeze. He leaned in toward Josie, looked up at her, and whispered, "What if my belly hurts while I'm here?"

Josie said, "I think if your belly hurts, you could tell your teacher."

Miss K nodded. "That's right. Anything that goes wrong, you tell your teacher and she'll bring you out here to me and then you know what I'll do? I'll call your mom."

Misty said, "And I'll come right away."

Josie's phone buzzed again. With her free hand, she took it out and looked at the display. Patrick. Harris said, "That could be important. A police call. You should answer it."

"I will," Josie said. "As soon as I know you're okay here."

He gave her hand one last final squeeze and went over to Misty, looping his arms around her neck. "Can my mom go to the classroom to meet my teacher for a little bit?"

"Of course," said Miss K.

"And you, too?"

Miss K clapped her hands together, delighted. "I'd love to!"

Josie swiped *answer* as she watched the two women escort Harris down the hallway to one of the classrooms. "Patrick, I'll be there as soon as I can."

"Thanks," he said. "I'm going to be heading over to the pool soon. That's where they have me working this week. Do you know where that is?"

"Hold on," Josie replied.

In the car, she turned on the ignition and found a napkin and pen to take down the directions Patrick gave her to the campus natatorium. She hadn't been on the university campus in a few months, but it was labyrinthian, and it didn't help that new buildings were being added with regularity. "I just have to drop Misty off at home first," Josie told him.

As she hung up, Misty emerged from the Tiny Tykes building, striding toward Josie's vehicle with her head down. Her long blonde hair hung across her face. It wasn't until she got into the passenger's seat that Josie noticed she was weeping.

"Are you okay?" Josie asked.

Tears streamed down Misty's face. She took a big, gulping breath. "It's just that I can't believe he's so big. He's in school now. He's just growing right up. I've never left him this long before in the care of strangers. It's just really hard. I didn't think it would be this hard."

She reached over and took the napkin from Josie's hand. Before Josie could object, Misty blew her nose into it. When she saw that Josie was staring at her, she said, "Oh, shit. I'm sorry. Were you using this napkin?"

Josie managed a smile. "No."

"Was it clean?"

"Yes."

Josie put the vehicle in drive and pulled out of the parking lot, headed back toward the center of Denton. "Listen, Harris is a smart little boy," she told Misty. "You've done everything you possibly could to prepare him for this."

Misty scoffed and dabbed at her eyes with the crumpled napkin. "*You've* done everything to prepare him for this. I just spent the last three months telling him everything would be fine when I don't really know that for sure."

Josie reached over and touched Misty's shoulder. "Of course it's going to be fine. You'll see. Do you remember your first day of kindergarten?"

Misty shook her head.

"Of course not. Because it wasn't traumatic. The same will be true for Harris."

From her periphery, Josie saw Misty raise a brow. "You're just saying this because you gave him that alarm. That's why you're so calm."

Josie shrugged. "Well, it does help."

# CHAPTER FOUR

A few minutes later, Josie left Misty at her home in much better spirits. As she drove toward the campus, she used the voice commands in her car to call Patrick and get the directions again. Denton University was located high above most of the city, in one of its hillier regions. The city itself spanned twenty-five square miles. Nestled among several mountains, the center of Denton was set out in a grid pattern with a large park butting up against the edge of campus on one end of the city. A branch of the Susquehanna River snaked through the heart of it. Quieter and more private neighborhoods sprawled along the perimeter of the city's historic district, leading out to the winding mountain roads that stretched like spindly spider legs to neighboring towns.

The campus itself was a maze of large brick buildings, beautifully landscaped courtyards and walkways, and blacktop parking lots that were far too small to hold all the vehicles trying to park there at any given moment. Josie found the flat-roofed red-brick building that housed the pool, and after following a line of three other cars circling the lot in search of parking spots that did not exist, parked illegally on the pavement in front of the building. This was only going to take a minute.

She snatched the bag with Patrick's red shirt from the backseat and jogged to the front of the building, pushing through a set of glass double doors. In the spacious lobby, she was overwhelmed by the smell of chlorine. A security guard clad in a brown uniform sat behind a crescent-shaped desk. He was an older man with thinning gray hair and a wiry frame. Craning his neck, he looked through the doors behind her. "You can't park there, Miss."

Josie took out her police credentials and flashed them at the guard even though she was not there on police business. "I'm looking for Patrick Payne," she said. "He should be working here this morning."

Mollified, the guard hooked a thumb to his right. "Vending machines."

Josie turned her head to see Patrick feeding a dollar into a vending machine in a cubby just off the lobby that was filled with various snack and drink offerings. He punched some buttons on the machine and then thrust his hand into the return slot, pulling out a granola bar.

"Hey," he said as he turned toward her. "Thanks for coming. You have my shirt? I'm already late. Thank God no one got here before me."

Together, they walked toward a set of solid blue doors on the other side of the lobby desk. Josie handed him the bag. As Patrick turned his back to push one of the blue doors open, he kinked an eyebrow at her. "Did Denton PD change its department colors?"

Josie glared at him. Tugging at her collar, she said, "You left your red work shirt in my washer. All my shirts look like this now, Pat."

Laughing, Patrick pushed all the way through the door. Josie had no choice but to follow him. "It's not funny," she told him. "These are expensive!"

"I'm really sorry," he replied.

The college's indoor swimming pool, with its eight racing lanes, took up most of the cavernous space. Large windows ran along the upper walls around the pool. Sunlight streamed in, reflecting off the blue water and causing the air in the room to shimmer. Tile floors stretched around the edges of the pool, lined with benches. It was hot and humid, and Josie felt a sheen of moisture cling to her face almost immediately. Patrick turned in the direction of a hall that was marked with a sign that read: Men's Locker Room. Josie pulled up short, her eyes drawn to the water. She took two steps closer to the pool's edge and then panic blossomed in her chest.

"Pat," she cried.

The woman's body floated face down, dark hair fanned out like a halo around her head. Josie took in the details like the rapid-fire clicks of a camera shutter. The woman bobbed fifteen to twenty feet from the edge of the pool. Second lane from the right. White tank top, blue shorts, white tennis shoes. Josie commanded her legs to run, but it felt as if someone had flipped a switch, setting her body on slow motion. Everything in the room seemed to stop. The stillness of the water before her was jarring. Some frantic part of Josie's brain howled. Her feet reached the lip of the pool's edge. Air pushed into her lungs again. She screamed, "Get help!"

Then she dove into the water.

# CHAPTER FIVE

The water was shockingly warm. Submerged, Josie carved her way toward the woman as quickly as she could, some dimmed part of her mind flashing back to the floods that had devoured Denton five months earlier. At least now she didn't have to fight a current or worse, a surge. Within seconds, she was beside the woman. Fitting her hands into the woman's armpits, Josie turned her onto her back. Positioning herself so that she was cheek to cheek with the woman, Josie worked her way toward the pool's edge. As she reached the wall, hands thrust out, relieving Josie of her charge. She recognized the security guard from the lobby as he and Patrick laid the woman on her back.

Josie climbed from the water and clambered across the tile. The guard's fingers pressed into the woman's throat. Patrick checked one of her wrists. "No pulse," he said, and looked at the guard. "You get one?"

The guard shook his head.

"Move," Josie told him. "Call an ambulance, campus police, and Denton PD. Now."

He hefted himself up and jogged back out to the lobby. Josie pressed the heel of one of her hands to the center of the woman's chest and then covered it with her other hand. Keeping her arms straight, she pumped, counting off the compressions under her breath. Once she reached thirty, she moved to the woman's head, lifting her chin and checking inside her mouth for any obstructions. Then she sealed her mouth over the woman's cold lips and gave her a rescue breath, then another.

Patrick said, "I don't think you're bringing her back."

Josie glanced at him long enough to see the strain in his face. Beads of sweat lined his forehead. "Gotta try," Josie said, resuming her compressions.

She felt Patrick's eyes on her as she worked, her arms and shoulders burning with the effort. Compressions. Breaths. Compressions. Breaths. His voice was small when he said, "Josie, I think she's gone."

"Shut up," she told him and went back to compressions.

Breaths. Compressions. Breaths. Compressions.

She was thinking about the time she'd pulled a four-year-old boy out of a pool while she was on patrol. His little limbs had been purple. She and the officer who had trained her had worked on him for almost ten minutes before the ambulance came. Josie had been sure that the boy was gone, but then he took a breath. That was all she needed. A breath. A heartbeat.

*Come on,* she commanded the woman silently. *Breathe. Just breathe.*

Sweat poured off her face, raining down on the woman's inert form. Her pink polo shirt and khaki pants were glued to her skin. Every muscle in her body clenched and ached. Josie had no idea how many minutes had passed until a rush of cool air hit her and footsteps drummed over the tile. The dark blue of the city's EMT uniforms flashed in her periphery. She kept counting off her compressions as she looked up to see two emergency medical workers she knew well: Owen Likins and Sawyer Hayes.

Owen dropped down next to her, muscling her out of the way, and took over the compressions. Opposite them, Sawyer felt for a pulse. "Nothing," he told Owen, removing a bag valve mask and placing it over her mouth, squeezing it to drive air into her lungs. He looked at Josie and then up at Patrick. "How long were you doing compressions?"

Patrick said, "At least ten minutes."

Josie's arms felt jellylike as she slumped, letting her rear end hit the tile.

Sawyer said, "How long was she in the water?"

Patrick looked at Josie and then back to Sawyer. "We don't know. We just walked in and Josie saw her floating and jumped in."

Patrick took Josie's hand and pulled her upright, keeping one arm slung around her shoulders. They watched as Owen and Sawyer worked. Unzipping one of their bags, Sawyer took out a pair of trauma shears and began to cut through the woman's shirt and bra.

Owen said, "If you're using the AED, we gotta get her good and dry."

Sawyer nodded and turned to Patrick. "I need towels. A lot of towels."

"This way," Patrick told Josie. She jogged after him into the men's locker room. They each grabbed a handful of rolled white towels and brought them back to the poolside.

"Let's lift her out of this puddle," said Sawyer.

Josie, Patrick, and Sawyer quickly lifted the woman to a dry patch of tile while Owen continued to squeeze the bag valve mask. Sawyer dried off her chest and readied the portable Automated External Defibrillator. Fear squeezed Josie's heart. The air was sticky all around them. Perspiration poured down her face. She wondered at the safety of using the AED in such a humid environment, but Sawyer and Owen managed it without electrocuting themselves. They were, of course, pros at what they did. When that didn't work, Sawyer used a bone drill to inject epinephrine directly into the woman's shoulder, its squeal just like that of a power drill. The noise sent a jolt through Josie's body.

She felt a terrible sinking feeling in her stomach as she watched them try to revive the lifeless woman. Every minute that passed was like another nail in her coffin. *Breathe!* Came the silent shout in Josie's head. But after twenty more minutes of valiant efforts, Owen sat back on his haunches and wiped sweat from his brow. "You wanna call it?" he asked Sawyer.

Sawyer looked up and met Josie's eyes for a brief second. His short black hair was soaked and stuck up in spikes when he pushed a hand through it. He looked at his watch. "Time of death 9:12 a.m."

Owen stood. Addressing Josie, he said, "I'm sorry."

"So am I," Josie said.

Patrick gave her shoulder a squeeze. "We don't know how long she was in the water. It's possible that reviving her was never going to work."

"That's true," Sawyer said. He looked around them. The guard pushed through the doors, letting in a brief but welcome breeze. Following him was campus police chief, Hillary Hahlbeck and two of her officers. Then came Josie's colleague, Detective Finn Mettner. Mett had started his career on patrol in Denton and moved up to a detective position. Of the four officers in investigative roles, Mett was the youngest and least experienced, but he had already taken the lead on some of the city's toughest cases, and Josie had full confidence in him.

Chief Hahlbeck pulled up short when she reached them. Petite and compact with shoulder-length curly brown hair and pale blue eyes, Hillary had been hired by the university almost a year ago. She was at least fifteen years older than Josie, in her late forties, and had experience working for a large police department elsewhere in the state. "Oh lord," she said in a regretful tone as she stared down at the woman on the tile. "This is not good. Not good at all."

Josie took a good look at the drowned girl's unlined face for the first time. Her olive skin had taken on a sallow hue, and her brown eyes were glassy, sightless orbs. She was obviously young, likely one of the university students, and she looked familiar, although Josie couldn't place her.

Mettner had his phone out and Josie knew that his note-taking app was open and ready to go. "What happened?" he asked, joining them.

Josie said, "I met Pat here because I had one of his work shirts. We walked in from the lobby. I saw her floating in the water."

Patrick said, "Josie jumped in, got her out, and did CPR until the paramedics got here."

Mett raised a brow and pointed a finger at Josie's shirt. "Is your shirt pink? Is that from blood?"

Josie pulled at the collar of the soaked shirt. Her sopping wet clothes hung heavy on her exhausted limbs. "No. No blood. This is from a laundry incident."

Mettner gave her a raised brow and then began tapping away at his phone. "No blood," he muttered to himself.

Hillary looked to the security guard. "Gerry?"

Josie turned to see that the guard's pale skin was flushed pink and his brown eyes were watery, broken blood vessels snaking through the whites of his eyes.

He was crying.

"Gerry," Hillary repeated, her tone firmer.

Gerry wiped at his eyes with the knuckles of his right hand. "That's Nysa," he choked out.

Hillary said, "I know who it is, Gerry. I recognize her from TV. What time did she get here?"

Immediately, Josie realized where she'd seen the dead woman before. Over the weekend, the local news station had run a story on Denton University's swim team. They had highlighted two sophomores, one of whom was Nysa Somers. She'd been touted as the best swimmer on the team and the recipient of a large scholarship awarded by a very rich Denton University alumnus. Josie remembered the videos of her swimming, her strong, lithe limbs cutting the water effortlessly. At the end, the video had cut to her standing beside the pool with several other teammates, a red swim cap covering her long brown locks. Her head was thrown back in laughter. The image came back to Josie now, in stark contrast to the corpse at her feet. Sadness floated up from deep within her, but she pushed it back down, trying to focus on the scene at hand. They still didn't know if this was some kind of horrific accident or a crime. Josie needed more information.

Patrick said, "I saw her on TV."

"I—I can't believe this," Gerry stammered. "I've been here twenty-seven years and I've never had anything like this happen."

Mettner said, "Gerry? You work in the lobby?"

Gerry nodded. From a breast pocket he produced a tissue which he pressed against one eye and then the other.

Mettner said, "All students enter through the lobby?"

"Yes," Gerry said. "That's the only way they can get in. There's two doors at the back of the building but only campus staff can get into those, with their key cards." His gaze drifted back toward Nysa. "Jesus. I had no idea. She was in here alone. She comes almost every day to swim. I had no reason to think—I should have checked, I…"

Hillary said, "Gerry, it's okay. You did your job."

"Did I? That girl is dead, and I don't even know what happened."

Josie wondered how close he had been to Nysa for her death to affect him so much. Or was he simply more sensitive to tragedy than some? Josie had seen countless reactions to sudden, tragic death from people with and without personal connections to the deceased. The reactions ranged from complete stoicism to hysteria. She looked at Mettner, silently communicating her question. He tapped away on his phone, likely making a note to investigate the connection between the guard and Nysa Somers. To Gerry, she said, "Did you see Nysa this morning when she came in?"

"Of course. That's my job. She was here earlier than usual but yes, she came in the front door. She said good morning to me, smiled, and went into the pool area."

Josie said, "What time was that?"

"Around six. I usually get here around five forty-five and then open the doors at six, even though on Mondays no one comes in that early. Nysa came in right after I unlocked the doors. Usually she comes in at eight."

Josie asked, "There wasn't anyone with her?"

"No."

Josie looked at Nysa's body again, her eyes moving from the white tennis shoes heavy on her feet to the white tank top and lacy pink bra underneath that Owen and Sawyer had carefully pulled back over her torso to cover her nakedness. "Was she carrying anything?"

Gerry's hand froze, tissue inches from his face. "What?"

"Did she have a bag with her? Swim bag? Purse? Backpack, maybe?"

"I don't—I don't remember. I don't know. I don't think so."

Mettner said, "Did you see anyone outside with her before she came in?"

"No. I can check the footage to make sure."

"Footage?" Josie asked hopefully.

Gerry looked around the perimeter of the room. "We've got CCTV cameras in the lobby and on the exterior of the building."

Disappointment stabbed at Josie. "But not in here? In the pool area?"

"I'm sorry, no," Gerry answered. "They tried a couple of times but with the humidity, they had problems. Cameras kept breaking. New ones are supposed to be installed next month."

Which didn't help them now, Josie thought.

Hillary said, "They'll want to see any footage we've got, Gerry. Probably need copies, too."

Josie nodded. To Gerry, she said, "Did Nysa seem like her normal self? Or did she seem different?"

"No, not different," Gerry answered. "She seemed the same as always. Maybe a little distracted. Sometimes she chats with me, and sometimes she just goes right in to swim. Today she just went inside. I figured she was focused on getting her swim in before her classes."

Josie asked, "Did anyone come in after her?"

"No. It was just her till you two showed up. Like I said, Monday mornings are really slow."

"So she was alone in this area?" Mettner clarified.

"Yes."

"No one else was here working or doing anything else in the building?" Josie asked. "The locker rooms, the back of the building?"

"No. Just me." He pointed to Patrick, still standing next to Josie. "Until he got here, but he went right to the vending machines. Then you showed up."

Mettner said, "You didn't hear anything after Nysa came in here? From the pool area?"

"No. Nothing." He pressed a palm down on the top of his head. "I keep going over it in my mind, wondering if I missed something. The doors were closed but even with the doors closed, sometimes I can hear the kids hollering to one another. I keep wondering if she screamed. Did she scream? Did I not hear her? But why would she scream? She's the best swimmer on the university team. She wouldn't need saving from the water. But maybe something happened, and she did. My wife always says that drowning is silent. I don't know what happened. I don't know what to think. I—"

Tears leaked from the corners of his eyes. Hillary tutted. "Gerry, I know you're upset but try to pull yourself together."

"It's fine," Josie said quickly. She put a hand on his shoulder.

"Thank you," he muttered.

"I know this is very upsetting, Gerry," Josie said. "You're doing great. Do you think you could pull up that footage for us now?"

"Oh yes," he said. "All the footage is in a room at the back of the building. I'll get it for you."

Hillary nodded at one of her uniformed officers who shepherded Gerry toward the back of the room and through a set of unmarked doors. Gerry used his key card to open the door. Josie could see a cinder block hallway beyond it.

Sawyer cleared his throat. "What's the plan?"

Josie looked at Mettner. "Call the ERT and Dr. Feist," she said, referring to Denton Police Department's Evidence Response Team and the medical examiner. "Get a patrol unit up here to have this place sealed off. One officer at the front door and one at the pool doors. No one comes in or out until further notice."

Mettner nodded and turned away from her, swiping at his phone and pressing it to his ear. Patrick sat down on a nearby bench. Everyone else stared at Josie, as though waiting for instructions. She was about to ask Chief Hahlbeck to station one of her officers at the door to the pool when a door between the pool and the lobby whooshed open. A female voice drifted ahead of its owner. "…nobody here. What the hell is going on?"

Josie pegged her for a student, given her shorts and oversized hooded sweatshirt. Her dark hair was pulled back into a ponytail. It swung from side to side as she strode toward them. As she drew closer, Josie saw a smattering of freckles across her face. Big brown eyes widened in shock as they landed on Nysa's form.

"Miss," said Chief Hahlbeck, blocking her way.

But the woman pushed the Chief aside and ran toward the body. "Nysa!" she cried.

Josie thrust her arms out and caught her before she could reach the body. Momentum sent the two of them into a half-twirl. Josie kept one hand clamped over the woman's upper arm as she tried to steer her back toward the exit. "I'm sorry, miss. You can't be here right now."

She contorted her body, trying to look back at her friend as Josie pushed her toward the door. "Nysa! That's Nysa, isn't it? Oh my God. What happened? What the hell happened?"

# CHAPTER SIX

Josie guided the young woman into the lobby. The cool air was a balm to her soaked and sweaty body. Steering the woman toward the benches lining one of the lobby walls, Josie told her, "I'm very sorry, miss. You'll have to wait out here."

Beneath her fingers, Josie could feel the woman's arm muscles tense. She sucked in a deep breath and on the exhale, said, "That was Nysa, wasn't it? Oh my God. Is she dead?"

Josie said, "Would you like to sit down?"

"I can't. I can't sit right now. What happened?"

Josie let go of her arm and immediately she hugged herself. Tears glistened in her eyes.

"What's your name?" Josie asked her.

"Christine. Christine Trostle. I'm Nysa's roommate. She didn't come home last night so I thought maybe she'd be here. Oh my God, is she dead?"

Christine's burgeoning hysteria was palpable. Josie kept her voice calm and even. "We haven't made a positive ID yet, but yes, we believe that the woman you saw inside is Nysa Somers, and I'm extremely sorry to tell you that she passed away. She was found in the pool. We tried CPR, but we were unable to revive her."

A small line appeared in the center of Christine's forehead. "CPR? For what? Did she, like, have a heart attack or something, while she was swimming?"

Josie thought about what they knew. The university's star swimmer had been found floating face down in the pool. No bag, no bathing suit beneath her clothes. She'd still had her shoes on when Josie jumped in to get her. Had she come to swim at all?

"We don't know," Josie told her. "I'm afraid we don't know much of anything at this point. My name is Detective Josie Quinn with the Denton Police Department. My team will be investigating her death. The medical examiner is on her way, but it may be days or even weeks before we have a definitive answer. What we really need right now is as much information as we can get about Nysa. You said you were roommates. How long have you known Nysa?"

Christine balled her fists inside her sleeves and used one of them to wipe at her tears. She looked around the room as if seeing it for the first time. Josie knew her brain was trying desperately to process what she had just seen and been told.

"Christine?" Josie said softly.

"Since freshman year," she said, swallowing.

"You're both sophomores now?"

Christine nodded and used her sleeve to dab at more tears. "Oh my God," she breathed. "This can't be happening."

Josie tried to keep her focused on answering questions. "Were you roommates during your freshman year?"

"Yes. We were in the dorms. We got to be really close, so when it was time to get housing for this year, we decided to rent a student apartment together."

"Where are you from?" Josie asked.

"Vermont."

"Is Nysa also from Vermont?"

Christine shook her head. Her eyes wandered upward to the ceiling. "No. New Jersey."

"I understand that Nysa was on the swim team. Are you on the team as well?"

Another shake of her head. "No. No way. I'm a terrible swimmer. Jesus. I can't believe this." One of her hands snaked out of its sleeve, reached up, and tugged hard at her ponytail. Finally, she met Josie's eyes. "You said she was in the pool. Now she's dead. Did she drown?" Before Josie could answer, Christine asked, "How in the hell does Denton University's best swimmer drown alone in a pool?"

"We're going to find out what happened," Josie assured her. "Christine, you said Nysa didn't come home last night, is that right?"

"Yeah. I was worried."

"She didn't come home from where?" Josie asked.

"The library. We had dinner in the commons last night and then I went back to our apartment, and she went to the library."

"What time was that?" Josie asked.

"Around six, six thirty. Nysa had a paper due in one of her English classes and things can get pretty loud over in our area of student housing, even on a Sunday, so she wanted the quiet."

"Did she walk? Or drive?"

"She walked," Christine said. "Her car is still outside our place."

"She walked from the commons to the library around six, six thirty and you didn't see her after that?" Josie clarified. "Are you sure she didn't come back to your apartment? Maybe after you were asleep?"

Christine shook her head. "I'm sure. I texted her at nine—the library is open till nine thirty—and she said she was finishing up. Then I was doing some reading for my history class, and I noticed it was eleven and she hadn't come back or contacted me so I texted her again." Christine reached into her sweatshirt pocket and took out her cell phone. She punched in a passcode and scrolled through a few screens. Then she turned the display toward Josie so she could read the text exchange between the two women.

At 11:03 p.m. Christine had texted: *where r u? everything ok?*

At 11:04 p.m. Nysa had responded: *Everything's good. Met up with a friend on the way back from library. Don't wait up.*

Then at 11:06 p.m. Christine wrote: *Friend? What friend???*

There was no response after that.

"I waited up until twelve thirty and then I fell asleep. I got up at seven fifteen because I've got a class at eight, but she wasn't home. I looked in her room, but I couldn't tell if she had been home or not 'cause her bed was a mess. She never makes it. Her toothbrush was dry as a bone though, which made me think she didn't come home. I called her phone, but it went right to voicemail." She swiped on her phone a few more times and then showed the display to Josie again. This time there was a call log showing that Christine had called Nysa three times between seven sixteen that morning and eight thirty. "I called a few times. Nothing. I didn't know what to do, so after my class I thought I'd check here. I mean, Nysa is in the water every chance she gets. If she's not home or in class, she's here. I figured that if she wasn't here, maybe some of her teammates would be. Maybe someone saw her. So I walked over here. Jesus. She's really gone?" Her voice went up two octaves. "I just don't understand. How can she be dead? This makes no sense."

"Do you have any idea who she might have met up with last night?" Josie prodded. "Who the friend was that she referred to?"

"No. I don't know. I just figured it was someone on the swim team. Those people are tight, you know? They hang out a lot."

Josie made a mental note that the swim team members would have to be interviewed. She said, "Christine, when you last saw Nysa, was she carrying a purse or a bag of any kind?"

"Her backpack," Christine said.

The lobby footage would show whether or not she still had her backpack when she walked into the pool building. They'd also need to check the locker rooms. That backpack and her phone had to be somewhere.

Josie continued with her questions. "Was Nysa dating anyone?"

"No. She said she didn't have time for it."

"Was she seeing anyone casually?" Josie asked.

"You mean, was she hooking up with anyone? I think that she might have been, but I'm really not sure."

"What makes you think she might have been?"

"Just, like, she would be late sometimes coming back from practice or class and she was all flushed, and—I don't know. Like, you know how someone looks when you walk in on them doing something they don't want you to see? She would look like that."

"Did you ever ask her about it?"

"Not directly. I asked her where she was or what was going on sometimes, but she always said she'd been out for a run or stayed late to ask a teacher for help or something like that."

"You didn't press the issue?" Josie asked.

"No. I'm not her mom. She's an adult. She can do what she wants. We live together and we're friends, but she doesn't have to tell me everything."

"If she was seeing someone but didn't want to talk about it," Josie said, "do you have any idea who it might have been?"

"None."

"Someone on the swim team, maybe?"

"I guess, but I don't know why she wouldn't just tell me that. It's not a big deal."

The cool air that was so wonderful a few moments earlier now sent a chill through Josie's limbs. "Was there anyone she seemed particularly interested in or someone who was interested in her, that you know of?"

Christine hugged herself again and started shifting her weight from one foot to the other. "I don't know. She always said she only had time for school and swimming and that dating was a waste. Maybe, after saying all that stuff all the time, she was embarrassed to admit that she was seeing someone and that's why she wouldn't tell me." Christine said this last part almost to herself.

Josie coaxed, "What about anyone who was interested in her?"

"Oh, I guess Hudson. He's on the swim team. He had a big crush on her last year, but Nysa shot him down. This year they're just really competitive with each other, like trying to outdo each other and stuff. He was part of the special they did on the news over the weekend. They're, like, the two best swimmers or whatever. They were supposed to just do the piece on Nysa 'cause she won the big scholarship, but Hudson's mom had a shitfit that they didn't include him, so he was on there too. That was kind of awkward. Anyway, he's a nice guy, and she liked him, but she said his family was a little intense for her."

"I saw the piece," Josie said. "Intense in what way?"

Christine shrugged. "I don't know, like overbearing, I guess. Nysa said he was one of those guys whose mom would be in the middle of their relationship the whole entire time, and she didn't have the energy for that."

"Any chance they could have been seeing one another in secret? Maybe not telling anyone?"

Christine said, "I don't think so. He still looks at her with those puppy dog eyes all the time. It's kind of sad."

Josie's list of mental notes grew the more that Christine talked. She pulled her phone from her back pocket so she could fire off some texts to Mettner. After the flooding in Denton five months earlier, during which Josie had been in the water more often than not, she'd purchased a Samsung Galaxy 9 which purported to be waterproof. Jumping into the pool with the phone in her pocket was the first test of its ability to withstand water. As Josie pressed the power button and then tapped in her passcode, she was relieved to see that the phone had, in fact, survived her plunge.

She tapped in text messages to Mettner even though he was still by the pool, telling him that they needed to interview all swim team members and, in particular, someone named Hudson. She asked Christine, "Was Nysa having any problems with anyone recently?"

"No. Everything's been great." Her chest rose several times in succession as a sob worked its way up into her throat. More tears streamed down her face. Josie gave her a moment to regain some of her composure, then asked, "How has Nysa's stress level been lately?"

"Fine. It's only the beginning of the year, so things aren't that bad yet."

"How about her mood?" Josie asked. "Was she upset or depressed lately? Distraught?"

Christine's body went still. "Why are you asking that? You think she killed herself or something? No way. Nysa wouldn't do that. She's one of the most upbeat and driven people I know."

"You've known her for a year. Did she ever mention any history of depression or anxiety?"

Christine shook her head vigorously. "No, no. Definitely not Nysa."

"Okay," Josie said. "I understand. How about drugs or alcohol? Did she use them at all?"

"You know we're not twenty-one yet, right?"

Josie gave a weak smile. "Christine, in my experience, that's never stopped anyone, certainly not on a college campus. It's okay if she did. We just need to know."

"Definitely no drugs. She rarely drank. She was very focused on her conditioning for swimming. I mean, there were times last year at parties where she had a drink or two, but she was really into healthy eating and staying fit. Especially with this swim scholarship. Her parents aren't rich or anything, so it was a big deal for her to get it. If she performs poorly on the swim team or falls behind academically, she could lose it."

"Christine," Josie said, "I've got to confer with my colleagues, but after that, I was hoping you could take me to see yours and Nysa's apartment."

"Sure."

Goosebumps erupted along Josie's bare arms. Her clothes were still wet, and she was getting colder by the minute. "Will you wait here for me?"

Christine nodded.

"Can I call anyone for you in the meantime?"

"Nysa's parents, maybe. They're still in town. They visited this weekend because WYEP was doing that special on the swim team. They're staying at the Marriott."

Josie was most certainly not going to call Nysa Somers' parents to come to the scene of her death, particularly while it was still in chaos, but she would have someone dispatched to the hotel to speak with them and ask them to come to the morgue to make a positive ID. Perhaps Noah or Detective Gretchen Palmer, either of whom would handle the death notification with compassion and sensitivity.

Through the glass doors, Josie could see the flashing red and blue lights of two police cruisers pulling up in front of the building. She stepped closer to the entrance and saw Dr. Anya Feist's small pickup truck pulling in behind them.

"I've got to talk to my colleagues," Josie told Christine. "If you wouldn't mind—"

Christine folded her arms over her chest. "I'm not going anywhere. I want to know what happened to Nysa."

# CHAPTER SEVEN

Josie met the other Denton officers and Dr. Feist at the doors. She stationed a uniformed officer just outside the front doors and another outside the pool entrance with a clipboard so that he could log anyone entering the scene. Then she led Officers Hummel and Chan of the ERT and Dr. Feist into the pool area. Josie felt a shiver in spite of the welcome heat in the room. A loose circle had formed around Nysa Somers including Sawyer, Owen, Chief Hahlbeck, one of the other campus officers, and Mettner. Glancing at the benches lining the wall, Josie saw Patrick still seated there, watching the emergency personnel. She walked over to him and asked if he was okay. He answered with a tired nod. Touching his shoulder, she told him he was free to go and that if his boss had an issue with him taking the day off, he could take it up with her. He squeezed her in a brief, unexpected hug and jogged off. Josie turned to the new arrivals and gave them the rundown of what had happened and what little they knew, including what she had found out from Christine Trostle.

"We're treating this as a suspicious death," she concluded.

Hummel and Chan began unpacking their equipment. Dr. Anya Feist knelt on the tile, peering down into Nysa's face. Josie took out her phone again and dialed Noah. It rang eight times and went to voicemail.

"Mett," she said. "Did you see Noah at the station this morning?"

He shook his head. "No. Try Gretchen."

As Josie scrolled her contacts for Gretchen's number, she said, "Was it busy this morning?"

"No," Mettner said. "Not particularly."

Noah was working the same shift as Josie. She was wondering where he was when Gretchen's voice came through the receiver. "Boss?"

Josie put the phone to her ear and quickly explained the situation, as well as her request for Gretchen to go to the Marriott to notify Nysa Somers' parents and bring them to the morgue. After she hung up, Hillary said, "Gerry is in the back, pulling footage. I checked the women's locker room to see if she'd left anything in there—perhaps a swim bag or something like that. Didn't find anything. Also checked her pockets. Nothing. I checked the men's locker room just to see if there was anything unusual in there. Didn't find a thing. I know you'll want to have a look yourself, though."

Josie nodded. The Evidence Response officers took photographs while Dr. Feist stood back. "I'll have a look now, if you don't mind."

Hillary followed her, first into the women's locker room, then the men's, answering Josie's questions as she asked them. There were no assigned lockers. The rooms were cleaned twice a day by custodial staff. Once mid-morning and once mid-evening. No custodians had yet reported to the building. Finding nothing of interest, Josie returned to the body.

Dr. Feist knelt on the floor beside the body once more, her gloved hands probing Nysa Somers' limbs. "Bag her hands, would you, Hummel? In case there's skin under her nails."

Hummel and Chan went to work as Dr. Feist stood and snapped off her gloves.

Josie asked, "You think there was foul play?"

Dr. Feist shook her head. "I don't know. I don't see anything that indicates she was trying to defend herself, but what are the odds that such a strong swimmer would drown? Unless she was under the influence of drugs or alcohol, which is the most likely scenario. We'll run toxicology, but you know that takes almost two months. We could also be looking at a sudden medical event like cardiac arrest or something like that. She could have come for a swim but gone into cardiac arrest and drowned."

Josie frowned, looking at Nysa Somers' clothes once more. "She wasn't dressed for swimming."

"Right," said Dr. Feist. "That's your department, not mine. However, I don't think a sudden medical event is very likely. We don't typically see those types of things in young, healthy people. It's not unheard of, but based on my experience, the most likely scenario is that she was intoxicated, thought it would be a great idea to go for a swim, and drowned accidentally."

Josie turned to Hillary. "Do you think Gerry's got that footage ready for us?"

"Come with me," she answered. She led Josie and Mettner out of the pool area toward the back, to the brown door Gerry had gone through earlier. Up close, Josie could see that it was marked with a large, intimidating red sign with white letters that announced: *Emergency Exit Only. Do Not Block. Door Alarm Will Sound.* From her belt, Hillary produced a laminated card attached to a retractable lanyard which she held under a silver box beneath the door handle. A swirl of red lights danced over the card and then a beep sounded. Hillary pushed through the door, no alarm sounding. Josie and Mettner followed her into a drab gray hallway. Josie looked right and then left. At the end of each side of the hall were two more doors simply marked Exit.

"This way," Hillary said, pointing left.

Josie and Mettner walked in single file behind her. Several feet before the exit, on the right, was an unmarked brown door with another scanner on its handle. Hillary scanned her card and they followed her inside. It was a small tile and concrete office with desks lining the walls. Each desk held two laptops, their screens lit up. One set of computers showed three views of the lobby, and the other showed multiple views of the exterior of the building.

Gerry sat at the closest desk, focused on the computer. He waved them over, clicking away until three equal-sized boxes filled up the screen. Each showed a different view of the building's lobby. As he worked back to find Nysa Somers on the videos, Josie asked, "How difficult would it be for someone to get into the pool area from these back doors?"

Hillary said, "As Gerry said earlier, you'd need a staff ID card to get inside the exterior doors as well as the door at the back of the pool area. That's exit only, so the alarm would sound if you opened it."

Mettner said, "If one of those doors was breached without a staff ID card, where would the alarm sound?"

"Inside the building, and an alert would go to our main switchboard as well as to the phones of any staff currently on duty. We've got an app."

"Even in the middle of the night?" Mettner asked. "Before Gerry came in?"

Hillary nodded. "Yes. In that case, the alerts would go to the main switchboard and our night patrols. But I can tell you that no alarms were triggered in this building last night or this morning. I already checked."

"How about a list of ID cards that were used to access the building?" Josie said. "If someone accessed it using a card last night or this morning, would you have a record of that?"

"Yes," Hillary said. "I thought of that. I checked, but no one except Gerry used a card to enter this building this morning, and he was here at five forty-five a.m."

"How about the guard from last night?" Josie continued. "What time did he or she close up the building?"

"Ten p.m.," answered Hillary.

"We'd like both those logs, if you wouldn't mind," Josie said. "The one showing the alarms for the last twenty-four hours and the ones showing key card use as well."

"Of course." Hillary walked over to a touchscreen tablet mounted on the wall and started punching and swiping with her fingers. A moment later, a printer beneath one of the desks whirred to life and began to spit out paper.

"Here's Nysa," Gerry said, motioning toward the laptop.

Over his shoulders, Josie and Mettner leaned in. On all three views, the timestamp at the bottom right read 6:02 a.m. One view showed a set of exterior lobby doors opening. Nysa Somers stepped inside, wearing her tank top and shorts, carrying nothing. She stopped midway through the lobby. Her head swiveled to the left and she smiled. She waved and said something. One of the other views showed Gerry behind his rounded reception desk, smiling and waving back. He said something to her in return. Then Nysa walked up to the doors to the pool area and pushed through them.

"Gerry," Josie said. "You said she came most days to swim. Did she usually have some kind of bag with her?"

His brow furrowed. He stopped the footage and met Josie's eyes. "Well, yeah. All the girls carry some kind of bag even if they come with their suits on under their clothes. Usually she has a duffel bag. Sometimes she has that and her backpack."

Josie said, "So she showed up at 6:02 a.m. wearing regular clothes with no bathing suit underneath, carrying nothing. She walked inside. What did she say to you, Gerry?"

"She said, 'Good morning, Mr. Murphy.' I said good morning back to her."

Mettner said, "She called you by name. Did you know her well?"

Gerry shook his head. "No, not well. I knew her better than most of the kids on campus because she's in here almost every day. I get to know the kids on the swim team, chat with them sometimes, but that's it. I don't know them well. Just names and faces, really."

"Do you know a student named Hudson?" Josie asked.

"Sure," Gerry said. "He's on the team too. I see him and Nysa together a lot. He's got a pretty big crush on her, I think, but mostly they're just real competitive with each other. They *were* real competitive. Jeez." He took a deep breath. "Sorry. It's just hard to believe something like this happened. It's so awful. So tragic. Poor Nysa."

"Do you know if Nysa and Hudson were dating?" Josie asked.

"Oh, I don't know. The kids don't talk to me about that kind of stuff."

Mettner said, "What time did Patrick get here?"

"I'll show you," Gerry said. He began to click, but Josie put a gentle hand on his forearm.

"Would you mind fast-forwarding through to the time Patrick appears so we can be assured that no one else came in between Nysa and him?"

"Of course," said Gerry.

He clicked a few times more, and the screens fast-forwarded until footage of Patrick entering the lobby came up on all three cameras. Josie noted that Gerry remained at his desk the entire morning, so there was no possibility that he had slipped into the pool area and done something to Nysa. On Patrick's arrival, the time stamp read 8:16 a.m. He carried a backpack which he set down beside him when he plopped onto one of the benches. They watched as he bent his head to his phone. A moment later, he stood, stretched his arms over his head, and headed toward the vending machine area. Two more minutes went by and then Josie saw herself on the screen.

The lobby was quiet. Gerry sat at his desk reading a newspaper. At 8:20, Patrick came running back out into the lobby, arms waving, mouth stretched open. Gerry jumped out of his chair, pulled his phone out of his pocket, and started running toward him. The doors swallowed both of them up.

"That's enough," Josie said. "Can you show us the footage from the exterior of the building?"

Solemnly, Gerry clicked out of the footage they'd been watching and returned the screen to the present views of the lobby, which showed one of Denton PD's uniformed officers standing sentry with a clipboard; a campus officer milling around; and Christine Trostle waiting on a bench.

Gerry wheeled his chair over to the other table and clicked away on one of the other laptops, bringing up four views of the exterior of the natatorium all crowded together on one screen. All four sides of the building were accounted for. In the front where emergency vehicles sat, Josie saw Sawyer Hayes removing equipment, including a stretcher, from the back of the ambulance. Beyond that was a parking lot with room for several rows of cars stretching out of view of the camera. In the back of the natatorium was a narrower lot with only a few spaces reserved for security and other campus workers as well as a dumpster. Beyond that was woods. Josie knew they extended down a small hill toward one of the city's main roads into campus. On either side of the natatorium were tree-lined courtyards with benches and tables for students to linger in nice weather. Josie also knew that, beyond those courtyards, on one side of the natatorium was the Health and Human Sciences center and on the other was one of the many buildings that housed athletics, but the camera views only showed the courtyards.

They watched as Gerry brought up footage beginning at five that morning. At 5:44, a small jeep pulled up out back. Gerry emerged a minute later and used his key card to enter. The courtyards and the front of the building were empty. At six, they watched Nysa emerge from the far end of the front parking lot, walking steadily toward the natatorium. She was alone, just as Gerry had said. They viewed the rest of the footage up until various emergency vehicles arrived. No one went in or out of the building besides those already accounted for. Josie felt a kernel of discomfort in the pit of her stomach.

"We'll need copies of all the footage you've got," she told Gerry. "If you could also give us anything you've got going back a full twenty-four hours, we'd appreciate that. Now, if you don't mind, I'd like to talk to Nysa's roommate again."

# CHAPTER EIGHT

The killing didn't start with me. It was true that part of me always enjoyed watching people suffer. Some people. People who deserved it—like the ones who called me names, outshined me at school, or received praise or rewards for something I had worked just as hard to get. I had found other ways to make them pay for what they did to me without anyone realizing I was behind it. Few things are more satisfying than watching someone who thinks they are better than you shit themselves from the laxatives you put into their lunch, or someone who criticizes the way you look make a sour face at the piss you mixed in with their smoothie. But I'm not sure the killing would have occurred to me. I'm not sure I would have even realized I could get away with it if I hadn't seen her do it first.

We both knew the kind of person he was—I just never expected her to do anything about it. Then one morning, I heard her call 911, speaking in a muffled tone. Maybe she was trying not to wake me. While she waited at the front door, I went into the bedroom and saw him. He had clearly been dead for a long time. I'd never seen a person so still before. Wherever his skin touched the bed or pillow, it had turned a purple so deep, it was almost black. I only saw edges of it at first, but when the paramedics arrived and moved him, I saw much more. They didn't bother with CPR. Two of them stood in the bedroom with her, asking countless questions. I don't think they noticed me there in the corner of the room, taking it all in. My attention was torn between him—finally gone forever—and the conversation between her and the paramedics. One of them asked about medications.

"A couple of different kinds," I heard her say. "For his heart and high blood pressure. Some for pain. He had a knee injury a while back. But he doesn't always take his pills correctly. Sometimes he gets them mixed up. Once he took six pills from the same bottle—all Vicodin. I had to take him to the ER to get his stomach pumped. Plus, he drinks. I've asked him so many times not to drink with these medications. He doesn't listen to me. Here, you can look at the bottles."

She motioned toward the nightstand where several orange prescription bottles sat, all arrayed for inspection. A paramedic went over and picked them up one by one, studying them.

She looked at me then. I knew damn well he didn't get his pills mixed up. She was the one who dispensed them. I said nothing.

The paramedic shook one bottle, but there was no telltale rattle of pills inside. "Digoxin," he said. "A high dose of this can kill you. The bottle is empty."

I waited for someone to figure out what she had done, but no one ever did.

# CHAPTER NINE

Hillary handed Josie a stack of pages containing the logs she had promised and then led her and Mettner back to the pool area. Again, the heat and humidity hit Josie like a wall. Her clothing was almost dry, for which she was grateful. Hillary said, "I'm going back to headquarters to make some phone calls, see if I can't get a list of swim team members for your department to interview."

"Thank you," said Josie.

Mettner pocketed his phone and took the stack of pages from Josie, tucking them under one arm. "The library was the last place we know for sure that Nysa went last night, so I'm going over there to see if I can get footage of her arriving and leaving. Try to nail down a timeline and see if she spoke to anyone or left with anyone."

"Perfect," Josie said. "I'm going to check out Nysa's apartment."

She watched as Mettner strode off. Then her gaze flicked toward Sawyer and Owen, who had secured Nysa's body in a body bag and lifted it onto the stretcher for transport. Josie felt sadness tug at her heart. Dr. Feist was gone, likely headed back to the morgue ahead of the body so that she could talk to Nysa's parents and ask that one of them give a positive ID. The thought that a family was about to be shattered cut deep, as it always did in her line of work. She pushed her own feelings down. Her job was to find answers for that family. She could never bring them peace, but she could discover what had happened to their daughter. It was a paltry offering in the face of their loss, but Josie would do her best.

As Josie's gaze lifted from the body bag, she met Sawyer's eyes. His thin mouth was set, and his blue eyes flashed—some combination of grief and anger. Like Josie, he had experienced loss in his personal life. Sometimes the job got to you, especially when the dead were young.

Noah stepped directly in her path, blocking her view of Sawyer. "That guy is everywhere," he groused.

She hadn't even seen Noah come in. "Hey," she said. "Where have you been?"

"At the station, why?"

"I called you. You didn't answer. Mett said you weren't at the station."

He looked over his shoulder, where Sawyer stood staring while Owen finished securing the body bag. "I was—I had—the Chief gave me something to do. Why is that guy staring at you?"

Josie said, "What?"

Noah turned back to her and lowered his voice although Sawyer and Owen had already started for the doors. "Sawyer. Everywhere we go, he's there. I know he left Dalrymple Township to come work for Denton, but still. Doesn't the city have other EMTs?"

Josie put a hand on her hip. "What are you even talking about right now?"

Sawyer and Owen disappeared into the lobby. The doors swung shut, leaving Josie and Noah alone. "He comes to our house for dinner. We see him at Rockview when we go visit your grandmother. Now we're at work, and here he is."

Josie said, "He's family now, Noah."

"Is he? He's not related to you, only to your grandmother."

Lisette Matson had raised Josie as her granddaughter for decades before the two found out they weren't blood-related. Josie had grown up believing that Lisette's son, Eli Matson, was her father. Eli had died when Josie was only six, leaving Josie in an abusive household with a woman she believed to be her mother. Lisette had made it her life's work to get Josie out of there and raise her. For years, Josie and Lisette had only had each other. Then a few months ago, Sawyer had shown up on the scene, claiming to be Lisette's grandson from a relationship that Eli had had with a woman he'd been seeing before Josie came along. DNA proved this to be true. Lisette was over the moon to have another grandchild. It had been a little more difficult for Josie, worrying that things between her and Lisette might change. She was doing her best to accept the new dynamic, though and welcome Sawyer into their lives. Anything less than that would break Lisette's heart, and Josie was not about to do that.

She said, "You were the one who encouraged me to get to know him."

"I think you know him well enough now."

"What's going on with you?"

Noah huffed. "Nothing. I'm just annoyed."

She regarded him with a raised brow. "Annoyed? Well, stow it. Right now, we have a case to focus on, Fraley."

Josie detected a slight flush in his cheeks. He waved his notebook in the air. "I am focused. I talked to Mett on the phone and also to Gretchen. What are you thinking? Accident?"

"I don't know, but this doesn't feel right."

Noah said, "You think this is a homicide?"

"No. I don't see how it could be. There was no one else here."

"Wasn't there a security guard?"

"He was at the desk the entire time Nysa was in the pool area."

"Could someone have slipped in through the back?"

"I don't think so," Josie said. "According to the logs Hillary gave us, no one but the guard used their key card to access the rear doors either last night or this morning."

"Is it possible someone could have come in here yesterday and spent the entire night?"

"I don't see how they would get out after the fact without setting off an alarm or being seen on camera."

"True," Noah agreed. "If no one killed her, then what? She accidentally drowned?"

"Unlikely. She's the university's star swimmer."

"She was intoxicated?"

"Given her behavior on the video we saw, she didn't appear inebriated," Josie said. "Certainly not enough to accidentally drown. If she was that messed up, I would have expected her to be stumbling or at least slurring her words. That leaves us with a sudden medical event. Although that doesn't explain why she came to the pool hours before her normal swim time without a bathing suit. We need more information. Once Dr. Feist does the autopsy and we talk to people who knew her and who were in contact with her in the last day or so, it might be easier to conclude whether this was some kind of accident or suicide."

"Suicide," Noah echoed. "We haven't touched on that yet."

"Her roommate doesn't believe she would commit suicide. Gretchen's on her way to the hotel to get the parents. They might be able to shed some light on Nysa's state of mind."

Noah sighed. "This is terrible. You okay?"

"I'm fine," Josie said.

It was her stock answer whether she was fine or not. Finding Nysa in the pool, not being able to revive her, had shaken Josie. But death and tragedy were the daily bread of her job. She was a professional, an expert at setting aside her own sadness so that she could do her work. Later, she'd have to meet with Nysa's parents herself. She wanted to be able to answer at least some of their questions.

Noah didn't press the issue. Instead, he said, "Where do you want me?"

Josie said, "Campus police headquarters. Work with Chief Hahlbeck to get as many swim team members and swim coaching staff as you can possibly get in there today for questioning."

"You got it."

# CHAPTER TEN

Outside the natatorium, Noah turned right and headed to upper campus where the police headquarters were located. Josie followed Christine Trostle through the parking lot, which had begun to fill up. In fact, the campus was far busier now than when Josie arrived. Some students stopped and gawked at the couple of police vehicles remaining out front of the natatorium but others went on their way, chatting to one another or on their phones, oblivious to the tragedy that had just occurred.

They came to the front of the Ervene Gulley Arts & Humanities building on the other side of the parking lot, the one that was just out of view of the pool building cameras. Josie said, "Christine, where are the commons?"

She stopped walking and pointed to her left where twin paths led downward to lower campus. "Over that way." She turned in the opposite direction and pointed to the tallest building on campus, which Josie knew was the library. "It's not that far a walk from the commons to the library. I'll show you the shortcut from here to our student housing complex."

They circled around the Ervene Gulley Arts & Humanities building. In the rear was a small parking lot, and on the other side of that, a wooded area with a cut-through in the brush. The path was one person wide and had obviously been made by hundreds of students trekking through it. Josie followed behind Christine, estimating the distance between the edge of campus and the small, unused street they came out on to be about thirty yards. When they stepped onto the asphalt, Josie saw the back of a row of several small houses. Each one had a postage stamp-sized backyard. Most were filled with grills, sports equipment, coolers, and trash bins. Josie knew from dealing with the university over the years that this area was called Hollister Way. It was a collection of six rows of tiny houses joined together and usually rented to sophomores who wanted a little more elbow room and privacy than dorms provided. Spots in Hollister Way were competitive because of its proximity to campus. Josie followed Christine as she walked around to the front of the closest row of houses. Each house was allotted two parking spots and nearly all of them were filled. Christine turned right down the third row of housing and Josie followed to a door marked with the number 14. As Christine worked the lock, she pointed to a light blue Honda Civic in front of the house.

"That's Nysa's."

Inside, the house was nothing more than a living/dining area, a tiny kitchen, and a set of steps, at the top of which was a bathroom sandwiched between two bedrooms so small, they looked like glorified walk-in closets. Christine showed her Nysa's room. An unmade twin bed with a laptop sitting at the foot of it took up most of the space. There was a tall dresser and a desk jammed beside one another along one wall. A stack of textbooks sat on top of the desk. On top of the dresser were two framed photographs. One was of a small white dog, and the other appeared to be Nysa Somers with her family at a swimming event. She wore a one-piece red bathing suit with a swim cap. A medal hung around her neck. Flowers were tucked in the crook of her arm. An older man and woman stood on either side of her, smiling widely. Beside the man was a grinning teenage girl with a more reserved smile who closely resembled Nysa. Parents and sister, Josie thought, before she had to look away. Her heart broke thinking of the news they were about to receive and how it was going to permanently destroy the happiness they'd known before this horrible day.

Christine stood in the doorway weeping quietly while Josie had a look around. There was nothing of interest other than the fact that three bathing suits were folded neatly in the top drawer of the dresser, and a small mesh bag with what looked like swimming supplies was tucked beneath the desk. Josie snapped on a pair of gloves and took a quick look through the bag. Inside were goggles, a swim cap, nose clips, a water bottle, protein bar, and a towel. She did not see a backpack anywhere or a cell phone.

Her phone rang and she took it out of her pocket to see Mettner's face flash across the screen. "Mett?" she said after swiping *answer*.

"I've got the library footage," he said. "Nysa left at closing time—alone. She had a backpack."

"Okay," Josie sighed. "Have you tried following her path using the other campus cameras?"

"Yeah. I'm with Hahlbeck and Fraley at the campus police building now. You'll want to see this."

# CHAPTER ELEVEN

Josie walked back through Hollister Way until she found the cut-through. She stood at the mouth of the path for a long moment, taking in the surroundings again. A few students trickled out of it, backpacks on, eyes on their phones, each one startled to find her standing at the end of the path from campus back to Hollister. One student came from behind Josie and took the path to campus. It was quiet and no one lingered. No residents poked their heads out of the backs of the houses facing the cut-through. People came and went without anyone noticing. A car pulled up along the wooded side of the small road. A male student stepped out, slung a bag over his shoulder, locked his vehicle and jogged past Josie up to campus. Along the side of the road, Josie noted a muddy divot where the asphalt ended and the forest began. Various tire tracks had imprinted in the mud. This was an area where students parked frequently to use the cut-through, which meant that someone could have been parked there the night before when Nysa emerged.

She had emerged, hadn't she? Josie wondered. She hadn't spent the entire night in the woods, had she? There were roughly eight hours unaccounted for in the last night of Nysa Somers' life. Josie wasn't sure why, but she felt those hours were vitally important to figuring out why Nysa was dead. Stepping onto the path, Josie walked slowly, panning from side to side to see if there were any breaks in the branches or brush alongside the path. She identified a couple of sycamore trees, two birch trees, and a maple tree. Most of the ground was thick with waist-high ragweed, crape myrtle, goldenrod and bull thistle.

Josie got almost to the campus side, which was on a slight incline, and turned to look back, surveying all she could see from the higher angle. There were no breaks in the brush on either side of the path, no places where it looked like someone had trampled down the plant life to get into the woods. However, from where she stood, there looked to be a break in a large thatch of bull thistle plants to her right, about thirty feet from the path. Most of the plants stood tall, their tips thorny green bulbs with purple or pink flowers thrusting out the top, like several hairs standing on end. Any casual observer would think the first thing that Josie did—an animal, likely a deer, had come through and trampled part of the thistle. But as Josie started back down the path toward Hollister Way, craning her neck to get a better view, she saw a flash of something dark. Not dirt. Fabric.

She took out her phone and took several photos before trying to find the least destructive way through the brush to the item she had spotted. As she picked her way through, a couple of female students came down the path from campus. "You okay?" one of them hollered.

Josie waved them off with a smile, pushing aside some goldenrod plants, as she worked her way closer to the thistle. A moment later, the object came into view. A black backpack. It looked as though it had been tossed there, rather than placed, as it rested unevenly on top of some partially snapped bull thistle plants. She looked back toward the path. It was feasible someone could have thrown it this far from there. Josie took several photos, carefully picked her way back to the path, and then called Officer Hummel.

"I think I found Nysa Somers' backpack. Could you and Chan come process it?"

She gave them directions and a few minutes later, the two officers traipsed down the path from campus carrying their equipment. "I'm going to shoot my way in," Hummel said as he pulled a large camera out of his equipment bag. "Chan can cordon off the area while I'm doing that. Once I've established the perimeter and checked the bag to see if there's any indication that it's Nysa's, you can come over."

Josie called Mettner and Noah as she waited on the path while Hummel and Chan got to work. Several more students passed by, each stopping to ask questions that Josie couldn't answer honestly. A cool breeze drifted down from the direction of campus, drying the last few wet seams in her clothing.

"Son of a bitch," Hummel said.

"What is it?" Josie asked.

"What the hell is this stuff?" He stood up straight and pointed down toward the thistles all around him. "It's got thorns."

"Bull thistle," Josie said. "Looks like a dandelion while it's growing, except it's thorny. It grows tall and flowers pink and purple."

Hummel held up a gloved hand and wiggled his index finger. A green thorn stuck out of it, and a drop of blood trickled from under it. "Hold on," he said. "I've got to change gloves. I don't want to contaminate anything here."

Chan handed him a new pair of gloves and then both their heads disappeared into the thistle. A few moments later, Hummel hollered, "Jackpot."

Chan's arm appeared over the top of the greenery, her gloved hand waving Josie toward them. Once Josie reached them, she found Hummel squatting beside the backpack, holding it open. Inside, Josie saw a lanyard with a student ID attached to it. Nysa Somers' face smiled at Josie from the photo. All innocence and enthusiasm for life. Josie sighed.

"What else have you got in there?"

As he riffled through the bag and listed off each item, Chan jotted it down on a notepad. "Two textbooks, a spiral-bound notebook, small cosmetic bag." There was the sound of a zipper. "Lipstick, foundation, mascara, make-up blender, rouge." He zipped the bag back up. "Pens, pencils, twenty-two dollars in cash."

"Cell phone?" Josie asked hopefully.

"Just a second," Hummel told her. He moved to the pockets on the outside of the bag. "Here. Cell phone." He pressed some buttons, but nothing happened. "Looks like it needs to be charged. We can take care of that when we get this back to the station."

"Great," Josie said. A small thrill of excitement took hold in her stomach. For modern-day investigators, there was nothing more valuable in solving a crime than a person's cell phone. People's entire lives were on them.

"What about that?" Chan said, pointing her pen toward the yawning pocket from which Hummel had just removed the cell phone.

Josie leaned over and peered into it. What looked like a piece of plastic was poking out. Hummel reached in and teased its squished form from the pocket, smoothing it out. "A Ziploc baggie," he said. "She must have had some kind of snack." He held it up, looking at the crumbs in the bottom of it. "Looks like brownies to me." He opened it and held it up to his nose, taking a whiff. "Yeah, smells like chocolate."

Josie noted a small white sticker at the lower left corner of the baggie. "What's that sticker?" she asked.

Hummel stood up and took a step closer to her so that she could see it. It was circular, black and white, about the size of a quarter with a crude hand drawing of a face. Its eyes were small 'X's, its mouth a toothy smile. Above the eyes, the forehead cracked open and squiggly lines jumped out in every direction.

"That's weird," Hummel said.

Josie nodded. "Move it around in the light. Can you see the impressions from a pen, or does it look like it's a copy?"

Hummel moved the sticker this way and that as the three of them studied it. Finally, he concluded, "Looks smooth. Must be a copy. Looks like one of those weird skater stickers or something. Like the kind kids put on their skateboards?"

Chan said, "Something like that on a baggie? That's not a skater sticker. Someone marked those brownies as edibles."

"What do you mean?" Josie asked. "The sticker is to indicate marijuana in the brownies?"

"The last city I worked in, we had a couple of cases of these. Locals would brand their drugs before they sold them. Sometimes stickers, sometimes stamps. Usually hand-drawn, so it couldn't be confused with anything else out there. Something cheap and easy so you remembered who to come back to for more. It's not always the smartest practice because it makes it pretty easy for the cops to track you down and also figure out who you sold to, but some people do it."

Josie took out her phone and took a photo of the sticker. "Have you ever seen this before?"

"No," said Chan. "I could be wrong. I'm just tossing out ideas. Maybe she made brownies at home and someone in one of her classes gave her a weird random sticker and it ended up on the baggie."

"I doubt that," Josie said. She wondered if marijuana would have put Nysa Somers into such a state that she would have gotten into the pool and drowned—either by falling asleep or by simply being in an altered state. Or maybe it had been laced with something stronger. Perhaps whatever was in the brownie had had more of an effect on her than she'd anticipated since, by all accounts, she didn't normally do drugs. But if she'd done drugs the night before, why? Why start taking them now? Josie knew that the university had drug testing requirements for all of its athletes. There was no way that Nysa would have been able to carry on a regular drug habit. Even a one-time thing would have been problematic for her since drug testing for university athletes was random unless drug use was suspected. Why would she risk it? Or maybe she hadn't known the brownies were laced with drugs. Had they come from the mystery friend she'd met up with? Perhaps she had trusted that person not to give her something with drugs? Or the friend had convinced her to let loose a little and try them? There was no way to know without finding the friend.

Josie said, "You can mass-produce your own stickers?"

Chan shrugged. "You can get blank stickers from any office supply place and run them through your printer, or you could upload your design to a website and have them print and send you a bunch."

To Hummel, Josie said, "Bag that up and get it to the state police lab, would you? I'd like to know what's in those crumbs. Also, print the bag."

She worked her way back to the path and then climbed up the rest of the way to the campus. Once in the parking lot, she called Christine Trostle. "You told me that Nysa never used drugs," she said to the girl. "Were you telling the truth?"

"Well, yeah, why?"

"She never tried anything?"

Christine made a noise in her throat. "Well, I never saw her try anything or heard her talk about trying anything, but I wasn't with her twenty-four seven. Maybe when she was at home she did, but it would have been really out of character for her. She drank sometimes, but drugs scared her."

"Scared her in what way?" Josie asked.

"She used to say that she knew what she'd get with alcohol. It was predictable, but with drugs, she didn't know what things would do to her body. In high school, one of her friends tried cocaine thinking it would be just fine, but it had PCP in it and ended up killing the girl. Heart attack, I think Nysa said. I guess the kid Nysa's friend got the coke from didn't even know about it. Nysa always said street drugs weren't regulated and you couldn't trust anyone, but if she had a beer, she knew exactly where it was coming from and what was in it. Plus, you know, 'cause she's on the swim team, she's subject to random drug testing."

"Okay," Josie said. "What about you? Do you or any of your and Nysa's mutual friends use edibles?"

"Like pot?"

"Or any food with drugs baked, cooked, or mixed into it."

"No," Christine said.

"You're not going to be in trouble if you or your friends use edibles," Josie told her. "I'm just trying to figure out what happened to your roommate."

Christine laughed. "I'm afraid that Nysa and I just weren't that cool, Detective, and like I just said, Nysa was an athlete and no way was she risking her body by putting crazy shit into it."

"Was there someone she might have risked taking drugs for?"

"What does that mean?"

"It means is there anyone you can think of who could have offered her drugs and, for whatever reason—peer pressure, or she liked the person—she wouldn't turn them down?"

"I don't think so."

"What about brownies? Did she like brownies?"

"Who doesn't like brownies? Yeah, she liked them. She had a weakness for sugary stuff."

"Had you two made any recently?"

"No."

"Bought any?"

"No."

"Had anyone brought you any brownies?"

"No. I promise you, Detective, we haven't had any brownies in this place since school started. Come back and look."

The autopsy would show stomach contents—if any—for the eight hours that Nysa was missing before her death. "That's okay," Josie said. "I believe you. I've got to get up to campus police headquarters. For now, I'm going to text you a photo of a sticker. I want you to tell me if you've ever seen it before."

"Why?"

"Just have a look, and then we'll talk."

She took the phone from her ear and quickly texted Christine a copy of the photo she'd taken of the sticker. Several seconds ticked by and then Josie heard an audible shudder. Christine said, "That's creepy as hell. What is that? Some kind of creepy doll with its head cracked open?"

"We're not sure yet," Josie answered. "I just need to know if you've seen it anywhere."

"No. Good God. I'd remember that. Where was it?"

"We located Nysa's backpack," Josie told her. "In the woods behind Hollister Way. There was a baggie with that sticker on it. There were crumbs in the bag. We believe from brownies."

Silence. Then, "Are you sure it was her backpack?"

"It had her student ID in it."

"Well, I've never seen the sticker before. I would definitely remember. I have no idea how it ended up in Nysa's things."

"Okay," Josie said. "If you do see this anywhere or hear anyone talking about it or even if anything else occurs to you that you think I should know, call me."

# CHAPTER TWELVE

Back on campus, Josie followed the directions that Christine had given her to find the campus police building. It was the smallest building on campus, Josie thought. Just a square, brick thing with four parking spots alongside it and two steps leading to the front door. Inside, a uniformed campus officer behind a metal desk waved Josie through the reception area down a short hallway. Only one door was open, and inside Josie saw Mettner and Chief Hahlbeck sitting side by side at a desk, their eyes glued to a laptop screen. Noah stood behind them, peering over their shoulders. Josie knocked lightly on the doorframe. The Chief waved her over.

Josie took up position beside Noah and reported on what she had found at Nysa's apartment—which amounted to nothing beyond the fact that her swimsuits and swim bag were still there—and more importantly, what she had found in the woods. She pulled up the photo of the baggie and sticker and showed each of them.

"Some kind of drug marker," Mettner said immediately.

"That's what Chan said," Josie told him.

"Yeah, when I was in college, we had a guy who sold stuff on campus. He marked all of his stuff with a drawing of a bluebird. It was a stamp though, not a sticker. Like his drugs were the bluebird of happiness or something stupid like that."

"No shit," said Noah. "We have no shortage of drug activity in this city. Hell, we're down under the East Bridge a few times a week, but I've never seen this. Chief, you ever see this drawing on campus?"

Hillary took a closer look at Josie's phone screen, her upper lip curling. "No, I haven't, but that doesn't mean much. I haven't been here long. Send that to me, and I'll start asking around, checking files."

Josie texted her the photo and pointed to the laptop on the desk. "How about you guys? What did you find?"

Mettner motioned to the laptop and asked Chief Hahlbeck, "Do you mind?"

She shifted her chair over a bit to give Mettner more room. "Not at all," she said.

He clicked around until he pulled up a screen showing the outside of the library. "Here we see Nysa leaving at nine thirty-two, alone."

Josie watched as a flurry of students exited the library, identifying Nysa immediately since she was wearing the same clothes as she was when they found her in the pool. A black backpack slung over her left shoulder, she walked off in the direction of lower campus. Mettner clicked out of the library footage and brought up several other screens showing the exteriors of various campus buildings. The footage was dim, since by that time of night it was dark and the outdoor lighting that presided over campus walkways wasn't very bright. Still, they could easily identify Nysa in the videos. Foot traffic was relatively light. Nysa moved alone, one of the only students out and about whose eyes weren't glued to her phone. She didn't greet or wave to anyone else. Another screen showed the exterior of the Ervene Gulley Arts & Humanities building.

Josie said, "The cut-through to her housing complex is behind that building."

Mettner nodded. "Yes, we found that." More clicking, and then another screen came up, this time from a camera set high up on the back of the building, taking in the parking lot and wooded area. They watched as Nysa walked through the parking lot and found the cut-through, disappearing through the trees. Alone.

"But we know she didn't make it home," Josie said.

Mettner held up a finger. "Here's where it gets interesting."

Josie and Noah watched as he fast-forwarded through the footage, each hour passing in a matter of seconds. No one used the cut-through during the night. Then at 5:57 a.m., a figure emerged from it.

Nysa Somers.

Dressed exactly as she had been the night before, but without her backpack, she walked steadily and seemingly with purpose. When she was out of the frame, Mettner closed out the window and opened another one. This showed the front of the Ervene Gulley building which was just across from the natatorium. The parking lot beyond it was empty, and no other students lingered in the courtyards as far as the camera showed. She walked straight ahead toward the natatorium until she was out of the frame.

It had taken her roughly five minutes to cover the distance from the cut-through to the pool building lobby. At 6:02, she had entered, said good morning to Gerry Murphy, and then gone to the pool. And what? Jumped in and never came out?

Noah said, "So she left the library alone at nine thirty, walked into the woods but didn't make it home. Then she comes out of the woods at six this morning wearing the same clothes but without her backpack. Roommate got a text saying she met up with a friend. Where?"

"It had to be on the other side of the cut-through," Josie said. "It comes out at the back of the last row of houses in Hollister Way."

Mettner looked up at Josie. "You sure the roommate is telling the truth?"

"As sure as I can be," Josie said. "I saw her phone, looked through the apartment, and the backpack was in the woods along the path."

Mettner said, "What if Nysa did go home? She and the roommate had some brownies laced with drugs. Things got a little crazy and Nysa took off?"

"Why would Christine lie about that?" Josie countered.

"Because her roommate ended up dead."

Noah said, "That doesn't explain the text from Nysa to the roommate saying she met up with a friend."

Mettner was silent.

"We need to find the friend she met up with," Noah said.

"Maybe we'll get something when Hummel charges up her phone. That's the real jackpot. There could be texts or calls to and from the mysterious 'friend,' and it if has GPS enabled, we could see where she was during those missing hours."

Mettner tapped away on his note-taking app as they talked through all the leads they'd need to run down.

"We should also canvass the houses in Hollister Way to see if anyone saw her last night, or noticed anything suspicious," Noah added.

Chief Hahlbeck said, "My officers are rounding up as many members of the swim team as they can find and bringing them back here. Coaching staff, too."

Mettner said, "You mind if we conduct interviews here?"

"Not at all," Hillary said. "We've got two rooms I can set you up in. If you'll excuse me."

She stood up from her chair and left the room.

Josie said, "Noah, how about you call in some patrol units and canvass Hollister? Mett and I will interview swim team members and coaches and then later I'll talk with Nysa's parents."

Noah said, "Sure. Have you heard from Gretchen yet?"

Josie shook her head and tapped Mettner's shoulder. "How about you?"

"Not yet," he answered. "I'll call her."

While Mettner tried to get in touch with Gretchen, Josie walked Noah outside. They moved around to the side of the building. Between two Japanese maple trees was a small clearing. The brick of the building had a green tinge to it, moisture causing a thin layer of lichen to grow in patches. A white five-gallon bucket, now gray with grime, sat upside down. Beside it was a smaller tin bucket filled with cigarette butts. Obviously, someone on the campus police used the enclave for smoke breaks.

Noah said, "What do you think?"

"I think that well-adjusted, relatively happy college swim stars who are so successful they've just won a major scholarship and been featured on the news don't normally spend a night with a 'friend,' eat brownies laced with some kind of drugs and then drown themselves."

"You think she drowned herself? Or did whatever she ingested make her pass out, and she accidentally drowned?"

Josie sighed. "I don't know, Noah. I just don't know."

"How many overdoses do you think they get on campus every year?" he asked.

"Two or three a year? I'm sure Chief Hahlbeck has the exact number. You really think this is as simple as a drug overdose? The roommate was adamant that this girl wouldn't take a thing."

Noah laughed. "No college kid takes drugs. That's like saying it never rains. Even the most dedicated students and student athletes try things from time to time. If I had to bet money, having seen all the things I've seen so far in my career, I'd say she met with a friend, the friend got her to try the brownies, she got messed up, walked to the pool for a swim and then passed out and drowned. Hell, maybe the friend didn't tell her the brownies were laced. Maybe she just thought she was getting a chocolate fix and then she got messed up, decided to go for a swim, passed out, and drowned."

Josie thought of the lobby video that Gerry Murphy had shown them. Nysa, steady on her feet, head swiveling. A smile spreading across her face. Her hand lifting in a wave. *Good morning, Mr. Murphy.* Josie said, "If she was under the influence of something that was strong enough to kill her once she was in the pool, wouldn't she have been, at the very least, stumbling or slurring her words?"

"Seems that way," Noah agreed. "But in the absence of evidence of anything else, that is the most obvious scenario."

"I guess toxicology will confirm it if that's the case," she said.

For a moment, she closed her eyes, thinking of what a tragedy it would be if Nysa Somers—who, by all accounts, didn't do drugs and rarely even drank—had decided to try some illicit drug, and it had led to her death. All the life she'd had ahead of her lost forever. She thought about Patrick. She'd have to give him a talk about not doing drugs, like a typical law enforcement officer or big sister. Then she thought about Harris getting old enough to go to college and try drugs, and her heart squeezed in her chest. Shutting down that entire train of thought, she opened her eyes.

Noah stared down at her. "You should go home and change."

She shrugged and fingered the collar of her polo shirt. "There's no time. Besides, I'm almost dry, and all my shirts look like this."

Noah asked, "How was Harris this morning at school drop-off?"

"Nervous. But I think it went well," she said, taking her phone out to check for any texts from Misty. There were none. No news was good news, Josie thought.

Noah stepped closer to her. He brushed a strand of her black hair away from her face. It hit her then how bedraggled she must look. She reached up to run her fingers through her hair, but Noah took her hand. "You look beautiful," he said softly.

"Did you hit your head this morning?" Josie joked. "While you were missing in action?"

Noah laughed. His thumb traced the inside of her palm. "I'm telling you, that salmon color really brings out your eyes."

"Oh piss off," Josie said, laughing in spite of herself. She tried to wrest her hand away so she could slap his chest, but he tugged her into him and kissed her. With no eyes on them, Josie sank into him, feeling some of the stress of the morning quieting. Then he released her and started walking away.

Josie said, "Don't disappear again."

Over his shoulder, he said, "I won't. We've got dinner with Misty and Harris tonight. I want to hear how the first day of Pre-K went."

"I'll see you there," she said.

He turned briefly and waved his phone in the air. "Text me the picture of that sticker so I can show it around Hollister."

She took out her phone and fired off the text to him. Then she watched him until he disappeared around the front of the building, headed toward one of the walking paths that led to lower campus. The moment of peace she'd felt while close to him leeched away, replaced by a deep ache thinking about how Nysa Somers' family would never get to hear how any of her days had gone ever again.

# CHAPTER THIRTEEN

Back inside the campus police headquarters, students had begun to arrive, most of them dressed in sweatshirts and shorts, some even in pajamas. All of them looked stricken and vaguely confused. Hahlbeck had corralled them into the reception area, which only had two guest chairs, both taken. The rest of the students leaned against the walls or sat on the tile floor. A low murmur found its way around the room. Josie heard the words "Nysa" and "dead" several times. A woman who appeared older than most of the students circulated around the room, giving out hugs and reassurances. One of the coaches, Josie thought.

"Boss." Her attention was pulled away from the tableau by Mettner. Josie looked over her shoulder and saw him standing in the hallway. He waved her back.

"You want to interview each witness together, or you take one and I take one in separate rooms?" he asked once they were out of earshot of everyone else.

"Let's do separate interviews," Josie answered. "We'll get through them faster."

Hahlbeck offered them each a room. The one Mettner went into was clearly an interview room, with only a table and some chairs inside it. Josie was stationed across the hall in a room with two desks, positioned opposite one another, each bracketed by a filing cabinet and a guest chair. She guessed this was where the officers did their paperwork. She chose the desk closest to the door and sat down. Hahlbeck had provided a pen and legal pad. As a campus police officer ushered in the first student, Josie patted the guest chair. "Sit," she said. "I just have a few questions."

Most of the interviews didn't take very long. Primarily because no one had anything to offer. No one had seen or heard from Nysa the night before—unless one of them was lying, but Josie didn't get that impression from any of them. The whole exercise felt more like giving a half dozen death notifications than anything else. Nearly all the students took news of Nysa's death extremely hard. She was well liked and known for her kindness and sense of humor. Listening to the other students talk so highly of her only made Josie's heart ache even more. All of them said the same things that Christine Trostle had said: Nysa didn't use drugs and rarely drank alcohol; they didn't recognize the sticker; Nysa hadn't seemed depressed; and none of them were aware of her having any history of anxiety or depression. None of them knew—or would admit to knowing—whether or not Nysa had been seeing anyone.

At some point, Josie and Mettner conferred in the hallway to compare notes. The results of his interviews were the same. They were getting nowhere. The only news had come from Gretchen, who had let Mettner know that Nysa's parents had made a positive ID and that they had returned to their hotel. "They're going to stay in town until her body is released," Mettner said. "Gretchen says she didn't ask them much. They were too distraught."

"I'm sure," Josie said. "We can talk with them later. Have you talked to any student named Hudson?"

Mettner scrolled down the list of students he'd made on his phone. "No."

"How many are left?"

Mettner walked to the end of the hall, peeked into the reception area, and returned. "Five," he said.

It was after lunch, and Josie was exhausted and starving. "See if we can get a pizza or something," she told him. "We still have a long day ahead of us."

He nodded and walked back to the reception area. "I'm sending the next person back to you."

Josie pegged her next candidate for the coach immediately because he looked older than everyone else. He was tall and solid, with large features, and dark hair trimmed close to his head. He wore a pair of khaki pants and a Denton U windbreaker. A lanyard hung around his neck. On closer inspection, Josie saw that it had a photo of him over the name Brett Pace, Head Coach. She recognized him then from the WYEP news story. WYEP had only given him a short sound bite, a few seconds, wherein he had praised Nysa Somers.

"Mr. Pace," she said, gesturing to the guest chair. "Please have a seat."

The chair creaked as he lowered himself into it. He put his elbows on his knees and rubbed his large palms together. His voice was husky when he spoke. "I guess it's true then. About Nysa? She's dead?"

"I'm afraid so," Josie said. "I'm very sorry."

"What happened?"

"That's what we're trying to find out," Josie said. "Tell me, how long have you been coaching?"

He smiled at her as if they were old friends, and she realized that he was used to getting his way using his looks and any charm he might possess. "Officer," he said.

"Detective."

"Detective, listen. I know you can't tell these kids anything, but I'm the head coach. I worked directly with Nysa almost every day. I promise you nothing that you tell me will leave this room."

Josie raised a brow at him. "I'm sorry, Mr. Pace."

"Coach," he said.

Josie smiled. "Coach, I'm not at liberty to give out any details of an ongoing investigation."

"So this is an investigation? Nysa wasn't… murdered, was she?" His brow furrowed.

Josie leaned in toward him. "Do you have reason to believe she was murdered, Coach Pace?"

He leaned away from her. "No. I don't. Unless it was some random attack. But she was found in the pool, wasn't she?"

Ignoring his question, Josie said, "How long have you been coaching here?"

"About six years." He scooted forward in his seat, flashing her a dazzling grin that quickly morphed into an earnest look of concern. He lowered his voice until it was almost a whisper. "Detective, we're two reasonable adults, aren't we? I'm telling you, I can keep a secret. I just can't believe that Nysa was found dead in the pool. She's the strongest swimmer on the team. Something had to have happened to her. Was she… beaten? Did someone…" He didn't finish, and Josie saw what she thought was the first flicker of true emotion flash in his eyes. "Did someone hurt her?"

"We won't know anything until after the autopsy," she told him. "I know this is very distressing and very shocking, but you have to let the process play out, and that means waiting on the autopsy and the results of our investigation. It would really help if you answered some of my questions. I understand that you're the head coach?"

He bit the inside of his cheek, and after a moment, decided to answer. "Yes."

"Did you know Nysa well?"

"I knew her as well as I know any of my students. I always encourage them to talk to me or come to me with any issues during the year, even if they're not swim-related. Sometimes these kids just need someone to talk to, you know?"

"Did Nysa ever need someone to talk to?"

"Sure. They all come to me at some point or another."

"When was this?" Josie asked.

He waved a large hand dismissively. "Oh, last year. She was worried about returning to school this year because of finances. Her dad had got laid off from his job. I knew that the Vandivere Alumni Scholarship had become available—they were looking for applicants for this fall—so I told her to apply. She was a sure thing. Strongest swimmer I've ever coached."

"She must have been thrilled," Josie said.

"We both were. She got to keep going to college, and I got to keep my star." He paused. Josie saw a range of emotions streak across his face. Then he lowered his head into his hands. From behind his palms, he said, "I'm sorry. I keep going from profound disbelief—like surely, this isn't really happening—to devastation. But acting like it's not real isn't going to bring her back, is it?"

"I'm afraid not," Josie said.

He lifted his head and slapped his palms onto his thighs. "I have to act strong for the kids. They're really freaked out. I'm sorry. What else do you need to know?"

"Does the university conduct regular drug testing of the students on the swim team?"

"Oh yeah. It's random. Twice a semester. More if we suspect something is going on. A positive result is an immediate suspension followed by an investigation. But we've never had any issues with my swim team."

"You ever have any problems with your swimmers using drugs? Edibles? Anything like that?"

Pace shook his head. "No, I haven't had a positive test come up in about four years. If these kids are doing stuff like edibles, they're either hiding it really well or getting lucky on random drug tests. We found a joint in someone's swim bag last year, but no positive tests."

"How about you? Any recreational drug use?"

His face went from a smile to a pinched expression. Incredulity, Josie thought, except it came off exceedingly fake. "Officer," he said.

"Detective."

"Detective, I'm the head coach of Denton University's swim team. Drug use is forbidden."

"Right," she said, noting that he didn't say that he didn't use drugs, only that the use of them was forbidden. She took out her phone and swiped until she found the photo of the sticker. Turning it in his direction, she asked, "Have you ever seen this before?"

He laughed but when he saw her expression, the sound cut off in his throat. "I'm sorry. You're serious. No, I've never seen it. What is it? A doodle or something? The drawing isn't half bad, but what the hell is it?"

"We don't know," Josie said. "It was found in Nysa's things."

He pointed a finger at her phone. "You found that in Nysa's things? Looks like whoever drew that was high. Is that why you're asking so many questions about drugs? You think Nysa was using them? Nysa didn't do drugs, and I can't see her drawing something as bizarre as that. She was more of a dogs and hearts kind of person. She was completely obsessed with her Havanese."

"Really?" said Josie, flashing back to the framed photo of a small white dog in Nysa's room. "What's her dog's name?"

"Oh, I, uh, I don't remember. The kids just always teased her about how much she loved her dog. It was her phone screensaver."

"When's the last time you saw Nysa?"

"Friday," he said. "That was our last practice."

"You were in the piece that WYEP did this weekend. You didn't see her then?"

"Oh, they taped my interview separate from the students, so no, I didn't see her Saturday."

"How did Nysa seem at practice on Friday?"

"She seemed like Nysa." A genuine smile crossed his face. "She was great."

"She didn't seem depressed or upset to you?"

One eyebrow kinked upward. "Upset? Why would she be upset? Listen, Nysa wasn't like the other girls, okay? She was driven and ambitious, sure, but not high-strung. She used to have this joke with the other kids where if they were whining about something, she'd say, 'But did it kill you?' The whole team started saying it. 'My roommate kept me up all night with loud music. But did it kill you?' or 'I tanked my history test. But did it kill you?' Man, and now she's dead. Shit. Why are you—why are you asking these things?"

"Standard procedure," Josie replied. "Did Nysa have any problems with anyone on the team? Any feuds or bad blood?"

"No, not at all. The kids get along pretty well. Also, I don't allow that kind of thing. If people have issues with one another, we address it head-on so it doesn't affect the rest of the team dynamic."

"Are there any team members she was particularly close with?"

"No, not that I can think of. She was friendly to everyone, but I don't think she had a best friend on the team."

"How about a boy named Hudson?"

"Hudson Tinning?"

Josie jotted down the last name. "I understand they're quite competitive, and that he may have had a crush on her."

Pace laughed. "He's always trying to impress her. He's had a thing for Nysa from day one, but he's kind of immature. Kind of a momma's boy. He's got a lot of growing up to do. Someone as independent as Nysa wouldn't have time for a kid like that."

Josie took down some notes. "Do you know if Nysa was dating anyone?"

"I doubt it," Pace said. "Like I said, Nysa was laser-focused on school and swimming. If she wasn't in class, she was at the pool. If she wasn't at the pool, she was at the gym doing conditioning exercises. If she wasn't there, she was at the library. If she managed to fit a relationship into her busy schedule, I'd be really surprised."

"Coach Pace, you said you hadn't seen Nysa since Friday. Had you heard from her, though? By phone or text? Social media? Anything like that?"

"Oh no," he said.

"Do the students have your cell phone number?"

"Well, yeah. All the kids on the team have it. They rarely use it unless they're going to be late or miss practice."

This was getting her nowhere.

"Do you live in Denton?" Josie asked, changing course.

"Yeah, a couple of miles from campus," he offered.

"Alone?"

"Does my dog count?" he laughed. "I'm divorced. No kids."

"What kind of dog?" Josie asked.

"Labradoodle."

"Where were you last night?"

"Last night?" he repeated. "I was—wait, why do you need to know?"

"We're asking everyone, Coach Pace." She gave him a big smile. "Standard procedure."

He didn't look convinced but said, "Last night I was at home."

"With your dog."

"Yeah."

"Right," Josie said. "After nine thirty. Still at home?"

"I was home all night," he replied. He slipped back into his overly friendly mode. "Mondays come quicker the older you get, know what I mean?"

Josie looked down at her pink shirt. "Yeah," she said. "I do."

# CHAPTER FOURTEEN

My first time killing came a bit later. It wasn't something I had planned initially, but living with other people can be difficult. They always disappoint, both in big ways and in small ones. He had disappointed me in a big way, but it was the constant wheezing that set my teeth on edge. You wouldn't believe the noises your lungs make when they fill up with fluid. At first, I was glad to see him in such discomfort. If anyone had ever deserved to die a slow death, robbed of air in increments each day while fever burned through them, it was him. It was divine luck that he got so sick in the first place. Then all I had to do was switch his antibiotics with something else. He almost caught on a few times, made some noises about how he wasn't "sure if these are the right pills," but by the fourth day he was so weak, and he had so little breath left to use on speech, he shut up. Of course, he went back for more antibiotics, and I had to switch those out, too. I had already decided by that time that if he wasn't gone within another week, I'd have to take drastic measures. The wheezing was driving me mad, but I didn't want him to get better. Not after what he'd done. He had lied and not just to me. He was a lot like Nysa in that way.

In the end, I didn't even get to see him die. I left him gasping for air and when I returned, there was only silence. I was giddy with delight—not just because he was dead but because he'd gotten what he deserved—until one of the doctors at the hospital mentioned an autopsy. Would it show that he didn't have any of the antibiotics he was supposed to have taken in his system? To my relief, they declined to perform one. Still, I waited for someone to figure out what I had done.

No one ever did.

# CHAPTER FIFTEEN

Josie followed Coach Pace into the hallway and watched him walk back to the lobby. She heard the campus officer at the reception desk say, "See you later, Coach." The smell of pizza wafted toward her from the other end of the hall, and her stomach growled loudly in response. Mettner poked his head out of the CCTV room. "Food's in here," he said. As Josie devoured two slices of pizza in short order, they exchanged notes on their most recent interviews, which had led nowhere.

Mettner said, "Hudson Tinning is the last interview. He's in my room. You want to talk to him together?"

Josie used a napkin to wipe pizza sauce from her mouth. "Yeah."

As they entered the interview room, Hudson Tinning stood from one of the chairs surrounding the small table. A black T-shirt hung on his tall, wiry frame. White letters proclaimed: *School Kills My Vibe.* The cuffs of his torn jeans brushed over the tops of his flip-flop-clad feet. He towered over Josie and even had a few inches on Mettner, who was almost six feet tall.

"You're the police?" he said, looking from Mettner to Josie and back. His pale blue eyes were wide. Stringy locks of blond hair hung down the sides of his face giving him a surfer look. "I mean, the real police," he clarified. "Not just the campus police."

"Yes," Josie said. She introduced herself and Mettner and they showed him their credentials. "Have a seat, Mr. Tinning."

He returned to his seat. Mettner sat across from him and took out his phone, pulling up his note-taking app. Josie remained standing. Hudson pushed a hand through his hair. "Is it true? Nysa's dead?"

"I'm sorry, Mr. Tinning," said Josie. "Nysa Somers passed away this morning."

"Oh Jesus." His head dipped as he took several deep breaths. When he looked back up at them, tears glistened in his eyes. "Are you guys serious? I mean, really? She's dead?"

"I'm afraid so," Mettner said.

"Oh God." He put his elbows on the table and lowered his face into his palms. A sob filled the room. Josie and Mettner gave him a moment. Then Mettner said, "Mr. Tinning, I know this is upsetting, but we really need to ask you some questions."

Lifting his face, Hudson wiped tears from his cheeks and nodded. "I'm sorry. Yeah, yeah. Go ahead. I just—what happened to her?"

"We're not sure yet," Josie told him. "That's why we're here."

"Someone said she was in the pool. Like, dead. That makes no sense. You know she's the best swimmer we've got, right?"

"We're aware," Josie told him.

"Then how could she drown?"

Mettner said, "As Detective Quinn said, we're really not sure what happened at this point. We'll know more when our investigation concludes."

Hudson said, "When will that be?"

Josie said, "It could take a couple of months, unfortunately, because the medical examiner is doing routine toxicology screening and that can take up to eight weeks."

"Eight weeks!" he exclaimed. "Why so long?"

Josie answered, "Not enough labs to do all the processing. The labs that are available are severely backlogged. Some of the tests require multiple steps and take time to process."

"But her family," Hudson said. "They'll want to know what happened. Her friends—all of us want to know what happened."

"I'm sorry, Hudson," said Josie.

"Her parents were just in town. Did anyone talk to them?"

"Our colleague was with them this morning," Mettner said. "They made a positive identification. We'll be speaking to them again later."

"Can you tell them I'm sorry? For their loss?"

"Of course," said Josie.

"'Cause I guess they'll have her funeral at home and not here."

Josie said, "New Jersey isn't a long drive from here."

Hudson nodded.

Mettner said, "I take it that you two were close?"

Hudson placed his palms down on the table. "Yeah. We've been training a lot together since school started. We were already friends but just spent a lot more time together since we came back to school this year. We're both on the swim team, both sophomores. We've had a few classes together."

"Were you having any kind of romantic relationship with Ms. Somers?" Josie asked him.

"No. We weren't. I wanted to. I liked her. She was cool, you know? Not like most girls here. But she was too focused on her schoolwork and the team to date anyone."

"Did Nysa know that you were interested in her in a sexual way?" Mettner asked.

He shrugged, his gaze on his hands. "I don't know. I guess. Maybe."

"Maybe?" Josie pressed.

Eyes still downcast, he mumbled, "Sure, I guess she knew I liked her. Everyone did."

Josie said, "Did you ever ask her out? Make any advances?"

"We kissed once at a party. Last year. We were both drunk. But after that she told me she wasn't interested in seeing anyone."

"Anyone?" Josie said. "Or just you?"

Several seconds ticked past. Hudson's fingers drummed against his thighs. "I don't know. That's what she told me. That she wasn't interested in seeing anyone."

"How were things over the weekend when WYEP taped their piece on the two of you?" Josie said.

"That," Hudson said, giving a slow shake of his head. "I didn't even want to be in it, but it turned out okay. We all went out to lunch after they shot the interviews—me, my mom, Nysa, and her parents. Everything was cool. WYEP shot the interviews and stuff Saturday morning 'cause that's when Nysa's parents could come. The other stuff was footage from the team archive from last year. I guess they edited all that day 'cause it was on the eleven o'clock news."

"So there were no issues between you and Nysa over the news story?" Mettner asked.

"No. Of course not. Everything was cool."

"Even though you're normally very competitive?" Mettner went on.

"No, everything was fine. I mean, yeah, my mom really wanted me to be included in the piece since I was born and raised here in Denton, but Nysa didn't care about sharing the spotlight. We had a good time."

Josie said, "Hudson, when is the last time you saw Nysa?"

He turned his gaze to her. "At, um, a party. Saturday night. It was in that student housing complex on the upper campus. Not Hollister, one of the other ones. A guy on the swim team—he's a senior—he and his roommate threw a party. I was there most of the night. Nysa stopped in but didn't stay."

"Was she drinking?" asked Mettner.

Hudson shook his head. "She didn't drink much. Hardly at all, really. She always came to parties, like, just to show face, or whatever, but she didn't like to drink so she'd hang for a while and then leave. I mean, sometimes she'd get drunk, like last year, but that was pretty rare."

Josie said, "Were there drugs at the party?"

"I don't know. Maybe. I didn't really notice."

Mettner asked, "Do you ever use drugs?"

Hudson looked from Mettner to Josie and back, eyes wide.

Josie said, "It's okay if you do. You won't be in trouble. We're not here for that."

"Oh, well, I might have smoked some pot last year."

"But not this year?" Mettner asked.

"Well, no. I, uh, I lost a scholarship last year because one of the swimming coaches found a joint in my swim bag. I'm also on academic probation. I can't afford to mess around this year, and you know they do random drug testing."

Mettner tapped into his phone. "Fair enough."

Hudson leaned forward until his chest brushed the edge of the table. "Look, if you could not mention that to anyone else on the team… It's kind of embarrassing. Obviously, the coaching staff know, but…"

Josie said, "There's no reason for it to leave this room, Hudson. Where did you get that joint?"

He shrugged. "Some kid in my English class."

"Do you remember his name?" Mettner asked.

Hudson raised a brow, his expression wavering on a smile, as though Mettner was about to drop a punchline. When he didn't, Hudson said, "I don't remember."

Josie said, "Tell me, have you seen this image before?" She took out her phone and showed him a photo of the sticker.

He stared at it for a beat and shook his head slowly. "No. What is it?"

"We're not sure," Mettner said.

"What does it have to do with Nysa?"

"We're not sure," Mettner repeated.

Josie moved on. "When you saw Nysa on Saturday at the party, was anyone with her?"

"Her roommate, Christine."

Josie said, "How did Nysa seem to you on Saturday?"

"What do you mean?"

Mettner said, "Was she upset at all? Distracted?"

"No, no. She was normal."

Josie asked, "Do you know if there was anything going on in her life that was causing her stress?"

"Nah," Hudson said. "She was pretty chill. Then again, it's so early in the semester, there's not much to stress over yet."

"Did Nysa have any problems with depression or anxiety that you know of?" Josie said.

His eyes moistened again, and his shoulders began to quake. "What? No. She was a happy person. Are you, like, saying she killed herself or something? 'Cause there's no way she did that. She was really ambitious. There was so much she wanted to do. She had plans for her life."

"Okay," Josie said, holding up a hand to silence him before he got hysterical. "I understand."

What she didn't tell him was that sometimes even the most driven and determined people had inner demons they couldn't escape. Sometimes people who were successful at most things in life weren't able to overcome those demons. Sometimes those demons led people to do things they might not otherwise do—like eat drug-laced brownies.

"Hudson," Mettner said. "Is there someone we can call for you? Your mom, maybe?"

"God no," Hudson said. "Please. Not now, anyway. I'll call her later today."

"Okay. We just have a few more questions," Josie said. "Where were you last night?"

"Home," he answered.

"Where's home?" Mettner asked.

"Oh, Hollister. Same as Nysa and her roommate. I live a couple of blocks away from them."

"Do you have a roommate?" Josie asked.

"Yeah. He was there."

Josie took down the name of the roommate and fired off a text to Noah to make sure he tracked the guy down to confirm Hudson's alibi.

Mettner said, "So you were home last night? Say, after nine, nine thirty?"

"Yeah. I had a chem test this morning, so I was studying."

Coming from someone wearing a shirt that said *School Kills My Vibe,* Josie found it hard to believe Hudson was studying on a Sunday night, but she didn't say that. Instead, she asked, "How'd you do on the test?"

"Oh, I won't know till later this week."

"Just one last question before we let you go," Josie said. "Do you know anyone who might have wanted to hurt Nysa?"

Hudson put his face back in his hands. "No, man. I don't. I don't know why anyone would want to hurt her. She was amazing."

# CHAPTER SIXTEEN

Before they left the campus, Josie checked with Chief Hahlbeck about the sticker. She'd been searching their database but hadn't found anything. She promised to keep looking and make some inquiries around campus. With nothing left to do on campus, Josie and Mettner returned to their own headquarters. Josie felt relief to see her beloved stationhouse after the intense chaos and sadness of the morning. It was a massive three-story stone building with an old, unused bell tower at one corner. When it was first built, it had been the town hall. Sixty-five years ago, it had been converted to the police station. Imposing, stately, and a study in gray, it had character. Josie loved the old building.

Mettner arrived at the same time as she did, parking next to her in the municipal lot at the rear of the building. Together, they trudged through the back door and walked up two flights of stairs to the great room where the detectives' permanent desks sat all pushed together in the middle of the room. Surrounding them were other desks used by various patrol officers needing to complete paperwork. There was now a new permanent desk for their press liaison, Amber Watts, to the right of the collective desks. Amber had decorated it in a teal and white theme—matching penholder, pens, stapler, and scissors. She had also put up a teal and white framed cork board on the wall beside her desk. It looked very un-corporate and cheery. It was a little out of place in the police station, but Amber's ever-present exuberance and her need to coordinate everything was growing on Josie.

Amber looked up from her laptop and pushed a long lock of her auburn hair off her shoulder. She grinned at Mettner, and

Josie detected two rosy pink circles in his cheeks as he said, "Miss Watts, nice to see you."

Amber nodded, flashing Mettner a megawatt smile, and stabbed her teal and white striped pen in the air. "The desk sergeant said to call him when you got here. He has something for you."

Josie went to her desk and dialed the front lobby where Sergeant Dan Lamay had been stationed now for almost five years. Dan had been with Denton PD longer than anyone currently on the force. He'd survived scandals and multiple chiefs. He was past retirement age, but when Josie was interim chief, she'd made him desk sergeant so he could continue to serve on the force. His family needed his income and his benefits. She'd been rewarded with his friendship, which had saved her hide on more than one occasion. "You're here," he said when he answered. "I'll be right up."

Josie was going to tell him that she would come to him, but he'd already hung up. Dan had bad arthritis in one of his knees that seemed to get worse each year. A minute later, he came huffing through the stairwell door, a paper evidence bag in his hands. Dan lumbered over to Josie's desk and handed it to her. "Hummel left that phone and charger. He said it's ready for you to examine. He already dusted it for prints. He said there was only one set, belonging to the owner of the phone."

"Did he say anything about a baggie?" Josie asked him. "I asked him to get prints from that, too."

Dan scratched his chin. "He said same prints on the baggie as on the phone. He'll have a report for you by the end of the day, but he wanted you to know that right away. Oh, and Gretchen called and got permission from the parents for you to examine Nysa Somers' phone."

"Where is Gretchen?" Mettner asked.

"She went over to Hollister Way to help Lieutenant Fraley canvass," Dan said. "She also told me about your shirts, boss. I ordered some for you. They'll be here in two days."

"Dan," Josie said. "You're a godsend. Thank you."

He waved a hand in a gesture that said it was no big deal. Turning to head back downstairs, he said over his shoulder, "This way you can spend your time on more important things."

Josie opened the bag and took the phone out. She pressed the power button. The screen said: enter passcode.

"Shit," Josie said.

Dan stopped. "What's wrong?"

"It needs a passcode."

Dan frowned. "Oh yeah. Gretchen said that she asked the parents if they knew her passcode, but they didn't."

"Thanks, Dan," Mettner said as the older man shuffled out of the room and back down the stairs. To Josie, he said, "I'll call Christine Trostle and see if she knows."

Christine didn't know the passcode but made several suggestions, none of which granted them access to the phone. Josie plopped into her chair with a sigh, put the phone on her desk and glared at it. From the corner of the room, Amber spoke up. "You said she was a swimmer, right? You should try something swimming-related. What was her event? The race she did the best at?"

Mettner flashed Amber a smile.

Josie sat forward and tapped away at her keyboard. "Great idea," she said. Pulling up the latest WYEP story on the Denton University swim team, Josie, Mettner, and Amber watched the short video, which focused almost entirely on Nysa. Hudson had been included, as per his mother's wishes, but his contribution had been pared down to short sound bites praising Nysa. The sight of her alive, well, and thriving was painful. Josie could still feel Nysa's cold, lifeless form beneath her hands as she tried to pump life back into her.

Mettner said, "Sounds like her best race was the hundred-meter butterfly."

Amber said, "I bet you her personal best time is her passcode."

Josie clicked off the WYEP story and did a Google search. It only took a few minutes to find it. "Amber! You're brilliant." She picked up the phone and typed in 5786. Immediately, the phone unlocked.

"Yes!" Josie said, drawing laughs from Mettner and Amber.

They crowded in behind her as she navigated through the phone. The home screen was a photo of the white dog that Josie had seen in a frame on Nysa's dresser. There were several unread texts, most of which were from Christine. Some were from other students who obviously shared classes with Nysa, wondering where she'd been that morning. There was one which Josie believed was from her mother, sent at nine that morning, asking how the paper was going. Josie swallowed over a lump in her throat. Clearly, Nysa had been very close to her family.

Josie had to find out what happened to this girl.

"There are no texts from last night except for the ones between her and Christine," she complained. "Whoever the 'friend' was that she met up with, they didn't text her. Unless she deleted the texts."

"Check the call log," said Mettner.

Josie did but there was nothing aside from Christine's calls, all of them missed. "There's nothing."

"There has to be something," Mettner said. "Let me see."

He took the phone from her hands, scrolling and swiping. Josie said, "Check her email and social media. There has to be some evidence of this mystery friend. You checked all the library footage, right?"

"Yeah," Mettner mumbled. "She went inside, went to the fourth floor, talked with the librarian and then worked at a computer station until the library closed. She didn't talk to anyone."

"Then she must have met up with the mystery person on her way out of the cut-through," Josie said. "I was down there today. She could have seen someone on the path or even walking back to her house. Also, people park there and walk up to campus. Someone could have even been waiting for her when she stepped off the path."

Mettner looked up from the phone. "So this is worthless."

Amber said, "Could I take a look?"

Mettner handed the phone off to Amber. To Josie, he said, "Didn't you say that the roommate thought Nysa was seeing someone secretly?"

"She implied it," Josie said. "Yeah."

"Maybe they met there and spent the night together. Maybe that's a place they routinely meet up—at the cut-through. If so, there would be no need for them to call or text one another."

"Could be, but Christine was expecting her to come home when the library closed. If the GPS is enabled on her phone, we might be able to find out where she was last night," Josie suggested.

"Her phone was in her backpack, which was tossed into the woods," Mettner said. "It was probably there all night."

"True," Josie said. "But it's worth checking."

"There's something in her calendar," Amber said. She held up the phone so that both Mettner and Josie could see the screen. Sure enough, the tiny square for that morning was filled with something. Josie took the phone from Amber and tapped to enlarge it. Her heartbeat sped up a fraction. "You're right," she said. "There was a calendar reminder set for five fifty-five a.m. today. It says: 'Time to be a mermaid.'"

"What does that mean?" Mettner asked. "Is that what she calls herself because she's a swimmer? A mermaid? Is that supposed to be some kind of joke? Like instead of 'time for a swim,' 'time to be a mermaid?'"

Josie scrolled through the calendar going back months, but the "Time to be a mermaid" alert was the only entry in it. "I don't think she used this calendar."

"She used it this morning," said Amber.

"Right. But there's nothing else on here going back a year, at least. Why would she suddenly put a reminder into her calendar app for a time she didn't normally even go swimming? Why would she stay out all night on a Sunday night with some mystery friend and then go to the pool with no suit and without her swim bag? Where was she between the time she left the library and when she came back out of the cut-through this morning? Who was she with?"

Mettner stared at her. "Should I be writing this down?"

Josie laughed drily. "No. I'm thinking out loud."

Mettner held out a hand and Josie gave him the phone. He tapped and scrolled. He frowned. "The GPS isn't enabled. Even if she had it with her all night, there's no way to find out where she went."

"Draw up a warrant," Josie said. "Send it to her provider so we can find out where the phone pinged last night."

"That's only going to get us to within one to three miles of where she was," Mettner pointed out. "And it could take a week to get it, depending on her provider."

"Still worth a try," Josie said.

The stairwell door swung open and Noah stepped into the room, looking tired. Behind him, Detective Gretchen Palmer shuffled in, a rolled-up polo shirt tucked beneath one of her arms. She handed it to Josie before lowering herself into her desk chair.

"Thanks," said Josie. "Dan ordered me some new shirts. I'll give it back as soon as they come in. Did you guys get anything?"

Noah, too, sat down. He took out his notebook and tossed it onto his desk. "No," he said.

"Not a damn thing," Gretchen added.

"You're kidding," Mettner said.

"I wish we were," said Gretchen. "But no one remembers seeing Nysa Somers last night or this morning. Or if they did, they won't admit it."

Noah said, "Sunday is one of the quieter nights, apparently. First classes on Monday don't start till eight. Nysa came out of the cut-through around six. There wouldn't have been many people out at that time on a Monday morning. We checked with Hudson Tinning's roommate. He says Hudson was home all day Sunday. His mom brought his clean wash over with some dinner. They all had dinner together around six thirty, then the mom left. The roommate says both of them were there the whole night. He went to bed around one in the morning, and Hudson was in their living room playing Xbox."

"Oh," Josie said. "I expect he scored high on that chem test then." Mettner laughed.

Noah said, "Where do we go from here?"

"I'd like to talk to her parents," Josie said.

"Not today," Gretchen said. "They asked if we could give them the rest of the day. Their other daughter is driving up tonight to be with them. She goes to Temple University in Philadelphia. Freshman year."

Noah looked at his phone. "It's almost five. We need to get home. We've got dinner."

Josie smiled in spite of the terrible mood the Nysa Somers case had put her in. "Oh yes, I can't wait. Let's get home then. I could use a shower. I just want to call Dr. Feist and see if she's had a chance to do the autopsy."

Josie dialed Dr. Feist's cell phone. After seven rings, the doctor answered, sounding out of breath. "Detective Quinn, what can I do for you?"

"We were just wondering if you'd had a chance to complete Nysa Somers' autopsy?"

She blew out a breath. "Best-laid plans. I had my assistant start the preliminary preparations, and then the emergency room got slammed. Three cases of seizures and two of acute heart failure, all in a row. They asked me to come up and help out. It's an 'all hands on deck' situation over here."

"I'm sorry to hear that," Josie said. "Don't let me keep you."

"Tomorrow, Detective," Dr. Feist said. "I promise."

*

At home, Josie took their Boston terrier, Trout, for a walk while Noah started dinner. Of the two of them, he was the only one who could cook a whole dinner without setting off smoke alarms. Misty and Harris showed up a half hour later. Much to Josie's relief, Harris had had a wonderful day at Pre-K and couldn't wait to return the next morning. He spent all of dinner regaling them with tales of the animals in the small petting zoo.

In spite of the pleasant dinner and the weight off her shoulders knowing that Harris had had a great—and safe—first day at Pre-K, Josie couldn't sleep. Thoughts of Nysa Somers, the potentially laced brownies, the creepy sticker, and the missing hours before her strange death whirled in her head. When she checked the clock for the third time that night, it read 4:57 a.m. This time last night Nysa had been… where? Josie wondered. Where had she gone for eight hours? Who had she been with?

Trout whined at her feet and jumped down from the bed, finding a place on the bedroom carpet as he sometimes did when Josie tossed and turned too much for his liking. Josie reached out for Noah, but his side of the bed was cold and empty. She got up and padded downstairs with Trout at her feet. Noah was nowhere to be found. Back upstairs, she saw that his phone and wallet weren't on the dresser where he normally left them. She called him. After six rings, he picked up.

"Where are you?" she asked.

"Got a call," he said. "I'll meet you at the station later."

"Why didn't you wake me up?" she asked.

"You were out cold. I thought you needed the rest. You can get the next one. Listen, I have to go."

Josie opened her mouth to say something: *Come home. I wish you were here.* She wasn't good at communicating those types of things. Things that uncloaked her vulnerability. She knew she was supposed to try. Everyone in her life had been pushing her to go to therapy for the past year. So far she had resisted. Reliving her vast and varied childhood trauma seemed like the least helpful thing to do. She preferred to push it down or out or into a compartment in her mind where she didn't have to remember any of it. Sometimes certain cases caused her demons to swirl. It was always better if Noah was there with her, especially since she'd given up drinking. But he had a job to do, just the same as her. She knew he couldn't come home, even if he wanted to.

"You there?" Noah said.

"Yeah," she said. "I—I'll see you later."

He hung up before she could say the one thing she was comfortable admitting: "I miss you."

# CHAPTER SEVENTEEN

Three hours later, Josie drove through the center of town and up the long road to Denton Memorial Hospital. The large, blocky brick building sat on top of one of the tallest hills in town. Josie parked and went inside, taking an elevator to the basement, which housed the city morgue. It was the quietest place in the entire building. A long hallway, once bright white but now dingy gray and complemented by yellowed floor tiles, led to Dr. Feist's domain. As Josie drew closer, the ever-present smell of chemicals combined with the rancid scent of putrefaction assaulted her senses.

She bypassed the large exam and autopsy room and went to Dr. Feist's office. The door was open, but Dr. Feist wasn't inside. Josie sat in the guest chair in front of her desk and waited. Dr. Feist had done her best to make the room warm and welcoming. The cinder block walls were painted a soothing periwinkle blue. The abstract wall art was awash in pastel colors. Dr. Feist kept the overhead fluorescent lights turned off in favor of two desk lamps, which gave the room a softer glow. A second potted plant had been added since Josie was last there, and now a white cylindrical air freshener sat on top of one of the filing cabinets, hissing out a spray of apple-scented aerosol every few seconds. It was a pleasant addition, but couldn't overcome the odor of the morgue next door.

"Detective Quinn," Dr. Feist said as she sailed into the office. She plopped into the chair behind her desk with a sigh, lower lip jutted out as she blew a breath of air upward, making her silver-blonde bangs flutter. "Are you alone?"

Josie checked her phone furtively. She hadn't heard from Noah all morning. His only response to her texts had been a terse: *Got caught up. Meet you later.*

"It appears that way," Josie said. "You look exhausted. Here." Josie handed her a cup of coffee from their favorite city café, Komorrah's.

"I haven't been home yet," Dr. Feist said. Her eyes closed as she sipped the coffee. "Heavenly," she added. "Thank you."

"They had you in the ER all night?"

She shook her head and put her coffee down on her desk. "Not the entire night. They had three more heart attacks after the other cases. I did what I could. I don't normally treat patients, but I made myself useful in any way I could. Then I figured I was up, so why not come down here and do Nysa Somers' autopsy? After meeting with her family yesterday, I don't want them to have to wait long for the body to be released."

"Thank you," Josie said. "For getting to it so quickly."

"Of course. I won't have a report ready for another day, and even then, it will only be preliminary, pending the toxicology results. I can't issue a final report until those are in, and as you know, toxicology testing can take up to eight weeks."

"I'm aware," Josie said. "Anything you can tell me now about your initial findings would be helpful."

Dr. Feist leaned back in her chair, resting her head against its back. "Before I go into those, you should know that while it is pretty clear that Nysa Somers drowned, it's not clear yet whether or not it was an accident. Her cause of death is drowning, but the manner of death—accident, homicide, suicide—I can't give you a firm answer on that right now. Sometimes, when we see drowning as a cause of death, particularly in a case where a body is found in water and we don't know how it got there, it's not always clear how the drowning happened. That's why toxicology tests are so important. I know it's frustrating to wait, but we have no control over the speed of the lab, unfortunately."

"I understand," Josie said. "What did you find on exam?"

Dr. Feist nodded. "She had no traumatic injuries, no signs of sexual assault, no bruising, no lacerations, no skin under her fingernails, and no evidence of disease or sudden medical event. Basically, on exam, Nysa Somers was as healthy as could be. The only things I found were consistent with death by drowning. Her lungs were very congested. Hyperinflated. On x-ray they showed what we call 'ground glass opacity,' meaning that the images of her lungs look as though they've got ground glass in them. She had fluid in her stomach and her paranasal sinuses. But as I said, the manner of death is undetermined. At least until we get toxicology back."

"Any other contents in her stomach?" Josie asked. "Any way to tell the last thing she ate and when?"

Dr. Feist's face lit up. "As a matter of fact, there was some type of food in her stomach at the time of her death. It was difficult to tell what it might have been but from having done autopsies for the last twenty years, my guess is chocolate. Some kind of candy bar, pastry—a brownie, maybe? I can't say that for certain. I've sent the stomach contents off to the lab as well for analysis but that, too, will take time."

Josie said, "The stomach takes about six hours to completely empty, doesn't it?"

"Well, it depends on the person," said Dr. Feist.

"We've got about eight hours of time unaccounted for in this case. From roughly nine thirty in the evening till six in the morning. Is it possible that Nysa Somers ate something during that time based on what you found?"

"Not just possible," Dr. Feist answered. "Probable. It's just difficult to pinpoint when she ate it. It would have had to be after midnight, I'd say."

"What about time of death?" Josie asked. "Were you able to narrow that at all? I know we're only looking at a two-hour window as it is—between six a.m. and eight a.m.—but I'm curious."

"Given the temperature of the room in which the pool was located as well as the pool water, both of which are at a constant temperature, and the measurement from her chest cavity on autopsy, I'd say she was dead approximately two hours."

"You're saying it's likely she died shortly after six a.m. when she entered the pool area, then?" Josie clarified.

Dr. Feist nodded.

Josie was silent.

"What is it?" Dr. Feist asked.

"Nothing," Josie said. "I'm just trying to work out how I'm going to tell her family that their star swimmer did, in fact, drown yesterday."

# CHAPTER EIGHTEEN

Chief Bob Chitwood stood in front of the detectives' desks, his arms crossed over his thin chest, staring down at Josie, Mettner, and Gretchen. His dark eyes peered at each one of them in turn over the rim of a pair of reading glasses. Strands of his white hair floated across his scalp. At least his acne-scarred cheeks weren't flushed with irritation or anger, Josie thought. Yet.

He stabbed the air with a finger. Josie couldn't tell if it was directed at one of them or all of them. "You're telling me," he said, "that the best swimmer on the college team drowned yesterday?"

The detectives looked at one another. Then Gretchen, who had the most calming effect on Chitwood of all of them, said, "Yes, sir. It appears that way. What caused it, we're not sure."

Mettner said, "The press has already gotten wind of it. Amber was fielding calls all morning. She's at lunch now, but she was pretty busy today. She gave them all the standard 'our investigation is ongoing' line for now."

"I'll make sure she keeps it that way. Quinn!" Chitwood barked. "You got anything?"

Josie told him about the brownie crumbs found in a baggie in Nysa's discarded backpack, as well as Dr. Feist's confirmation that Nysa had eaten said brownies before her death. Then Josie handed him a printout of the sticker.

Chitwood pushed his reading glasses higher onto his nose and stared at the picture. He said, "This is weird." Then he sighed, handed it back to her and shifted his glasses lower so he could look over them. "So she took something, got high, went for a swim while she was intoxicated and drowned. It's damn sad but not unique to young people. Open and shut."

Josie said, "Sir, I'm not sure—"

"Let me guess," he cut her off, leaning over and bracing his hands against her desk and staring closely at her face. "You think this is something more than some college kid doing an incredibly dumb thing and paying the ultimate price for it?"

Josie braced herself for one of his signature tirades. "Actually, a couple of things do seem off."

"Meaning what?" Chitwood demanded.

"Meaning, sure, she ate the brownies and yeah, they were probably laced with something, but I don't think she would voluntarily or knowingly take drugs."

Picking up on her train of thought, Mettner said, "Everyone we spoke with said that Nysa Somers didn't use drugs and rarely drank. If she was under the influence of something, I can see Detective Quinn's point. It would be odd if Nysa had chosen to eat those brownies knowing they had something in them."

"Also," Josie said. "The 'time to be a mermaid' calendar notification makes no sense."

"It does if she was high as a kite, Quinn," barked the Chief. "You know people do crazy, nonsensical shit when they're under the influence."

"I just don't think she ate those brownies knowing they had something in them."

Chitwood made a noise of frustration. "Did it ever occur to you that maybe she was depressed and just didn't care anymore? Maybe she was suicidal and didn't care if the drugs killed her."

Gretchen picked up a stack of pages on her desk and set them back down. "When I got here today, I drew up some warrants and served them on the campus health center in person and then her doctor's office in her hometown in New Jersey, by email. Mett and I spent all morning looking through her medical records.

There isn't a single suggestion of her struggling with depression or anxiety."

"Even extremely high-functioning people get depressed. They don't always go to the doctor for it. You talk to her parents yet?"

"I'm going to their hotel now to speak with them," Josie said. "But I have a feeling they're going to say the same thing that everyone else who knew Nysa Somers said. She wasn't depressed. She would never willingly or knowingly take drugs."

Chitwood said, "Quinn, college kids do dumb shit all the time. Even the most promising ones. Sometimes things are just exactly what they appear to be."

"What about the sticker?" Josie asked. "Whoever made those brownies and that sticker gave Nysa something that killed her. Or made her kill herself."

Mettner said, "You think she got into the pool and drowned herself? Wouldn't that be really hard to do?"

"Not if you're under the influence of something really powerful," Gretchen noted. "New drugs are coming onto the scene all the time. Maybe it wasn't pot in the brownies. We could be looking at a variation or combination of drugs. I saw the video you guys got from the lobby. She didn't appear intoxicated in the least and yet, Dr. Feist told Detective Quinn that she likely died soon after entering the pool area. How do you explain that?"

Mettner looked at Gretchen. "Maybe whatever substance she ate didn't hit her until she was in the pool."

"Then why would she get into the pool in regular clothes?" Josie asked.

Gretchen, eyes still on Mett, raised a brow. "We're not talking about tranq darts here, Mett. Dr. Feist said she ate the brownies sometime after midnight, not right before she walked to the pool."

"You don't know that—" Mettner began.

Chitwood held up his hands and yelled, "That's enough. All this speculation is a waste of time. We can say with ninety percent certainty that this girl had something in her system. We'll wait for toxicology. It's as simple as that. Quinn will go tell the parents today that their daughter ate brownies we believe had an illicit substance in them and then drowned. Once the toxicology comes in, Dr. Feist finishes her report. Case closed."

"But the sticker," Josie said. "Sir, what if more students get their hands on whatever was in those brownies?"

"You just said that the campus chief of police had no other drug-related incidents involving these stickers. We have no idea if anything was in the brownies. This is all speculation. Hell, it's speculation that the sticker is an indicator of drugs. I'm not starting a public panic until we have more information."

"But sir," said Josie. "Don't you have a contact in the DEA? You could get in touch and ask about the sticker."

"Or we could wait until toxicology comes back," Chitwood repeated. "Like I just told you."

Josie opened her mouth to respond but Chitwood held up a hand to stop her. "Quinn, I know you've got that feeling you get. I know your instincts rarely fail you, and I know that you want to run with this, but you can't. There's nothing to run with. I can't expend this department's time and resources on a case that's going to turn out to be a tragic accident."

Josie kept her tone calm and even. "Sir, just let me try to track down the person Nysa Somers was with the night before she died."

He folded his arms across his chest again and stared at her. Josie knew she had him. This was a reasonable request. A loose end that should be tied up no matter what the outcome of the investigation. "Fine," he said grudgingly.

"And follow up with Chief Hahlbeck about drug activity on campus. She didn't see any instances of the sticker in any of her files, but she said she was going to keep looking and make some inquiries on campus."

"Quinn—"

Gretchen stood up from her chair, drawing Chitwood's attention. "It's just a conversation, Chief. That's all."

He waved his finger at Gretchen, Josie, and Mettner. "Thin ice," he said. "You three are on thin ice."

Then he stalked off to his office, slamming the door behind him. After a moment of silence, Gretchen said, "He didn't say no."

Josie smiled.

Mettner said, "How are you going to find the person Nysa was with?"

Josie said, "I need you to get that warrant to see where her phone pinged the other night. That's a place to start. Also, given the probable drug angle, I think we should talk with the guy who threw the party that Nysa and Christine were at Saturday night. Hudson said he didn't know if there were drugs there or not."

Mettner scrolled through his phone. "I interviewed that guy already yesterday. He's on the swim team. He hadn't seen the sticker and said he wasn't aware of any drugs at the party."

"Of course he said that," Josie said. "See if you can track down some other people who were at the party."

"You think she got the brownies there? Without her roommate even knowing?"

"I have no idea, Mett. It's another avenue, and we don't have many right now. Someone should also go down to the East Bridge and show the photo of the sticker around there. See if anyone recognizes it."

Beneath Denton's East Bridge was where much of Denton's drug activity was concentrated. "Will do," Mettner said.

Josie said, "While you do that, I'll go see her parents."

Gretchen stood up. "I'll go with you. Let's grab some lunch first."

# CHAPTER NINETEEN

I did it. It worked. I didn't even have to be there. It was contactless death. I was still shocked by the reality of what I had pulled off, by the genius of it. Nysa Somers was dead. My euphoria was tempered by the realization that the aftermath was so much bigger than I anticipated. Not only did the press jump on the story, but the police did as well. There had been times in the past that the police had gotten involved, but in those cases, their role was perfunctory. They showed up, found nothing out of the ordinary, and closed the case. I had always covered my tracks well enough in the past to elude suspicion. This time, things felt different. The police were taking this way more seriously than I expected. I knew I should have felt frightened. Maybe I should have been more cautious, but the truth was that I felt exhilarated. Nothing had ever felt this good. I had always been invisible before. Only I knew the impact that I had made with each death. Now I was being *seen.* This was the best and biggest thing I'd ever done.

I wanted to do it again.

I could do it again. It would be so easy. But who was left? My list had grown shorter over time. My next victim couldn't be just anyone. It had to be someone who would make just as big a splash as Nysa.

Otherwise, what was the point?

# CHAPTER TWENTY

Josie and Gretchen ate lunch at Sandman's and discussed the case before stopping by the campus again to talk with Chief Hahlbeck. It was a short conversation, as Hahlbeck hadn't found any instances or mentions of the sticker in any of the police files or during her inquiries on campus. Mettner called to say that no one from under the East Bridge had seen—or would admit to having seen—the sticker before. The local drug trade was a dead end.

Josie hung up with him, relayed the news to Gretchen, and then the two of them set off for the Somers' hotel. The Marriott was out past the college campus, just on the outskirts of the city of Denton. It was one of the hotels that filled up completely every year at graduation time and was the hotel of choice for visiting parents. A small café opposite the lobby boasted comfortable seating, low lighting, and the nutty aroma of coffee. Gretchen and Josie found a table, and Gretchen called Mr. Somers, offering him and his family the option of meeting them in the café or having them come up to their room. Ten minutes later, a man and woman in their fifties and a teenage girl shuffled out of one of the elevators and toward the café. Josie recognized them from their photo in Nysa's room and from the news story she had seen. Except now they no longer looked happy and vibrant. Nysa's death had sucked their vitality away. They looked broken, like their skin was barely holding their bones together as they walked.

Nysa's father slid into a seat across from Josie and Gretchen first. He was tall and stocky with a sizeable paunch, a combover, and calluses on his fingertips. A mechanic, Gretchen had told Josie on the way over to the Marriott. Nysa's mother was a dental assistant. She was smaller and thinner than her husband with dark shoulder-length hair. Josie immediately saw the resemblance between her and Nysa. Sitting beside her husband, she patted a chair at the end of the table, indicating for her other daughter to sit. Where Nysa had been lithe and rangy, her sister was curvy, with wide hips and an ample bosom. Where Nysa's hair had been straight, her sister's was curly. After Gretchen made the introductions between Josie and the parents, Nysa's sister extended a hand. "Naomi," she said. "Thank you for coming."

Naomi held their gazes while her parents looked down at the table. There was a fierceness to her that Josie immediately respected, and yet, knowing the task that Naomi was already taking on—of carrying her family through this horrific loss—Josie felt sympathy for her as well.

"We're very sorry for your loss, Naomi," said Josie. "Also, we spoke with several of Nysa's teammates yesterday and many of them, including Hudson Tinning, send their condolences."

Mrs. Somers nodded. "Hudson's a good boy. We were just out to lunch with him and his mom, Mary, on Saturday. We had a lovely time. It was such a great weekend. I don't understand how…" she drifted off, blinking back tears.

"Have you found anything out?" Naomi asked, getting right to the point. Josie's appreciation of her expanded.

Gretchen said, "The autopsy showed that the cause of her death was drowning."

Both Mr. and Mrs. Somers' heads snapped upward, eyes searching. Mr. Somers said, "How is that possible? There is no way my daughter drowned. No way. What kind of incompetence is this? I want another autopsy."

"Dad," Naomi said, her tone quiet but commanding.

Josie said, "It's your choice to have another autopsy performed, and we can certainly discuss the logistics of that."

"But," Naomi said.

Mrs. Somers slid a hand across the surface of the table toward her daughter, and Naomi took it without looking away from the two detectives.

"But our investigation is still very active, and there are some other things that you should know."

A tear slid down Mrs. Somers' face. She said, "Go on." Then she closed her eyes.

Taking a deep breath, Josie went over all they had learned, managing to keep her tone matter-of-fact, trying not to draw conclusions for them, merely presenting what they'd uncovered to that point and relaying their plans for the future of the investigation.

"May I see the sticker?" Naomi asked.

"Of course," said Gretchen. On her phone, she pulled up the photo that Josie had taken and texted to all members of the team, and showed it to the family. Mrs. Somers opened her eyes and gazed at it. Her husband gave it a cursory glance before shaking his head and looking up at the ceiling.

Naomi said, "I've never seen that before. More importantly, you should know that Nysa would never take drugs. Yes, she might drink—"

Her father shot her a stunned look. Addressing him, she said, "Really, Dad. We're in college, we're not saints." She turned her attention back to Josie and Gretchen. "But Nysa would never take drugs."

"She had that friend in school who died from using cocaine once," Mrs. Somers said. "What was her name?"

"Regina," said Naomi. "Now listen. Whoever gave her those brownies or convinced her to eat them did not tell her what was in them. There is no other way that things could have gone down. I know my sister, and she—"

For the first time, emotion overtook her. Naomi shut down and her throat quivered as she fought to regain her composure. Mrs. Somers placed her free hand over both their hands and squeezed.

Josie said, "I believe you."

Naomi nodded. Josie and Gretchen waited for her to get her emotions under control.

"You'll find the person she was with? The person who made that awful sticker and gave her the brownies?"

"We'll do everything we possibly can to find that person," Gretchen assured her.

Naomi said, "There's a law in Pennsylvania now. The death by distribution law. If a person gives another person drugs, and the person taking them dies, the person who provided them can face murder charges."

Josie was aware of the law. It was primarily targeted at drug dealers, and she wasn't sure that Nysa's case would fall under it, but she wasn't about to argue the point with a grieving family. Besides, that was the district attorney's purview, not Josie's. Her job was to do whatever she could to figure out exactly what happened to Nysa.

Gretchen said, "You're right, Naomi. All the more reason to find the person who gave Nysa the brownies."

"If you don't mind," Josie said. "We just have a few questions. We know this is the worst possible time to be asking them, but it will really help our investigation."

Mr. Somers let out a shuddering breath and put his large hands on the table. "Fine," he said.

"Any time you want to stop, you say so," Josie added.

Mrs. Somers nodded.

They went through the series of questions they'd posed to everyone who'd known Nysa. Had she been depressed or anxious? Stressed? No. Did she have a history of anxiety, depression, or suicidal ideations? No. Had she been dating anyone or seeing anyone casually that they knew of? No.

"One last thing," Josie asked. "Did Nysa ever refer to herself as a mermaid? Or did any of you ever call her that?"

Mr. and Mrs. Somers shook their heads. Naomi said, "No. We called her our superstar."

Mr. Somers' shoulders began to quake. Abruptly, he pushed his chair back from the table and stood. Wordlessly, he headed for the elevators. "I'm sorry," his wife whispered. "He's just…"

Josie said, "You never have to apologize for your grief, Mrs. Somers, or your husband's. I'm so sorry."

"Thank you," she answered. Relinquishing Naomi's hand, she heaved herself to her feet and went after her husband.

Naomi, Josie, and Gretchen watched her go. This was the worst part of the job, Josie thought.

"There is something you need to know that I didn't want to say in front of them," Naomi said.

Josie and Gretchen looked at her.

Naomi folded her hands on the table and shifted her weight in her chair. "Nysa was seeing someone. It started right at the beginning of the semester. It wasn't serious. In fact, she instantly regretted it. That's how I know about it. She called me crying the morning after the first time it… happened."

"Happened?" Gretchen said. "Naomi, was your sister raped?"

Naomi's fingers dug into the flesh of the backs of her hands. "No. She made that very clear to me. That was my first question as well."

"Why was she so upset?" Josie asked.

"You have to understand, Detectives, my sister was the ultimate rule-follower. Dedicated, disciplined, ambitious. The first time she ever had a sip of beer, she thought the entire world was going to end. She was upset because the fling she was having—or whatever you want to call it—was with someone much older than her. I am pretty sure it was a professor."

Which would explain Christine Trostle's characterization of Nysa's secretive and unusual behavior, Josie thought.

"So it wasn't Hudson Tinning," Josie said.

Naomi rolled her eyes. "Mommy's boy, Hudson? No. She liked him, a lot, actually, but it definitely wasn't him. Like I said, the person she was seeing was older than her."

"She didn't tell you who it was?" Gretchen asked.

"She said she didn't want anyone to know. She was going to end it and that would be that, and he would never get in trouble for it and neither would she."

"But she didn't end it," Josie said.

"No, she did," Naomi said. "I talked to her on Friday afternoon. She said she'd broken things off. She felt better, was even going to party over the weekend. Well, party as much as Nysa could party, so that probably meant going to a party and having a half a cup of beer."

Gretchen said, "Did she ever confirm that it was a professor?"

"She never said that outright," said Naomi. "I just assumed it was because she was so freaked out."

"What did she actually say?" Josie asked.

Naomi unlaced her fingers and rubbed her palms together. "She said he was a lot older than her and that it was inappropriate."

Josie's cell phone rang. A glance at the screen showed the face and phone number of Mrs. Quinn, her late husband's mother and Harris's grandmother. "I have to take this," she said. Gretchen gave her a nod, indicating that she'd finish the interview with Naomi while Josie stepped away from the table.

Josie walked out into the lobby and swiped *answer.* "Cindy, is everything okay?"

"I'm at Tiny Tykes," Cindy Quinn answered. "I had to pick up Harris because Misty picked up another shift. Pre-K is expensive, you know."

In fact, Josie did know. She'd helped Misty pay for it. "Is Harris okay?"

"Oh yeah, he's fine, but they won't let me take him. Something about an approved list. I'm not on it. I know Misty put me on it, but this woman swears up and down that she didn't."

"Misty must have forgotten," Josie said. "Have they tried calling her?"

Annoyance edged Cindy's words. "They can't do that, apparently. I have no idea why but they're refusing. They'll only release him to Misty or to you. Misty's working in the call center, and I can't get through to her, although even if I could, she'd tell them the same damn thing I've been telling them, which is that she put me on the list when she enrolled Harris. I've been arguing with this woman here for fifteen minutes. Josie, she's like a power-drunk tyrant. She won't let me take my own grandson!"

Josie sighed. "Unfortunately, Cindy, that's a standard policy at these kinds of facilities. It's meant to protect children."

"From what? Their own damn families? Josie, I've just about had it with this lady here. I'm telling you this is a clerical error on their part."

"I'm sure it is," Josie said quickly. "But regardless, we have to address it. We just have to get you back on the list, is all. I can help." The last thing Misty needed was for Cindy to cause a scene at Tiny Tykes. "I can be there in ten minutes. I'll ask if they'll let me put you on the list for future pickups."

"Well, hurry," Cindy said. "I can't be held responsible for what I say to this awful woman in the meantime."

Josie hit *end call* and blew out a breath. She looked up to see Gretchen walking toward her. "I'm sorry. I have to run up to Harris's school."

"It's fine," Gretchen said. "Naomi told me that her whole family is on the same cell phone plan. I'm going to have Mett email the concierge some consent forms. They'll print them here at the desk and then one of Nysa's parents can sign them. This way we don't have to wait for a warrant to see where her phone pinged on Sunday into Monday. I'll get the coordinates and then cross-reference those with the home addresses of her past and present professors. If any of their addresses fall into the area where she was during the time she was unaccounted for, then we'll go have a talk with them."

"Great idea," Josie said. She started to walk out the sliding glass doors but stopped and turned. "Gretchen, put the head coach on that list, would you?"

"You got it, boss."

# CHAPTER TWENTY-ONE

At Tiny Tykes, only two cars remained in the parking lot. In one of them sat Cindy Quinn, window rolled down, her sharp features set in an expression of anger. Josie parked beside her and got out, walking up to the window. Cindy said, "I'm not going back in there."

Josie suppressed a sigh. "I'll get him and see that you're put on the list."

Inside, only Mrs. D remained, sitting at the desk that Miss K normally commanded with Harris in a chair next to it, his large backpack on his back. His legs swung back and forth, not reaching the hardwood floor. When he saw Josie, he jumped up and ran toward her. She caught him expertly and scooped him up, hugging him to her, bulky backpack and all.

"Miss K wouldn't let me go with Grandma," he told her immediately, a frown on his face.

Josie laughed. "I know that. It's okay. Remember how we talked about this place having special rules to keep you safe? Just like your mom and I have special rules to keep you safe?"

"I guess," he mumbled.

Josie set him down and took his hand, walking toward Mrs. D. "You can only leave here with adults that your mom and I say are okay. We forgot to put Grandma on the list. It was a mistake. But I'm going to tell Mrs. D to put her on and everything will be fine. Got it?"

This seemed to cheer him up. He rocked up on his toes. "Got it!"

Mrs. D stood and shook her head. "I'm very sorry about all this. I thought Miss K explained this to Harris's mom during registration. We can't allow anyone to take custody of a child unless they're approved in our system by the child's parents or guardians. We don't know what kinds of custody disputes people have. Terrible things have been known to happen. I can't put my kids at risk that way."

"It's fine," Josie said. "I'm not upset, and I'm sure Misty won't be either. But may I add Mrs. Quinn to the pickup list?"

Mrs. D smiled. "Sure. Of course. Let me get Harris's file."

She disappeared into her office and returned with a thin folder. "You still have physical files?" Josie asked.

"Only for our original enrollment paperwork. Most things are in the computer system, but we keep originals of certain forms."

Josie smiled as Mrs. D opened the file, turned a few pages, and slid it across to Josie. She pointed to a form that had several boxes for parents and guardians to list authorized people for school pickup. "Just fill out the one on the bottom of that page," Mrs. D said.

Josie was still looking at the top of the form where Misty had filled in the parental information. She had told Misty to put her on as one of the emergency contacts, but Misty had listed her as a guardian. It had no legal standing, of course, but it was obvious that the Tiny Tykes staff were not questioning it since they would allow Josie to put Cindy Quinn on the pickup list.

Mrs. D pointed again to the box at the bottom of the page. "This one."

Josie went to add Cindy's name, address, and phone number when the box above it caught her eye. "Mrs. Quinn is already listed here."

"What?"

Josie tapped her pen against the box that Misty had already filled out, just as Cindy had said, listing her as an authorized person for picking Harris up from school. Mrs. D turned the folder toward her and leaned down, studying it. "Oh dear," she said. "Oh no. I'm so sorry. This isn't in the computer. It's supposed to be entered. I guess Miss K didn't check the physical file. Things are so hectic here at the end of the day. I've told her not to leave her post, so maybe that's why she didn't go into the office for the file."

Josie put the pen back on the table and gave her a tight smile. "I hope this means there won't be any problems in the future with Mrs. Quinn picking up Harris?"

"Not at all, I promise," Mrs. D assured her. "I'll talk with Miss K about it in the morning to make sure there are no issues going forward."

"Great," Josie said. She turned to Harris and held out a hand. "Let's go."

In the parking lot, Harris wasted no time entertaining his grandmother with tales of Pre-K. He hardly noticed when Josie kissed the top of his head and told him she'd see him soon. Josie explained the error to Cindy, who was satisfied to be proven correct. Josie watched her drive away and then got into her own vehicle, checking the dashboard clock, thinking about how she hadn't seen Noah all day. It was extremely odd. Longing to hear his voice, she called him, and was relieved when he answered right away.

"Where have you been all day?" she blurted out.

"The Chief has me doing something," he answered vaguely.

She couldn't help the annoyance that edged into her tone. "Really? Like what? Because we briefed him this morning on the Somers case, and he didn't say anything about more pressing assignments."

"It's not a big deal, Josie," Noah said. "I'll tell you about it tonight."

"Fine," she huffed. "I'm headed back to the station now."

"Yeah, I probably won't see you till later tonight. At home." As if he could sense her disappointment through the phone line, he added, "I'll get takeout. Your favorite."

Accepting his peace offering, she said, "Okay. I'll see you then," and hung up.

She was halfway down the mountain road leading back into the city proper when she smelled smoke. Slowing her vehicle, she searched the trees on either side of the road and looked to the sky to see if there were any signs of fire. Out here, people did sometimes burn their trash in metal barrels or fire rings made from old tire rims. They weren't supposed to do it within the city limits, but it happened. Josie didn't see anything out of the ordinary and wasn't looking to give out any citations, so she sped back up. Moments later, she rounded a bend in the road and saw a large black mailbox beside a tree-lined driveway. Josie couldn't see where it led due to the thick foliage. Beside the mailbox was a girl with long, dark hair. She was tall and reed thin but as Josie drew closer, she realized that she was probably only ten or eleven. She wore a pair of jeans and a T-shirt with an anime character on it. Both arms waved wildly over her head. As Josie pulled over, her movements became more frantic. Her feet lifted from the ground, as she jumped in place, then ran over to Josie's vehicle.

"Help!" the girl said. "I need help. My grandpa's house is on fire. Him and my sister are still in there."

"Where?" Josie said.

The girl turned and pointed to the driveway. "Up there. Can you help?"

"Get in," Josie told her.

The girl climbed into the passenger's seat and the moment the door slammed shut, Josie gunned it, her Ford Escape lurching forward and roaring up the long, winding driveway.

"What's your name?" she asked the girl.

"Dorothy." The girl looked shell-shocked but not dirty or streaked with soot or grime.

"Dorothy, do you know your grandpa's address? So I can tell the fire trucks?"

The girl rattled it off and Josie used the voice commands in her car to call 911 and alert them to what was going on. The smell of smoke grew stronger. As they crested the hill, Josie's heart caught in her throat. A two-story house stood in the center of a clearing, one side of it fully engulfed in flames. Stone steps led to what Josie assumed used to be a front porch but now looked like a melted candle. Flames shot out of the windows above it. Thick black smoke rose into the sky. From the other side of the house, flames burst from the first-floor windows but not the second floor.

Yet.

Josie knew several firefighters from the city's department. The words of one of those firefighters echoed in her head: a fire doubles in size every thirty seconds.

If there were people still in the house, Josie couldn't wait for the trucks. The entire structure would be gone in minutes. She pulled up as close to the house as she dared, threw the SUV into park, and turned to Dorothy. "Where are they inside? Do you know? First floor? Second floor? Front? Back?"

Tears glistened in her eyes. She pointed to the wall of flames that used to be the front porch. "My grandpa was in the front room."

"What's your sister's name?" Josie asked.

"Bronwyn. She's five."

A band of fear tightened around Josie's chest.

"I thought she was behind me. I told her to follow me."

"It's okay," Josie said. "Who else was in the house besides your grandfather and Bronwyn?"

"No one."

"Okay. Stay here."

She jumped out of the vehicle and ran toward the house, circling it to see if she could find a way inside. The first-floor windows were elevated far too high for her to climb into without a ladder. Rounding the back of the house, she heard a shout. She looked behind her, expecting Dorothy, but there was nothing. The shout came again. Josie looked up. From one of the second-floor windows, a girl's face, framed by golden-brown hair, poked out. A small hand waved.

"Help!" she hollered.

"Shit," Josie muttered. She couldn't reach the first-floor windows, let alone the second-floor windows. The house was almost fully engulfed. Even if she could find a way inside, there was no telling whether or not she'd be able to get to the second floor. For all she knew, the stairs had already burned away. She took a second to gauge the distance from the ground to the window.

"Wait there!" she yelled to Bronwyn. "I'll be right back."

She sprinted back to her vehicle and yanked open the passenger side door. "Get out," she told Dorothy. "And go to the end of the driveway to signal the fire trucks just like you signaled me, okay?"

Dorothy jumped out. Tears streaked her face, but she nodded. "Did you find my sister?"

"Yes," Josie said. "There's not much time. I need you to go *now.*"

Dorothy took off at a run. Josie scrambled to the other side of her vehicle and hopped into the driver's side. Engine roaring, she punched the gas pedal and sped across the grass, around to the back of the house, plowing right through a plastic playhouse and coming to a stop beside the house—so close that she heard the house's siding scrape her passenger's side paint job. The heat of the fire pulsed, consuming every last molecule of air around her. She got out and went to the hood of her Ford Escape, climbing on top of it and running up her windshield onto her roof. The metal roof sagged under her weight but from this height, she was much closer to Bronwyn.

Josie held up both arms and yelled. "I need you to jump, Bronwyn."

The girl leaned out the window and looked down at Josie, her expression uncertain.

"I'll catch you," Josie promised. "But you have to jump now."

As if to punctuate her words, a window to their right blew out, glass exploding, flames licking the outside air hungrily. Both Josie and Bronwyn instinctively threw their arms and hands up to block any glass or fire that might reach them. Glass sparkled on the sleeves of Josie's jacket, but she lifted her arms again, imploring Bronwyn to climb to the window's edge and jump. "We don't have much time," she said. "Jump now!"

The heat blasted at her from every direction, the thick air clogging her lungs. It felt like an eternity before the girl climbed into the window frame, knobby knees sticking out of her shorts, blackened with grime.

"Come on!" Josie coaxed.

Finally, the girl jumped, landing awkwardly in Josie's arms with one arm around Josie's neck, her waist over one of Josie's arms and a leg over the other. Josie teetered and lost her footing, crashing down onto the roof of the car. Instinctively, her arms held tight to any bony body part she could grasp, hoping they didn't roll off the top of the car. Together, they slid down onto the hood of the vehicle. Quickly, Josie righted herself, sitting up and checking the girl over for injuries.

"Are you okay?" she asked.

Bronwyn nodded, her big brown eyes sorrowful. "Did my grandpa get out?"

Josie jumped off the hood of the car and guided Bronwyn to the rear driver's side, pushing her inside. "I don't know, Bronwyn. We have to wait for the firefighters. It's too dangerous for us to go in there. The fire trucks are on their way. Right now, we have to get you away from the house."

The heat inside the vehicle was so intense, Josie momentarily considered abandoning it altogether. The headrest of her passenger's side had begun to melt, leaving a horrible burned plastic smell. But the car was the fastest way to get them away from the house. Plus, Josie didn't want to cause an explosion by leaving her vehicle so close to the fire. The engine sputtered to life. Josie threw the car into gear and slammed her foot onto the gas. The Escape bucked violently and pitched forward. She pushed harder on the gas pedal, the movement of the car like a lumbering beast with a lame leg. The tires closest to the house had probably started melting, too, she realized.

"Come on," she mumbled under her breath, pushing the car as far as it would go.

When she was several yards from the house, she got back out and snatched Bronwyn from the back of the car. The girl was small and immediately wrapped herself around Josie—arms latched onto Josie's neck and spindly legs cinched around Josie's waist. Josie ran toward the front of the house, past the detritus of the playhouse, along the tree line to the welcome sight of the driveway. She followed it to the road, lungs burning, legs aching, holding tightly to the girl. As she reached the road, she saw Dorothy waving at a fire truck on the road headed in their direction.

Relieved, Josie set Bronwyn down beside Dorothy, who immediately dropped to her knees and threw her arms around her sister. The two held each other and sobbed. Josie gathered them to her and shuffled them farther onto the shoulder of the driveway so they would be well out of the path of the emergency vehicles. Three trucks passed them and then an ambulance went past, lumbering up the driveway toward the house. A second ambulance pulled up, stopping on the other side of the driveway across from Josie and the girls. Two paramedics jumped out—Owen and Sawyer. Sawyer went directly to the two girls while Owen opened the back doors of the ambulance.

Josie pointed to Bronwyn. "She was still inside when I got here."

He nodded his understanding. Josie was concerned about both girls' lungs but especially Bronwyn's, since she had been in the burning house longer. She watched as Sawyer and Owen got the two girls into the back of the vehicle, covered them with blankets, checked their vitals, and gently placed nasal cannulas on their faces to give them oxygen. Sawyer broke away momentarily when the radio in the front of the ambulance squawked. A tinny voice came over the line. They could all hear it. "We've got an adult male. Back of the house, near the woods. Badly burned. Looks like he got out and tried to put some distance between himself and the fire. Unresponsive, but we've got vitals. Taking him to Denton Memorial, but he might need to be life-flighted to Philadelphia. Somewhere with a burn unit."

Sawyer picked up the radio. "Copy that. Do you need assistance?"

"Just clear the driveway."

"You got it."

Turning, he stopped when he saw Josie. "You hear that?"

She nodded. Sawyer went back to the girls. Dorothy asked, "My grandpa got out? Is he alive?"

Sawyer said, "Yes and yes."

Owen added, "They'll get him to the hospital right away."

While Owen secured the back doors, Sawyer hopped into the cab and steered the ambulance a few more feet onto the shoulder of the driveway, just in time for the other ambulance to come roaring past, lights blazing, siren wailing. It turned toward town and disappeared into the night.

As Owen threw the doors to the back of the ambulance open again, Josie heard Bronwyn's small voice say, "Do you think Grandpa will live?"

All of the adults froze. Josie noticed her lip quiver, saw Dorothy watching all of them, and said, "The doctors are going to do everything they possibly can to save him, and if they think they need more help, they'll send him to a bigger hospital with even better doctors."

This seemed to placate both girls. Sawyer and Owen began asking them questions like their names and ages and telling them how brave they were. Josie hung back, listening for details in case she needed to report them to the fire chief later. Sawyer asked their mother's name and phone number. Michelle Walsh. Bronwyn didn't know her number, but Dorothy did. As she rattled it off, Josie punched it into her phone and made the call, a little piece of her heart breaking as she gave Michelle the news about the fire. But she felt a small swell of relief that she was able to tell the mother that both her daughters were safe and that her father was still hanging on.

"I am only a few minutes away. Can you wait there for me? I'm on my way," Michelle told Josie.

"Sure," said Josie.

# CHAPTER TWENTY-TWO

Sawyer monitored the two girls' oxygen saturation and kept them company inside the back of the ambulance while Josie stood just outside with Owen.

"You know whose place this is, right?" he asked her.

"No," Josie said. "You do?"

Owen nodded. "Clay Walsh."

The name sounded familiar to her, but she couldn't place it.

Owen said, "He's a retired firefighter."

Josie felt as though someone had punched her in the stomach. She glanced inside the vehicle. Both girls rested on the gurney together, Bronwyn wrapped in Dorothy's arms. Neither seemed to have overheard, but Sawyer stared at Josie with a penetrating look.

"A firefighter almost dies in a fire," Josie murmured.

She climbed inside the vehicle. Sawyer adjusted the oxygen cannula on Dorothy's nose and asked her, "Do you know how the fire started?"

Both girls' eyes widened. Bronwyn looked up at her sister, as if seeking guidance of some kind.

Josie said, "It's okay. Whatever happened, you won't be in trouble with us. We just need to know."

Dorothy swiped at a tear running down her cheek. "Grandpa… he…"

She looked away from them and squeezed her eyes closed, her entire body quaking with a long sob.

Sawyer looked at Dorothy's vitals. Her heart rate jumped. He said, "It's okay, girls. We don't have to talk about it. Just rest now."

But Bronwyn extricated herself from her sister's embrace and sat up straight.

"Bron," Dorothy cautioned, opening her eyes again.

"Grandpa said it's not tattling if you think someone's gonna get hurt," she announced.

"That is true," Josie said carefully.

Through her tears, Dorothy glared at her sister. "Grandpa's still alive, Bron."

Bronwyn gave a little pout. "Grandpa said we should always tell the truth."

"Not about this," Dorothy croaked.

Sawyer opened his mouth to speak, but Josie shook her head almost imperceptibly. To the girls, she said, "I think that Mr. Hayes is right. You two need to rest right now, okay?"

Dorothy looked relieved and nodded. Bronwyn's cheeks filled with air, almost as though she was bursting to tell what she knew. Sawyer followed Josie outside of the ambulance. Owen went inside to keep an eye on their vital signs. Josie led Sawyer several feet away before speaking. "We need to wait for their mother," she told him. "They're minors."

Sawyer looked back at the ambulance. "The little one is about to spill. Besides, this is a fire, not a homicide or something. Do those rules about having a parent present even apply here?"

Josie raised a brow at him. "We're waiting for their mother."

He held her gaze for a long moment. The sound of wheels over asphalt and then a door slamming tore Josie's attention from him. From the road, Mettner jogged toward them. "Hey," he said when he reached them. "Are you okay?"

"I'm fine," she said. "What are you doing here?"

"It was on the radio," he said. "You called in the fire. Everyone was worried so I said I'd come out and see. Hey, you've got glass in your hair. What happened?"

Josie wondered if everyone included Noah. She hadn't checked her phone but wondered if he, too, had heard and tried to call her. Sawyer left them alone, climbing back into the ambulance with the girls. Josie shook her hair to try and rid it of some of the glass and checked her phone as she updated Mettner. No calls or texts from Noah. She concluded with, "Also, I think my car is totaled, so I'm going to need a ride back to the station—or home. Have you seen Noah?"

"Uh, no," Mettner said. "Your car is totaled? The one you bought only five months ago?"

Josie pressed her lips into a thin line and nodded. This wasn't her year for cars.

"Girls?" a female voice cried. "Girls? Where are my girls?"

From the road, a woman in her thirties, dressed in jeans, a fitted black shirt, and a long, cream-colored sweater ran toward Josie and Mettner. Long sandy hair flew behind her. Her hands tugged at the lapels of her sweater, stretching them until her fingers left distortions in the fabric.

"Michelle?" Josie asked.

She almost ran straight into Josie, gripping Josie's upper arms to stop herself. "It's me," she said. "Where are my girls?"

"The ambulance," Josie said. "Come on."

Michelle ran ahead of her, jumping up inside the ambulance without warning, muscling Owen and Sawyer out of her way to get to her children. She gathered them tightly to her, leaning over the side of the stretcher and holding their upper bodies against hers until one of them said, "Mo-oom."

Josie, Mettner, Sawyer, and Owen waited while Michelle fussed over her girls and took a few minutes to hold them before Josie climbed into the cab, seating herself on one of the benches along the side wall. Mettner, Owen, and Sawyer stood just outside, eyes and ears focused on Michelle and her kids.

Michelle said, "Where's my dad? Did they take him to the hospital?"

"Yes," Josie answered. "To Denton Memorial—although they did say he may have to be life-flighted to a hospital in Philadelphia if his burns are too severe."

Michelle pressed a fist against her mouth and nodded.

"We started to talk to the girls about what happened," Josie explained. "But I thought it was best for you to be present."

"Thank you," Michelle said. She looked down at the girls. "But I don't see the harm in you talking to them about this. I want to know what happened as well."

Dorothy reached up and tugged on her mother's sweater. "Mom, I don't think we should talk about this. I think it should be private."

Michelle's head reared back. "What? Dorothy, Grandpa's house burned down." Her lower lip quivered as she tried to maintain her composure. "Grandpa—" she broke off and sucked in several deep breaths before continuing, "Girls, this is not something we can keep private. Do you understand? This is a tragedy. A terrible, terrible tragedy. I need to know what happened. The firefighters who came today? They probably know Grandpa. Some of them might have worked with him. They need to know what happened."

The sadness in Dorothy's voice when she spoke next was a spike through Josie's heart. "But you always said Grandpa was a hero."

Michelle tucked a lock of Dorothy's hair behind her ear, fiddling with the cannula tube. "He is a hero, honey. He always will be."

Bronwyn said, "Not anymore, Mama."

All eyes focused on the five-year-old. Michelle's voice trembled when she said, "What do you mean, Bron?"

Dorothy grabbed Bronwyn's hand and squeezed it, snapping her eyes shut at the same time, as if she were waiting for someone to do something painful to her. It reminded Josie of Harris when he had to get his shots.

In a voice so low, all the adults leaned in to hear it, Bronwyn said, "Grandpa set the fire."

A beat of silence passed. Then Michelle said, "I'm sorry. What?"

Bronwyn said, "We were all playing out back. Grandpa went inside. He didn't come back out, and we were getting hungry, so we went inside. He wasn't in the kitchen, so we went into the living room and he was in there. He had a towel all rolled up and he was catching it on fire with a lighter."

Michelle nudged Dorothy's shoulder. "Dorothy, look at me."

Dorothy didn't move.

Michelle shook her shoulder. "Dorothy. Open your eyes and look at me. Is this true?"

Dorothy's eyes opened. From under her lids she looked up at her mother, jaw clenched with fright. "Y-yes. Grandpa started the fire."

Michelle drew her hand back and crossed her arms under her ample breasts. "This is not funny, girls. Grandpa would never intentionally set a fire. You know that. If you two did something and it got out of hand, you need to just tell me right now. Don't lie. You'll be in more trouble if you lie, especially when Grandpa wakes up and tells me what really happened."

Bronwyn wiggled on the stretcher. "We are telling the truth, Mommy. Grandpa caught the towel on fire and then he started putting the fire all over the place. On the curtains and the furniture."

"Bron!" Michelle shrieked. "Stop! I mean it."

Dorothy talked over her mother. "It's true, Mom. We're not lying. I thought Grandpa was, like, sick or something. I asked him what he was doing, and he said 'time to be a match.'"

The words gave Josie a jolt, but she kept silent.

"A match?" Michelle asked. "What does that mean?"

"I don't know," Dorothy said. "He just kept saying it over and over again." She mimicked a low, monotone voice. "'Time to be a match. Time to be a match.' I told him to stop and he did, but by that time the whole downstairs was on fire. He looked at me and told me to take Bron and get out. So I did. Except Bron wasn't behind me. I thought she was, but she wasn't. I tried to go back in, but the porch fell down."

Bronwyn said, "I went back for Grandpa. He was in the kitchen. I told him to come with us and he said he would, but we got to the front of the house and the floor was gone. I asked Grandpa what we should do, and he just looked at me all funny like he didn't know what I was saying. The fire was getting worse. I didn't know what to do. Then there was a noise, a bad noise, and Grandpa picked me up and threw me. I landed at the bottom of the stairs. I looked back and more of the floor was gone—like the whole floor from the living room to the kitchen. I didn't see Grandpa at all. I didn't know what to do, so I went upstairs."

Tears streaked Michelle's face. "This doesn't make sense. None of it makes any sense." She turned toward Josie and Mettner. "My dad wouldn't do something like that. He was with the fire department for thirty years. He saved lives. He's the best man I know."

"Maybe he was sick," Dorothy offered. "Like he had one of those things in his brain. What are they called?"

"Storks," Bronwyn said. "Like my camp teacher had over the summer."

"Strokes," Michelle corrected. She pressed a hand to her forehead. "I don't know. Maybe. I can't—this doesn't—Dad just wouldn't… something had to be very, very wrong."

Every fine hair on Josie's body stood to attention. She leaned forward and met Dorothy's eyes. "Was your grandpa acting strangely at all today?"

"No. I mean, except for when we came in from outside, and he was lighting the fire."

"How long were you outside with him?"

Dorothy shrugged. "Since we got home from school. I don't know."

Josie tried to calculate. Most local schools ended their day between two thirty and three. She'd been at Tiny Tykes with Harris and Cindy until four thirty. Although Pre-K ended significantly earlier in the day, Misty had enrolled Harris in their aftercare program. It had been approximately four forty when she came upon Dorothy on the side of the road.

"What school do you girls go to?" Josie asked.

Bronwyn said, "I go to Tiny Tykes 'cause I'm not six yet, and you have to be six to go to kindergarten."

"I know it," Josie said. She didn't remember seeing Bronwyn or Michelle there the day before, but there had been dozens of students and parents, and Josie's full focus had been on Harris. "Do you know what time your grandpa picked you up from there?"

"Same time as every day," Bronwyn said simply. "Then we came to his house and watched TV until it was time to get Dorothy."

Michelle said, "He picks Bron up at one o'clock. We chose it because it's close to Dad's house so it's easy for him to get her. He doesn't mind helping out with the cost since he doesn't have to go very far to get her. She went to summer camp there, too."

"What about you, Dorothy?" Josie asked.

"I go to Wolfson Elementary."

The school was about twenty minutes from Clay's house.

"Did you girls and your grandpa stop anywhere after school?"

Both girls shook their heads.

By Josie's calculations, they would have gotten back to Clay's house after picking up Dorothy by three thirty. Given the state of the fire when Josie arrived and the time it would have taken Dorothy to get down to the road to flag Josie down, Clay must have set the fire sometime between four and four twenty, although it was possible he had started it closer to four fifteen.

Josie said, "Was he outside with you for very long?"

Dorothy shrugged. "No, I guess not."

Bronwyn added, "He only had time to blow bubbles twice and he had to go back inside."

"Why did he go inside?" Josie asked.

"He thought he heard a car in the driveway," Dorothy answered. "Did he?"

Bronwyn said, "I don't know. That's just what he said. We were playing out back."

"Did either of you hear a car?"

Dorothy said, "I thought I did but I couldn't be sure either. Grandpa said he would go check and he did."

"You didn't go after him?" Josie asked. "To see for yourself?"

"No," Dorothy answered.

Bronwyn said, "He said to stay where we were and he told Dorothy to blow the bubbles, but she's not as good at it as Grandpa. She doesn't make the big bubbles like he does."

Michelle let out a little gasp and clamped her hand over her mouth, fighting a sob.

"Bron," Dorothy choked.

"What?" Bronwyn said. "It's true."

"How long was your grandpa in the house?" Josie asked.

"I'm not sure," Dorothy said. "But I used up almost all the bubbles while he was gone."

"A long time," Bronwyn added.

Josie asked, "Did you hear anyone else? See anyone? Hear him talking to another person?"

Both girls shook their heads.

Michelle tore her eyes from Josie to look at her girls. "But you went back inside because you were hungry. Dad always has dinner on the table at four fifteen."

"He didn't make dinner," Dorothy said.

"Yeah," Bronwyn added. "No dinner but he made brownies. I really wanted some, but then we saw he was catching the fire."

"Brownies," Josie said. "He made brownies? Are you sure?"

"They were on the table when we went inside," Bronwyn said.

Josie looked at Dorothy. "Is that true?"

Dorothy said, "I don't remember."

Bronwyn rolled her eyes. "They were on a paper plate right on the kitchen table."

"I didn't see them, Bron," Dorothy said angrily. "Grandpa was setting his house on fire!"

"Okay, girls," Josie said. She turned to Michelle. "Did your dad make brownies for the girls on a regular basis?"

Michelle shook her head. "I never knew him to bake."

Josie was, quite arguably, the worst baker on the planet. She turned to Mettner. "How long does it take to make brownies?"

He shrugged. "I don't know."

Michelle said, "Out of the box—which is the only way my dad would make them if he baked—twenty to twenty-five minutes."

Josie looked at Dorothy. "Do you think he was inside that long?"

One thin shoulder shrugged. "I don't know."

Kids had little sense of time. Josie knew this wasn't something they'd be able to pin down.

Mettner said, "Did you girls see anything else? Anything with the brownies? Did they have wrappers on them or anything? Maybe a sticker?"

Bronwyn said, "No. They were just on a paper plate on the table."

"Was someone in the house with him?" Michelle asked.

Both girls looked from one adult to the next until Dorothy gave a one-shouldered shrug and answered for both of them. "I don't know. I didn't see anyone else. Did you, Bron?"

She looked at her little sister who said, "No. Only you and Grandpa."

Josie said, "Dorothy, you got out first and ran down to the road. Did you see anyone?"

"No," she said. "If I did, I would have asked them for help."

"Did you see any cars? Either leaving the driveway or going up or down the road? Maybe too far away for you to get their attention?"

She shook her head.

Josie thought back to when she'd pulled out of the Tiny Tykes parking lot. She didn't remember seeing any vehicles coming her way, from the direction of the Walsh property, and no one had been in front of her either. If they had, they would have seen Dorothy first. She was going over everything the girls had told them in her head when she felt the heat of Michelle's gaze on her. She met the mother's eyes.

Michelle said, "Where did the brownies come from?"

"I don't know," Josie said. "Let's get over to the hospital and see how your dad is doing. Maybe he can tell us."

# CHAPTER TWENTY-THREE

Darkness fell like a blanket over the mountain as Sawyer and Owen secured the girls in the back of the ambulance. Above them, light from a half moon sliced through the trees, giving everything a silver glow. All around, the sounds of crickets, cicadas, and about a half dozen different types of frogs called, whistled, peeped, and sounded off like rattles. The sound of life continuing on, oblivious to the tragedy that had just happened a quarter mile up the driveway. They could still see and smell smoke from the house, as well as the lights of the fire trucks. Raised voices of the firefighters reached them now and then. Michelle agreed to follow the ambulance to Denton Memorial Hospital. Josie and Mettner walked back to his car and joined the caravan.

The ER was quiet on the outside. Inside was a different story, the waiting room packed with bodies of Denton City firefighters waiting for word on Clay Walsh. Josie and Mettner weaved their way through the men and women, offering sympathetic shoulder pats and nods. Finally, they came to the security desk right before the locked, glass double doors that separated the waiting room from the treatment area. They flashed their credentials, and the guard passed them through.

It took only seconds to find Clay Walsh. All of the noise in the unit was concentrated behind a glass enclosure. Nurses and doctors hurried about, shouting out vital signs and orders. Medical waste littered the floor at their feet. Monitors bleeped and blared. Josie looked around but didn't see Michelle or the girls. Someone would have put them on the opposite end of the ER, she realized, so they wouldn't have to witness the desperate flurry of medical personnel trying to keep Clay alive. The sight of him made her heart flutter, seize, and flutter again. His head and most of his upper body had escaped the flames, but the color of the skin on his lower body and one of his arms was a combination of black and a red the hue and consistency of raw meat. Josie had seen a lot on the job, but this was hard to take. Turning away, she drew in a deep breath, and then returned to her position beside Mettner, looking on. He seemed unaffected. Then again, one of the things that made him an excellent detective was that nothing ever got to him—or if it did, he never showed it. After several minutes, the activity in the glass room became less frenetic and a doctor slipped into the hallway, tugging off his blue skull cap to reveal thick, dark hair. Josie read his name tag: Dr. Ahmed Nashat.

"Doctor," she said as she and Mettner produced their credentials again. "Is he able to talk?"

The doctor shook his head. Pocketing his skull cap, he looked back into the room, where nurses rerouted wires and fed medication into an IV. "He won't be talking anytime soon. We've stabilized him for now, and we've arranged for a life flight helicopter to fly him to the Hospital of the University of Pennsylvania in Philadelphia, but he's got full-thickness burns over sixty percent of his body. His airway and lungs are a mess. Smoke inhalation. You probably already know this, but that's a bigger killer than burns in fire cases. I'm sorry to tell you, Detectives, but Mr. Walsh may not survive the trip to Philadelphia. Even if he does, I'm not sure they'll be able to help him."

Mettner said, "He hasn't been able to say anything? To communicate in any way?"

Dr. Nashat frowned. "I'm afraid not." He stared in at Clay Walsh once more, and then seemed to remember something. He turned his gaze back to them. "You're the police. You wouldn't be here unless a crime was committed. Was this arson?"

Josie said, "It's going to take some time for that to be officially determined. We really can't say. We're looking at every possibility."

Dr. Nashat crooked a finger, beckoning them into the room. The smell of burned flesh turned Josie's stomach. She glanced at Mettner and saw that this affected him—physically, if not mentally. His face turned a pale shade of green.

Dr. Nashat motioned them toward a tray table on one side of the room. On it were several basins which held scraps of clothing which they'd obviously removed from Walsh's burned flesh. In one basin was what appeared to be a melted piece of plastic. "This," Dr. Nashat said, holding the basin up for their inspection. "He was clutching this in his good hand, so tightly it took some effort to uncurl his fingers. If you would, look closer."

He picked up a pair of tweezers and used them to point at a portion of the plastic. Something white lay in contrast to the pink plastic basin. Josie and Mettner leaned in simultaneously. There, affixed to what Josie could only conclude was a piece of Saran wrap, was half of a sticker. One half of a sinister face, its eyes the shapes of the letter X, its head broken open and wayward, frenzied lines extending out of it.

"Son of a bitch," said Josie. "Dr. Nashat, can you run a tox screen on Mr. Walsh before you transfer him?"

He raised a brow at her but didn't argue. "Sure, I suppose. Why not? You'll have a warrant?"

"Yes," said Josie, looking over to see that Mettner was already pressing his phone to his ear. "Gretchen?" he said as he walked out of the room. "Can you do something for us?"

Josie turned back to Dr. Nashat. "Thank you," she said. "We'll be back."

Outside the room, she waited until Mettner had given Gretchen all the information she needed. When he hung up, Josie said, "We need to talk to Michelle again."

It took a few laps around the halls of the emergency department to find Michelle Walsh. She stood outside a curtained-off area, talking in low tones on her cell phone. Her eyes were red and glassy from crying. She hung up as Josie and Mettner approached. "Were you able to talk to my dad? They said he was in really bad shape. They're sending him to a hospital in Philadelphia, but I thought maybe you got him to talk?"

Josie shook her head. "I'm sorry, Michelle, but no. He wasn't able to talk."

Mettner said, "Miss Walsh, we just need to ask you a few more questions."

"Of course. What's going on?"

Josie took out her phone and brought up the photo of the sticker they'd found in Nysa Somers' backpack, since it was intact and not half-melted like the one that Clay Walsh had clutched as he tried to escape his house. "Does this look familiar to you?"

Michelle grimaced. "Ew, no. What is that?"

Mettner asked, "Did your dad ever use drugs?"

"Of course not. Even if he wanted to, he couldn't."

"Isn't he retired?" Josie said.

"Oh, well, yeah. He retired about five months ago. After the flooding. That was a lot on everyone. Plus, I'd just started a new job, and I needed help with the girls. Dad retired so he could help me with babysitting and school pickup. My mom died when Dorothy was a baby. I'm a single mother. All I've got is my dad."

Josie sent up a silent prayer that Clay Walsh would have a miraculous recovery.

"What about edibles?" Mettner asked. "Did he ever try them?"

Michelle raised a brow. "You're thinking of the brownies, aren't you? What do you think? Some drug dealer showed up while my kids were there and sold him some pot brownies? Are you crazy?"

Her voice had reached a shriek. Calmly, Josie responded, "We have to ask."

"Why? Why do you have to ask that? You think my dad ate a pot brownie and burned his house down with my kids there? Are you listening to yourselves? First of all, what the hell kind of pot would make a person do that? Second, my dad is one of the most highly decorated firefighters in this city. He served for decades. He's saved hundreds of lives and done more community service than almost anyone else in the department. I know that you heard what my kids said, but I'm telling you, what happened today was as out of character for my dad as you could possibly get."

"You don't believe the girls?" Mettner said.

Michelle's chin dropped to her chest. A shaky breath rattled her frame. She looked back up, crossing her arms over her chest. "Of course I believe my girls. But you heard them: Dad heard a car in the driveway. He didn't make those brownies. Someone brought them to him. Whatever he did today wasn't his fault. He had to be under the influence of something, or else he would never intentionally set a fire, and he would absolutely never, ever put my kids in danger." She lowered her voice and took a step closer to Josie and Mettner. "We're talking about arson here. Arson. I'm already wondering how the hell to explain this to the guys he worked with. Do you think they're going to believe a couple of kids, even his own grandkids, that Clay Walsh—the legendary Clay Walsh—set his own house on fire? They'll never accept that."

Josie asked, "Do you think that your dad would have eaten a brownie if he knew they had something in them?"

"Of course not."

Josie said, "Michelle, I believe you. I think there's more to what happened than we know. We're going to do everything we can to get to the bottom of it, that I promise you. Can you tell us, was your dad feuding with anyone? Having trouble with anyone?"

"No, no."

Mettner asked, "Was he dating anyone? Had he just broken up with anyone?"

Michelle barked a laugh. "Dad? Date? Please. No. He hasn't been on a date in years."

"Does the name Nysa Somers mean anything to you?"

"No. Who's that?"

Mettner said, "She was a student at the university."

Michelle didn't pick up on his use of the past tense. She shook her head rapidly and pushed her hands through her hair. "No. My dad doesn't know anyone from the university. Unless there was a fire there, he would never be up there for any reason."

Josie said, "Can you think of anyone who might have wanted to hurt him?"

Michelle's hands dropped to her sides. She sniffled. "No. Jesus, no. Everyone loves my dad. He's the best."

# CHAPTER TWENTY-FOUR

Sleep didn't come easily, but mostly because I was so keyed up, there was no way I was going to get any rest. For hours I refreshed the WYEP website, looking for news of Denton's felled hero. Not only had he been brought down, now he would be disgraced. Not for the first time, I wished I could share my brilliance with someone. But that wasn't really an option. My earlier excitement about being *seen* faded. Maybe I wasn't truly being seen—that wasn't possible—but my actions were being noticed. For the first time, they weren't being written off as unfortunate accidents. Now everyone knew my power. It was a very different, very heady feeling, than the quiet satisfaction of knowing I had given someone their comeuppance.

I kept refreshing. Finally, sometime after midnight, the story appeared. *Local Firefighter Badly Burned in House Fire.*

My heart jumped into my throat. "Badly burned?" I muttered.

It wasn't right. Then I realized it wouldn't matter. That was the beauty of my new and improved method. Even if he survived, he wouldn't remember what happened. He wouldn't remember starting the fire or even seeing me.

How badly burned, I wondered? Badly enough for him to pay for how harshly he had treated me during our encounter months earlier? My face flushed red as I remembered how rudely he had spoken to me. "Get out of my damn way," he had growled. Then he had pushed me aside, like I was nothing. He hadn't even apologized. Hadn't even given me another glance.

Brain buzzing, I read on. Had I at least managed to kill one of those little brats he took with him everywhere?

"Shit."

Everyone had survived. Not that it mattered. None of them had even seen me. Still, it chafed. Every last one of them had made it out of the fire and yet, WYEP reported that the "city was reeling" over the "tragedy that unfolded at Clay Walsh's house."

A city reeling.

They had no idea. Even before I chose Clay, I had set other things in motion.

# CHAPTER TWENTY-FIVE

Toxicology panel in hand, Josie and Mettner returned to the stationhouse. Noah had finally answered Josie's texts, promising to be there and to drive her home. As annoyed as she was with him for not responding to her most of the day, she couldn't wait to see him. Part of her wanted to keep working on the case—or cases—until she had nothing left and all the answers to her questions had been laid bare. Another part of her wanted nothing more than to go home with Noah and make him use his hands and mouth to make her forget everything about the past two days.

It was late, and all of them except Gretchen—who had volunteered to work late—should have been at home, but in the great room at the stationhouse, they convened: Josie, Mettner, Gretchen, Noah, and the Chief. Even Amber Watts was there, now dressed casually in jeans and a light sweater with her auburn hair twisted up in a loose bun. When Mettner sat down at his desk, she drifted over and stood behind him.

Chief Chitwood's face was already beet red, and none of them had spoken a word yet. "I just got off the phone with the city's fire marshal. His team of investigators won't be able to assess the Walsh house for the cause of the fire until tomorrow. I didn't tell him that a couple of elementary school kids told my detectives that one of the most decorated firefighters in this city set his own damn house on fire. I don't want to have to tell him that. Am I going to have to tell him that?"

No one dared answer. Clearly, he was on a roll. He continued, "Palmer brought me up to speed after she prepared the warrant for toxicology on Clay Walsh, which was a bitch to get a judge to sign, by the way, because we're talking about a city hero. But I understand you've got the tox screen, so please tell me what we're dealing with here because I need something more to tell the fire marshal and everyone who works for him besides that Clay Walsh lost his mind and burned his house to the ground."

Mettner and Josie looked at one another, silently trying to decide which of them was going to give the news. Finally, Mettner sighed and said, "The tox screen was clean."

A collective gasp went up around the room. The Chief hollered, "What?"

Josie noticed Amber slide a hand onto Mettner's shoulder and squeeze.

Noah said, "How is that possible?"

Gretchen said, "You said there were brownies and a sticker just like we saw with Nysa Somers. That's how I got the warrant—by convincing the judge that a championship swimmer doesn't drown herself on Monday and a decorated firefighter doesn't nearly kill himself by setting a fire on Tuesday, but that something else is going on. Like someone going around getting people to eat brownies laced with some kind of drug that would make them do these things. The only reason I could sell that to the judge was because the sticker was present in both cases."

Josie held up her hands to silence Gretchen. "I know, I know."

The Chief said, "You're telling us the brownies had nothing in them? That these two people just lost their minds within a day of one another?"

"No," Josie said. "That's not what I'm telling you. Not at all. We all know tox screens don't test for everything, only the most common drugs."

"Right," Mettner said. "This just means we can eliminate amphetamines, cannabis, cocaine, opioids, barbiturates, benzos, PCP, Quaaludes, methadone, and Darvon."

Noah said, "Which leaves what? Date rape drugs? GHB? Rohypnol?"

"That makes more sense," said Gretchen. "Those drugs have short half-lives. They don't stay in your system that long. If it's one of those, then Nysa Somers' tox screen will be clean, too."

"But if it was one of those," Josie said, "it still might have shown up in Walsh's tox screen. There wasn't that long a time period between when we believe he ate the brownie and when his blood was drawn. Also, I've had the misfortune of seeing people who've been given GHB and Rohypnol. I'm not sure they would be as steady as Nysa Somers was on video. It's possible. Some people take GHB recreationally, but mostly date rape drugs are meant to incapacitate. Nysa Somers wasn't incapacitated. Clay Walsh wasn't incapacitated."

"Let's go over this again," said the Chief, looking directly at Josie.

Josie gathered all the facts in her mind, drew in a breath, and began. "Nysa Somers went to the library on Sunday night. She left but didn't make it home. Told her roommate via text that she met with a friend. Approximately eight hours went by. She then reappeared along the path between her housing complex and the campus. At some point, she got a calendar notification on her phone that said, 'Time to be a mermaid.' She or someone else threw her backpack with her phone in it into the woods. When we recovered the backpack, there was a sandwich bag with what appeared to be brownie crumbs inside and on that baggie was the creepy, cracked skull sticker. Autopsy confirmed that Nysa had brownies in her stomach and that she drowned."

Mettner interrupted, "She walked into the pool under her own steam, said hello and smiled at the security guard, and called him by name before going into the pool area and drowning."

Josie picked back up. "Clay Walsh was home playing in the backyard with his granddaughters. Both he and his eldest grand-daughter, Dorothy, thought they heard a car in the driveway. Clay went inside. Never came back out. An indeterminate amount of time passed. The girls came back in and he was going around the house setting things on fire and saying, 'Time to be a match.' Just like with Nysa's phone reminder, 'Time to be a mermaid.' The younger of the two granddaughters said there were brownies on the kitchen table. At the hospital, he was found to be clutching what we believe is Saran wrap with a partial cracked skull sticker on it."

"Someone showed up at Walsh's house," Mettner said.

"Right," Josie said. "That's our theory. Mystery person shows up and gives him brownies. We believe he ate one. Then he started acting weird and set the house on fire. The girls thought he was sick. Bronwyn said that toward the end, before she lost sight of him—after he threw her out of the way of the collapsing floor, he looked at her 'funny.' He might have been disoriented. There had to be something in those brownies. We just don't know what."

"The mystery person," the Chief said. "That's the connection we need to pursue." He rubbed his temples with his index and middle fingers and blew out a breath. "Where are we with finding the person who was with Nysa Somers the night before she died?"

Noah said, "No one at Hollister Way remembers seeing her the night before she died, or seeing anyone out of place."

Mettner said, "But we sent paperwork to Nysa Somers' cell phone provider this morning to have them see where her phone pinged during the hours she was missing. We're going to cross-reference the area with addresses of all her professors and the swim team's coaching staff."

"Right," Josie said, "Because her sister said she'd been seeing someone older than her and referred to the relationship as 'inappropriate.' Also, she'd just broken things off with this person on Friday."

Chitwood said, "All right, here's what you're going to do. All of you but Palmer are going home and getting some damn rest. I want to know the moment those phone records come in and you've got your list of possible older, inappropriate men. Tomorrow I want you talking to people who knew Clay Walsh. All of you. I want to know who came to his house before he set it on fire. I know his daughter said he wasn't feuding with anyone and didn't have a girlfriend he might have just broken up with, but I want to hear that from everyone he knew before we let that avenue of inquiry go. I also want you to try to find any connection at all between Nysa Somers and Clay Walsh. I don't care how small it is. Find it. Find something! You got that?"

They all nodded. Mettner tapped notes into his phone.

"I'll get in touch with my DEA contact and see if he knows anything about this sticker or maybe other drugs we should be looking at," Chitwood added.

Amber cleared her throat, drawing attention to herself for the first time. Chitwood said, "What are you even doing here, Watts?"

She didn't miss a beat, offering him a cheerful smile. More and more, Josie admired how unflappable she was when it came to Chitwood. "I'm still getting a lot of questions about the Nysa Somers case and tonight, the reporters are going nuts wanting to know what happened with Clay Walsh. What should I tell them?"

Chitwood grunted. "Nothing. Nothing at all. You press types are good at using a lot of words to say nothing. Do that."

Mettner opened his mouth to say something, but Josie quickly jumped in. "Both cases are open investigations which we cannot comment on. They're pending. We don't have enough information to comment yet."

Chitwood pointed his index finger and fanned it around the room at each of them. "Not one detail gets out about this brownie or sticker business, you got that? Not until we get a handle on what the hell's going on in this town."

Without waiting for an answer, he returned to his office, slamming the door behind him.

# CHAPTER TWENTY-SIX

At home, Josie and Noah took their dog, Trout, for a long walk. It was dark and quiet in their neighborhood, but the streets were well lit. Trout was so happy to be outside, Josie was sure he didn't care whether it was night or day. Guilt pricked at her as she thought about all the hours he'd been home alone that day. Normally, one of them stopped in a couple of times during the day to walk him and throw his Kong.

Noah walked beside her in silence. She tried to muster the energy to interrogate him about his day, but she didn't have much left to expend. Her mind replayed the scene at Clay Walsh's house again and again. The stricken, tear-streaked faces of Michelle, Dorothy, and Bronwyn Walsh floated to the front of her mind every few minutes.

"I'll take you to get a rental car in the morning," Noah said. "Did you call to get your car towed from the Walsh place yet?"

Josie shook her head, eyes on Trout as he sniffed a telephone pole, peed on it, sniffed it again, and then repeated the process four more times.

"Josie?"

She looked up at Noah, whose face was illuminated by a streetlight. "What?"

"What's going on?"

A voice in her brain shot back: *I don't know. Why don't you tell* me *what's going on? Where have you been lately?* But her mouth said, "I'm fine."

"Josie."

"It's the case," she blurted out, mostly because she didn't want to say anything that would lead to a fight. Not tonight. Not after two days of horrific death and grieving families.

"It's always the case," he said, laughing softly.

"It's not funny," she snapped. Trout paused in his walk to stare back at them.

Noah looked down at him. "It's okay, buddy," he reassured the dog. Trout resumed his walk. "I'm sorry," Noah told Josie. "I didn't mean it like that. Sometimes I just think that there might be other things on your mind, but you talk about work because that's easier."

Josie was glad for the darkness so he couldn't see the flush creep into her cheeks. "If this is another one of your campaigns to get me into therapy, you can just forget it."

"Paige Rosetti is a psychologist, and you've already got an in with her," he noted, mentioning a woman Josie had spoken with on a previous case.

"Noah, please. Just drop it."

"I would, except sometimes I don't think you talk to me either. Sometimes I feel like I don't really know what you're thinking or how you're feeling."

Josie stopped in her tracks, and Trout's leash gave a little snap. The dog paused and then trotted back to Josie's feet, staring up at her with his tongue lolling from the side of his mouth. "I'm thinking that yesterday I pulled a twenty-year-old woman out of a pool, and I tried to revive her and I couldn't. She died alone, and I had to sit at a table with her broken family and tell them I'd try to make sense of her death even though I'm not sure I can do that. I'm thinking that no sooner did I walk away from that table than I had to rescue a little girl from a burning building because her grandfather—a man she trusted—set the house on fire with the kids inside. Then I had to see his burned, blistered body that looked like someone had taken a hot meat tenderizer to it, and after that, I had to tell his grieving daughter that I'd do my best to make sense of what happened to him even though I don't think I can. What I'm feeling is afraid that we won't solve this one because it's too slippery and there are no leads. What I'm feeling is fear that even if we figure out what the hell is going on, we won't be able to prove anything because what kind of drug makes people do things like Nysa Somers and Clay Walsh did? What I'm feeling is terror at the idea that there's nothing good in the world anymore."

Noah touched Josie's cheek, and it was then she realized she'd twisted Trout's leash around her fingers so tightly that it was cutting off her circulation. A paw scratched against her shin. Trout trying to get her attention. Somehow, he always knew when she was upset. She supposed Noah did as well, and yet, he'd been inaccessible to her for the last couple of days when she wanted him most.

"Josie," said Noah. "You *are* the good in the world."

She unwound the leash from her fingers and shook her head, trying not to smile. It should have sounded trite or cheesy, but coming from Noah it only sounded sincere. That was the thing about him. He had always seen her in a completely different light than anyone else saw her—most importantly, herself. At first it had made her uncomfortable, but more and more she leaned on it. It felt like emotional progress, but part of her hated herself for needing him so much.

Noah didn't wait for her to respond. Instead, he said, "I know you're not going to sleep tonight, so let's do something."

"What?"

"About the case."

"Like what? It's almost eleven o'clock at night."

"Come on," he said. "We'll go home and call Shannon. She'll still be up. Ask her what kind of a drug could make someone pliable without incapacitating them. Make them do things they wouldn't normally do."

Shannon Payne was Josie's biological mother. She was a chemist for a huge pharmaceutical company, Quarmark. She lived two hours from them.

"Shannon wouldn't know street drugs, though," Josie pointed out.

"Not necessarily," Noah agreed. "But I'm fresh out of DEA contacts, Chitwood hasn't yet heard back from his DEA guy, and talking to her would be a start."

They hurried Trout along the rest of the way. At home, they settled at the kitchen table and put Josie's phone in the center, on speaker. Josie pulled up Shannon's number and punched the call icon. Shannon picked up after three rings. After exchanging the usual pleasantries, Josie asked if they could pick Shannon's brain in her capacity as a chemist for Quarmark.

Shannon laughed. "I'm not sure how helpful I'll be since I've been working on the same cancer drug for the last four years, but go ahead."

"Are you aware of any drugs that could make a person extremely suggestible? Something that would make them do things they wouldn't normally ever do? Even something harmful to themselves?"

There was a beat of silence. Then Shannon said, "Are we talking about street drugs? Josie, I don't have a lot of knowledge about those."

"I realize that," Josie said. "But you develop drugs for a living. If you wanted to develop a drug that would make people pliable but not incapacitated, what would you do?"

"Pliable but not incapacitated?" Shannon echoed.

Josie thought about Nysa and Clay. How they'd been functioning perfectly normally by all appearances and yet had taken such nonsensical words to heart: time to be a mermaid; time to be a match. Bronwyn had said that Clay continued setting things on fire until they told him to stop. She said, "Something that if you gave it to a person—in the right dose, of course, because I know that would be an issue—you'd be able to tell them what to do, and they'd do it. Anything at all. But they wouldn't be sick or disoriented or appear intoxicated."

"Hmmm," Shannon considered. "This really sounds like a question for someone on an illegal drug task force, but okay, I'll play along. Let me think a minute, would you?"

They waited several minutes, listening to the sounds of Shannon typing away on a keyboard while she mumbled inaudibly to herself. Then her voice became sharper and more distinct. "Josie, Noah? You there?"

"We're here," answered Noah.

Shannon said, "I'd start with scopolamine, although it's not a controlled substance. It's used mostly to treat seasickness."

Noah said, "Is that the one that comes as a patch? You put it behind your ear?"

"Right, exactly," said Shannon.

"How did you know that?" Josie asked.

Noah gave a little smile. "I've used those patches to go deep sea fishing."

"That patch is an extremely low dose," Shannon explained. "It's released over a three-day period so the absorption is slow. Scopolamine is also known as hyoscine. In small doses, it's used to prevent nausea and vomiting. Your body naturally produces a chemical compound called acetylcholine, which basically transmits nerve impulses in the central and peripheral nervous systems. It's the main neurotransmitter responsible for contracting muscles, dilating blood vessels—many things. Basically, it can have an inhibitory effect on your nervous system or an excitatory effect. It causes your nerve signals to go faster or slower. Scopolamine blocks the acetylcholine from the central nervous system. No one is really sure why, but it works on the body's vomiting center. Like I said, usually as a result of seasickness or post-op nausea. Sometimes it's used for gastrointestinal distress—like spasms. We've used it in some drugs to prevent nausea caused by chemotherapy. In fact, my team developed a very effective drug in that vein several years ago, which is now used for multiple indications."

Before Shannon could launch into a full description of Quarmark's drug, Josie asked, "What would happen if you used scopolamine in larger doses? Or if you ingested it?"

"Well, you can ingest it, that's not an issue. It comes in pill form. In large doses, however, you'd start to see side effects like drowsiness, itching, headache, rapid heartbeat, confusion, dilated pupils. It would very likely cause amnesia. At extremely high doses, you're looking at psychosis, seizures, hallucinations and of course, death. Side effects would vary from person to person, naturally. Everyone's body chemistry is different. There are a lot of factors that make a drug effective for one person but not for another."

Noah said, "You said you'd start with scopolamine. Why?"

Shannon sighed. "Well, I work in pharma, and that was the first thing that came to mind because I've worked with it before. Also, as I said, it blocks the neurotransmitter acetylcholine from doing what it's supposed to do in the nervous system. This would lead to cognitive issues and memory loss. In some studies, higher doses caused docility, extreme suggestibility, almost a hypnotic state."

Josie asked, "A hypnotic state. Is it possible that a person who had ingested a high dosage—but not enough to cause things like drowsiness, confusion, psychosis, seizures, and such—could appear to be in a normal state but actually be highly suggestible?"

"Sure, I guess," Shannon said. "The conditions and dosages would have to be just right, but I suppose it is possible. You know, the government used scopolamine as a truth serum in the early 1920s. I believe a country in Europe used it for the same purpose more recently."

Josie laughed. "I didn't know that. Oh, one last thing—how long does it stay in the bloodstream? For toxicology purposes?"

"That I couldn't really tell you. I'm pretty sure the answer is not very long, but you're better off asking a toxicologist."

They chatted a few more minutes, with Shannon asking after Patrick. Josie didn't mention the laundry incident but promised to tell him to call Shannon, and they hung up.

"Patrick," Josie said. "That's who we need to talk to. Tomorrow."

Noah raised a brow. "Is he some kind of scopolamine king? Is there something you're not telling the rest of us about your little brother?"

Josie laughed. "No, but he's a student. He lives on campus. Hahlbeck gave us the 'official' information. But she won't know the same things the students know."

"You mean the things the students don't want her to know."

"Exactly."

# CHAPTER TWENTY-SEVEN

The next morning, Josie sent a text to Patrick, inviting him to dinner that evening. Then Noah took her to get a rental car. He left her at the rental company, telling her he'd meet her at the station, but when she arrived at work, he was nowhere to be found. Using her desk phone, she called the hospital and asked for Dr. Nashat, hoping he could give her some kind of an update on Clay Walsh. Relief washed over her when he told her that Walsh had survived the flight to Philadelphia and that, as far as Dr. Nashat knew, he was still alive. Hanging up, Josie remained at her desk, staring at her phone, trying to decide whether or not to call Noah and check on him. Was she overreacting? She couldn't help but feel he had been strangely distant lately. Maybe not distant, but inaccessible. He was probably just out working on one of the many more minor calls the detectives were responsible for other than homicides. Where the hell else would he be? The stairwell door slammed, and Mettner walked into the great room with a sheaf of papers, including what looked like a rolled-up poster. "Oh good," he said. "You're here." He handed her the rolled-up paper which turned out to be a map. "I've got those coordinates from Nysa Somers' phone."

Josie put her phone down and grabbed up some tape. She hung the map up on one of the walls of the great room and used a Sharpie to mark the area in which Nysa's phone had pinged throughout the night. Holding the list of addresses he had compiled of the older males of Nysa's acquaintance that could potentially be her mystery boyfriend, Mettner watched Josie work. She said, "At ten, her phone pinged these three towers, which puts her here—which includes the campus and Hollister Way."

"And part of the area north of campus," Mettner added.

"True, but this was never going to be precise. However, at 11:03 her roommate texts her wondering where she is, and she replies saying that she met up with a friend, at which point her phone pings these towers over here." Josie pointed to an area roughly six miles away from the campus which encompassed part of a shopping district, a portion of the interstate, and two different residential neighborhoods.

"Well, that's interesting," said Mettner.

"And at two a.m., her phone pings again back here," Josie made a circular motion with the Sharpie, indicating the first area she had marked which included the campus and Hollister Way.

"So she went somewhere and came back."

"Right," Josie said. "Her phone pings in the campus/Hollister Way area up until Monday afternoon, after which Hummel retrieved and charged it. Then it pings over here in the center of Denton where we are, which is after Hummel brought the phone to us."

"But the roommate says she didn't make it home."

"The roommate also said she was seeing someone. So did her sister. That someone probably met her in the street where the cut-through comes into Hollister. No one would have been out there at that time of night. Even if they were, I watched these kids walk back and forth along that path. They never take their damn eyes off their phones long enough to look around. Nysa Somers could have been standing right there with her lover and no one would have noticed."

"Okay," said Mettner. "The older, inappropriate male lover picks her up at the cut-through, takes her somewhere and then brings her back at two-ish. Then what? The roommate said she never made it home. Then at close to six a.m., she gets a calendar notification telling her it's time to be a mermaid, her bag is tossed into the woods, and she comes out of the cut-through onto campus and walks to the pool. We're still missing four hours."

Josie touched the cap of the Sharpie to her chin, studying the map. "The roommate said she wasn't sure if Nysa had made it home or not. She didn't wake up until seven fifteen."

"So it's possible that Nysa came home for four hours, got the notification on her phone, and went back out?"

"I suppose."

"But when does she eat the brownie? Could the person she was with have gotten her to eat it before two a.m. with the effects still working by six a.m.?"

"I don't know," Josie said. "We still don't actually know what drug was in the brownie. Shit. So much of this is speculation."

"Well, not really," Mettner said. "We know she wasn't on campus or at home between 11:04 and 2:00, so let's look at these addresses."

He handed her a page with half the addresses on them. Together they began marking them on the map. When they were finished, they stood back and studied the map. Mettner said, "Son of a bitch. This makes no sense."

None of the seven men lived in the area in which Nysa Somers had been between 11:04 p.m. and 2:00 a.m.

"No," Josie said. "It makes perfect sense. He didn't take her to his home. Not at first, anyway. They went for a drive and then he brought her back. He lives in this area—near campus."

There were two push pins in the first area of triangulation. One was for a professor and the other was for Coach Brett Pace.

Mettner reached forward and pulled the push pin representing the professor out of the map. "This guy's married. His wife was home all night. Maybe he was able to sneak out while she was asleep, but he couldn't have brought Nysa back with him."

"Which leaves Coach Brett Pace," Josie said. "Let's go have a chat with him."

\*

Brett Pace wasn't at the athletic center on campus. They checked various buildings but didn't find him. One of the assistant coaches said he'd left practice early the day before and hadn't returned. Josie and Mettner drove to his address—a white rancher on an acre of land along a rural route just above campus. A jeep sat in the gravel driveway. Empty flower beds lined the front of the house. A Denton University camping chair sat on the front stoop beneath a set of windchimes. The house had a sad air about it, and Josie had the sense that Brett Pace's divorce hadn't been an amicable one. As they approached the door, music could be heard from inside. Mettner rang the doorbell, setting off a frenzy of dog barks from inside. The music stopped abruptly. They heard Pace's voice and then the dog's barks receded to a low growl. The door swung open and Brett's large form filled the space. In two days, he had become a different man. Stubble covered his jaw. Dark circles smudged the skin under his eyes. Instead of the neat, jaunty coach's uniform, he wore torn jeans and a black T-shirt with holes in the collar. Even though he clearly hadn't slept much in the last two days, he somehow looked younger in his disheveled state than when he had projected his clean-cut image. Josie wondered if Nysa had seen this side of him and been intrigued by it. Or was it the grinning, smooth-talking coach persona spouting off about team dynamics that had drawn her in?

Wordlessly, Pace stepped out of their way and ushered them inside. An enthusiastic labradoodle greeted them, tail wagging, nose nudging their hands. Josie patted its head. Pace told it to go lay down and reluctantly, it walked to the corner of the room and curled up on a ratty white dog bed. Josie panned the room, which held only a television mounted to the wall and a leather couch. She wondered if his ex-wife had gotten the bulk of the furniture in the divorce or if he was moving. A peek behind him into the kitchen revealed two cardboard boxes on the counter with unused bubble wrap beside them.

"Have a seat if you want," Pace said.

Mettner said, "We looked for you on campus. One of your assistant coaches said you left yesterday and didn't come back."

Pace stood in the center of the room, shoulders slumped. "I handed in my resignation last night."

Josie lifted her chin in the direction of the kitchen. "You're moving?"

Pace sighed. "I'm not staying here. My, uh, dad has a place up by Penn State. A little cabin, out of the way. Figured I'd lay low there for a while."

"Lay low?" Josie said. "How come?"

"Look, let's just cut to the chase, okay?" Pace said. "You're here about Nysa. Once that comes out, I'll lose my job and be a pariah. I'm just heading things off at the pass, okay?"

"Once what comes out?" Josie asked.

He rolled his eyes. "You're going to make me say it?"

Mettner said, "Yeah. That's our job."

"The affair. Well, I guess it wasn't really an affair, since we were both single and both consenting adults. But I was her coach, so it's a scandal, and I'm a bit older than her, and then she killed herself because we broke up."

Mettner gave Josie a quick side glance. Then he said, "Tell us about the break-up, Mr. Pace."

Pace turned and walked into the kitchen. Josie and Mettner followed him. From the fridge, he pulled a Guinness. He waved it in the air, silently offering them one. "We're on the clock," Josie said.

Pace opened the beer and took a long swig, using the back of his wrist to wipe his mouth afterward. "Right, right." He walked over to a small table in the center of the kitchen and sat down. "Look, there's one thing you need to know. One thing that everyone needs to know, okay? Like when it comes out and her parents find out.

They need to know: she dumped me. I was into her, you know? I had a couple of other women on the hook—women my age—and I deep-sixed them once things started happening with Nysa. Things between us were hot."

Josie hid her disgust, keeping her face blank. She was sure it was no coincidence that Pace thought things were "hot" with Nysa, and she just happened to be younger than him. She said, "If she dumped you, why do you think she killed herself?"

He took another swig of beer. "'Cause of what I said to her on Sunday. But you have to understand, I didn't really mean it."

Josie said, "When we spoke on Monday, you told me that the last time you saw Nysa was Friday at practice."

"Well, yeah," Pace said. "I wasn't going to blurt out that I was banging a dead student. Christ."

"You're not lying now," Mettner said. "Why did you lie on Monday?"

Pace started peeling the label from his beer. "Because I had just found out Nysa died. I didn't know what the hell was going on. I was trying to cover all my bases. But your lady friend here—"

"Detective Quinn," Mettner corrected.

"Yeah, yeah," Pace said. "She already knew Nysa was with someone on Sunday night. It was only a matter of time before you figured out it was me. Look, I watch crime shows, you know? I know you've got all kinds of technology now that tells you where everyone is all the time, and I'm right because here you are. Also, I don't know who Nysa told about us. She said she never told anyone but these chicks, they lie all the time. It's like it's in their DNA."

For a moment, Josie felt repulsed by the fact that Nysa had let this creep touch her. Then she remembered how nice and genial he'd been on Monday when she interviewed him. That had been him playing the role of a college swim coach. He probably played a lot of roles—whichever benefited him most in the moment.

Although in this moment, Josie was sure she was looking at the real man beneath the veneer, and she didn't like him one bit.

Mettner pulled out a chair and sat across from Pace. "What happened on Sunday night, Brett? Start at the beginning."

Josie said, "Actually, start with Friday. You said she dumped you."

He sucked down the rest of his beer. "Yeah. We had been seeing each other after practices and sometimes after her classes if no one was around my office. Friday after practice, I asked her to stay late, like usual. We went back to my office. Things started to get hot and heavy and all of a sudden she stops, you know? She starts saying all this stuff about how what we're doing is wrong and inappropriate, and she's worried about her future. I tried to tell her it didn't matter. No one would find out."

"But she dumped you anyway," Josie filled in.

He went back to trying to peel the label off the empty bottle. "Yeah. She said she felt bad about it, but she couldn't keep doing it. Then she left."

"You didn't try to call or text her?" Mettner asked.

"No way, man. The first rule when you're hooking up with a student is not to leave any trail—" He broke off, as if just realizing who he was talking to.

Josie let the uncomfortable silence play out until he started squirming in his chair. Then she said, "How did you know where she was going to be on Sunday night?" she asked finally.

"She always used that path behind the Gulley building. The one that goes from campus right into the back of Hollister? We met back there a few times. She didn't like it, didn't want us to be seen there, but no one ever noticed. I knew she usually ate on campus, so I went over and waited. Except she didn't come out till almost ten o'clock."

"You waited for her for three hours?" Mettner asked.

"Listen," Pace responded, meeting Mettner's eyes. "When I tell you it was hot with Nysa, I mean it was hot. Yeah, I waited three hours. Besides that, she was my star swimmer. I didn't want her to be upset with me. We still had the whole year to get through."

Josie said, "What happened when she came off the path?"

"I told her to get into the car, and she did. I told her to come home with me so we could talk, but she didn't want to. So I said 'just go for a drive with me and hear me out.' She said that was fine. We drove around for a few hours but there was no convincing her. Things got a little… ugly."

"Ugly how?" Mettner asked.

"I might have said some things to her that I didn't really mean, but you have to understand she was saying ugly things, too, like I wasn't really who I seemed to be and how the nice-guy coach thing was just an act and she felt duped, and I was just using her."

"You weren't?" Josie asked pointedly.

"Using her how?" he scoffed. "What would I possibly be using her for?"

Ignoring his question, Josie said, "What did you say to her?"

He swiped a hand down his face. "I might have said that if she dumped me, I would tell people about her, like how she was in bed and stuff."

"What else?" Josie asked.

"I also might have said I would tell people she slept with me to get me to recommend her for the Vandivere scholarship."

Josie had to concentrate hard on neither physically recoiling nor punching Pace in the throat.

Mettner said, "That's sexual harassment. Surely, you know that."

"Well, if I didn't, Nysa made sure I knew. Like my career would be destroyed if people found out about us. I gave her this whole line about how maybe I'd have to coach elsewhere, but she would forever be humiliated, and her reputation would be tarnished for life. I might have made it sound pretty bad 'cause she started crying and made me take her home, except she wouldn't even let me drop her off at her place. I left her at the entrance to her complex."

Josie said, "She told you to take her home and you did."

"Well, yeah. She was hysterical. Plus, I started to feel a little bad, you know? She was right. Telling people about us would have been worse for me than her. But I just wanted to keep seeing her. I thought if I scared her…"

"Yes," Josie said. "Every woman loves to be scared into continuing a relationship."

Pace gave her a sour look. "Yeah, I get that. It was a dumb move. I'm not proud of it. It was a shitty thing to do, but I didn't think she'd kill herself over it. I didn't think she was like that."

Mettner and Josie exchanged another furtive look. Mettner asked, "What time did you drop her off?"

"I don't know. Around two, maybe?"

"You dropped her off at the entrance to Hollister Way at two in the morning and went home?" Josie said.

"Yeah. Next thing I know, I get to work and find out she drowned in the pool. Shit. I never meant for anything like that to happen."

Mettner said, "Did you give her anything before you dropped her off?"

"Like what?"

"Something to eat," Josie said.

"Something to eat? Like what?"

Mettner said, "We believe Nysa was under the influence of something when she went into the pool."

"Yeah, well, that was kind of obvious since you two asked everyone on the team about drugs. I figured she was so upset, she went home, got messed up and then drowned in the pool."

"But you didn't give her any drugs," Josie said. "To calm her down? Get her to come back here with you? Maybe without telling her you were giving her something?"

"Where would I get drugs?"

"I don't know," she countered. "You tell me."

"I didn't give Nysa any drugs. I didn't bring her back here."

Mettner said, "Your closest neighbors can't really see your house from where they're at, can they?"

"What's that got to do with anything?"

Mettner shifted in his chair, leaning his elbows on the table. "Well, it's just that you say you dropped Nysa off around two at Hollister, but you don't have anyone who can confirm that you were here alone all night, do you?"

Pace shook his head. "No, I don't, but I'm telling the truth. Nysa did not come home with me Sunday night."

Considering he lied as easily as he breathed, Josie was skeptical. She tried a different tack. "You and Nysa had been seeing each other in secret for a few weeks. Did you have nicknames for each other?"

His brow furrowed. "What? What kind of question is that?"

Mettner said, "Just answer it."

With a sigh, Pace said, "I had one for her, but she didn't have one for me. She liked to call me by my first name. Brett. Made her feel like we were really two adults on even ground, she said."

"What did you call her?" Josie asked.

His gaze flicked to the table. "I called her my sexy mermaid."

Neither Josie nor Mettner reacted to this. Mettner picked up the questioning. "How do you know Clay Walsh?"

"Who?"

"Clay Walsh," Mettner repeated. "How do you know him?"

"I don't know anyone named Clay Walsh. Who is he?"

Josie said, "Where were you yesterday afternoon around three thirty, four o'clock?"

Brett waved his hands to indicate his kitchen. "I was here."

Josie asked, "Do you like brownies, Mr. Pace?"

His entire face puckered momentarily, like he'd eaten something sour. "What the hell kind of interrogation is this? You guys are some weird cops, you know that?"

Without missing a beat, Mettner said, "Do you? Like brownies?"

Rolling his eyes, Pace said, "Sure. Who doesn't?"

Mettner stood up. "Do you mind if we have a look around?"

"For what? The drugs you think I've got? Go for it. Not many places to look. My ex-wife took just about everything."

He was right. Besides the kitchen table and chairs and the couch, the house held almost no furniture. Only a bed and a dresser. A folding chair served as Pace's nightstand. There was nothing to indicate that Nysa had been there; that Pace was hiding or making drugs; or even that he had recently cooked anything. Takeout containers overflowed from his trash bin. Then again, he would have had a pretty good idea of what the police would be looking for from their first interview.

"I think we're done here," she told Mettner once they'd had a thorough look around.

Pace walked them to the door. Mettner handed him a business card. "I wouldn't go far, Mr. Pace. We'll be in touch."

They were halfway to their vehicle when Pace came out onto the front stoop. The windchimes swung toward him, brushing his head, and he stepped to the side. "Hey," he said. "I didn't do anything wrong."

Josie and Mettner stared at him for a beat before turning back to the car.

Pace called, "This is going to ruin my life, isn't it?"

Josie turned back, a faint smile curling her lips. "That's not really the question you should be asking yourself, is it?"

A line of confusion creased Pace's forehead. "What?"

Josie said, "This is going to ruin your life, yeah, but will it kill you?"

# CHAPTER TWENTY-EIGHT

Josie and Mettner made it back to the station by lunchtime. She was relieved to see that Noah was there with Gretchen, and they'd brought lunch as well. They convened at their desks and ate until Chitwood emerged from his office for a briefing. Noah and Gretchen had nothing to report yet. They'd done several interviews with Clay Walsh's friends, coworkers, and acquaintances but hadn't yet turned up any red flags or connections to Nysa Somers. Josie and Noah told the team about the conversation they'd had with Shannon the night before, including her suggestion that scopolamine, or something similar to it, in large doses, could cause docility and suggestibility. Chitwood promised to ask his DEA contact about the drug. Josie and Mettner then outlined their conversation with Brett Pace.

"What a sorry excuse for a human being," Gretchen said.

"No shit," Mettner replied.

"Quinn," said Chitwood. "You believe Pace is good for this?"

"I really don't know, sir," she said. "He's a proven liar. He's got no alibi. He's admitted to being with Nysa on Sunday night, and his nickname for her was 'mermaid.'"

"We can't rule him out," Chitwood said. "He gives me a bad feeling, especially since he's trying to get the hell out of here only a couple of days after this woman died. I want you all to be looking for connections between Pace and Clay Walsh, you got that? Maybe one of you can go back down to the East Bridge and show Pace's photo around. See if he ever bought drugs down there."

"Chief," Josie said.

He held up a hand. "I know, I know, Quinn. I've put in three calls to my DEA friend already. As soon as I hear from him, you'll know."

Josie opened her mouth to thank him, but the door to the staircase slammed open. All heads swiveled in the direction of the doorway where a breathless Sawyer Hayes stood, chest heaving, one hand holding out a cardboard cupholder with four cups of Komorrah's coffee in it. He thrust it toward them and said, "Did you send your desk sergeant into the bell tower for some reason?"

"What?" Chitwood and Josie said at the same time.

Sawyer took a few steps into the room and handed the coffees to the closest person, which happened to be Mettner. "He's up in the bell tower. What's his name? Lamay?"

"Dan," Josie said, springing from her seat. She looked at her colleagues. "Anyone know why Dan is in the bell tower?"

Mettner said, "I didn't even know you could get to the bell tower."

Sawyer said, "I was coming out of Komorrah's—I got you all coffee since it's been a rough week and I was in the area—when I saw him up there, leaning out the window. Scared me because I thought he would fall. He keeps leaning further and further out. I have no idea what he's doing."

Josie pushed past him with her colleagues in tow. "Then let's not leave him up there. Come on."

She raced into the stairwell and took the steps two at a time to the third floor. The bell tower was on the east side of the building. Josie navigated two hallways until she found the door. She pushed through it and scrambled up the narrow, twisting steps to the top of the belfry, which extended almost a full floor length above the third floor of Denton's police station. Another door, this one made of heavy wood, waited at the top of the belfry. It creaked as Josie opened it. Stepping onto the wooden platform that formed a pentagon around the enormous bell, she hesitated. Only once had she been in the bell tower and that was during her tenure as interim chief, when she had had a structural engineer assess the tower and the integrity of the structure holding it all in place lest the two-ton bell topple onto the city street below and cause a catastrophe. She hadn't been comfortable in the tall, confined area even though the windows were open with no screens or shutters. It was at least ten degrees cooler up here, and noises from the street carried upward—the sounds of tires over asphalt, beeping horns, dogs barking, people shouting greetings to one another.

Josie made the mistake of looking down, a wave of dizziness instantly assailing her. Wooden scaffolding ran the length of the shaft beneath the belfry. Thick beams had been fitted together in a Jenga-like pattern, all designed to support the weight of both the bell and the structure built around it. Josie was relatively certain there was a ladder along one of the walls below the belfry but from where she stood, she couldn't see it.

The platform surrounding the bell, which stood between the bell and the windows, had only a thin, rough-hewn wooden rail along the bell side. For a terrifying moment, all Josie could focus on were all the openings she could easily slip through on either side of the platform. There was at least a person-sized gap between the stone walls and the stand. The gap on the bell side was slightly larger. A fall from the belfry to the bottom of the tower shaft would definitely kill her. Taking a deep breath, she placed a foot onto the platform, noting it looked like nothing more than a few two-by-fours pushed together. She placed another foot onto the wood, letting all her weight rest on it as her left hand clutched the rail, splinters digging into her palm. It didn't bow beneath her but still, it seemed far too flimsy for her taste.

She inched around the large, weathered bell. The enormous wheel beside it loomed over her, easily twice her height. Josie quickly took measure of all of the mechanisms. The structural engineer had been most enthusiastic about his job and had explained to her that the large block of wood to which the bell, the wheel and the stay were attached was called a headstock. Metal loops called cannons held the bell fast to the headstock. On one side of the bell, fixed to the headstock, was the stay, a piece of wood that held the bell in place so that it rested on a slider beneath it. On the other side of the bell, also connected to the headstock, was the wheel which held the rope one needed to pull to ring the bell. The rope hung down the shaft and out of Josie's view. The bell hadn't been used in ages. It was merely decorative at this point. Josie couldn't think of any reason for Dan to be in here, although having been on the force nearly fifty years, he was probably one of the only officers, other than Josie and the Chief, who knew how to get into the bell tower. Josie remembered him telling her that when he was a rookie, they used to ring it any time a police officer died—on or off the job.

Taking more tentative steps, her eyes were again drawn to the center of the belfry. For all her lovely knowledge of the mechanisms of the giant bell, all Josie could think about was how disastrous it would be if the headstock or any piece attached to it failed, and everything in the belfry—including herself and Dan—went tumbling down the shaft.

Shaking those images from her mind, Josie concentrated on the task at hand, taking more careful steps along the wooden platform that circled the bell. Dan came into view as she rounded the bell on the Main Street side of the tower. A cool wind blew through the arched windows, caressing her face. Dan stood with his back to her, leaning out of one of the windows, one of his feet lifted from the ground.

Josie stopped a few feet away from him. "Dan?"

If he heard her, he made no indication, instead leaning further out of the window, his paunch resting on the stone sill. Josie stepped closer. Behind her, the wooden platform creaked. She turned to see Noah and motioned with one of her hands for him to go around the bell the other way. He gave a nod and disappeared behind the bell. "Dan," Josie said again.

No response.

Dan thrust a hand out the window, as if trying to grasp something. "Dan!" Josie said, more sharply, but his other foot lifted from the ground. His upper body levered over the window sill. Josie dove for his feet, only managing to catch one of them before he went into freefall out the window. Her own legs scrabbled to gain purchase on the narrow platform. She felt her right leg slip into the gap between the platform and the stone wall. Only emptiness and a long fall to concrete waited beneath.

"Noah," she cried.

She tried to use her left knee on the wooden floor to steady herself and bring her right leg back up, but above her, Dan flailed, making it impossible for her to find any stability. "Dan!" she shouted. "Stop."

He froze, his legs sinking back to the floor inside the tower but causing Josie to drop, her left leg now slipping into the gap, only a pantleg and a grasp between her and a plummet to her death. Finally, a hand slid under her armpit. She looked up to see Noah, one hand clutching the belt of Dan's pants while the other scooped under her arm to try to get her back onto the platform. Josie took one hand from Dan's leg and latched onto Noah. He pulled and she scrambled, using his body to climb back onto the platform. Keeping hold of Noah's shoulder, she dared not look down again. Her heart pounded so hard in her chest, it felt like each beat rattled her bones.

She looked at Noah for a beat, silently thanking him. Then she let go of him and turned her attention to Dan. Placing a gentle hand on his shoulder, she said, "Dan, are you okay?"

His upper body still leaned slightly out the window. He pulled himself back in and turned to her. Eyes blank, he stared into her face, sweat beaded along his receding hairline and his upper lip. "I have to get it," he mumbled.

Noah kept hold of Dan's belt. Josie met his eyes and gave a small shake of her head to indicate that Dan was not okay.

"Dan," she said. "What is it that you have to get?"

"Here," he said, turning back toward the window. "I've got to get this here."

Josie caught the look of concern that crossed Noah's face and gently squeezed Dan's shoulder. "There's nothing up here."

"I have to put it back," Dan said into the breeze flowing past outside.

Josie turned his upper body, and he let her, facing her once more. "Dan, do you know who I am?"

Another blank stare. Josie leaned in closer and noted that his pupils were dilated. Still, she managed a smile for him, trying to stay calm. "It's me, Dan. Josie Quinn."

Noah shuffled around behind Dan, blocking off his access to the window.

"Josie Quinn," Dan said, mystified.

"Lieutenant Fraley is right behind you," Josie said. Gently she pulled him toward her. "Why don't we go downstairs and talk, okay, Dan? This isn't a good place to talk. It's a little dangerous up here."

"Dangerous," he repeated.

Josie turned so that he could squeeze up beside her. She put an arm around his shoulders. "Walk with me."

Obediently, he walked alongside her, the platform now bowing slightly beneath their combined weight. He let her guide him through the door, back down the twisting steps to the door into the third floor where a crowd of their colleagues waited. Noah followed closely behind. Chief Chitwood said, "Sergeant Lamay, are you all right?"

"He needs to go to the hospital," Josie answered, an arm still wrapped protectively around Dan's shoulders.

Sawyer muscled his way between Mettner and Gretchen. "What's going on?"

"He's disoriented," Josie said. "He's talking but not making sense. Doesn't seem to know where he is or who I am."

Dan looked around at all the faces. Josie felt him tense beneath her arm. "I have to get it," he repeated, except that now his voice was far more high-pitched, a note of panic making it crack.

Noah drew up on Dan's other side and linked arms with him. "Everything's fine, Dan. We're going to call your wife and take you to the hospital, okay?"

Josie squeezed his shoulder. "Let's walk down the steps, okay, Dan?"

He hesitated a beat and then took a small step. "Walk."

"Yes," Josie said. "We'll walk down the steps and to the parking lot."

As Chitwood, Mettner, Gretchen, and Amber parted to let them through, the Chief said, "I'll call the hospital to let them know you're on the way."

Mettner added, "And I'll call Dan's wife."

"Go get her," Josie told him. "They only have one car and Dan drives it to work. Their daughter is away at school."

"You got it, boss."

Sawyer said, "I'll drive."

"No," Josie said. "I will."

Sawyer went ahead of them down the stairwell. "This is my job, you know."

An edge to his voice, Noah said, "If Josie said she'll drive, then she'll drive."

"I'll get there faster, Sawyer," Josie explained as they proceeded down the stairs to the ground level with Dan sandwiched between her and Noah, walking dutifully. "I assume you didn't come here in an ambulance."

Sawyer held the door to the parking lot open. "No, I didn't. At least let me ride with you. I can assess him."

They reached Josie's vehicle. "That would be great," she said. "Let's go."

# CHAPTER TWENTY-NINE

I checked the WYEP news site for two days to see if there were any more stories about me—or rather, about what I had unleashed. I was disappointed to see nothing at all. Not yet, anyway. Had I miscalculated the effectiveness of my newest tool? Surely not. It was the easiest, most effective method I had used to date. It made my previous efforts seem so unsophisticated—even my second killing, which I had always found so clever.

It wasn't as spectacular as what I'd done to Nysa Somers and Clay Walsh, but I still recalled that day fondly. Waiting outside on her front step, nervous but also excited. Remembering all her sins against me as I stood there, hurt, but it was nothing compared to the knowledge that I was about to get payback.

"Did you clean yourself off?" she asked after I walked in.

"Yes," I said.

"Why were you at the shelter today anyway?"

I didn't answer. Instead, I reached into the brown grocery bag dangling from one arm and held out the carton of orange juice she asked me to bring by. Extra pulpy.

She took it without thanks. Always without thanks. She ambled into the kitchen, and I followed. I watched her pour a glass. Glancing back at me, she said, "You know, if you were at the shelter today, you should have taken a shower before you came here. I told you I'm allergic to cats."

"I know."

She touched the glass to her lips. Hesitated. Her eyes locked on me. "Extremely allergic," she reminded me.

"Yes," I said. "I know."

She didn't even get through the whole glass before the anaphylaxis took hold. Her lips and tongue swelled first. Then came the clutching of her throat, the wheezing, the falling, the writhing, and finally, stillness. The last bit of life was bleeding from her eyes when I walked over and stared down at her—one of the only times I saw someone take their last breath. I had loved her once.

"I deserved better," I said.

Smiling, I walked over to the counter, dumped what was left in her glass, and rinsed it out. Then I took out the other carton of orange juice from my grocery bag. No pulp. I filled the cup halfway with that and left it on the counter. I took out the last item in my grocery bag: broccoli soup made with cashew cream. She was also highly allergic to cashews.

I took the extra-pulpy orange juice with me when I left. I didn't expect anyone to raise any questions, but it was just good practice not to leave behind a carton of orange juice with finely shaved cat hair in it.

# CHAPTER THIRTY

An hour later, Josie paced in the waiting area of the Emergency Room. Dan Lamay's wife had just been allowed back to see him. The doctors said he was stable, and although they hadn't found any evidence of a stroke or heart issue, they were running additional tests to see if they could pinpoint a reason for his behavior. They'd also taken blood. Since he presented with disorientation but no immediate signs of a stroke or heart attack, they'd run toxicology, but it had come back clean. She couldn't shake the feeling that the unusual event with Dan was somehow connected to the Nysa Somers and Clay Walsh cases. Chief Chitwood must have agreed because he had immediately ordered Mettner to track down every place Dan had been that morning, every person he'd come into contact with, and everything he'd ingested. He'd also sent Noah and Gretchen out to do the work on the Clay Walsh case, as they'd previously discussed before Sawyer had burst into the great room to alert them that Dan was in the bell tower. No one had wanted to leave the hospital, but the Chief insisted.

"There's work to be done, people," he had hollered outside of Dan Lamay's room, causing nearby nurses to startle.

Everyone had scattered except for Josie, who stood resolute before the Chief, hands on her hips, chin jutted forward. Chitwood looked at her, cheeks pinkening. "That means you too, Quinn. You are one of my detectives, are you not?"

"I'm not going," Josie said.

"The hell you're not."

Her heart did a double tap, but she didn't move. Dan Lamay was more than a colleague to Josie. He was a friend. Three years ago, she'd hit rock bottom, personally and professionally, and Dan had come to her aid. He'd put his own job at risk for her even though his wife was battling cancer and their daughter was in college. He had helped her when no one else would or could. Josie was not walking away from him now that he was in trouble.

Chitwood sighed and said, "Quinn, they'll call if there's any news or any change."

"Sir," Josie said. "You saw how Dan was acting. His eyes were dilated. He wasn't making any sense, but he did whatever we told him to do. I told him to come down from the bell tower, and he did. I told him to walk, to get in the car, to walk into the hospital with us, and on the ride over, Noah made several suggestions—kind of like a field sobriety test—and Dan did them all without question. He was suggestible, docile, but not incapacitated. Medically, he's fine. No stroke, no cardiac issues. His tox screen was clean."

"You think I didn't notice, Quinn? After the last two days? What's your point?"

"I'd like to get Mrs. Lamay's permission to have Dan's blood samples tested for scopolamine," she said. "I know it's a long shot based purely on speculation, and that we haven't even talked to your DEA contact yet, but if somehow what happened with Dan today is related to what happened to Nysa Somers and Clay Walsh, we've only got a narrow window of time, from a toxicology standpoint, to test Dan's blood. If I can get her permission, we wouldn't need a warrant, and in this instance, I'm not even sure we could get a warrant. We've got an opportunity here. If it turns out to be nothing, the only cost would be an extra lab test."

"Fine," Chitwood said. He started to walk away but stopped. Turning back to her, he said, "Quinn, if Dan's incident today is somehow connected to Somers and Walsh, and we've got someone going around this city giving people an unknown drug with a half-life so short it doesn't stay in their system long enough for medical professionals to test for it, this whole thing is going to be hard as hell to prove."

"Yes, sir."

"Quinn, you do love uphill battles, don't you?"

"Those are my favorite kinds of battles, sir," she answered.

He gave her a strange look and then a slow smile spread across his face. Josie's breath stopped in her throat. It was only the second time she'd ever seen him smile, and no one was there to witness it.

Chitwood said, "Keep me posted on Lamay's condition, would you?"

She nodded and watched him leave.


Josie spent the rest of the afternoon in the hospital, monitoring Dan's condition. Dan's wife readily agreed to a test for scopolamine. The only problem was that Denton Memorial didn't have the capability to perform such a test. It would have to be sent to an outside lab, which was going to take two to three days at the most. Noah, Gretchen and Mettner worked the rest of the day, splitting up to cover as much ground as possible. They maintained a group text message thread to keep one another informed of who had been interviewed and whether any leads popped up.

Mettner found out that Dan had stopped at a local mini-market that morning for gas, coffee, and a pastry. Josie asked him to bag anything that remained at Dan's desk and send it to the state police lab for analysis. Mettner also pulled footage from the mini-market for the few hours before Dan came in until after Dan left, but so many people had bought coffee and pastries that morning, it was impossible to tell if anyone had tampered with anything. Interviews with the mini-market employees turned up nothing. Mettner even pulled footage from the station lobby where Dan was usually posted to see who had been in or out and if any of those people had acted suspiciously. He found nothing. Gretchen and Noah continued to provide their own updates throughout the day as they each worked their own list of people from Clay Walsh's life, trying to find connections between him and Nysa Somers as well as him and Brett Pace. They turned up nothing. They had also shown Brett Pace's photo around beneath the East Bridge, but no one had ever seen him before, or if they had, they wouldn't admit to it.

Just before dinner time, after being assured by the medical staff that Dan was just fine and that they'd keep him overnight for observation, Josie returned to the stationhouse, exhausted and no closer to figuring out what the hell was happening in her city. She dropped into her seat and threw her feet up onto her desk. Gretchen straggled in, followed several minutes later by Mettner. Each of them looked just as worn out as Josie felt.

"Where's Noah?" Josie asked.

"A couple of last-minute interviews," Gretchen said. "I don't expect them to turn anything up though."

The door to the Chief's office banged open. "Quinn!" he barked. "Get in here! Now!"

Josie stood, smoothed her Denton PD polo shirt—the one she'd borrowed from Gretchen still—and khaki pants and walked into the chief's office. "Sir?"

He motioned toward the door behind her. "Who else is here? Get them in here, too."

Josie called for Mett and Gretchen, who joined her. They gathered around the Chief's desk, and he punched a button on his desktop phone. "Josh?" he said. "You still there?"

A voice answered, "Yeah, Bob. I'm here."

"I got my people here. Can you tell them what you told me?"

"Sure thing."

Chitwood looked up at his detectives. "You're talking to DEA agent, Josh Stumpf. He's been with the agency over twenty years. Seen it all. We worked on three task forces together. He knows his shit. I called him and talked to him about what's going on around here. Rather than repeat everything he told me, I figured I'd just have you talk with him directly so you can ask any questions you have. Josh?"

"Hey there," Josh said. "Who've I got on the phone?"

Josie, Gretchen, and Mettner introduced themselves.

"All right then," Josh said. "Bob sent me a photo of the sticker you found. I ran it through our database, talked to a few people. It's not something we've ever seen before. Bob also told me you were looking into the possibility of a street drug that would make a person suggestible, docile, and pliant but without completely incapacitating them. He also mentioned that one of you had brought up the drug scopolamine. Turns out there is a street drug that's very similar to scopolamine. It's called Devil's Breath."

Josie looked at Mettner and Gretchen. Both were taking notes—Gretchen in her trusty notepad and Mett on his phone app.

"We have a fair amount of drug activity here," Josie said. "And Detective Palmer worked in a major city for fifteen years. We haven't heard of Devil's Breath before."

"Because it's taken on a kind of mythological status," Josh explained. "Here in the U.S. it's considered an urban legend. It's mainly found in South America. Colombia, to be exact, although we've had reports of it being used in Europe and Thailand. Comes from the flowers of the borrachero shrub which is found, guess where?"

"Colombia," Josie filled in.

"Right. There's a chemical process used on the seeds, turns them to powder, and leaves you with burundanga, which is extremely similar to scopolamine. There's this myth—you can google it—that offenders are able to put the powder on a business card and hand it to you. Once you touch it, the burundanga absorbs into your skin and you lose your memory and your free will. Wake up a day or two later naked in a strange place with no idea what happened to you. The other legend is that an offender would blow the powder into your face with the same result. Hence the name Devil's Breath. That's the urban legend part. It's much more likely that an offender would slip it into your drink. It's odorless and tasteless so it's easy to slip to people without them knowing it. There is a real problem with it in Colombia and when I say problem, I mean cases of people coming into emergency rooms for burundanga overdoses. Symptoms include rapid heartbeat, dilated pupils, confusion, hallucinations, heart failure, seizures, psychosis, that sort of thing. So while Devil's Breath is, as I said, a bit of an urban legend, it is certainly real and being used with regularity in South America. Down there, they use it sometimes to facilitate sexual assault, but mostly to rob people."

Mettner said, "It's used to rob people?"

"Yeah. Guy goes to a club, gets approached by a beautiful woman. When he's not looking, she slips it into his drink. He wakes up with no memory of anything at all—sometimes no memory of even going to the club—but turns out the woman convinced him to go to the ATM machine and withdraw every cent he's got to give to her. And they'll find video of themselves going to the ATM and taking out the money. They'll track down people who saw them the night before and those people will say, 'Hey, man, you weren't out of it or anything. You said you were going to help this chick out by getting her some cash from the ATM.'"

Gretchen said, "But there are no known cases of Devil's Breath being used here in the U.S., are there?"

"No, not in that capacity that I'm aware of, but here's the thing: it only stays in your system for about four hours. So if someone wakes up twelve hours later, disoriented, with no memory of the night before and they go to the hospital to have blood taken, doctors won't find anything. Also, standard tox panels here would only test for the usual suspects like roofies, ketamine, and GHB. Blood wouldn't be tested for burundanga or even scopolamine unless someone specifically asked for a test and even then, I'm not sure hospitals would be prepared to test for it. That's outside of my purview."

Josie asked, "If you wanted to get Devil's Breath here in the U.S., how would you do it?"

A sigh came over the line. Then Josh said, "Well, the easiest and most direct way would be the dark web. Or you could try making something similar to it using scopolamine. It's also found here in the U.S. in jimsonweed. That stuff is everywhere. I guess if you knew what you were doing, you could make it from one of those two things. It would be hard, and dosing would be an issue as well, but I guess if you're making this stuff with the intention of doing harm to people, you don't much care whether you give them too much or not. That help?"

"Yes," Josie said. "Thank you."

Chitwood thanked Josh and they hung up. He looked at Josie. "Happy?"

"Not particularly," Josie admitted. "This is going to be hard to prove, just like you said. We're only speculating that we're dealing with a drug that could be either some sort of homemade scopolamine concoction or actual Devil's Breath—or some derivative—bought from the dark web. We still need proof of the drug. We know they're very similar which means that they'd both have the same or similar adverse effects, but we need actual evidence."

Mettner said, "We should try to get a warrant to have Clay Walsh's blood samples tested for scopolamine, Devil's Breath, or some derivative of it—if they have anything left from the blood samples they took when he was first brought in. We can have it sent to the same outside lab Denton Memorial is using to test Dan's sample."

Gretchen said, "I can work on that."

Mettner continued, "When I checked Dan's desk today, I bagged a half a doughnut and a quarter cup of his coffee. Hummel took it into evidence and sent it to the state lab for analysis. I can give them a call and ask them to test for burundanga or some derivative. We've also still got the brownie crumbs from the bag in Nysa Somers' backpack. They went out to the lab on Monday. Now that we know what to look for, we can alert the lab and maybe they'll find something."

"Which lab?" Josie asked. "Do you know?"

Mettner looked at his phone, scrolling through his notes. "The one in Greensburg."

"I have a friend there," Josie said. "Someone who owes me a favor. Let me give her a call and tell her what's going on. She might be able to speed up the testing process."

Chitwood was still seated behind his desk. He patted a stray piece of white hair down onto his scalp. "If what happened with Dan today is connected to Somers and Walsh, we have a real problem. We need to move as fast as we can."

Something in the back of Josie's mind shifted, calling attention to itself. "The hospital," she muttered.

"What's that, Quinn?"

"Both Shannon and DEA agent Stumpf said that scopolamine and Devil's Breath overdoses could cause dilated pupils, rapid heartbeat, psychosis, hallucinations, and seizures."

"Right," Gretchen said, flipping the pages of her notebook.

Josie continued, "The day of Nysa Somers' death, I called Dr. Feist to see if she'd had a chance to do the autopsy, and she said the Denton Memorial ER had been inundated with seizure cases and heart attacks."

Chitwood stood up. "I'll go over there and talk to the administrator myself. This is going to be a nightmare in terms of privacy of health information. I'll talk to him, and then one of you can draw up the warrants and see if we can get our hands on some of the names of these patients Dr. Feist told you about. I believe Mett and Palmer here are on for the rest of the evening. Quinn, you go home."

"Sir—" Josie said.

He raised his voice to a shout. "Dammit, Quinn. Did you or did you not pull a grown woman out of a pool on Monday and try to resuscitate her?"

"I—yeah."

"Did you or did you not rescue a five-year-old girl from a burning building yesterday, sacrificing your own damn car to do it?"

"I—I did, sir," Josie stammered.

His voice boomed across the room. "Did you or did you not almost fall to your death getting Lamay out of that tower today— that's right, Fraley told me what happened—well?"

"Sir, I—"

"Go the hell home, Quinn! Find Fraley, wherever the hell he is, and take him with you. And do not stop to save any drowning kids, lost puppies, or adults in distress, do you understand me? Call 911 like every other reasonable person, and wait for help. Now go eat and get some damn sleep!"

Josie stood up and wiped sweaty palms on her jeans. She turned toward the door but Chitwood said, "Wait."

"Yes?" she said, looking back at him.

"Just don't eat or drink anything you didn't prepare yourself, you got that? Just, you know, for the time being."

Josie smiled and left the room.

# CHAPTER THIRTY-ONE

Josie texted Noah but he said he was busy on an interview and that he'd meet her at home. Before she pulled out of the municipal parking lot, she called Misty to tell her to avoid any foods that she didn't prepare herself until further notice. Misty gave a long, heavy sigh. "Let me guess, you can't tell me why you're making this bizarre request, can you?"

"I'm sorry, I can't," Josie said.

There was a long silence, then another sigh. Misty said, "I'm too tired to argue with you about this. What about Harris?"

"I thought you packed his lunch," said Josie.

"I do, but sometimes they give out snacks there. I'm asking if you if my son is safe at school, Josie."

"Yes," Josie said. "This is probably just me being overly cautious. I mean, I know it is. Just—indulge me, would you?"

"Fine," Misty said and hung up before Josie could say more.

Josie fired up her rental car and drove home. It wasn't until she pulled into her driveway that she remembered that she had invited Patrick to dinner and had not planned for it at all. "Shit," she muttered to herself as she unlocked her front door. In the foyer, Trout raced toward her, throwing his fat little body at her, anxious for pets and belly rubs. As she knelt to give him attention and assure him that he was the very best dog in the world, she noticed the television in the living room was on. She heard the hum of her washer from the laundry room.

"Pat?" she called.

He poked his head out of the kitchen. "Hey, hope you don't mind. I used my key."

"Of course not," Josie said. "You're doing more washing?"

"Yeah, sorry," he said sheepishly. "But I promise not to leave anything behind this time."

Trout followed Josie into the kitchen, his nails clicking on the tile. Patrick stood at the kitchen table, peeling three paper plates from a larger stack of them and placing them where he, Josie, and Noah usually sat. The smell of pizza filled the air. Josie's stomach growled loudly. She looked over to the countertop to see two large pizza boxes.

"I'm so sorry, Pat," she told her brother.

"I know," he said, cutting her off. "Work. I figured that when I got here and neither of you were home. I was going to head back to campus, but I brought my wash, so…"

Josie went over to the counter and opened one of the boxes. Cheesy deliciousness stared back at her. All slices were accounted for. She lifted the lid of the other box which was also untouched.

"I used your emergency twenty," Patrick said. "For the pizza. But I also took Trout for a w-a-l-k."

"It's fine. Thank you. Where did you get this pizza?"

"Girton's."

"Did you pick it up or have it delivered?"

He raised a brow at her. "What's going on?"

"Pick up or delivery, Pat?"

"Delivery."

Josie looked back at the pizza. She was so hungry. With a sigh, she picked up one box of pizza and took it to the trash bin, emptying the slices into it.

"What the hell are you doing?" Patrick exclaimed.

She got the other box and threw those slices away as well. Then she turned on the oven. "I've got pizza in the freezer. It will take twenty minutes to heat it up," she told him.

He stood at her table with a pile of paper plates in his hand, looking mystified. "That was perfectly good pizza. What's going on with you? Do I need to call Noah? Or 911?"

Josie took the stack of plates from his hands and put them away. She found two pizzas in the freezer and peeled their packaging off, preparing them for the oven. "I know it seems like I'm acting crazy," she told her brother. "But trust me. I've got my reasons."

Patrick sighed. "Are you going to tell me those reasons?"

Josie slid the frozen pizza into the oven and set the timer. "I'll tell you as much as I can, but it stays between us, okay?"

"Sure."

The two of them sat at the table, and Josie told him as much about the theory that Denton PD was working under as she could without giving away any details that could later get her in trouble. He already knew something was up with Nysa Somers' death. Not only had he been there, but he'd been subject to rumors about her death since then, he said.

"What kinds of rumors?" Josie asked.

"Oh, I've heard it all, but basically no one believes she drowned, so people are saying her body was badly beaten when it was pulled from the water or that her skull was crushed in. I even heard one rumor that she wasn't found in the pool at all—that she was brutally murdered—but the powers that be at the university don't want bad press, so they're just saying she drowned. I didn't know whether to say anything or not. I saw her, but it seemed wrong to talk about it."

Josie fought the urge to roll her eyes. Rumors and death were never a good combination. "I think keeping quiet for now is best," Josie said. "Regardless of what you say to set the record straight, rumors will still spread. None of them are about drugs though, huh?"

Trout walked up beside her chair and nudged her hand. She scratched between his ears.

"No," Patrick said. "I guess that's weird, considering you found that sticker. Can you show it to me?"

"I don't see why not," Josie answered. "I know Chief Hahlbeck showed it around campus."

She pulled up the photo on her phone. He studied it a long moment, pursing his lips. Josie said, "You've seen it before?"

"I don't know. I don't think so, and yet, something about it is familiar. It's pretty gruesome though, isn't it?"

"Yeah," Josie said. "Listen, Pat, if you've been using drugs, it's okay to tell me—"

He held up a hand to silence her. "Please, don't. You don't have to worry about me. Believe me, even if I was doing drugs and knew something about that—" he motioned toward her phone just as the screen went blank and the sticker disappeared. "I would say something, especially since people are dying—well, almost dying. Is that firefighter still alive?"

"As of this morning, yes," Josie said.

"So what are we talking about here? A date rape drug? If I knew anything about those, I'd report it."

"I'm glad," Josie replied. "But not date rape drugs. Something like those drugs in the sense that after taking them, people wouldn't remember anything that happened. What we're looking for is to see if anyone here in Denton has been using a drug or giving a drug to other people that—I'll spare you the scientific version—makes them compliant, docile, and extremely suggestible."

The oven timer went off. Patrick stood and grabbed an oven mitt, pulling the pizza out and leaving it on the counter to cool. He tossed the mitt back into a drawer and returned to his seat. "What do you mean?"

"I mean a drug that puts a person into a state where you can tell them to do anything, and they'd do it. Anything at all, from something as simple as telling them which direction they should walk to telling them to harm someone, maybe even themselves."

He frowned and pushed a shock of dark hair off his forehead. "But not necessarily hurting someone?"

"No," Josie said. "Not necessarily. The drug we're looking into basically wipes away a person's free will. Also, I'm told they wouldn't remember anything afterward. Used with ill intent, as I'm sure you can imagine, it could be extremely dangerous."

He nodded as she spoke. "There were these videos circulating last year on campus. Right after school started."

"Circulating how?" Josie asked. "Via social media?"

Patrick shook his head. "Text message. Only people on campus. No one knew where they originally came from or who took them. Even the people who were in them didn't know, mostly because they didn't remember having done the stuff they did in the videos. There was like this unspoken thing where you didn't post them anywhere, but people on campus were sending them to each other."

"What kinds of videos, Patrick?"

"The first few were just really dumb stuff. Like one of them was of this guy—he was a senior last year—walking through the middle of campus, late at night. Whoever was taping him was following him—it was a dude's voice. He would tell him what to do, and the guy would do it. He said things like 'act like a chicken' and the dude would start clucking and waving his elbows. He told him to lay down in the middle of the street and so the guy did. Stupid shit like that. Do handstands—which the guy clearly couldn't do. Then you heard the person taping say something like, 'The police are coming, run!' and the video ended."

"Did the student who was being taped seem disoriented? Was he stumbling? Slurring his words? Anything like that?"

"No. He seemed totally normal. Actually, when the video first started going around to people's phones, they were like, this is all fake. I guess it was supposed to be, like, 'look what I made this dumb drunk guy do,' and everyone who watched it was like, 'that guy's not drunk!'"

Josie said, "What about the other videos? How many were there?"

"Four." Patrick stood and grabbed his and Josie's plates, going to the counter to get them both two slices of pizza. Beside Josie, Trout gave a low whine, and she told him to go lay down, which he did, finding his bed in the corner of the kitchen and giving a heavy sigh as he plopped down on it. Patrick set the pizza down in front of her but neither of them ate. He said, "I only remember four. There was one of a girl sneaking onto the roof of one of the athletic buildings in the middle of the night and doing some cheers—I think she was a cheerleader for the football team—and the guy taping had her strip down to her bra and underwear and do a cheer he made up about how sports suck. It was kind of funny. Except then she almost fell off the roof, and the camera dropped and went out. I think she got in trouble with the cheerleading squad, but she said she must have gotten drunk and done it because she didn't remember. They put her on probation, or something like that."

"But didn't kick her off the squad?" Josie asked.

"I don't think so, but everything I'm telling you, I heard second and third hand. Rumors. I don't know if any of what I heard is even accurate."

"I understand," Josie said. "What about the last two videos?"

Patrick leaned his elbows on the table and swiped his hands over his face. "I'm trying to remember now. I don't remember the third video that well, other than that some guy was stumbling around a little bit. It was, like, him going around licking stuff."

"Licking stuff?" Josie said. "Like what?"

"Like anything. The pavement, telephone poles, door knobs. Anything that would make you cringe. But that guy really looked drunk. That one was probably the one the students on campus found the funniest. I mean, it wasn't funny in the sense that it's never funny to make a drunk person do stuff they wouldn't normally do, but that one got forwarded more than any other one. I think it did. It seemed like more people saw that one. I'm saying that anecdotally, by the way. It's not like I've got data."

Josie laughed a little. "You sound like Mom. How about the last one? Do you remember it at all?"

Patrick grimaced. "Yeah, that one wasn't funny at all. It was kind of sad. It was actually a freshman girl. I didn't know her but people in my dorm did. I think Brenna might have known her. We weren't dating then but after we met, the subject of the videos came up at a party once, and Brenna got really upset and said that the last video wasn't funny because it almost ruined that girl's life."

The pizza, which had smelled so delicious earlier, now seemed completely unappetizing. Josie picked at the crust. "Tell me about that video."

"The girl was walking down the street. It was dark. The guy taping was following her. She had on a dress and heels, like maybe she was out at a party or something. It was really creepy though, 'cause you couldn't tell if she knew the guy was following her or not."

"Could you tell where they were?" Josie asked.

"I don't remember. It didn't look like campus. I just assumed it was somewhere in Denton, though. Anyway, she gets a little way down the street, near this streetlight, and he tells her to stop walking and just like that, she does. She doesn't even turn around, she just stops. Then he has her do all this dumb shit, like five squats, and jump on one foot, and it was like she was a robot."

"Did she seem intoxicated?"

"No. Well, at one point you could see her eyes up real close and her pupils were huge. So she must have been on something, but she wasn't stumbling around or anything. The video goes on, with him telling her to do progressively dumber shit, like look up her own ass—which made him crack the hell up. He couldn't even keep the camera steady."

"This was all in public?"

"Yeah," Patrick said. "You could hear people in the background who must have walked by either laughing or asking the girl if everything was okay, and she'd always answer yes. The guy taping would say they were drunk and just messing around."

"But he took it too far, didn't he?" Josie said.

"Yeah," Patrick sighed. "He did. He told her to take off her clothes. All of them. She did it, too. No hesitation at all. Then he made her do more stupid shit. It was really painful to watch at that point. For his finale, he made her get up onto the hood of someone's car and urinate."

"Good lord," Josie said. "Did the videos come to your phone?"

He nodded.

"Who sent them?"

"One of my friends got them from someone in one of his classes who had gotten them on a group text, and then my friend blasted it out on another group text which included my number. No one really knew where they were coming from, but they still shared them."

"Do you have any of them still?"

"No," Patrick said. "I didn't keep them. I wasn't even that interested in them except everyone was talking about them. The last one really made me sad. It was hard to watch, and it felt… wrong, you know? To watch it? Like, it wasn't funny. It was disturbing."

Josie gave him a pained smile. "I know," she said. "You're a good kid, Pat. Do you know whether any of them were ever posted anywhere online?"

"I don't think so, but it's not like I looked or anything."

"Do you know or remember any of the names of the students in the videos?"

"No. I'm sorry."

"No idea who took the videos?"

He shook his head.

"There were only four?"

"That I know of, yeah, but I think that really was the last one. Most people who saw it were pretty upset by it. I reported it to the campus police."

"What did they say?" Josie asked.

"That they'd 'look into it' but that they didn't even know whether the girl in the video was a student or not and that unless she made a complaint herself, there wasn't much they could do."

It sounded exactly like something that Hillary Hahlbeck's predecessor would have said. The man had been incompetent and lazy and a constant source of frustration for Denton PD, who often ended up investigating the crimes that he dismissed, and then when Josie's team asked for campus police assistance, he would block them at every turn. Hahlbeck had been a welcome change.

"Do you think anyone you know might still have one or more of the videos that I could see?"

"I doubt it, but I can ask around."

"You said you thought Brenna might know the girl in the last video? Do you think you could talk to her for me? Try to get a name?"

"I can try," Patrick said. "But she's really weird about it. Protective. I got the sense that the girl in the video's been through so much that Brenna doesn't want to add to it."

"Understandable," Josie said. "And I'll definitely talk to the new campus police chief to see if she can find out for me without the need to go through Brenna. But Pat, we're working some cases right now where a lot of people could be in serious danger. If the person who made those videos was slipping that drug I told you about to those people to get them to do whatever he said and we were able to locate him, it could crack the case. I wouldn't ask if it wasn't extremely important. We're not exactly neck-deep in leads. Any small piece of information could help."

"Yeah," Patrick said. "I get it. I'll talk to her tomorrow. Hey, where's Noah?"

Josie checked her phone. He should have been home hours ago. "I don't know," she said. "I'll text him."

She fired off a message. His answer came back less than a minute later. *Still chasing leads. Don't wait up.*

Josie tried not to wait up, but her brain wouldn't shut down. Patrick left once his wash was finished, and his absence only made things worse for her. Her mind wouldn't let go of the case. The thought that someone was deliberately giving a drug to people that made them so pliant chilled her blood. She kept imagining Noah wandering around, drugged, at the mercy of someone who was so cold and cruel they'd tell a swimmer to drown herself and a firefighter to set his house on fire.

Time to be a mermaid.

Time to be a match.

Lamay was the outlier but still, it was awfully coincidental that he'd had such a strange episode so close in time to what happened to Nysa Somers and Clay Walsh. What if the person responsible for the drug was now targeting random people and giving them no instructions at all? Alone in bed, the events of the last few days went through her mind again and again on a loop. She got up and turned on both nightstand lamps as well as the overhead light. Trout whined and tried to burrow his head beneath one of the covers. Josie took her phone off the charger and checked it for notifications, even though she would have heard it chirp had there been any. As she expected, there was nothing.

At eleven thirty, she punched in a text message to Noah. *Please come home. I need you.*

She stared at the words for a long moment. Naked on the screen. She bit her lower lip, erased the words 'I need you' and pressed *send.* His response came back a few seconds later: *On my way.* Her relief was so profound that a gasp escaped her lips. She ran down the steps and stood before the front door. Disgusted, Trout stayed in bed. The sound of Noah's vehicle in the driveway made her heart skip. He unlocked the door and stepped through it. Josie was relieved to see his easy smile and that his pupils were normal size.

"Hey," he said. "I'm really sorry. I got caught—"

Josie threw her arms around his neck. "I don't care," she said, and pulled him down to her in a hungry kiss.

# CHAPTER THIRTY-TWO

Josie and Noah's first stop the next morning was Denton Memorial Hospital to visit Sergeant Dan Lamay. He was alert and sitting up in bed with the television remote in his hand. When Josie and Noah entered, he tossed it aside and beckoned them closer. They both hugged him, and Josie was stunned by the stress that immediately lifted from her shoulders knowing he was okay.

"How do you feel?" Josie asked, as she and Noah took up position on either side of Dan's bed.

"I feel great. Just really 'freaked out,' as my daughter would say. I woke up here this morning. Had no idea what the hell was going on."

"You don't remember coming here yesterday?" Noah asked.

Dan shook his head. "Not at all, and before you ask, the Chief was here about an hour ago and he told me the whole story, and no, I don't remember the bell tower or any of that either."

"What do you remember?" Josie asked.

"I remember kissing my wife goodbye yesterday morning and walking out my front door and the next thing I know, I'm in this bed. 'Bout gave myself a heart attack when I woke up here. But they said all my tests are negative. I've got a clean bill of health, and I can leave later today."

"That's great," Josie said.

Noah asked, "Did the Chief mention anything to you about how we think you ended up here?"

"Yeah, he said Josie thinks we might have someone peddling some kind of drug in the city somewhere. Maybe lacing people's food with stuff. Like a poisoner, I guess. So I won't eat or drink anything my wife doesn't make me until you guys get this straightened out. I sure don't like losing time like that."

"You don't remember stopping at the mini-market, or anything you ate yesterday morning?" Noah asked.

"No, but it was probably the same thing I have every morning. Yogurt and granola at home and then coffee and a pastry from the mini-market on my way to work." He laughed. "I was kind of hoping the wife wouldn't find out about my mini-market habit."

A knock on the door interrupted them. One of the nurses shooed Josie and Noah out so she could check Dan's vital signs. Certain he was in good hands, they left the hospital and checked in at the station. Gretchen and Mettner weren't due in until later in the afternoon, but the Chief was waiting with a list of updates. He stood in front of their desks, reading off a stack of pages clutched in his hand. Amber, who had been sitting at her desk, focused on her laptop, looked up as he talked.

"I talked to the hospital administrator last night. He wasn't happy, but after he reviewed the ER records from Monday, he agreed that it was an unusual number of similar cases in a short amount of time. Before she left for the night, Palmer wrote up a warrant for the names of the seizure and heart attack patients who came in to the ER the day that Nysa Somers died. That's been served. The hospital's attorneys and compliance officers are looking it over. I'll get Palmer to follow up on that later today when she gets here.

"Neither Mettner nor Gretchen found any connections among Nysa Somers, Clay Walsh, and Coach Brett Pace or between any of those three and Dan Lamay—other than the obvious connection between Somers and Pace. Fraley." He raised his eyes to look at Noah. "You were out all day on interviews and here late, as I understand it, writing up reports. You didn't find anything either, did you?"

"No, sir," Noah answered.

"Right," Chitwood said with a sigh, shuffling the pages in his hands. "The only good news I've got is that Clay Walsh is hanging on. He is in stable condition at the hospital in Philadelphia. I also talked with the Fire Chief this morning. The Walsh fire was set intentionally, and they want to know who the hell burned down the home of one of their most decorated firefighters."

He looked over the rim of his glasses at Josie and Noah. Neither of them spoke. The Chief took a step closer to their desks. "So I told him it was Walsh, and he told me I was full of shit and threw me out of his office before I could float our drug idea. Watts!" He looked over at Amber. "I know you're eavesdropping 'cause that's all you damn do around here. None of this gets out to the press, you got that?"

She nodded.

Chitwood said, "What've you two got?"

Josie recounted her conversation with Patrick for the Chief. When she finished, he said, "Well, don't sit here staring at me. Get the hell up to campus and see what else you can find out! Go, go, go."

At the campus police station, Josie and Noah found Chief Hahlbeck in her office. Josie explained what Patrick had told her about the videos circulating on campus the year before.

Hillary frowned as she clicked away on her computer. "As you know, that was before my time," she said. "But if any report was made, it should be here in the system."

It took several minutes before she hit on anything. "This is a complaint made by Patrick Payne about a lewd video taken of a potential student."

She clicked a few more times and printed the report for them. There wasn't much to it. There was a copy of a handwritten statement by Patrick where he described the video and how he had received it, as well as the previous three videos. The second document was a typed report from the prior Chief stating that Patrick's report was "unfounded," and that no other complaints had been made about it— including from the subject of the video. The report went on to say that, after viewing the video, he was of the opinion that it was impossible to verify if the woman in the video was even a student, noting that the video was clearly not taken on campus.

"This is all?" Josie said. "There aren't any other reports or complaints about any of the videos?"

Hillary shook her head. "I'll run the searches again, but no, I don't see anything else. That's it."

Noah said, "Do you have a copy of the video?"

Hillary clicked a few more times, her frown deepening with each one. "It doesn't appear that my predecessor made a copy of the video. Or if he did, he didn't save it into our system. I'm really sorry."

"What about the cheerleader?" Josie asked. "Pat said that the girl in the second video was a cheerleader and that she got in trouble with the squad after the video circulated."

"Well, that wouldn't be within our purview. For that, you'd have to contact the cheerleading coach. I can tell you where to find her, if you'd like?"

"Yes, please," Josie answered just as her cell phone chirped. She took it out of her pocket and punched in her passcode to find a text from Patrick.

*No one I talked to still has copies of any of the videos. Sorry.*

Disappointed, Josie typed back: *Thanks for trying. What about the name of the girl in the last video? Did Brenna tell you?*

His reply came back within seconds. *Her name is Robyn Arber. She goes to Bloom U now. Brenna said she'll talk to you but only you. Robyn starts her shift as a waitress at Rose Marie's at noon.*

"Shit," Josie said. She turned the phone to Noah so he could read the text. If she wanted to be in Bloomsburg by noon, she'd need to leave immediately.

"I'll take the cheerleading coach," Noah said. "You track down Arber."

"Okay, great. Chief Hahlbeck, could you just look up a name for me in your system? Robyn Arber?"

"Sure thing," Hillary said, tapping at her keyboard. After a solid minute of searching, she found nothing.

"It's okay," Josie said. "I didn't think she'd be in your system."

# CHAPTER THIRTY-THREE

Josie arrived in Bloomsburg just before noon. It was a quaint town, like Denton on a smaller scale, with beautiful historic brick buildings lining its well-tended Main Street, which led from the Bloomsburg Fairgrounds right up to the university's Carver Hall, the college's iconic red-brick edifice with white pillars holding up a portico and above that a domed clock tower. A few blocks from Carver Hall, Josie found Rose Marie's tucked away in a parking lot behind the buildings that faced Main Street. A single door stood beside a hedgerow. Beside it was a black dry-erase board listing the day's specials. After feeding the parking meter in the lot, Josie went inside, telling the hostess she needed only a table for one. The restaurant was nearly empty, with just one guy seated at the bar and one table on the right-hand side of the large open floor plan occupied by a couple in their twenties. The hostess seated Josie near them. "I was hoping to talk with Robyn," Josie told her.

"Robyn's the only waitress on right now," the hostess said. "She'll be right with you."

Josie opened her menu but didn't peruse it. A few minutes later, a young woman appeared at the other occupied table. Her blonde hair was pulled into a tight bun, and she was dressed all in black, her jeans and T-shirt clinging to her curvy form. A large name tag over her right breast proclaimed that she was, indeed, Robyn. She smiled warmly as she took the couple's order, but that smile slipped from her face when she approached Josie's table.

"I'm Detective Quinn," Josie told her.

"I know who you are," Robyn said. "I've seen you on TV before."

She folded her arms under her breasts and waited for Josie to speak.

"I need to talk to you about the video that was taken of you last year in Denton while you were a student at the university."

"I know why you're here," Robyn said. "I shouldn't even be talking to you. What is it that you want to know?"

"I was hoping you could tell me what happened," Josie explained.

"What happened? I don't remember any of it. I was at a party with friends and the next thing I know, I'm naked in my bed and there's some horrible video of me on every phone on campus. It was humiliating. I knew I had to have been drugged. I know I had a couple of drinks at my friend's house, but not that much. Even if I had been drunk, I would have been throwing up or stumbling or passed out. Not… doing all that horrible stuff in the middle of town."

"Did you report it?"

"Not at first. I was so embarrassed. I didn't know what to do. I kind of hoped that if I ignored it, it would just blow over. I mean, if you had seen it…" She shuddered. "But then one of my professors apparently saw it." Her face reddened at the memory. "At first, he was, like, scolding me for it. I broke down in his office and told him that I didn't remember it at all. That's when he said I had to report it. I was in the Secondary Education program. He was my advisor. He said I wouldn't want something like that out there because it could ruin any chances I ever had at getting a job. That put me into a panic."

"Did you go to the police?"

Robyn scoffed. "The campus police? Are you serious? No. Listen, I had friends who got roofied, all right? They went to the campus police and those douchebags did nothing. They were all like, 'well, if you can't remember anything, who are we supposed to arrest?' Like it was the victims' job to investigate. No way was I going to the campus police with this unless I had some proof of who did it.

Even then, I wasn't going to bother with them. I was going right to the real police."

Josie said, "You filed a complaint with Denton PD?"

"No. I never got that far. Once I figured out who did it, I couldn't—he begged me not to involve the police. I accused him of date-raping me, but he swore he never touched me. He said he didn't even give me a date rape drug, just something he learned how to make from the dark web or something like that. I asked him if he was the one who took the other videos. He admitted it. He said he was just having fun. It was an experiment. He thought it would be funny, and he never planned to hurt anyone."

"What was his name?" Josie asked.

"You really need to know his name?"

"Yes," Josie said. "I really do. This is important, Robyn, or I wouldn't be here."

Robyn leaned in toward Josie and whispered, "You have to understand, he's the Dean's son, okay?"

"The Dean of Students?" Josie asked. No wonder there was no campus police report, no follow-up to Patrick's complaint.

"Yes, and believe me, the Dean wanted this to go away. Badly. I'm not even, like, supposed to talk about this ever, with anyone."

Josie raised a brow. "Did you sign a non-disclosure agreement?"

"No."

"Then you can tell me his name now, or I can look it up when I get home."

"It was harmless. Everyone agreed," Robyn tried.

Josie found it hard to believe that any reasonable person could think that the video was somehow harmless. She also found it deeply disturbing that any person would think drugging someone without their knowledge or consent under any circumstances was just fine.

"Even you?" Josie asked. "Did you agree?"

Robyn's mouth snapped shut.

Josie waited a long moment, but the girl didn't speak. She was one of the few witnesses Josie had ever interviewed who was able to withstand the uncomfortable silence. Josie said, "What if I told you that there is a possibility that this kid you're talking about didn't stop? That maybe he stopped taking videos, but he didn't stop doing what he did to you to other people and that now a girl is dead?"

Robyn's fingers fidgeted with her name tag. "No. That's not possible. He wouldn't. He promised. That was part of the deal."

"The deal?"

Robyn's name tag fell from her shirt. She quickly grabbed it up, holding it in both hands. "When I found out it was him, and we talked, I told him that I couldn't just let it go—especially since the video was already out there on campus and my advisor knew about it. We came to an agreement which included me not going to the police. My parents were completely on board with that. My dad thought that if we pursued it criminally, it would become a matter of public record, which would mean that even more people would see the video, and the main thing I wanted was for the video to go away."

"His name, Robyn," Josie prompted.

Robyn's eyes shifted to the front of the dining area, but neither the hostess nor the bartender were paying her any mind. The couple nearby were engrossed in a private conversation. One of her index fingers pressed into the point of the pin on her name tag, drawing a tiny bead of blood. "Doug," she said. "Doug Merlos. His dad was the one who arranged our agreement. He brought my parents in, even though by that point they wanted me to transfer to another school, get a fresh start, which was fine with me. Thank God no one ever posted the video anywhere—that I've seen—but you can't unring a bell. Plenty of people saw it at Denton U. So I came here this year. I actually love it here, so I'm glad I made the change."

"What was the agreement, Robyn?" Josie asked.

"Doug got expelled. He was no longer able to set foot on campus, had to stay away from me and most importantly, he had to destroy any copies he had of the video."

"That's it?" Josie blurted out. "Robyn, what he did to you was a crime. He should be in prison. He should also be on the sex offender list."

Robyn sighed. "But, like, I was underage drinking that night."

"So?" Josie said. It was hard not to jump out of her seat and shake the girl. "Regardless of that, what he did was wrong. You understand that it's wrong to give someone a drug, especially an illicit drug, without their knowledge or consent, right? It's also dangerous. What if you had some kind of underlying medical condition? He could have killed you."

Robyn threw her hands up. "Whoa, lady. I don't need this, okay? What's done is done. I agreed to talk to you because Brenna's a friend of mine, and she said you were a good person. I would never have agreed if I knew you were going to be all judgy."

Josie took a deep breath and tried to slow her racing heart. The couple nearby shot her and Robyn dirty looks. She lowered her voice when she spoke next. "Robyn, I'm very sorry. I'm not judging you. I didn't mean to sound that way. Also, the statute of limitations has not expired. You could still press charges."

Robyn started to walk away. Quickly, Josie caught her wrist. "Please. Robyn. I'm sorry. I'm truly sorry. I'll stop. Just—can I just ask a couple more questions?"

It killed her to clamp her mouth shut. Everything she wanted to say blasted through her mind. Who were the adults in Robyn's life who had allowed things to be handled this way? Her parents, the Dean, her advisor? What had they been thinking? How could they have let Doug Merlos get away with something so violating? Josie shuddered to think that he might have gone from making disturbing videos to actually killing people. If he had been properly dealt with at the outset, would Nysa Somers still be alive? Would Clay Walsh still be in good health?

Robyn stared at her and then twisted her wrist from Josie's grasp. "What?"

"Did you know Doug before he made the video?"

"I had a class with him. We traveled loosely in the same social circles, so yeah, I knew him."

"How did you figure he was the one who took the video?" Josie asked.

"My plan was to talk to everyone I could find who had been at the party. I started by talking to people I knew—including people I knew but didn't know well, like Doug. Before I even had a chance to talk with him, someone else I spoke with mentioned that she had seen Doug following me down the street after I left the party. Then I confronted him, and he came clean right away."

"That's good investigative work," Josie noted, internally flinching at how difficult it must have been for Robyn to track down the person who had violated her by herself. "Do you know if he knew the people in the other videos as well?"

"He said he knew of them, whatever that means. I think he just picked people at random. Like I said, he swore it wasn't malicious."

Josie took out her phone, swiping and tapping until she found the picture of the sticker. She showed it to Robyn. "Does this look familiar to you?"

Robyn's skin turned to ash. Josie tried not to show her excitement. Clearly, the girl recognized the sticker. Robyn drew herself up straight, carefully pinned her name tag back onto her shirt, and pulled her phone from her jeans' back pocket. Josie waited for her to speak, not sure if she was about to walk away without another word or if she just needed more time before she answered the question. But then she placed her phone on the table in front of Josie. On the screen, a video had been queued up. The still showed a street that Josie recognized from Denton. Several feet ahead of the camera was the back of a woman in a short red skirt and halter top. Not just any woman. Robyn Arber.

"That video is three minutes and thirty-seven seconds long," Robyn said, her voice carefully modulated to reveal no emotion whatsoever. "What you're looking for appears at one minute and sixteen seconds."

"You know the exact second?" Josie said.

The life in Robyn's eyes shuttered away. "I know every second in that video. Every horrifying second."

Josie felt a weight on her shoulders. You didn't get to know every second of a near four-minute video unless you watched it a lot. Maybe even every day. Quietly, Josie said, "I may need this video for evidence in our current case, Robyn. I would need your permission to make a copy of it."

"Whatever," said Robyn. "I really need to get to work, so if you're going to order, be ready when I come back."

She walked away, back to the other couple, plastering on a smile. Josie looked down at her phone and with a stomach full of cement, pressed *play*. The video was exactly as Patrick had described. When Doug Merlos instructed Robyn to look up her own ass, she calmly contorted every which way, trying to do so. Doug's laughter was uproarious. He lost control of the phone. It wavered and tumbled, showing nothing but blackness rotating with the glare of a streetlight. Then it stopped, a finger covering the lens. He must have caught it before it dropped to the ground. The finger came away, showing blackness. As the phone moved away from the black, it revealed itself to be a canvas messenger bag. In the corner of it was a white circle. Josie set the video back and let it play twice more before she captured the second in which the white spot came into view. When it did, it was clear she was looking at the cracked skull sticker.

Josie didn't watch the rest of the video. It felt wrong to do it in the same room where Robyn Arber was working, putting on a fake smile and serving people wine and food. Instead, she sent it to her own phone and from there, sent it to the rest of the team, along with Doug Merlos' name. By the time she got back to Denton, they'd have a location on him, and Josie was going to be the first one of them to knock on his door.

She pulled two twenties from her jacket pocket and put them on the table. Then she placed Robyn's phone face down over the top of them. She panned the restaurant but didn't see Robyn anywhere. On her way out she told the hostess, "Please tell Robyn thank you."

# CHAPTER THIRTY-FOUR

There was still no word on the goodies I had distributed randomly. It didn't make sense. Why weren't more people dying? At the very least, more people should be acting strangely enough for the police or the news to pick up on it. What had I done wrong? Or maybe it wasn't my fault at all. Maybe the product just hadn't been distributed as I had hoped. That was the problem with being invisible. Everything was easier and went more smoothly when I had direct contact with the victim, like the first time I used the drug. I remembered sitting in my car, hands shaking with excitement. They trembled so badly, I almost spilled the powder. Once I got it into the paper coffee cup, I used a stirrer to dissolve it completely. No chunks. No residue. Best of all, no odor. I capped the cup and looked around, relieved none of the drug had gotten on the console or the seats. It was potent and extremely dangerous, which was what made it so much fun. My feet tapped against the floor mat while I waited for him to emerge from the building. For a few minutes I worried that the coffee would get cold before he came out, but then he was there, striding through the double doors, clipboard under his arm like always.

I got out, jogged over to him, made the necessary small talk. Given how badly things had gone the last time we'd seen one another, he was happy to accept my gift of hot, fresh coffee. I wanted to throw it in his face. It was clear he saw it as a peace offering, when in fact he should have been the one extending an olive branch or an apology. He had made fun of the way I did things, going on and on, insulting me and then laughing about it. Who laughed at his own jokes? I had told him to shut his damn mouth, and it had only made him laugh harder.

I never forgot it. In fact, he was the first person on my list once I realized just what the drug could do. It didn't disappoint. It didn't even take long for it to kick in. I'd had to do a lot of research to figure out the exact moment when a person was completely in the thrall of it. When I knew he was there, I leaned closer and whispered instructions into his ear. Then I made sure that he had his keys in his hand, walked him to his car, and waited for him to start it up.

I leaned in through the window. "Remember," I told him. "Go as fast as you can. Don't stop until you make a dent."

# CHAPTER THIRTY-FIVE

On the interstate on the way back to Denton, Josie had to consciously and repeatedly remind herself to stay within the speed limit. Anger coursed through her body. She hadn't even watched the worst of the Robyn Arber video, but she felt sick to her stomach. Breathing through her rage, she tried to work through things more clinically in her mind. Doug Merlos had told Robyn he'd 'learned to make' the drug he gave her from the dark web. It stood to reason that he had also created the creepy sticker. He'd had it on his messenger bag when he took the video of Robyn. The videos had stopped after a deal was struck between the Dean and the Arber family. A deal that included Doug being banned from campus. Josie assumed that also meant Hollister Way, since it was managed by campus housing. Although the only person who really knew that Doug had been banned from campus was his father. Robyn had left the university. It stood to reason that Doug could go anywhere on campus at any time, more or less, and no one would sound an alarm. On the other hand, maybe Doug had sold his branded drug to someone else. Maybe Brett Pace. Although, given the content of the videos that Doug had made, it seemed more likely that he was behind the Somers drowning and the Walsh fire.

Josie pressed the voice control button on the steering wheel and through gritted teeth said, "Call Noah."

"I'm sorry," the vehicle's robotic voice replied. "I do not recognize that command. Please try again."

"Shit." Her cell phone wasn't synced to the rental vehicle. She put on her turn signal and pulled over onto the shoulder of the highway, using her cell phone to call him. After eight rings, it went to voicemail. Without leaving a message, she hung up and called Gretchen.

After two rings, Gretchen answered. "Boss? I've already got Doug Merlos' current address. I'm just running some background on him now. No criminal record that I could find."

"Great," Josie said. "You have a photo?"

"I've got a driver's license photo, yeah. His license was suspended over the summer for his second underage drinking/DUI charge, but I've got a photo."

"I'm wondering if you can check the surveillance we have from Sunday night and Monday morning on campus and see if you can find him on any of it."

"I can certainly look," said Gretchen. "The Chief brought me and Mett up to speed on the leads your brother gave us when we got here today, and Noah told us he checked in to the cheerleader from one of the videos, but neither she nor her friends or the cheer coach knew who took the video. Noah also told us about Robyn Arber. What else did she tell you?"

Josie recounted her conversation with Robyn Arber.

"What a sack of shit," Gretchen said. "Two sacks of shit. Him and his dad. Where are you now?"

Josie read off the upcoming exit sign. "Give me Merlos' address, would you?"

She heard the pages of Gretchen's notebook turning. Then she rattled off the address to Josie.

"I'm bringing him in," Josie said.

"Or," Gretchen said evenly, "I bring him in and let him sit in an interview room for an hour and sweat. Then when you get here, he'll be good and freaked out about why he's there."

Josie liked this idea even though they technically could not detain Doug Merlos. They couldn't force him to come into the station or even to talk with them. Even if he agreed to go with

Gretchen, he could actually leave at any time. Of course, oddly enough, they rarely ran into a situation where people refused to come to the station or, once there, demanded to leave. They had no idea if Doug Merlos was one of those people.

Gretchen's voice interrupted her thoughts. "Boss? You still there?"

"Yes," Josie answered. "Fine. Bring him in. I'll meet you at the station. Also, see if you can get some alibis for him for Nysa Somers' death and the fire at Clay Walsh's house. If he's got them, we'll need to check them out."

For the rest of the ride, she went back over every detail of the case in her mind. The name Doug Merlos had never come up. Not once. That didn't necessarily mean anything, especially if he was picking his victims at random as Robyn had suggested. As she drove into Denton, a beep from her console alerted her that she was low on gas. She pulled into the nearest gas station to fill up. It was only once she was pumping the gas into her tank that she realized she was at the same mini-market that Dan Lamay had stopped at yesterday morning. Like it had been on the CCTV video they'd pulled from yesterday, it was busy now. Its central location ensured that it always got a lot of traffic. Josie finished up her transaction at the pump and got back into her car, ready to pull away, when something at the front entrance caught her eye.

A card table sat several feet to the left of the double doors. A banner stretched across the front of it, which read: *Support Precious Paws Rescue & Adoption Center.* Atop the table were a number of what looked like pins, brochures, magnets, and pens, all featuring the Precious Paws Rescue logo as well as several boxes of baked goods. A small handwritten sign next to a box of cookies, Rice Krispie treats, and brownies read: "50 Cents per Baked Good or 5 for $2." Beside that was a small metal lockbox which was being manned by a woman in her sixties. A tingle started at the base of Josie's spine. She pulled into one of the parking spots in front of the mini-market and got out.

"Hello," said the woman at the table as Josie approached. "Would you be interested in supporting our local animal shelter? We've got cookies, brownies, Rice Krispie treats."

Josie appraised her. She carried some excess weight around her middle, and her brown hair was shot through with gray and pulled back in a bun. She wore navy slacks and a bright fluorescent-green shirt with the Precious Paws logo on it. A handmade name tag said Terri.

"Terri," Josie said. "What's your last name?"

Terri's smile stiffened on her lined face. "It's Cassavettes. Do I know you?"

"Do you work for Precious Paws?" Josie continued.

"I volunteer. Are you interested in volunteering? You can volunteer at the shelter with the animals, or do community outreach and fundraising like this."

"How long have you been out here selling baked goods?"

"All week."

"Just you?"

"Well, yes, I volunteered this week."

"Did you make the baked goods?"

"No. I pick them up from the shelter each morning and bring them here. Did you want to donate baked goods for our fundraising efforts?"

Josie stared at the boxes. "No," she said.

Terri's face fell.

"I'd like to give you a property evidence receipt."

"I—I don't understand," said Terri.

Josie said, "How much for all of these?"

Josie deposited the boxes of baked goods onto her desk at the station. Mettner stood up from his own desk and reached for a brownie. She smacked his hand. "No one eats these," she said.

"In fact, get me a Sharpie and some tape. I'm marking them and taping the boxes up."

He looked at her as if she'd lost her mind. "I'm serious, Mett. Sharpie. Tape. Now. I might have another lead. Is Gretchen here? Did she bring in Doug Merlos?"

Mettner riffled through his desk drawers until he came up with a marker and some tape. "He wasn't home. She's over there staking out his place. She'll call as soon as she sees him. What's with the baked goods?"

"Precious Paws Rescue has been fundraising outside the mini-market that Dan went to yesterday morning. You didn't see the table there when you went to pull their CCTV footage?"

"Well, yeah," Mettner said. "I saw it. So what?"

"He didn't hit it up that morning though, did he?"

"The Precious Paws table? No. I watched the video, boss. I would have mentioned something like that to the team."

"That's what I thought," Josie said. From her jacket pocket, she produced a flash drive. "But when I saw Dan at the hospital this morning, he told me that he stops at the mini-market every day. Gets something sweet with his coffee but doesn't want his wife to know. The volunteer from Precious Paws, Terri, told me she'd been there all week."

Mettner folded his arms over his chest and looked down at her. "Did the mini-mart manager pull the footage from the rest of the week for you without a warrant?"

Josie grinned. "He sure did."

She plopped into her chair and plugged the drive into her computer. A moment later, Mettner leaned over her shoulder as they watched footage of the Precious Paws table just outside the mini-market doors on Tuesday morning, the day before Dan had gotten disoriented and gone into the bell tower. Josie fast-forwarded through some of the footage until Dan emerged from the doors, a coffee in one hand and a doughnut in the other. The doughnut already had a large bite taken out of it. Terri must have called to him, just as she had to Josie, because he froze, and his head turned toward her table. He took a slow walk toward the table and spent over a minute looking at Terri's selection. Then he thrust a dollar at her and snagged two brownies from the box before shuffling off to his car.

"But he didn't have his incident until the next day," Mettner pointed out.

"Because maybe he stashed the brownies in his car until the next day. He was already eating the doughnut. It's possible he didn't remember that he had those brownies until yesterday morning. I bet if you call his wife and ask her to check in the car, you'll find a brownie still left in there. He bought two."

"I'll go over there and check," Mettner said. "If there's one in there, we'll need to have it tested. But boss, you don't think this is a stretch?"

Josie taped up the boxes and wrote DO NOT EAT in huge letters on each one. "I know. But it's the only thing we didn't account for in Dan's situation. Where are we with the warrant for the hospital? The one for the names of all the patients who came in the day Nysa Somers died?"

Mettner tipped his head back and let out a long breath. "I see where you're going with this. The names came in a half hour ago. Fraley's downstairs in the break room. I'll get him and we'll run these people down, see if any of them stopped at the mini-market that morning or any time this week. If we can connect any of the seizure or heart failure cases to the Precious Paws table, then we can prove that someone—maybe your Doug Merlos—is running around Denton poisoning people. But boss, why give Nysa Somers and Clay Walsh specific instructions: 'time to be a mermaid' and 'time to be a match' but then poison a bunch of people randomly with the drug using Precious Paws?"

Josie's cell phone chirped. It was a text from Gretchen. Doug Merlos had just arrived home to his apartment.

"To throw us off, maybe?" Josie suggested, pocketing her phone. "To break up his pattern? That was Gretchen. Merlos is home. I'm going to drive over there. I don't have all the answers, Mett, I'm just following leads."

"Got it," he replied.

Josie pointed to the pastries she'd confiscated. "I'm giving you custody of these pastries. Call Hummel," she told him. "Get him to drive these out to the lab along with anything you find in Dan's car. I talked to my contact in Greensburg. She said the tests for scopolamine can be done in twenty-four hours in urgent cases."

"Is this an urgent case?"

Josie raised a brow. "In the span of only a few days, we've potentially had a half dozen poisonings."

"But we don't actually know that," Mettner pointed out. "We haven't gotten any lab results back. All we've got is a sticker found at the Somers and Walsh scenes."

"That is true," Josie conceded. "But within the next twenty-four hours we could potentially have proof that the brownies Nysa Somers ate were laced with Devil's Breath or something similar, that both Dan and Clay had it in their bloodstream, and that these pastries I confiscated from Precious Paws also have Devil's Breath or some derivative in them. If I'm right, and someone is poisoning people in this city, I don't want to waste a single second." The sight of Clay Walsh's charred legs flashed through her mind. "It could mean the difference between life and death, Mett. If I'm wrong, then all we've wasted is time—"

"And some of the department's money," he said with a smile and a sideways glance at Chief Chitwood's closed door.

Josie nodded. "Yes," she said. "But I'm not Chief anymore. My job is to solve this case, and that's it." An image of Nysa Somers' parents plodding through the lobby of the Marriott, their grief so heavy it weighed them down, came back to her. "It will be worth it. If I'm right and all these lab reports come back positive for Devil's Breath, or something like it, I want to be ready to go."

"You got it," Mettner said.

"Also—"

"I know, I know. I'll find out everything there is to know about everyone associated with Precious Paws," Mettner filled in. "I'm on it."

# CHAPTER THIRTY-SIX

Doug Merlos lived in an apartment in one of Denton's seedier areas, where a number of the tall, forgotten buildings were condemned, and the ones that were occupied—by storefronts on the bottom and roach-infested apartments on top—always looked on the verge of being condemned. A pawn shop inhabited the first floor of Merlos' building. A glass door to the side of it led to a set of stairs that spit Josie and Gretchen out into a lobby above the pawn shop.

"An elevator!" Gretchen exclaimed. "This has got to be the only building in this part of Denton with an elevator. Let's see if it works."

She punched the button and something behind its doors screeched to life. What felt like an eternity later, the blue doors lurched open, and a cloud of unpleasant odors filtered into the lobby. Josie waved a hand in front of her nose. "You sure you don't want to take the stairs?"

"He lives on the eighth floor," Gretchen said. "We're taking this elevator."

Surprisingly, they arrived on the eighth floor without incident, although Josie swore the odd mixed scent of sewage, cigarettes, weed, and piss clung to her shirt even after they made their way down the hall to Doug Merlos' door. "This is where the Denton University Dean of Students' son lives?"

Gretchen snorted. "Apparently, the campus isn't the only place he got banned from."

Josie knocked on the door. Behind it, a voice called, "Just a minute."

They heard movement inside, footfalls coming toward the door, and then nothing. Gretchen took out her credentials and held them up to the peephole. A muffled "shit" could be heard from the other side of the door.

"Doug Merlos," Josie said loudly. "Denton Police. We just have a few questions for you."

They heard another muttered, "Shit."

Under her breath, Gretchen said, "I am not chasing this guy."

Josie thought of the foot chase they'd had five months earlier during a homicide case they'd worked only a couple of blocks from where they now stood. "We might have to chase him," Josie whispered.

From behind the door, they heard the sounds of rustling and glass clinking.

"You know what we need?" Gretchen said. "A dog. A big dog. Like a German shepherd. He could do the running, no problem. I'm getting too old for this shit."

"You're never too old to take up running," Josie suggested. "You should try it. It's good for you. Releases endorphins. Makes you feel better."

Something inside made a loud thud. They heard a muffled, "Son of a bitch."

"This kid better not be a runner," Gretchen groused. Making her voice louder, she yelled, "Mr. Merlos, please open the door." Then, lowering her voice, she replied to Josie, "You know what else makes you feel better? Therapy. You should try it."

Merlos shouted, "Be right there!"

Josie said, "Guess that means he's not a runner." As the door swung open, Josie got one last mumble out the side of her mouth. "And I'm not going to therapy."

Doug Merlos was not at all what Josie expected, although she hadn't had time to ask Gretchen to show her the suspended driver's license photo. He was short—even shorter than Josie, which put him somewhere between five foot two and five foot four. He had shaggy black hair that hung in hanks around his head. Almost like someone very angry had given him a haircut and quit in the middle of doing it. Close-set dark eyes stared at them over a long nose that hooked at the bottom. A gray sweatsuit hung on him. His skin had the pallor of someone who rarely saw the sun. "What do you want?" he asked.

Gretchen said, "We need to talk to you."

"About what?"

Josie said, "About Robyn Arber, for a start."

"Oh shit," said Merlos. Before they could ask him to come down to the station, he disappeared into the apartment, leaving the door open behind him. Josie put a hand on the butt of her gun and unsnapped her holster.

Gretchen called, "Mr. Merlos, may we come in?"

"Yeah, yeah," came his voice from another room.

With Josie in the lead, hand still at the ready on her gun, they walked through the door. A short, dark hallway led into a square room that might have been a living room at one time but now looked like something from NASA's control center. Josie counted four desks, each with at least two laptops on them. Cords and wires snaked every which way along the floor and up walls and even beneath some closed doors on the opposite side of the room. Two windows were covered with garbage bags, held in place by duct tape. The room was lit by purple LED lights lining the crease where the walls met the ceiling. Josie blinked to adjust her vision. A chemical smell hung in the air, but she couldn't quite place it. Merlos sat in an elaborate, high-backed office chair with headphones attached to one of its arms.

He said, "Does my dad know you're here?"

"No," Josie said.

"Robyn decided to press charges, or whatever?" he asked.

Josie wished she had. "Maybe," she told Merlos. "It depends on what you tell us right now."

Merlos pushed a hand through the front of his hair and his black locks stood up in a wall. Josie waited for them to fall back into his face but they didn't. She couldn't decide if the effect was comical or sinister. Gretchen pulled up a photo of the cracked skull sticker on her phone and showed it to him. "Did you create this?"

Merlos took a long look at it. "It was a failed venture," he said.

"Your venture?" Josie asked.

"Yeah. Are you really here about a sticker?"

"It's your brand, isn't it?" Gretchen said.

"Was," he said. "It was going to be my brand. Like I said, it was a failed venture."

"So you did draw it?" Josie said.

"Yeah, I drew it." He leaned back in the chair, and his right hand slipped down under the seat. Josie's gun was halfway out of its holster when a footrest popped out from under the seat of the chair and Merlos set his feet, clad in blue slides, on top of it. "Hey," he said. "Don't shoot me, lady."

Gretchen told him, "Just keep your hands where we can see them, okay? Your failed venture—what was it?"

"Aw, come on," Merlos said. "If you talked to Robyn, then you know what it was."

"A drug," Josie said. "Is that right?"

"Not just a drug. *The* drug. Something we don't have here. Something we've never had here. People talk about the dark web all the time, but no one actually knows how to use it."

"But you do," Gretchen said.

"Damn right. You wouldn't believe the shit you can get from the dark web."

"You mean the drugs."

"You gonna arrest me if I say drugs?"

"I'm still thinking about it," Josie told him, her hand still on her Glock. "Doug, I think it would be best if you came down to the station with us to talk."

He looked down at his hands clasped in his lap, then around at his monitors. "Nah," he said. "I'd prefer not to."

They couldn't make him. Not at this juncture. They needed a lot more information, and if they wanted to arrest him, a warrant. "Okay," said Gretchen. "We can talk here. But I'd like to read you your rights, if that's okay."

"Sure, whatever."

Gretchen recited his Miranda rights and, once he acknowledged that he understood them, she asked, "Where were you on Sunday night?"

Doug chuckled. He waved his hands in the air, indicating the room around him. "Where do you think?"

"Here?" Gretchen said. "Alone?"

"I'm not much for company, and shocker, but girls don't really dig me that much."

Josie couldn't imagine why. She asked, "Where were you between three and four p.m. on Tuesday?"

Again, he spread his hands and laughed. "Here. Alone. Let me save you some time. Except for this morning when I walked down to the corner store for some smokes, I've been here alone for the last two weeks. Okay? But if you're really into this alibi thing, or whatever it is you're trying to do here, the pawn shop has exterior cameras that show the walkup to the apartments, okay? They get broken into like twice a month. You can ask them for their footage."

"We'll do that," Gretchen said. "Do they have footage of the rear entrance as well?"

Merlos laughed. "You can't get out that way. Dumpster's in front of it."

"That's against the city codes," Gretchen pointed out.

He laughed again. "Does this look like the kind of place that gives two shits about city codes?"

Changing the subject, Josie asked, "You drive?"

"My license is suspended."

"In my experience, that rarely stops people," Josie told him.

"Nah. Don't have a car."

"Borrow one?" Gretchen asked.

"Nope. What do you want to talk about next? Planes I don't fly? Helicopters? How about trains?"

"Names," said Josie.

Merlos smiled. His dark eyes glittered in the purple light. "Okay. Go."

"Nysa Somers."

"She's that swimmer who just died, isn't she? From the college? Yeah, I watch the news. Don't know her. Never knew her. Robyn should have told you I got expelled and banned from campus, so it's pretty unlikely I'll know any of the names associated with the university."

"Clay Walsh," Josie said.

"The firefighter. Also on the news." He giggled, the sound disconcerting. "Are you really cops or are you from the local news station, conducting some freaky poll to see how much viewers are paying attention?"

Josie wondered if he was high. "Brett Pace," she said.

He stabbed the air with an index finger. "Now there's one I don't know. Never heard of him."

"Okay, let's talk about 'the' drug," Gretchen said. "You got it from the dark web?"

Josie added, "Robyn Arber says you told her you learned to make it from the dark web."

"Oh well, yeah, the dose I gave her, I made myself. But as you know, the drug thing didn't turn out the way I hoped."

"Because you got caught?" Gretchen said.

"Well, yeah," he said. "What I was hoping to do with those videos was get my brand out there, show people how much fun they could have with it and then they'd start buying it, but my dad came down so hard on me, it was clear that it wasn't going to work out. I mean, I was lucky to get off with an expulsion. Dude cut me off completely. I'm not even allowed to see my mom or my brother anymore. He didn't appreciate the brilliance of it, you know? Like, he worked his whole life for the university and what's he got? A big house, some shitty IRA, and a mountain of debt? I could have been living large. Start here at the university level, get the drug out there, let people have fun with it, work out the kinks, dosages, and all that, and then take it to the dark web. There's a completely untapped market here in the U.S. People don't know what they're missing."

Josie said, "You said the dose you gave Robyn you made yourself. What about the other doses? There were four videos total."

"Yeah, rad, huh? They were all my shit. My drug. I got some of the real deal from the dark web and then I recreated it."

"What was the real deal?" Gretchen asked. "What are we talking about here, Doug?"

The chair creaked as he leaned forward, extending his hands until his fingers curled over the toes of his slides and tapped the bottom of his shoes. "Devil's Breath." He licked his lips and grinned, as if waiting for some grand reaction from them. It occurred to Josie then why he was telling them all this, even though he was confessing to illegal activities and they'd already read him his rights—he was proud of himself. He wanted to tell someone. He'd probably been waiting for the opportunity to brag about what he'd done. When he didn't get a reaction from Josie and Gretchen, he shook his head and sat back in the chair. "You don't know, but it's a big deal. In Colombia, they give it to people and—"

"We know what it does," Josie said, cutting him off. "If you could get it from the dark web, why did you try making it yourself?"

"Because it's expensive as shit, and you know, we've got some stuff here in the U.S. that isn't even illegal, like scopolamine and jimsonweed, and you can basically make a synthetic of it if you know what you're doing."

Gretchen asked, "How did you know what you were doing?"

He smiled again. "Research, my friend. Research. You can find anything on the web, especially the dark web."

Again, Josie was surprised by his honesty. She wondered briefly if he didn't understand the law or maybe, she thought with a sudden chill, he understood it perfectly. In her mind, she went over what she knew about the Controlled Substances Act in Pennsylvania. Doug had used ingredients that were legal to create his drug. Neither scopolamine nor jimsonweed—or any combination thereof—was on the controlled substances list according to the Crimes Code, as far as Josie knew. The drug trafficking and distribution laws in Pennsylvania applied to very specific controlled substances and usually took into account the severity of those substances as well as the amount in the person's possession. There was a chance that drug charges against Doug would never stick to begin with, and if they did, a good defense attorney could get them dismissed. They would have better luck charging him with reckless endangerment for what he'd done to Robyn Arber, but the district attorney would likely need her testimony to successfully prosecute him, and even then he might end up doing no time at all since reckless endangerment was a misdemeanor.

They were on a slippery legal slope, and in spite of Doug's willingness to confess to what he'd done, Josie wasn't sure it was going to do them any good. Still, she wasn't about to stop him from talking to them, especially since he had already been advised of his rights.

"If you could make it yourself," Josie said, "why buy the real stuff? Why the need to recreate it?"

"'Cause I had to know what it felt like, you know?"

Gretchen said, "You took it?"

He nodded proudly. "Damn right I did."

Josie said, "Doug, we know that Devil's Breath causes amnesia. How did you know what it felt like?"

"I didn't. I had to tape myself. Lock myself in a room and tape myself. Then once I had done that, I started making my own and taking that. Took me a few tries to work out the dosing and all."

Gretchen's tone was skeptical. "You were doing all this on your own? With no help? You could have died."

"Yeah, I know," he said. "That's part of the thrill of creating something, don't you think?"

"I don't know about that," Josie said. "When you gave people the drug, how did you slip it to them?"

"In their drinks. Like a powder. Took me a while to get it to the point where it was totally dissolvable, but I did it."

"You said you stopped giving people the drug after you got in trouble over the Robyn Arber video," Josie continued. "Did you still have some of your knock-off Devil's Breath left?"

"I dumped it," he said. "I had to. That was one of my dad's conditions. He talked to a lawyer who said since my drug wasn't a controlled substance, I would probably get off if the police ever got involved, but still, he thought it was best to just destroy everything. He didn't want anything leading back to me, you know? Well, back to him, really."

"You dumped it?" Gretchen said, her tone disbelieving. "What? Flushed it down the toilet?"

"Yeah. What else was I gonna do with it?"

"How about your stickers?" Josie asked. "What'd you do with them?"

"Threw 'em out. It was a shame, too, 'cause that was one of my best pieces."

# CHAPTER THIRTY-SEVEN

"You think he's telling the truth?" Gretchen asked once they were back at the station.

Josie sat at her desk and looked around. They were the only ones there. The Chief's office door was closed. "About most of it. I'm astounded by how much he confessed."

"He obviously knows that the best we could do is charge him with reckless endangerment, which carries almost no time at all, and that we'd only be able to charge him on the Arber case because that's the only video we've got," Gretchen said.

"Right, and without her testimony, the charges won't stick. Even if we went ahead and arrested him anyway for recklessly endangering Robyn Arber, he'd be out in a few hours."

"You think?" Gretchen said. "Daddy cut him off."

"Because Daddy was worried about his own reputation. If his son got arrested for this, he'd do everything he could to keep it quiet and make it go away as quickly as possible, which means he'd have his son out on bail in a few hours and then he'd be pulling all kinds of strings to get the charges dropped. He'd probably contact Robyn Arber's family to make sure she kept quiet. Then Doug would still be out on the street, and he'd know just how aggressively we're prepared to come after him. It's not going to do us any good to bring him in now, especially with the risk of his dad and a high-powered defense attorney getting involved immediately. I would rather he think we were only there to talk to him today while we keep working the case. He told us a lot, but he's definitely leaving something out."

"Like the part where some of his buddies helped him test the product?" Gretchen said.

"Yeah, exactly that part. Also the part where he might still be selling this shit."

"How?" Gretchen asked. "He's not exactly the most personable guy, and if he's right about not leaving his place, where's he distributing it?"

"Maybe people are coming to him?"

"But if they were, wouldn't we have seen or heard about the sticker on the street already? Like Noah said, there's no shortage of calls to the heavy drug areas. This has never come up before."

"Maybe he's only selling it to a few close friends, then," Josie suggested.

Gretchen waved a flash drive in the air. "In that case, we might have to return to the pawn shop for more footage to see who's been coming and going. For now, let's see what they have for us in terms of alibi."

The pawn shop footage was a lucky break. The place looked cheap and run-down, but they'd sprung for an expensive Rowland Industries security system which stored footage going back months. Josie and Gretchen only needed it going back to Sunday. The owner hadn't asked for a warrant because he didn't want them coming back, if at all possible, as police hanging around tended to make his customers uncomfortable. Once he'd copied the footage they requested to a flash drive, Josie and Gretchen had made their way around the back of the building to find that Doug Merlos had been telling the truth. The single rear exit was blocked by a large, slime-covered dumpster that smelled worse than the city morgue. A fire escape crept up the side of the building, which would have allowed Merlos to leave unseen, except that the drop from the ladder to the ground was such that he would never have been able to reach it if he wanted to return to his apartment via the fire escape.

Josie wheeled her desk around to sit beside Gretchen, and together they reviewed the footage, which confirmed exactly what Doug had told them. Since Sunday morning, he'd only left his apartment once and that had been earlier in the day just before Gretchen showed up and knocked on his door only to find out he wasn't home.

"All right," Josie said. "He's telling the truth about his alibi and we can't disprove it, but it is no coincidence that he created this drug and the stickers. I think we need to find out who he was hanging out with when he was in school last year."

"Call Robyn Arber and ask her if she remembers any of his friends."

"Good idea," Josie said, wheeling her chair back around to her own desk and fishing her cell phone from the pile of paperwork on its surface. Her call to Robyn Arber went to voicemail. Josie left a message, but she was doubtful she'd get a return call.

Gretchen said, "I'll contact Chief Hahlbeck about getting a list of Merlos' classes and the names of people in them."

"Find out if he had a roommate," Josie said.

"I'm sure he did," Gretchen said. "Given his age, he had to have been a freshman last year." She started tapping away at her keyboard.

Both their phones chirped with a text. Josie snatched hers up and studied it. "That's a text from Mett," she said. "He and Hummel found one brownie and one plastic baggie with brownie remnants in Dan's vehicle."

Gretchen kept typing. "Which gets us closer to confirming your theory that the Precious Paws brownies were laced."

"Yeah," Josie said. "Now we just have to wait for results. Hummel's already on his way to the lab with the baked goods I got from the Precious Paws table and what they found in Dan's car today."

Josie typed in a quick response thanking Mettner. It took her a few seconds to realize that Gretchen had stopped typing. When

Josie looked up from her phone, Gretchen was staring at her. "Hey, your shift was over hours ago. Why don't you go home?"

Josie wanted to argue, but she was exhausted. The scope of the case—or cases—kept getting larger with every person they talked to and every lead they followed, and still they had no hard proof that Devil's Breath—or Doug Merlos' synthetic version of it—had actually been used on any of their victims. She made a mental note to call her contact at the state police lab the next day about the food analysis.

"Boss," Gretchen said. "Your eyes are glazing over."

Josie shook herself to attention and laughed. "Sorry. This one is getting to me."

"It's a lot," Gretchen agreed.

Josie finished typing up her reports for the day. She texted Noah before she left to see where he was—still out with Mettner running down leads on the hospital patients and the animal shelter. She was relieved when he followed up with: *Won't be much longer.*

Josie pulled into an empty driveway but her downstairs lights were on. In her mind, she catalogued the people who had a key to her house. If any of them were inside, it stood to reason that their car would also be in the driveway. At the front door, she unsnapped her holster, keeping one hand on the butt of her pistol while she turned the key in the lock as silently as possible. She heard the telltale clickety-clack of Trout's nails on the foyer floor and the huffing sound he made when he got really excited.

Wouldn't he have gone crazy if someone was inside? Had she or Noah left the lights on all day?

She turned the knob and pushed the door so that the latch didn't catch anymore but it still looked closed. Then she drew her Glock, holding the barrel toward the sky. With her foot, she nudged the door open and stepped inside, using one of her legs to keep Trout at bay while she panned the foyer, steps, and living room.

From the kitchen doorway, a male voice sounded. "Hey, Trout. Where are you, boy?"

The dog stopped his excited wiggling, ears pointed, head turned. Josie called, "Who's there?"

FBI agent Drake Nally appeared in the kitchen doorway, a fork in one hand and a plate topped with a slice of cheesecake in the other. "Quinn," he said. "Nice to see you too."

Josie let out a breath and holstered her weapon. "You scared the shit out of me, Drake. I could have shot you. What are you doing here?"

She knelt to give Trout some attention. Once he was satisfied, she walked over to Drake. He stared down at her. He was taller than most men she knew, wiry and rangy, and very serious about his work. He was also very serious about his relationship with Josie's twin sister, Trinity Payne, a famous journalist based in New York City. Drake said, "What? Trin and I can't come to visit? She wanted to get out of the city for a while. She misses you."

"You could have called," Josie said. "Not because you're not welcome, but so I didn't shoot you. Speaking of Trinity, where is she? There's no car out front."

"She went to see Pat, I think," he told her as she studied the cheesecake on his plate, noting that it was still completely intact.

"You think?" Trinity had been kidnapped several months ago, and Josie knew for a fact that there was no way in hell Drake would lose track of her sister.

"No, I'm sure. She went to see Pat. On campus. That's what she said."

Josie was about to ask more questions when he stabbed at the cheesecake with his fork and lifted a bite to his mouth. She reached up and placed two fingers on the stem of the fork before it could reach his mouth.

"Where did you get that?" she asked.

Consternation crossed his features. "What?"

"The cheesecake. Where did you get it?"

"We picked it up at Sandman's. Trinity wanted some. She said it's the best in Denton. We got a whole pie. Expensive as hell, by the way, but she had to have it. You're welcome to have a slice."

"No," Josie said. She took the fork and the plate from him and pushed past him into the kitchen in search of the rest of the cheesecake. Relieved to see his was the only slice missing from it, she picked up the entire container and threw it into the trash bin, then scraped Drake's slice in after it.

"Hey," he protested. "What the hell are you doing? Have you lost your mind?"

"No," Josie said. "Just trust me."

"You're weird," he said. "You got weird since the last time I saw you."

Josie opened the fridge and shuffled some things around until she found a banana cream pie Misty had made and dropped off over the weekend. She put it on the table. "You can eat this."

"Okay, food inspector. You want to tell me why I can't eat the delicious, creamy, really expensive cheesecake that my girlfriend bought?"

Josie took two forks from her silverware drawer and plopped into a chair. "Because I think we've got someone going around the city slipping a very dangerous drug into people's food."

Drake straightened up a little. He took two strides and sat down at the table beside her, accepting the fork she offered him. "A poisoner?"

Josie took the Saran wrap off the banana cream pie and plunged her fork into the center of it, digging out a large forkful and stuffing it into her mouth. She closed her eyes, reveling in the rich, creamy taste of it. Misty really was the best cook she knew. When she opened her eyes, Drake was regarding her with an amused look on his face. "That bad, huh?"

Josie swallowed and went in for another forkful. "I think so."

Drake started on the edge of the pie and worked his way toward the center. "This is really damn good," he noted. "You have any suspects?"

"A college kid," Josie said. "Actually, ex-college kid. And possibly a swim coach. Since you're here, you've worked a lot of different cases, right? Worked with the Behavioral Sciences Unit out of Quantico?"

Around a mouthful of pie, Drake said, "Yeah, well, we call them in sometimes to lend assistance developing profiles of criminals. Speaking of which, I worked a poisoning case before. Pretty big one, too."

"Strictly speaking," Josie said, "I'm not sure this constitutes poisoning."

"Tell me about it."

"We believe that someone is using a drug called Devil's Breath, or a synthetic of it, and putting it into baked goods which the victims then consume. Some appear to be targeted and others appear to be random."

"Devil's Breath like the shit they have in Colombia?" Drake said.

"You know about it?"

"I've heard some tall tales. But listen, this still sounds like a poisoning case to me."

"Tell me about the case you had," Josie prompted.

"Okay," said Drake. "I handled one early on in my time at the New York field office. Someone was hitting salad bars at city fast food restaurants and lacing the dressings with drain cleaner. The SAC asked the BAU for a profile."

"That's awful," Josie said. She used her finger to dislodge a small piece of flaky crust from the edge of the pie and fed it to Trout, who waited eagerly at her feet for any scrap of table food Josie might be willing to share—or drop.

"They did an in-depth profile for a suspect in our particular case and a more generalized one that applied to poisoners. Every case is different, but there are some aspects that are the same or similar across the board a large percentage of the time."

"Like what?" Josie asked.

Drake swallowed another bite of pie and said, "A pretty good percentage of poisoners are female," he said.

"I've got no female suspects," Josie said.

"That's okay. I'm not saying poisoners can't be male—most of the large-scale medical poisoners we see are male—it's just that with poisoning there's a pretty even split between male and female offenders. I've heard some criminal psychologists refer to it as a 'female crime' because it typically takes careful planning, patience, and cunning. Plus, it's not as overtly violent as, say, stabbing or beating someone. That's the difference between male and female offenders—a male is more likely to bludgeon someone to death, whereas a female is more likely to kill someone in a gentler way, if you get what I'm saying."

Josie thought of Nysa Somers drowning and of Clay Walsh nearly burning to death. "The way the murder victim in this case died was not what I'd describe as gentle," Josie said. "And our other victim is clinging to life. His experience was also far from gentle."

"No death is really gentle, is it?" Drake said. "My point is that with poisoning, the offender isn't always right there to see the outcome. That's why to them it doesn't feel as brutal as if they stabbed someone or strangled someone up close. There's a distance there. Plus, the fun for the poisoner is the sense of power and control they get knowing they've wreaked all this havoc but being removed from it. It's about manipulation, not confrontation. I'm talking about serial poisoners, mind you."

Josie pushed the pie away from her and put her fork on the table. "I can see that. What else does the profile say?"

"Poisoners are sneaky, lack empathy. They're emotionally stunted. Almost childlike in the way they think, sometimes. Entitled."

Coach Brett Pace immediately came to mind. "Go on," Josie said.

"There is sometimes a history of trauma or abuse in childhood, but what's more likely is that they were spoiled. Extremely, extremely spoiled."

"Really?" Josie said. "That seems odd."

"It does, but that's what they've found, and yet, poisoners often have feelings of inadequacy, although they hide it well because, again, they're non-confrontational and very cunning. They tend to be extremely immature so, while you or I might want revenge on someone who killed a loved one, for example, they're going to want revenge on someone who did something pretty insignificant to them. There was a case in Idaho where a fifteen-year-old girl dumped a Tide pod in her mother's coffee because the mother banned her from social media for a month."

"My God," Josie said.

"Yeah, and there was a case in Florida where an intern at a web design company was going into the fridge in the company break room and putting rat poison into people's lunches because he didn't feel he was getting enough credit for his ideas."

"That's horrifying."

Drake nodded, lifting more pie onto his fork and taking a bite. After he finished, he said, "We had one in Alabama where a mother-in-law was slowly poisoning her daughter-in-law with arsenic because the daughter-in-law didn't like her cooking. You get the gist here, right?"

Josie gave a dry laugh. "The gist? That if I cut one of these people off in traffic, they'd want to poison me to death? Yeah, I get it."

"Well, it's just that the infraction doesn't match the response. These people think they deserve everything, regardless of their own behavior. They're used to getting everything they want because they've been spoiled. They grow into adults who expect the world to spoil them like their parents did and when it doesn't, they have to get revenge. Then there are people who work in healthcare who poison large numbers of people. Those cases are a little different, but usually we see the same psychological markers: non-confrontational, clever, entitled, spoiled, lacking in empathy, and just absolutely ruthless. Regardless of which column the poisoner falls into, they crave the power they get from doing what they do."

Yet, neither Brett Pace nor Doug Merlos struck Josie as power-hungry, ruthless, or even cunning. Certainly, Brett Pace was manipulative and lacked empathy. Merlos was wanting in the empathy department as well. No one who could do what he had done to Robyn Arber could be empathetic. By his own admission, though, he hadn't taken any of the four videos last year as a type of revenge. In his mind, he was starting some grand enterprise, a "get rich quick" scheme of sorts. *Buy this drug and have fun with your drunk friends* might have been his slogan if he'd gotten things off the ground—if he hadn't gone too far with Robyn. If, a year later, he had slipped Nysa Somers or Clay Walsh his iteration of Devil's Breath and told them to harm or kill themselves, what was the motive? There didn't seem to be a revenge element that Josie could glean. Brett Pace obviously had a cruel streak, but was he callous enough to slip his star swimmer—and his lover—an illicit drug and then convince her to drown herself? Doing so would have ruined his own life as well by exposing their affair. Even if he had, where was the connection to Clay Walsh or the animal rescue? Was the animal rescue even in play? Without lab results from the pastries Josie had confiscated from the charity table or the brownies found in Dan Lamay's car, the connection between the Somers and Walsh cases and the animal rescue was tenuous at best.

Before she and Drake could continue their conversation, Trout jumped up and ran toward the front door. Seconds later, they heard Noah and Trinity. Josie hadn't seen her sister in weeks. She forced thoughts of the case out of her mind and sprinted into the foyer to embrace Trinity.

# CHAPTER THIRTY-EIGHT

The next morning, the sounds of pots and pans clanking downstairs woke Josie a half hour before her alarm went off. Sitting up in bed, she yawned and looked around. Trout was nowhere to be found, which meant whoever was in her kitchen was definitely cooking. The scent of something delicious—pancakes or French toast—wafted up into Josie's bedroom. Noah's side of the bed was cold. A glance at his dresser told her he had already left the house for the day since his wallet, phone, and gun were all missing.

With a sigh, Josie padded downstairs to find her twin sister, Trinity, cooking pancakes. On the floor next to Trout's food bowl was a plate with tiny squares of dough lightly covered in maple syrup. Trout rooted, sniffed, and gobbled, the noises coming from him like those of a percolator. He glanced up when Josie entered the room, and then quickly went back to work, eating even faster this time, like he was afraid she'd take the plate away. Which she did.

"Trin," Josie said. "Are you trying to give my dog diabetes, or what?"

"Oh, hey," said Trinity, turning to Josie. A pair of sweatpants and an NYU T-shirt hung on her lithe frame. She held a spatula in one hand. No make-up. Her long black hair was twisted into a bun at the back of her head. Still, she looked shiny and glamorous, like she'd just stepped off the set of the morning show after doing a piece on cooking for college kids or the perfect sleepover. Trinity always looked like the movie star version of Josie, and Josie wondered if it was the hair and skincare products she used, or if years as co-anchor on a national news show had left some kind of residual celebrity glow on her. Josie patted the back of her own head where her matching black hair was tangled and matted from a night of uneasy sleep. Then her fingers traveled self-consciously to the thin scar along the right side of her face that ran from her ear, down her jawline, to the center of her chin. It was a memento from her traumatic childhood. One Trinity hadn't shared because, although it sounded like something out of a cheesy movie, they'd been separated at birth.

Trinity looked at the half-eaten plate in Josie's hand. "I thought you gave Trout people food."

"Very rarely," Josie said. She shot a look at Trout, who now lay on his bed in the corner of the room, a look of perfect innocence on his little face. She deposited his plate into the sink and moved to the coffeemaker, relieved to find it half-full.

Trinity flipped a pancake in the frying pan in front of her. "You said he was food motivated. I want him to like me."

Josie laughed. "There are dog treats in the pantry. Where are the men?"

"Drake's still in bed. Noah left already."

"Left? For where?" Josie said as she finished preparing her coffee. Taking a seat at the table, she sipped it slowly.

"Work," Trinity said. "That is the only thing either of you do, you know—work."

"That's not true."

Trinity slapped the pancake onto a nearby plate already piled high with pancakes and turned the stove off. She turned to Josie with a hand on her hip. "Really?"

"Yeah, really. We, uh…" she floundered, trying to think of the last time she and Noah had done anything together, besides jogging, that didn't involve work. "Shit."

Trinity grabbed her own mug of coffee from next to the pancakes and sat across from Josie. "Maybe you guys need to make some time for one another."

Josie narrowed her eyes at her sister. "You've been dating Drake for what? Eight or nine months? Suddenly you're an expert? Besides, Noah's the one who's not here right now. He didn't even leave me a note."

Trinity sipped her coffee. "He said to check your phone."

Josie wrestled her cell phone from her pajama pants and keyed in her passcode. A series of text notifications popped up. All from Noah.

*Sorry I left so early.*

Trinity said, "I'm not saying I'm an expert. Far from it. I'm just saying that the past year has taught me that you really need to make time for the people you love, that's all."

*Wanted to get a jump on the day.*

"You two should have—I don't know—like a date night or something."

*Already took Trout for a jog and fed him.*

"You could start this weekend. Maybe today you and I could go get our hair and nails done or something. You could get a new outfit. Something slinky."

*Mett and I are getting a warrant to search Doug Merlos' apartment. Will let you know how it pans out.*

"I know you've got this whole thing about not eating outside food right now, but you know what would be really romantic?"

*Call Denise at the lab and see if she's got anything yet.*

"A picnic," Trinity said. "You make the food—well, actually, probably not you guys. We could ask Misty to prepare something really good, and you could pack it up and have a picnic. I heard that they revamped the outdoor area in the city park. Right near Lover's Cave. They even have tables there now. Wouldn't that be amazing?"

Josie looked up at her sister. She thrust her phone at Trinity so she could see the flurry of texts from Noah. "Romantic?" she said. "Look at these. I didn't even get a standard 'I love you.'"

Trinity pursed her lips as she scrolled through the texts. Then she put the phone down on the table between them as if it was something explosive. "Sometimes in relationships you just get into a rut or a routine that's hard to get out of, and you just forget to really pay attention to one another. Plus, this case you guys are on is a lot of pressure. That's why I'm suggesting—"

Josie held up a hand to stop her in mid-sentence. "I've been here," she complained. "I've been here all week. I've wanted him to come home. I've wanted to see him. But as you can see, he's not here."

Trinity stood up and took her mug to the sink, dumping the rest of its contents and rinsing it under the faucet. "You two have to take a day off sometime. Or even an evening off. A few hours. How about Saturday? Late afternoon, early evening? I'll call Misty. We'll get everything ready and send the two of you off on your date. You'll be forced to reconnect."

Josie rolled her eyes and picked up her phone, looking for Denise Poole's phone number. "Fine. But I'm not getting my hair done. I have to be at work in two hours, and salons aren't even open this early."

Trinity turned back toward her, looking crestfallen. "At least get your nails done. Come on. There's a nail place in South Denton I used to go to when I worked for WYEP. I know the owner. All I have to do is make a call, and she can get the two of us in before you have to be at work. Drake and I won't be in town much longer.

I know you're on a big case. Spend a half hour with me so I can tell you all about my new show!"

Josie punched the call button beneath Denise Poole's name. "Fine," she groused. "Let me make this call and then I'll get ready."

Trinity clapped her hands with delight and hurried out of the room, no doubt to set up the nail appointment.

Denise didn't answer, so Josie left her a voicemail. While Trinity was out of the room, Josie tried Robyn Arber again to see if she could come up with a list of Doug Merlos' friends, but got her voicemail as well.

Making sure that her volume was on in case either woman called back, Josie scarfed down a couple of pancakes and went to get ready to get a manicure with her sister. She was pulling into the stationhouse two hours later with freshly painted pale pink nails when her cell phone rang. Denise Poole's face appeared on her phone screen.

Josie parked her rental car in the municipal lot and answered.

"Quinn," Denise said. "This better be important. You called pretty damn early."

As surly as Denise sounded, Josie knew it was a lot of bluster. They'd helped each other out on a major case five years earlier—one that nearly cost them both their lives—and that was a bond that couldn't be broken.

"I wouldn't call if it wasn't important," Josie replied. "I'm calling about the food samples we sent in."

"Yeah. Hold on, would you?"

Josie heard shuffling and rustling and then Denise came back on the line.

"I've got brownie crumbs from the bottom of a baggie. I've got stomach contents from a twenty-year-old female. Also brownies, by the way. Then I have… let's see… more brownies and brownie crumbs from a vehicle belonging to Daniel Lamay, and a large bag of baked goods from a non-profit called Precious Paws which includes brownies. I'm seeing a theme here. Anyway, the cookies and Rice Krispie treats were negative but guess what all the brownies and brownie residue have in common?"

Josie held her breath.

Denise didn't wait for her to answer. "They all had varying but significant levels of scopolamine and datura stramonium in them."

Josie closed her eyes, relief washing over her. Proof. They had proof. Opening them, she said, "What's datura stramonium?"

"Jimsonweed," said Denise. "In addition to scopolamine, you asked me to look for derivatives of scopolamine or any substances—naturally occurring or man-made—similar to it. That's what I found. You want this report emailed?"

"Yes," Josie breathed. "Please. Denise, I owe you big time."

"No," Denise said. "No you don't."

Josie raced inside, but none of the team were there yet. Chitwood's door remained closed. She was bursting at the seams by the time the team got there—Noah and Mettner returning from having served the warrant on Merlos' residence, and Gretchen, whose shift started late that day. She knocked on the Chief's door and then waited until everyone was seated at their desks in the great room with Amber lingering nearby and the Chief standing before them, arms folded across his chest as usual. "Quinn," he barked. "You look like you're gonna shoot right out of that chair. You go first."

Josie gave them the news, passing around copies of the report she'd received from Denise. After that, she briefed Chitwood on what she'd learned from Robyn Arber the day before. Gretchen recapped their interview with Doug Merlos and noted that she was waiting to hear back from Chief Hahlbeck about Merlos' roommate and other known associates on campus. When she finished, Josie turned to Mettner and Noah. "What about you guys? You were on Merlos this morning, and Mett, you were supposed to track down the patients from the hospital yesterday. Did you get anywhere with that?"

Noah said, "Merlos had a number of powdered substances in his apartment that we could not identify. He refused to tell us what they were, but the bedroom in his apartment looks like a damn high school chem lab."

"Meth?" Gretchen asked.

Noah shook his head. "No, I don't think so. We pushed pretty hard, trying to get him to tell us what he'd been making and when we brought up meth, he said it was beneath him."

Gretchen laughed.

Chitwood said, "We'll find out for sure when the lab results come back in, and then hopefully we can nab that little shit on drug charges. What else did you two get?"

Mettner held up a finger to draw their attention to him. Looking at his phone, he read from his notes. "I tracked down five of the hospital patients yesterday evening, and they were willing to talk to me. I could connect all but one of them to the Precious Paws table outside the mini-market where Dan was last seen before he came to work the other day. All of them stopped at the table and all of them bought—guess what?"

"Brownies," everyone filled in.

Mettner picked up a stack of pages from his desk and handed one to each of them. "In light of that, I thought I'd take a closer look at the animal rescue, as per the boss's suggestion. What you've got in your hands is a list of employees and volunteers. The ones with the asterisks are the people involved in the last couple of weeks of fundraising efforts and community outreach, meaning they set up these tables throughout the city and try to get people to donate or buy baked goods. The names that are circled are volunteers who baked things for the fundraising. I got in touch with their director this morning and she said that basically, anyone on the schedule to make a batch of cookies or brownies or what have you, is instructed to drop their goods off by seven thirty in the morning at the shelter.

Then the volunteers who are actually going out into the community come in before eight thirty and take what they need."

Josie looked at the seven names circled: Lori Guerette, Neil Sidebotham, Mary Lyddy, Samantha Vogelpohl, Jen Rector, Joanne McCallum, and Darlene Skwara.

Chitwood said, "Is there any way to tell who made the brownies?"

Mettner sighed. "Lots of people made brownies, just like lots of people made cookies and Rice Krispie treats as well. It's a city-wide fundraiser. They don't keep track of who makes what. People just drop off as much as they can bake at the shelter, the more, the better."

"What about any way of telling whose baked goods were at the mini-market the day that Dan was there?" Chitwood asked.

Mettner shook his head.

"It doesn't matter," Josie said. "We have proof that some of the brownies from the batch I removed yesterday as well as the brownies that Dan bought earlier in the week had scopolamine and jimsonweed in them. We could have the results from the blood tests from Dan as soon as today."

"Quinn's right," Chitwood said. "One of you should track down the bakers on that list. See what you can come up with."

The phone on Gretchen's desk started ringing. She snatched it up and said, "Palmer here."

"Maybe talk to the director of the rescue again, or go over there and see if they've got cameras that might have caught people dropping things off for the bake sale."

Gretchen hung up the phone and cleared her throat. All heads swiveled in her direction. "Hahlbeck found out the name of Doug Merlos' roommate."

"Yeah," said Noah. "What's the name?"

"Hudson Tinning."

# CHAPTER THIRTY-NINE

I tried to move through my day as if everything were normal, but one word loomed in the back of my mind. Failure. Had I failed? Why hadn't the baked goods I dropped off at the shelter been distributed? Or had people eaten them, but because no one was there to give instructions, they just sat around like a bunch of duds? I thought it would be so fun for the drug to pop up all over the city without any rhyme or reason—people acting bizarrely and doing anything anyone told them to do. Still, there was nothing. Either the police had figured out a lot more than I anticipated and confiscated the brownies, or the dosing had caused other problems. I'd only run into other problems once.

She was only the second name on my list. I had to see her every day for months, and every day for months she nitpicked at every little thing I did, from the way I parked my car to the way I organized things before classes. She was intolerable. Really, not killing her right away showed amazing restraint on my part. The final straw was the day she complained about the way I talked to a student. I was condescending, she said. That was rich, coming from her. I had to do something to shut that bitch up. She wasn't a coffee drinker. I had to come up with something else.

I baked the powder into some cookies. I had to make sure she got the right one, but I made several different kinds, including her favorite. She actually thought I had done it for her. That's how important she thought she was and how self-centered she actually was. She smiled at me so sincerely before she gobbled it down and gave me a patronizing "thank you, that was wonderful" after she wiped the crumbs from her mouth. I waited for the drug to take hold. I had my instructions prepared. But she never reached any state of docility at all. Death still came for her, luckily, so it wasn't a complete waste. It just didn't go off the way I planned. Still, it was deliciously dramatic. Lots of flair, even if it was unintentional. The left side of her body just stopped working. Her mouth drooped. She tried to speak but all that came out was gibberish. She was having a stroke, I realized. It was a rare side effect—extremely rare—but it did happen. For the briefest second, I considered whether she would survive or not. Then I threw caution to the wind and leaned close to her face. "You got what you deserved," I whispered. Then I grinned. I'm not sure if she registered my words or the grin, because at that moment she collapsed, and the screaming started all around us.

I wondered now if scenes like that were popping up all over the city, and I just didn't know it.

# CHAPTER FORTY

Josie paced the great room while they waited for Gretchen to drive over to the campus, find Hudson Tinning, and bring him in for questioning. Mettner had gone off to run down the Precious Paws leads. Noah sat at his own desk, tapping away at his computer. She knew he was preparing a warrant to search Hudson's residence, but every so often he glanced up at her, his eyes moving like two metronomes in time with her movements.

"Son of a bitch," she muttered.

"You know," Noah said, "none of us had any reason to suspect him."

Josie stopped walking and pointed to the map she and Mettner had left on the wall showing the coordinates from the triangulation of Nysa Somers' cell phone. "He lives in Hollister Way too. I looked back over all the notes in the case file. His current roommate can only account for his whereabouts up to one a.m., and Nysa was dropped off at the entrance to Hollister Way at two a.m."

"That's weak, Josie, and you know it." He went back to typing.

"He was in love with her. Maybe even obsessed for all we know. She had rejected him."

Without looking up, Noah said, "Lots of women reject men. Not all of those men poison those women. You followed all the evidence where it went, and here we are."

"Did I?"

The clicking of his keyboard paused. "You're wondering if you could have prevented the fire at Clay Walsh's house or Dan's incident? No. These investigations don't move at warp speed. You know that better than anyone. We're not psychics. We follow the leads. Nothing pointed to Hudson Tinning until now."

"You and Mettner and Gretchen have been running all over this town looking for connections between Nysa Somers and Clay Walsh, between those two and Brett Pace. No one's been trying to connect them to Hudson Tinning."

"We already know he's connected to Nysa Somers. We can go back and try to connect him to Walsh now—and the animal rescue."

"Or we can see if he owns a vehicle and get the GPS coordinates to see if he was at Clay Walsh's house the day and time of the fire."

Noah grinned at her. "As soon as I finish what I'm doing, I'll check for a vehicle registration and get a warrant for that."

An hour later, Hudson Tinning sat at the interview table with an untouched cup of coffee in front of him. He slouched in his chair, shoulders rounded, his blond hair falling across his face. This time he wore a Denton University T-shirt and distressed jeans. Flip-flops completed his surfer look. Josie turned away from the CCTV in the adjoining room and asked Gretchen, "Did he give you any trouble?"

"No, not at all. Noah's over there with Officer Chan executing the search warrant for his residence. Kid didn't even care. As for the car, he doesn't have an active navigation system, so Hummel had to impound it to get the GPS coordinates. Hummel should have the car back here by the time we're done with the kid. Hudson wasn't thrilled about losing his car for a couple of hours, but other than that, he was perfectly willing to come down and talk to us. In fact, I asked for his phone and he gave it to me." Gretchen held up a sleek black Android phone.

Josie's brow furrowed. "Really?"

Gretchen set it back down on the table. "Yeah. But the GPS isn't enabled. There's nothing on it. Nothing useful, anyway. Nothing incriminating and nothing that would lead you to believe that this kid is the kind of garbage human being who would randomly drug people with a potentially fatal substance for fun."

"Calls to and from Nysa? Texts?"

"Nothing recent. The ones that are on here are all about practice times and meeting up for the piece WYEP did on her."

"What about Merlos?" Josie asked.

"Nothing. Merlos isn't even a contact in his phone."

"He could have erased anything even remotely incriminating," Josie pointed out. "He's had plenty of time."

Gretchen slid her reading glasses up her nose and looked at the phone, swiping and scrolling. "I'll tell you what. If he was going to erase something, he should have erased all these messages from his mother. This kid doesn't stand a chance of having a relationship other than with her. Listen to this text: 'I talked to your professors today to let them know you're too distraught to turn in any assignments. They've all agreed to a week's extension.' Heart emoji, smiley face emoji."

"Wow," Josie said. "Way to foster his independence."

"Yeah," said Gretchen with a sigh. "To his credit, he texted back and asked her to stop interfering in his life and that he's perfectly capable of talking to his own professors. There's a shit-ton of calls, too, although mostly from her to him. He called her Sunday night around ten. They talked for forty-nine minutes. Then Monday afternoon for an hour." She put the phone back onto the table. "You ready?"

"Let's go talk to him."

Hudson smiled at Josie when she and Gretchen walked in. Josie took the seat closest to him. Gretchen sat further away, her notebook out in front of her.

"Hey," Hudson said. "Did you find anything out about Nysa? Like what happened to her?"

"That's why we asked you to come down here today, Hudson. I need to advise you of some rights first, okay?"

"Oh, like on TV? Am I under arrest?"

"No," Josie said. "Not at this time, but if we're going to talk, I'd like you to be aware of your rights before we get started. How's that sound?"

"Uh, sure, okay."

Josie read him off his Miranda rights. He bobbed his head in agreement as she spoke. When she finished, she waited a few beats to see if he'd demand to leave or ask for an attorney, but he simply stared at her, waiting.

"Hudson," Josie said, "we asked you to come down here because we were hoping that you could tell us what happened with Nysa."

"Wait, what? I thought you said you were investigating. Why are you asking me?"

"I think you know why we're asking you, Hudson," Josie said. "Nysa was with someone between two a.m. and almost six a.m. on Monday morning. Right before she walked into the pool and drowned herself."

Hudson's eyes widened. He leaned in a fraction with each word Josie spoke, as though he were listening to a riveting story. "Who was it?" he asked.

"You don't know?" Gretchen put in. "Hudson, we don't have time for lies. Nysa is dead and her family wants answers."

"Lies? What do you mean?"

Josie said, "Cut the shit, Hudson. This doe-eyed act isn't going to work on us. Where did you take Nysa Somers on Sunday night? Back to your house? Somewhere else?"

"Take her? I didn't take her anywhere. I didn't even see her. Listen, I didn't want to say anything before, but you should know that Nysa was sleeping with Coach Pace."

"We're aware of that," Gretchen said. "We've already spoken to him."

"What did he say? He was with her that night, wasn't he? Who else would have been with her? If you're looking for who she was with, I'm telling you, it was him."

"How do you know about them?" Josie asked.

He sighed and looked down at the table. "I, uh, saw them once. After practice. In his office. Believe me, Nysa wasn't the first student he slept with. I just didn't think it was anyone's business. I don't think Nysa would want people to know about it."

"That must have been difficult for you," Josie said. "Knowing they were together."

He lowered his gaze. "I wasn't thrilled about it. Nysa deserved better than that jerk."

Gretchen said, "You didn't think this was information that the police needed to know?"

"Detective Palmer is right, Hudson. You lied to me and Detective Mettner when we spoke to you on Monday," Josie said. "How can we believe you now when you say you didn't see Nysa on Sunday night or Monday morning?"

"Doesn't matter," Gretchen said dismissively, addressing the words to Josie. "We'll get the GPS coordinates from his Nissan Versa. We'll be able to tell where he took Nysa from that. Let's move on."

"Wait a minute," Hudson said. "Why do you keep asking me about this? What does it even matter who saw her on Sunday or Monday?"

Josie leaned in closer to him. "Because, Hudson, whoever was with her had a hand in her death. But you already know that, don't you?"

He splayed a large hand over his chest. "Wait, you think *I* did something to her? Like what? I told you already—I saw her Saturday at a party and the next thing I know, one of the assistant coaches is calling me saying she's dead, and I need to come to the campus police station."

"We know what you did to her, Hudson," said Josie. "The same thing your ex-roommate did to Robyn Arber, except you took it way too far."

He sucked in a sharp breath. His entire body stiffened, reminding Josie of prey in the wild, freezing in the hopes that a nearby predator would move on instead of attacking. He managed a choked, "What did you say?"

"Do you remember Robyn Arber, Hudson?" Josie asked.

"No, I mean, yes. I mean, Doug mentioned her. She was the reason he got kicked out of school—"

"She was the reason?" Josie asked, cutting him off, shifting her chair closer to him, deeper into his personal space. "Are you sure about that, Hudson?"

His lips worked but no words came.

Josie said, "You sure it wasn't the drug that you and Doug developed?"

His voice rose an octave. "What?"

It was an assumption on Josie's part. It was entirely possible that Hudson hadn't helped in the development of Doug's version of Devil's Breath, but there was no way in hell he hadn't known anything about it.

"Listen," he pleaded. "I didn't agree with what Doug did to Robyn. That was messed up. But it wasn't my idea, okay? I told him no one would think those videos were funny."

Gretchen said, "So you knew about the drug?"

"Well, yeah, we lived together. He was always doing all this weird shit like some kind of mad scientist, but I wasn't involved in that. That was his thing. I found out about the videos after the fact."

Josie glanced at Gretchen, who gave her a barely perceptible nod. Moving even further into Hudson's personal space, Josie said, "We talked with Doug yesterday, Hudson. He told us everything. Everything but your name. I guess he didn't think we'd be able to figure that out. But the old campus Chief is gone, so no more cover-ups or lost files. The new campus Chief of Police, Chief Hahlbeck, checked for us and found out you were Doug's roommate freshman year. Guess what else she found out?"

He said nothing.

"You didn't get in trouble last year just for having a joint in your swim bag."

A muscle ticked in his jaw.

Josie went on, "You got in trouble because you and Doug had an extremely large amount of your knock-off Devil's Breath in your apartment. Doug got expelled, banned from campus. You got off a little easier, though, just losing your scholarship."

He scratched the side of his nose with an index finger. "Yeah, well, my mom went batshit crazy on the Dean. My dad passed away in my senior year of high school, and that scholarship money really helped. The Dean said affording tuition was the least of our problems since he wanted to kick me out of school. Losing the scholarship was a compromise. I got to stay in school."

"What scholarship was that, Hudson?"

His hand fell back to his lap. He didn't look at her. Didn't speak.

"Hudson?" Josie said.

"The Vandivere Alumni Scholarship," he mumbled.

Josie turned to Gretchen. "Detective Palmer, what was the big scholarship that Nysa Somers received over the summer? The one they were talking about on the news when WYEP did that piece on her?"

Gretchen made a show of flipping pages in her notebook and adjusting her reading glasses. Josie noticed Hudson watching from beneath lowered eyelashes. "Um, the Vandivere Alumni Scholarship," said Gretchen.

"So Nysa got your scholarship," Josie said. "I bet that didn't sit very well with you, now did it?"

"Nysa deserved it," Hudson said.

"You weren't angry about the fact that you lost it and she got it?" Josie said.

Finally, Hudson met her eyes. "No, I wasn't."

Gretchen said, "Hudson, it's really hard to believe you when you have a track record of lying. You lied about not knowing who Nysa might have been with the night before she died. You lied about not knowing whether or not she was seeing anyone. You lied about why you lost your scholarship. You lied about not recognizing Doug's creepy little sticker. At this point, Doug Merlos has more credibility than you. He didn't hold anything back." Gretchen winced. "Even Coach Pace came clean with us."

Here they let the silence stretch on until the ticking of the wall clock became thunderous. Josie had counted ninety-seven ticks when Hudson finally said, "What do you want me to say?"

"We don't want you to say anything," Josie said. "We want you to tell us the truth."

"I am telling you the truth."

"Not about the Devil's Breath," Josie pointed out.

He blew out a long breath. "Fine. You're right. I wasn't completely honest about that, but I didn't help Doug make the drug. All I did was help him test it out, okay?"

"Test it out how?" Josie asked.

"I took it so he could see what happened, if it was for real."

Gretchen said, "Doug gave you Devil's Breath and taped you?"

He looked at her. "Yeah. We wanted to see if it was real. 'Cause Doug said it made people into zombies and you could get them to do whatever you said, and they wouldn't remember anything. So I took it and he taped me and then he did it, and I taped him. Then he got the idea to make his own, like try to start some stupid business or something, and so I took a couple of doses of the Devil's Breath he made—it wasn't real, it was like some combination of an over-the-counter drug and some plant or something—and he taped me while I was on that. It wasn't a big deal since I didn't remember anything, and Doug said it wouldn't stay in my system so I wouldn't run into any problems with drug testing for the swim team. We kept testing it until he had something that did pretty much the exact same thing as the real Devil's Breath. He was obsessed with it."

"What happened to those videos?" Josie asked.

He shrugged. "I don't know. I'm sure he deleted them. We took them on his phone. I mean, that shit fucks you up. Anyway, he started making the videos and then he got in big trouble, and we both got screwed and that was it."

"You never gave the drug to anyone?" Gretchen asked.

"No."

"What about Nysa?" Josie asked.

"What? No. I didn't—you think I gave Nysa Devil's Breath?" He touched his chest. "I don't even have any. We got rid of it. We had to. We couldn't keep it. Doug flushed his down the toilet after shit went down with Robyn. Even if I had some, I wouldn't give it to anyone. Especially Nysa. She was a good person. I would never do that to her. I wouldn't even do it to someone I didn't like, let alone someone I cared about, like Nysa."

"Don't bullshit me, Hudson," Josie said, pushing. "Doug knew how to make this stuff. He'd done it before. He still lives in Denton. It would have been no problem for you to get more of it. Hell, maybe he didn't flush it all down the toilet. Maybe you took some before he could get rid of it all. You dosed Nysa just like Doug did to Robyn and then you put an alert on her phone. You knew damn well that when she read it, she'd likely die."

"What? No, no, no. What are you even talking about? An alert on her phone for what? I didn't do anything. I didn't even see her. I didn't give her anything. I didn't hurt her. I wouldn't. I couldn't."

"But you did, didn't you?" Josie said. "You baked the Devil's Breath into some brownies, and you gave one to Nysa and sent her to the pool to drown. Then you stopped at the house of a decorated firefighter the next day, gave him a brownie, and told him to burn his house down. You used Doug's stickers so the investigation would lead back to him, but you lied about having seen them so we wouldn't suspect you. Then, sometime after Detective Mettner and I interviewed you on Monday, you dumped the rest of the brownies at a charity bake sale so it would all look random."

With each accusation, more and more color left his face. His mouth hung open. It took several seconds of him opening and closing it before he was able to say, "I don't know what the hell you're talking about."

"Where's the rest of the Devil's Breath?" Gretchen said, her voice cool to Josie's hot anger.

"I told you. I don't have any. I got rid of it. That shit already messed up my life enough. I lost my swimming scholarship."

"What about Clay Walsh?" Gretchen asked. "Would you give it to him?"

Confusion creased his brow. "Who's that? I don't know anyone by that name."

A beat of silence passed. Then Josie said, "What about Precious Paws Rescue and Adoption Center? Does that name sound familiar to you?"

The faintest flicker of shock passed over his features. His voice was shaky as he answered, "No. I don't know that place."

# CHAPTER FORTY-ONE

"Another Oscar winner," Gretchen mumbled as they stood in the Chief's office, watching from the window as Hudson walked out onto the sidewalk where Hummel had left his car. "What do you think?"

Josie massaged her temples where a dull ache was turning into a full-bodied throb. "I don't know. I don't know what to think."

Below them, Hudson took out his phone, which Gretchen had returned to him before letting him go. His fingers punched angrily at it and then he pressed it to his ear.

"Three guesses who he's calling," said Gretchen. "You think his mom's going to come down here all 'batshit crazy' and try to clean up the mess he's gotten himself into?"

Pacing back and forth beside his car, Hudson's mouth moved, spittle flying. They couldn't hear his words, but it was obvious he was shouting.

"I hope not," Josie said. "Maybe he's not calling her. Maybe he's calling Doug Merlos? Maybe he doesn't keep Doug as a contact in his phone because he's Hudson's drug dealer? Or maybe after we found the sticker on Monday and showed it to him while we were interviewing him, he removed all evidence of his association with Doug."

"Maybe," Gretchen said. "You think this kid is good for this?"

Hudson continued to pace, phone against his ear, now biting the fingernails of his left hand. Listening. Who was on the other end? "I think he's as good a suspect as Brett Pace or Doug Merlos. He's got no real alibi from one a.m. onward for the night that Nysa was missing. If we could connect him to the Clay Walsh fire, that would go a long way."

Gretchen said, "Hummel should have those coordinates in a report for us within the hour."

"He was definitely lying about not knowing the animal rescue."

"Yeah. I saw that."

Hudson stopped pacing. His mouth moved, more calmly now. One fist hung clenched at his side.

"I think we should follow him," Josie said. "Now he knows exactly what we're after. If he's got any tracks to cover, he's going to do it now."

"Agreed," Gretchen said. "Let's go."

Josie drove, in her rental car. They followed Hudson Tinning through the center of town and toward the campus. But instead of turning onto the road that led to Hollister Way, he kept going. For a few minutes, Josie wondered if he was headed to visit Coach Pace, but then he turned off into a development about a mile before Pace's house. It was a quaint little neighborhood, built by developers twenty-five years earlier, and it attracted mostly working-class homeowners: teachers, tradespeople, nurses, and even some of Denton's patrol officers lived there. They stayed back as far as possible while Hudson weaved his way through the tree-lined streets. It was midday, so there weren't many people out and most of the driveways were empty, including the one Hudson pulled into. The driveway belonged to a bungalow with deep-blue siding and white trim. The tiny yard was well kept and boasted a small flower bed awash with brightly colored flowers. It was cheery and warm. Inviting.

"His mom's place," Josie said. "Can you check?"

Gretchen said, "We don't have a mobile data terminal in here, boss."

"Use your phone," Josie told her. "You can log in to the county property records search site." She rattled off the address as Gretchen put on her reading glasses and started tapping away at her phone. Josie drove around the block once and then parked three houses down but within full view of the house. Hudson stood near the front door, fiddling with his keys.

Gretchen said, "This house was purchased by Bradley and Mary Tinning twenty-five years ago."

"I knew it."

Hudson used one of the keys on his keyring to unlock the door. He disappeared inside the house, closing the door behind him. Josie looked at the dashboard clock, noting the time so she could say for certain how long he was inside.

It turned out not to be very long. He emerged fifteen minutes later carrying a Vera Bradley tote bag. Tossing it into the passenger's seat of his Nissan, he hurried around the front of the car and got in.

"He's in a hurry," Gretchen observed. "How much you want to bet he's got some of Doug Merlos' Devil's Breath in Mom's tote bag there?"

Josie watched Hudson back out of the driveway so fast that the tires squealed. Something in the back of her mind flashed and disappeared, like lightning, trying to illuminate some detail she'd overlooked in the investigation.

"Boss?" Gretchen said.

Josie threw the rental in drive and took off after Hudson, trying to remain inconspicuous but keep up with him. They followed him back out of the development and into town. He skirted the city park and turned north, heading out of Denton proper.

"Where's he going?" Gretchen asked.

"I don't know," said Josie. She kept her eye on Hudson's vehicle as she searched the inner sanctum of her mind for what she was missing. She needed that lightning flash again. Just one more time and she might be able to see what she'd missed.

Gretchen said, "Should we call for backup?"

"No," Josie said. "Not yet. I don't want to spook him. Let's see where he's headed."

Her stomach tightened when he turned onto the road that led to Tiny Tykes. He picked up speed as they went higher up the mountain. They passed Clay Walsh's driveway, now cordoned off with yellow caution tape. It was only after Hudson passed the entrance to the Tiny Tykes parking lot without even slowing down that Josie let out a breath of relief.

"Where does this go?" Gretchen asked.

"It doesn't go anywhere," Josie said. "It's like this for miles and miles. Eventually, we'll cross some highways, a couple of tiny towns, a state park."

Josie hung further and further back so Hudson wouldn't get suspicious. No other vehicles followed them or passed from the other direction. Trees closed in on them from both sides of the road. Occasionally, there was a break where a driveway or a house sat along the side of the road.

"What's that?" Gretchen said, pointing at a blinking red light visible in the distance.

"Railroad crossing," Josie said.

As they drew closer, they saw where the railroad tracks crossed the road. Lines had been painted on either side of them and a railroad crossing signal stood sentry on the right, its red lights blinking steadily, and its arms pointing skyward, ready to lower should a train cross. Josie expected Hudson to fly right through it but instead he slowed. Without using his turn signal, he turned right. Josie slowed, still several car lengths behind him on the road.

"It's a service road," Gretchen said. She had her phone out and her reading glasses on. "Let me see if I can get Google Maps."

"You won't get cell service out here," Josie told her.

"Sure I will. I'll make a mobile hotspot."

"Good luck with that."

Josie crept along the road until they were only a few feet from the crossing, now glad no one was behind her. Just as Gretchen said, there was a small, paved, one-lane road that ran alongside the railroad tracks on the right-hand side. As they drew closer, Josie craned her neck to peer around the trees right at the bend, but Hudson's vehicle wasn't visible.

Gretchen said, "I got it! Here we go. I've got the satellite view. It's a small service road that leads to… that looks like a bridge."

Josie hadn't spent much time north of Denton. Whenever she'd been out here, it was to get somewhere else. She knew the railroad weaved through the mountains, but she wasn't familiar with this particular area. "Let me see," she said, stopping the vehicle just before the turn.

Gretchen turned her phone screen toward Josie. There were no houses. Just trees, the service road, the railroad, and then more trees. Josie said, "The service road drops off where the bridge starts. This dead-ends at the abutment."

"Right," said Gretchen. "You want to wait for him to come out, or you want to see what the hell he's doing on a railroad bridge?"

Josie gunned the engine and took the turn. "From the aerial view that looks like a damn big valley. My guess is he's tossing whatever Devil's Breath he's got left into the abyss."

The rental car barreled down the service road until Hudson's Nissan came into view. Josie slammed on the brakes and then maneuvered her vehicle so that Hudson couldn't drive away without asking her to move it—or crashing into it. Once the gearshift was in park, Josie and Gretchen hopped out and ran toward the bridge abutment. Josie said, "Now we should call for backup."

Gretchen fell a few steps behind Josie as she called dispatch to request a patrol unit for assistance—or a unit from the state police, since they were likely outside Denton city limits. The service road terminated in a waist-high stone wall. Next to it was a small hill of stones leading up to the railroad tracks. Josie still didn't see Hudson anywhere. Heart in her throat, she leaned over the wall and looked down. The effect was dizzying. The drop-off was significant, easily a football field, but beyond that, the sharp V of the valley below was inaccessible by any type of vehicle. A swollen creek ran through it. The Tamanend Creek, Josie remembered, a tributary of the larger Swatara Creek. She didn't see any evidence that Hudson had either jumped or fallen into it.

Gretchen said, "I think I see him!"

Josie looked over to see Gretchen laboring up the small incline, trying to keep her balance on the stones. Josie scrambled up behind her. They reached the tracks, and Josie was relieved to find firmer footing on the ties and off the track ballast.

"There," Gretchen said.

Turning in the direction of the valley, Josie saw Hudson in the middle of the bridge, the bright purples and pinks of the tote bag on his shoulder flashing in the sunlight. "Jesus," Josie said. "What's he doing? If he's got something to dump, he could have thrown it over the wall."

"Let's go," said Gretchen.

Josie went first, staying inside the rails and stepping only on the ties. The bridge ahead was an open spandrel arch bridge. Under other circumstances, it would have been breathtaking. The floor system sat atop steel spandrel columns which were supported by a wide arch rib. The bridge consisted of a single arch connecting two abutments, each one built into the side of a mountain. Hudson Tinning stood in the middle of it. As Josie and Gretchen drew closer, Josie saw that the deck expanded a few feet on either side of the railroad tracks, ballast rocks bleeding into two narrow concrete walkways which were hemmed in by steel parapets. Hudson stood to their right, his waist pressed against the top of the parapet. The tote hung from his shoulder. One hand held it open while the other hand riffled inside. He began to pull out what looked like Saran-wrapped brownies and toss them into the void below.

"Hudson!" Josie shouted, breaking into a jog. "Stop."

Momentarily, he froze, his pale blue eyes widening, panic turning his face ashen. For a split second, Josie thought he might cooperate. Then he turned away from her, slung the tote bag over one shoulder, put both hands on the parapet railing, and climbed over the top of it.

Josie sprinted toward him. Behind her, she heard Gretchen huffing, feet smacking the railroad ties in an effort to catch up. "Hudson, stop!" Josie said. "Please!"

Holding onto the railing, he carefully rearranged himself so that he was facing her, both his feet on the outer edge of the bridge. "Don't come any closer," he yelled. "I'll jump!"

# CHAPTER FORTY-TWO

Josie stopped and threw her hands up in surrender. She was only four or five feet from him, but not close enough to try to catch him if he let go of the railing. "Hudson, please. Come back onto this side of the railing, would you?"

He shook his head. With his palms wrapped around the railing, he levered himself back and forth, his upper body extending out into the air, the tote bag swinging back and forth violently. A small plastic bag, maybe two inches by two inches, fluttered out of the bag's opening and into the valley below. From where Josie stood, it looked like it had white powder in it.

Gretchen drew up behind Josie, and Josie could hear her tapping the screen of her cell phone. Trying to get more help, Josie thought, but without alerting Hudson. Staying in place, Josie kept her hands in the air. "Hudson, look at me. Look at me."

He stopped moving and met her eyes.

"I'm only here to talk, okay? That's it. I just don't want you to get hurt. Why don't you come back over to this side of the railing?"

"No."

"I won't come any closer, I promise. I'll stay right here."

He lifted his chin to indicate Gretchen. "What about her?"

Josie turned to see Gretchen throw up both of her hands. She must have put her phone into her pocket. She said, "I'm not moving either. We'll do this your way, Hudson. Obviously, you're pretty upset. We don't want to upset you further. Like Detective Quinn said, all we want to do is talk. We can do that from right here, but it sure would make us feel a lot better if you were on this side of the railing."

He considered this for a moment. Then he looked over his shoulder, into the chasm. Turning back to them, he squeezed his eyes shut. His knuckles were white. "No, no, no. I have to do this."

Josie said, "Have to do what, Hudson? Jump? Because you don't have to jump. We can work this out."

His eyes snapped open. Angry lines creased his face. "Don't give me that cop bullshit. I watch TV. I know what happens. You tell me everything will be okay, I tell you everything I know. I go back to the station with you, or whatever, and the next thing I know, I'm sitting in jail. No. No way. That's not going to help. The only thing that will stop this is if I jump."

Gretchen said, "No, Hudson, the only thing that will stop this is you. You can stop it. Right now. But you're right. You will go to jail. We can't help that. Nysa is dead. Clay Walsh is barely hanging on and even if he survives, he'll be disabled for the rest of his life from his injuries. That can't go unpunished, Hudson, but you can stop anyone else from getting hurt."

A tear slid down his cheek. He looked from Gretchen to Josie, then to the sky, shaking his head. "You don't think I've tried to stop it? You don't think I've always tried to stop it? I didn't even know—" He broke off and Josie's heart stuttered as he took one hand off the railing to wipe his eye. She couldn't breathe until he gripped the railing once more. "I loved Nysa," he continued. "I know she didn't love me. I know she was never going to be into me, but I loved her. I would never hurt her. I would never hurt anyone. I'm not like that. I'm not like them. But this happened because of me. Things have… happened because of me. If I'm not here anymore, no one else gets hurt."

"You're not like who, Hudson?" Gretchen asked.

The kaleidoscope at the back of Josie's mind shifted, bringing the flash from earlier into better focus. Drake's poisoner profile came back to her. *They're sneaky, lack empathy.*

But Hudson didn't lack empathy. Josie had thought that he was faking it—his concern over how the Somers family was taking Nysa's death, and his assertion that he hadn't agreed with the videos that Doug Merlos had made—but maybe he wasn't a really good actor. Maybe he truly felt empathy.

"I don't want to talk about this," he yelled. "Talking about it won't help. Things have gone too far."

Gretchen responded, "Okay, Hudson, okay. Let's just take a minute, all right? Take a deep breath."

*They're emotionally stunted. Almost childlike in the way they think... extremely immature.*

But Hudson was none of those things. Certainly, he had lied about several items, but when confronted about his lies, he had been very mature in his response. When they'd questioned him about how it felt for him to lose his big scholarship and for Nysa to get it, his response had been that Nysa deserved it. While he hadn't wanted people to know what he'd done to lose the scholarship, clearly in his own mind he took responsibility for it. That wasn't the mark of someone who was emotionally stunted or immature.

Josie locked eyes with him and nodded. "Yes," she said. "Let's just calm down for a second. We didn't come here to upset you, Hudson. Like we told you, we only came to talk, but we can take a break." She took in several exaggerated deep breaths and after three, she saw him mirroring her unconsciously. "That's good," she told him.

*What's more likely is they were spoiled. Extremely, extremely spoiled... entitled.*

There was no doubt Hudson was spoiled. She remembered that Christine Trostle had said that his mother had "thrown a shitfit" when she found out he wasn't going to be included in the WYEP piece. Pace had called him a Momma's boy, and then there were the texts from his mother about having spoken with his professors on his behalf. But Josie couldn't see the sense of entitlement that might form as a result of his mother being so overbearing. Hudson took no pleasure in her machinations. He had even responded to her text message about smoothing the way with his professors by asking her not to talk to them. When Josie had brought up the WYEP piece in their initial interview, he'd said he hadn't even wanted to be in it. He wasn't the one who was entitled.

Josie said, "Hudson, the 'them' that you're not like. Do you mean your parents?"

He levered himself back and forth again. "My dad's dead," he blurted.

"Right," Josie said quickly. "But your mom's not."

He said nothing.

Josie used one hand to motion toward the tote bag on his shoulder. "Your share of the Devil's Breath is in that bag, isn't it?"

His voice went higher. "My share? I never had a share! This was all Doug. I went along with it when it was just him and me testing it out 'cause, I don't know, we were dumb college kids. I never wanted it. I was never going to use it."

Gretchen said, "When we talked to you at the station today, you said, 'Doug flushed his down the toilet.' If you didn't each have a share of it, why did you say that?"

His knees began to tremble. Josie tried to stay focused on talking to him instead of the image of him toppling into the valley below. When he didn't answer, she said, "It wasn't your share, was it, Hudson? It was your mother's."

Again, he squeezed his eyes closed. Still, tears slid down his cheeks.

Josie continued, "Your mother was the one who cleared things up with the Dean—who is Doug's dad—when the fallout from the Robyn Arber video happened. You were going to be kicked out of school completely. Your mom negotiated with the Dean and got you a much lighter punishment. She would have been very involved in the entire thing. She's very involved in every aspect of your life, isn't she, Hudson?"

He opened his eyes, took one of his hands off the rail again to swipe at his tears. "She only does it because she loves me. You have to understand. Her and my grandmother, they—well, when my mom was a little girl, her dad did things to her, you know?"

Gretchen said, "Your grandfather sexually abused your mother?"

He bobbed his head in agreement. "Yeah. My mom didn't tell me till I was older. He did it for years and my grandmother knew but instead of trying to stop him, she overcompensated by giving my mom everything, you know? Everything and anything she wanted."

Josie said, "She spoiled her."

"Well yeah, I guess. Until my grandfather died—this was before I was born—and my grandmother used the life insurance policy to live from. My mom told me that she had to stay close to me no matter what to make sure no one ever hurt me the way that her dad hurt her. So she's always been, like, you know, there. I want her to stop but I feel guilty. I know she loves me and now with my dad gone, I'm all she's got."

"Hudson, I'm glad you're telling us these things," Gretchen tried. "But could you come to this side of the railing? Please? We can keep talking just like this. We stay here, you stay there."

"No," he said, pushing his upper body violently back and forth.

"Okay," Josie said. "Fine, fine. Stay on that side but just keep still. How's that?"

The rocking slowed. Josie counted off a few seconds and tried to restart the conversation. "Your mother was there when you and Doug had to clean out your room to vacate campus, wasn't she?"

He nodded. "She came and took over, did most of the cleaning and packing. Doug was flushing the Devil's Breath, and she told him to stop. She said that she'd take it and dispose of it—that it was a job for a responsible adult, not a boy. He didn't care."

"But she didn't dispose of it, did she?" said Gretchen.

He glanced over his shoulder at the bag which dangled over the valley beneath him. "I thought she did. But then on Monday, you told me Nysa died and you showed me that sticker, and I got really scared. I saw Nysa on Sunday night getting into a car with that shithead, Pace. I was upset. I called my mom. I just wanted to, I don't know, vent. I wanted someone to tell me that I wasn't a total loser because Nysa chose him over me, even after she said she broke up with him. My mom said not to worry about it, that Nysa wasn't worthy of me, and didn't deserve me, and that she'd get what was coming to her."

Josie said, "Did you see your mom later that night? After you talked to her on the phone? After your roommate went to bed?"

"No. I went to sleep after that. I never would have thought that Nysa and my mom—or that my mom would—but, well, people tend to—" He stopped. Again, he glanced behind him, this time with more courage, it seemed. Either he was mentally committing to the jump, or he was just becoming inured to the danger he was in. Josie couldn't say the same. Her heartbeat was all over the place.

"People tend to what?" Josie coaxed.

"My grandfather died of an accidental overdose," he blurted out.

"Overdose of what?" Gretchen asked.

"His heart medication, I think."

"You think your mom had something to do with that?" Josie asked, trying to keep his focus on her and not the drop.

"Or my grandmother. She's dead now, but what I'm saying is that people tend to die around her and around my mom, too."

Josie said, "What people, Hudson?"

His voice was very small when he said, "Like my dad. He died in his sleep. He had a bad cold, a little bit of pneumonia, but it didn't seem like enough to kill him. Then I found out he had been having an affair with a lady where he worked."

"You think your mom did something to him?" Gretchen asked.

"I don't know. She's always been weird and sneaky, you know? Like putting stuff in food if people don't treat her right, or if they say something she doesn't like."

"What kind of stuff?" Josie asked.

"Like spit or laxatives or dirt."

From just behind her, Josie heard Gretchen whisper, "Jesus."

Hudson said, "Right before my dad died, I saw her doing something with his antibiotics. I thought maybe she was switching them with something else, but I couldn't be sure. When I asked her about it, she told me I was crazy. But I don't think I am crazy."

"Who else has died around your mother, Hudson?" Josie asked.

"There was a driving instructor. Her license had expired because my dad used to drive her everywhere and so she decided to take driving lessons because it had been so long, she didn't feel comfortable driving on her own. But he made fun of the way she held the wheel or something. He said she looked like she was clutching her purse on a subway or something like that. Next thing I know, he's dead. Drove himself into a tree. She said he was drunk, but now I don't know. If she had the stuff Doug made—which she would have had by then—she could have made him drive into a tree."

The words were a punch to Josie's solar plexus. She had to work hard to get her own words out. "I took that call," she said. "Right before the floods. He had a six-year-old daughter. It was classified as a DUI until two months later when his tox screens came back negative. His wife asked for another autopsy, but it didn't turn anything up. The medical examiner said he could have had some kind of mini-stroke that wouldn't show up on exam." She was going to ask Hudson if he remembered the man's name, but Josie couldn't recall any other driving instructors in Denton who had driven themselves into trees in recent years.

"Yeah, and my grandmother. She passed right after my dad. Anaphylactic shock. She was allergic to cats except she didn't have a cat. But my mom volunteers for this shelter."

"Precious Paws," said Gretchen.

"Yeah. My mom was always careful about cleaning herself off before she went over there, but what if she didn't? She always resented my grandmother for what my grandfather did."

Josie said, "Your mom baked for the Precious Paws fundraiser this week, didn't she?"

"Yeah."

In her mind, Josie called up the list of bakers Mettner had given her. There wasn't a Tinning on there. Josie would have seized on that immediately. Mrs. Somers had said that Hudson's mother's name was Mary. There had only been a Mary Lyddy on the list. "Does your mother use her married name still?" she asked him.

"No. She uses her maiden name. Lyddy. Mary Kate Lyddy."

Josie said, "Hudson, you've told us a lot of really helpful things, and I don't believe that you did anything wrong. You don't need to jump. Please come back onto this side."

He ignored her, plunging on with his story. "Then there was this teacher where my mom works. Over the summer. My mom hated her because she always criticized everything my mom did with the kids. One day she had a stroke right in summer camp and died."

A rushing started in Josie's ears. With perfect clarity, she envisioned little Bronwyn Walsh's face as she suggested that her grandfather had had a "stork" like one of her teachers had had over the summer. "A stroke," Michelle had corrected. Josie hadn't even considered whether scopolamine could cause a stroke. But it worked on the central nervous system. Or maybe that teacher had been misdiagnosed on autopsy. But none of that mattered right that second. Josie took a step closer to Hudson. He pushed his arms out straight, as if to put some distance between them. Josie froze again. "Hudson," she said, her voice husky. "Does your mom work at Tiny Tykes?"

He looked momentarily confused. "Yeah," he said.

Josie took another step closer to him.

"Stop," he said.

"Hudson," Josie said. "You've done a good thing today by talking to us. I know you don't believe it, but I can tell you that everything really is going to be okay—for you. Not your mother, but for you. It's safe for you to come back onto this side of the bridge. We don't need to take you to the station. We don't need to put you in jail. Give us that bag. You got that from your mother's house, didn't you? It's got the Devil's Breath in it, right?"

"I called her after I left the police station. She wouldn't admit it at first but then she told me that she still had it, and that she'd used it recently. I went to her house and found it in the closet in her bedroom." He made no move to come back over the parapet. "I want her to stop, but she's my mom. She's all I've got."

"I understand," Josie told him. "When I was your age, all I had in the entire world was my grandmother. It's an impossible situation that your mother has put you in, but you did the right thing. So why don't you come back over to this side now? You can go home, to your campus apartment. We're going to investigate all of these allegations, but more importantly, we're going to put together an arrest warrant for your mom. We can stop her."

"No, you can't."

Josie beckoned him toward her. "Yes, Hudson. We can stop her, but first I need you to be safe. Just step back over. Here, I'll help you."

She got closer and extended a hand, only a few inches from his wrist.

He said, "She'll find a way to hurt you, though. Don't you get that? She always does. You won't be safe. You'll think you are, but you won't be. She's sneaky, and she can wait. I told her Nysa shot me down last year, and she waited until now to hurt her. You'll never know when it's coming."

Gretchen said, "Hudson, really, there's not much she can do in prison. I know she seems almost God-like to you because she's your parent, but she's just a woman who's made some very poor choices and hurt a lot of people, and she needs to be held accountable. Help us do that, Hudson. Don't you think that's what Nysa would want? For you to keep doing the right thing by helping us?"

Josie inched closer, hand out, ready to grab, while his eyes stayed on Gretchen.

"If I had done the right thing the first time I thought she hurt someone, like when my dad died, maybe Nysa would still be alive. I'll never forgive myself for that. I can never—" The rest of his words choked off in his throat. His mouth worked to form more words. Finally, he said, "I'm sorry."

Then he let go of the railing.

# CHAPTER FORTY-THREE

Josie lunged forward, her hand seizing his wrist, but his momentum yanked her upper body over the parapet railing. Her other hand shot out, scrabbling for a grip on the railing as her legs whipped up and over the barrier. The railing slipped from her grasp. A blurred collage of foliage, Hudson, and the tote bag whipped past her vision. For one lightning-fast second of complete lucidity, she thought, "This is how I die." Then her body halted abruptly. Gretchen's hands clutched Josie's calf, digging in so hard, Josie felt the muscles spasm. Josie looked up to see Gretchen's face, red with the effort of holding Josie upside down by one leg. Below her, Hudson dangled. Josie's right hand held onto his wrist. It wouldn't have been enough to keep him aloft given the size and weight difference between them but sometime after she grabbed him, his survival instinct kicked in and his free hand came up and clamped over her forearm. They were locked together, dangling over the narrow fissure, and Josie felt like her limbs were being torn from her body.

Through gritted teeth, Gretchen said, "I can't hold on much longer, boss."

Josie had to conserve her energy and every tiny movement for survival. Slowly extending her other hand toward Hudson, she said, "Grab on. You're going to have to climb my body, and fast. It's the only way."

Gretchen said, "No, boss. It won't work! I can't hold onto you."

Hudson released one hand and quickly grabbed Josie's other arm. Above them, Gretchen let out a yelp, and Josie felt Gretchen's grip on her leg slip a little.

Hudson said, "I think I can swing onto the top of the arch. There's room."

"No, Hudson," Josie said. "It's too dangerous."

"Boss," Gretchen said, a sound in her voice that Josie had only heard once or twice before: hysteria. "I can't. I can't hold on."

Josie could feel Gretchen's hands sliding down her calf to her ankle. She leaned over the railing and slipped an arm across Josie's boot where it bent at the ankle, pinning Josie's heel against the parapet railing. She used her other arm to effectively put a chokehold on Josie's leg with the railing as an anchor.

"That's better," Josie told her.

Hudson said, "I promise, I'll try to make it to the arch. It's either that or both of us die. Or maybe if I fall, I'll land in the water."

"You don't know how deep that water is, Hudson. You could still die. I don't know if Gretchen can withstand the motion if you start swinging around. You're an athlete. Can't you just climb up my body?"

Josie lifted her other leg, lining it up with the one Gretchen clung to. Gretchen lifted one elbow in a flapping wing movement and pulled Josie's other foot under her armpit, pinning that one to the parapet railing as well.

Hudson said, "I am an athlete, and I think I can make it. I need one good swing toward the bridge, and I can grab onto one of the columns. I know I can do it."

"You could die," Josie told Hudson.

But they both knew there was no time left. Hudson was the tallest and heaviest of all of them, and he was the one dangling. Josie's arms were going numb, and she could feel tremors beginning in Gretchen's upper body as she tried to hold on. They had seconds.

"Go," she told him. Then she closed her eyes, trying not to focus on his movements, on the merciless tugging on her limbs, on the pain that coursed through her body, on the cool fall breeze caressing her cheek as she swung back and forth through empty air, completely at the mercy of gravity. Strangely, all she could think about was Trinity's stupid picnic idea. In the seconds before Hudson let go, images of herself and Noah at a picnic table in the park, snuggled side by side watching the stars appear in the night sky, flooded her mind. Then the weight pulling her downward was gone, she heard Gretchen cry out, and she thought, *I should have taken more time with Noah.*

Just as her mind accepted the freefall, Gretchen's voice broke through the protective bubble her brain had erected. "Boss, use your abs!"

Her eyes snapped open to see that Gretchen was still holding onto her feet but now one of her hands extended toward Josie's upper body. "Use your abs!" Gretchen repeated. "Can you reach my hand?"

A sit-up was going to save her life, Josie thought. She tightened her abdominal muscles and focused all of her energy on levering her upper body toward Gretchen. Their hands locked, palm to palm, like they were about to have an arm-wrestling match, and then Gretchen pulled. Josie was able to grip the railing with her other hand. With Gretchen's help, she made it back over the railing. The two of them collapsed onto the ground, gasping for breath. Black spots invaded Josie's vision. Her arms and legs felt loose and floppy. As she tried to even out her breathing, all she could concentrate on was the glorious solid feeling of the deck beneath her. Every muscle in her body screamed when she stood, dragging herself back up, both hands on the railing. Leaning her head over, she saw only the unbroken surface of the creek below. She screamed, "Hudson! Hudson!"

No response.

Josie looked down at Gretchen, whose face was crimson and covered in sweat. "Did he fall? Did you see if he fell?"

Gretchen held one of her arms against her chest like a broken thing. "I don't know. I lost sight of him once he let go of you."

"Jesus," Josie said. She leaned over further but saw no sign of him. "Hudson! Hudson!"

She went completely still, and they listened. Nothing.

Josie started to limp away, back toward the service road. "Come on," she said. "We'll be able to see the arch from the wall next to the abutment."

"I think I injured my shoulder," Gretchen said, grimacing.

Josie went to her good side and put a hand under her armpit, helping to lift her. They leaned on one another and lurched up to the rail ties, walking inside the rails again until they were clear of the bridge and could climb down to the access road.

"I'm getting too old for this shit," Gretchen told her.

"Nah," Josie huffed as they made their way down a small embankment of ballast stones. "You saved my life. That means you've still got it."

Gretchen laughed. Once they reached the service road, Josie let go of her and ran to the stone wall. She put her palms on the edge of it and leaned out as far as her upper body would reach without giving herself vertigo. Her eyes searched the creek below and its banks, but found nothing that looked like a body. Then again, if he had fallen all the way to the creek, he might have washed downstream already—too far for her to see. She counted the spandrel columns between the arch and the bridge deck, trying to figure out which one Hudson might have been able to reach.

"Hudson!" she shouted one more time.

"Someone's here," Gretchen said as the sound of wheels over the asphalt reached Josie's ears. "Backup," Gretchen huffed. "Of course they show up now."

Josie panned the creek again when a flash of color caught her eye. Downstream, next to a large boulder, something flapped. Pink and purple. Josie pointed. "It's the bag! The tote bag!"

Gretchen ran over, still holding her arm, and looked. "I see it! Is that him?"

The bag stopped moving, and Josie saw Hudson using his forearms to drag himself onto the bank of the creek. After going only a few feet, his upper body collapsed. His head turned to the side, resting on stones. From where she stood, Josie couldn't see any more movement.

"He survived," Josie said. "But I don't know whether he's going to make it or not. He must be badly injured. We need to get someone down there immediately. We might need the state police—a helicopter, something."

She turned to see two state police officers, Mettner, and Noah, jogging toward them. Josie pushed off the wall and staggered toward Noah, wrapping her arms around his waist the moment she reached him. He gathered her into him. Into her hair, he said, "What the hell is going on?"

Josie looked up into his hazel eyes, dark with concern at the moment. "I'll tell you in the car. Right now, I need to call Misty and then we have to drive over to Tiny Tykes."

# CHAPTER FORTY-FOUR

I knew it was over when my son called from the police station, angry and upset, accusing me of so many things. All of them were true, I told him proudly, unapologetically. But he was always a soft-hearted thing. I should have known he wouldn't appreciate the genius of what I had done. He never knew the feeling of absolute power over someone's life the way I did. He never knew what it felt like to right the wrongs people perpetrated against you. Making people pay was like heroin for my soul.

Hudson had too much of his father in him. I loved him and had done everything in my power to both shield him from the bad things in life and ensure that he had every good thing, but he would never understand me. He would never *see* me. Not really. Just like my father, who had never really seen me. To him, I was just a body to abuse. Just like my mother, who had taught me to be clever and cunning and to kill with impunity, but who had never really seen me. If she had, she wouldn't have let my father do the things he did. She wouldn't have killed him after the fact, when the damage was already done. She would have apologized to me, at the very least. I had hopes early on in my marriage that my husband would be different, but he was a disappointment as well, taking up with his secretary the moment I put a little weight on, got a few wrinkles around my eyes.

Maybe I would never have been properly seen, but at least now, thanks to my sweet, stupid, spineless boy, everyone would know my power. They were already on to me.

I just wasn't going with them. If life as I knew it was going to end, then it was going to be on my terms. Even if I was on the run, I was still the one with power over life and death—and not just my own.

# CHAPTER FORTY-FIVE

Leaving Hudson's rescue in the capable hands of Gretchen, Mettner, and the state police, Josie climbed into the passenger's seat of Noah's Toyota Corolla. As he fired up the engine, she got out her cell phone to dial Misty. Her fingers shook as she stabbed at the green *call* button. After three rings, Misty answered. Josie let out a strangled cry.

Misty said, "You okay?"

"Misty," Josie said. "I don't have time to explain anything. I just need you to go to Tiny Tykes right now. Right this very second and get Harris. Do you understand?"

Misty's voice became high and reedy. "Josie, I don't like this. Is everything okay? Is Harris in danger?"

"I don't think so," Josie said. She hadn't met Mary Lyddy either of the two times she'd been at Tiny Tykes. There was really no reason to think that Lyddy would target Harris. But Josie was about to detain her at the school, and it would be better if Harris wasn't there. That, and Josie had learned the hard way throughout her life and career to always follow her instincts, no matter how crazy they seemed at the time. "Just please go get him, Misty, okay? I'll explain later."

"Okay," Misty said in a small voice. "I'm leaving work now."

Josie hung up. Noah made a left onto the main road and headed back toward Denton. "She's not there," he said.

"What do you mean?" Josie asked.

"Mary Lyddy. Mett and I were tracking down everyone on the baking list, including a Mary Lyddy. We figured out that she was

Hudson's mother because her home is still listed under the names Bradley and Mary Kate Tinning. Mett did some digging in the TLO database and found out her maiden name is Lyddy. I tried calling you, but you didn't answer. I texted you. We figured you were out running down leads, so we went to Lyddy's house first but no one was there. One of her neighbors said she worked at Tiny Tykes. We drove up there but the receptionist said she wasn't there. Left early because she wasn't feeling well."

"Shit," Josie said. "Where would she go?"

"No idea," Noah said. "We were going to start running down people who knew her when the call from dispatch came in from you and Gretchen. What the hell happened out there?"

Josie told him.

His hands twisted on the steering wheel. "Josie," he said.

She had been in a lot of dicey situations. She'd almost died more times than she could count, but today had been the first time she ever truly believed she was going to die. Today was the first time that she had let go and accepted it, waiting to fall. For that, she felt guilty. "You said one of the reasons you loved me was because I always run toward the danger," she blurted out.

Josie's cell phone chirped. A text from Misty. *I've got him. We're going home. Call me ASAP. I'm totally freaked out.*

He was silent for several seconds. Outside the vehicle, tall trees flashed by on either side of them. "I did say that," he muttered. "And it's true, but for the love of God, Josie, I don't want you to die."

"There," Josie said, pointing ahead and to the left. "Tiny Tykes is coming up. See the sign?"

"We're still going there?"

She was glad he didn't try to keep her on the subject of her almost falling to her death.

"Who better to tell us where Mary Lyddy might be than her coworkers?"

He nodded his agreement. Just as he slowed and put his turn signal on, Misty's vehicle pulled out in front of them, turning left and away from them.

Noah parked in a visitor's spot, and they got out and headed for the main building. It was still an hour before dismissal time, so the lobby was empty and silent. From the halls leading to the classrooms, the sounds of children laughing, clapping, singing, and squealing with delight could be faintly heard. Mrs. D sat at the reception desk, typing on the computer. She smiled at them, but as they got closer, her smile faltered. She made a gallant effort to keep it in place. "Can I help you, Ms. Quinn? Misty just left with Harris. She seemed a little distraught, if I'm honest. I hope there's no problem. Is this Harris's father? We don't have him on the list." She stood up, folding her hands over her bosom. Even though they were alone in the lobby, she lowered her voice. "I don't know what kind of custody issues or arrangements you all have, but if there is a dispute, school isn't the place to address it."

Josie glanced at Noah, clocking his look of confusion, then looked back at Mrs. D, trying to muster a smile. "No, no, Mrs. D. We're not here about Harris. Actually, as you may remember, I'm a detective with the city. This is my colleague, Lieutenant Noah Fraley. Lieutenant Fraley and one of our other colleagues were here earlier to talk to one of your teachers, but were told she had left early, sick. However, she didn't make it home. We were wondering if you or anyone else on your staff might know where she might be?"

Mrs. D's eyebrows kinked. "None of our teachers went home sick today. Are you sure?" she looked at Noah. "You came here? Today? Who did you speak with?"

"Your receptionist," he said. "Miss K."

"Oh, well, she was the one who left early," Mrs. D told them. "Right around the time Harris's mom came to get him. Who is the teacher you're looking for?"

Josie's stomach dropped.

Noah said, "Mary Lyddy."

Mrs. D laughed. "Oh, Mary's not a teacher. You talked to her. We call her Miss K. Her full name is Mary Kate Lyddy. When she started working here, we had two Marys on staff so she said to just use her middle name, Kate. Over time it got shortened from Kate to Miss K. But I don't know why she would tell you that she wasn't here. She said that to you? The police? Did she know you were the police?"

Josie looked at Noah. A muscle in his jaw rippled. "Yes, we told her," he said.

Mrs. D wiped a thin sheen of sweat from her forehead. "Oh dear. This is very unusual. I don't know why she would have lied to the police. How strange. Do you mind if I ask why you were looking for her? Has she done something? You know what… maybe we should go into my office."

Noah said something in response, but Josie wasn't listening. She was replaying the incident on the first day of school in which she had snapped at Miss K for suggesting that they sneak out while Harris wasn't paying attention.

Drake's words drifted through her brain. *The infraction doesn't match the response.*

"Shit," Josie said.

Hudson had called his mother, clearly upset, immediately after leaving the interview with Josie and Gretchen. Had he mentioned Josie by name? Or had she asked? Had she put it together that the detective accusing her son of poisoning people was Harris's other caretaker? Miss K had recognized Josie the first day of school. She had known the police were on to her because Noah and Mettner had just been there looking for her. She had lied right to their faces.

"Noah," Josie said. "We have to leave right now."

Noah and Mrs. D stared at her, open-mouthed. Clearly, she had interrupted some conversation between them.

"Noah!" she said, her voice high-pitched. "Now. Now. We have to go now!"

Without waiting for a response, she took his hand and dragged him out to the car. He stopped by the driver's door. "Josie," he said. "Calm down. What the hell is going on?"

"Drive to Misty's house. Now. Please. As fast as you can."

He didn't argue. Instead he went to the trunk and got out his blue emergency beacon light. He threw it onto the roof of his car, the magnet catching instantly, and turned it on. Blue light strobed in every direction. "Let's go," he said.

Josie used one hand to dial Misty on her cell phone and the other to clutch the interior door handle as Noah tore into the central part of the city, weaving in and out of traffic. The call went to voicemail. She tried again. Voicemail. Noah's car screeched to a halt in front of Misty's large Victorian home. Josie jumped out and ran up the driveway. Noah jogged behind her. A peek inside the garage door windows showed nothing but empty space.

"Her car's not here," she yelled to Noah as she raced to the porch. The front door was closed and locked. "They're not here," she said. "Jesus, Noah. They're not here. I don't think they even came home. You heard what Mrs. D said. Lyddy left right around the time that Misty picked Harris up. What if Lyddy asked Misty for a ride? Misty would have no reason to be suspicious of her. What if Lyddy is with them? Oh my God. Harris. I promised him nothing bad would happen to him."

Some rational part of her mind recognized that she was falling fast over the brink of hysteria and yet, she was powerless to stop it. Everything began to spin, only stopping when Noah's hands squeezed her upper arms. "Josie. You need to calm down. Take a breath."

"I can't," she squealed. "I can't. Harris. What did she do with him? Noah, we have to find him."

She wasn't sure if he did it on purpose or not, but his hands gave three gentle squeezes. Just like Harris. Josie looked up into Noah's face.

"You have the Geobit you gave him, remember?" he said.

"Oh my God," she breathed. "Yes, yes. My phone is in the car. Let's go."

As they climbed back into their seats, Noah said, "What is that?"

"What?" Josie said, searching the seat and then the floor for her phone.

"That sound," Noah said. "What is that sound?"

Her hand closed around her phone, which had fallen between her seat and the center console. As she pulled it out, the sound grew louder. Like a tiny car alarm sounding from her phone. "Oh my God," she gasped. Her hands shook so badly she dropped the phone. Noah snatched it from the seat and handed it back to her. "Calm down, Josie," he said. "You need to stay calm."

"Come on," she muttered, swiping at the screen. Finally, the keypad came up. She punched in her passcode, and the screen filled with the notification from Geobit. Harris had pressed the alarm button.

Noah put the car in drive. "Where are they?"

Josie punched the *locate* icon. Immediately, a map appeared with a small blue figure representing Harris, which moved steadily across the lines of the map.

Noah pulled away from Misty's house, the blue light on his roof still flashing. "I'll drive. You tell me where to go."

"Go straight," Josie instructed as they pulled away from the curb. She studied the map and then used two fingers to pinch the map tighter onscreen to zoom out so she could figure out where they were in relation to Harris.

"Left here," she told Noah. "Then right."

She watched the blue figure cruising through the map.

"Can you tell where they're headed?" Noah asked.

"Right. Right, another right."

Her body bumped against the door as Noah made a sharp turn. She zoomed out again. "It looks like they're turning onto that road that leads to Bellewood."

"The rural route?" Noah asked.

"Yeah."

Noah's hand disappeared into his jacket pocket and came up with his own cell phone. He tried looking at his phone and the road—back and forth—while he attempted to punch something into the screen, but the car kept swerving.

"What are you doing?" Josie shouted.

He handed her his phone. "Lyddy's cell phone number is on there. I tried calling her earlier when she wasn't home. Call her." He rattled off the last four digits of the number, and Josie found it in his call log. She punched the *call* icon and set it to speaker so they could both hear, and so she could keep monitoring Harris's location on her own phone.

After three rings, a female voice said, "Hello?" So bright and cheery. Not at all like the kind of person who would try murdering a half dozen people and who would put a four-year-old at risk.

"Miss K," said Josie. "It's Josie Quinn."

"Detective Quinn," she said smoothly. "I'm glad you called. I wanted to talk to you about my son."

Ahead of them, Misty's black Chrysler 300 came into view, still traveling through the residential area at the bottom of the rural route. There were two cars between their vehicle and Misty's. Josie couldn't tell if there was someone in the passenger's seat.

"Your son tried to jump off a bridge today," Josie told her bluntly. "He fell. The last time I saw him, he was still alive but badly injured. Because of you."

Silence.

Josie said, "Did you hear me? He told me everything. It's over, Mary."

"Is it over? My son wasn't upset because of me. He was upset because of you. He called me, nearly crying, and said two female detectives had badgered him and accused him of awful things. I asked him for their names and when he said yours, I instantly recognized it. Surely you don't think I would let what you did to my son go unpunished."

Josie signaled for Noah to try to get closer. He craned his neck to see if there was any way to get safely around the other vehicles. Even with his blue beacon flashing, the other vehicles made no move to pull over.

"I think you've doled out enough punishment. This game you're playing is over." She took a chance that Mary was in the car with Misty and Harris. "Tell Misty to pull over."

More silence. The car directly in front of them slowed to make a right turn. It seemed to move so slowly that for a split second, Josie wondered if the driver had suddenly passed out at the wheel. The tires of Noah's vehicle screeched as he tore around it halfway through the turn.

Mary's voice came over the line, less sunny now. "I most certainly will not tell her to pull over."

Hearing confirmation that Mary was in the car made Josie's stomach churn.

Mary continued, "You don't get to say when the game is over. I do. I say. Misty, see that row of mailboxes ahead?"

"I see them, Miss K," came Misty's voice, sounding much farther away.

"Plow right into them."

"No!" shouted Josie.

But it was too late. Misty's boxy Chrysler swerved violently to the left, crossing the oncoming lane of traffic and crashing directly into a row of mailboxes standing along the shoulder of the road.

Josie's heart stopped briefly and then skittered back into overdrive when they heard Harris's tiny voice. "Mommy, no!"

The car behind Misty stopped.

"Keep right on going, Misty," said Mary.

Misty didn't stop the vehicle. Wooden stakes and dented metal mailboxes crumpled beneath the tires of her car as she pulled back onto the road and continued. Clearly, despite Josie's warnings about not eating food unless she prepared it herself, Misty had taken a brownie from Mary. Either that, or Mary had slipped it to her some other way—perhaps in the bottle of water that Misty always kept in the center console.

Noah leaned on the horn as the driver who had stopped got out of his car. Jerking the wheel, Noah nearly hit him as he went around the parked vehicle in the middle of the road. He sped up, gaining on Misty's car.

"I think you should stop following us now," Mary said. "If you stop now, I won't hurt the boy. I know what it means to have a son."

"Then you shouldn't be asking me to stop," Josie told her. "Tell Misty to pull over immediately."

This time, Mary's voice had a sharp edge. "You're not listening to me, Detective. I don't like it when people don't listen to me. It's rude. You're rude. You need to be taught a lesson. Just like that swimmer who rejected my son, took his scholarship, and slept with the coach. People need to be held accountable for their poor choices."

"Their poor choices as they pertain to you," Josie accused. "You hurt people because you don't like their choices, not because they make poor ones. Nysa Somers did nothing wrong."

Mary laughed. "Nothing wrong? She was a liar. Everyone thought she was so pure and perfect, but she was just a slut who slept her way to a scholarship and a news story. She was not a good person. She was stupid, too. I waited for her near the front of Hollister, and the coach dropped her off in the middle of the night. She was so upset about something he'd said, it was easy to get her into my car. I made sure she got what she deserved."

Josie felt nauseated. "What about Clay Walsh? What did he ever do to you?"

"He wasn't on the pickup list," Mary said. "Just like Harris's grandmother, Cindy, he had a fit over it. Came right around the desk and pushed me out of the way! He put his hands on me. I should have called the police, but Mrs. D didn't want a scene. He should have thought about how he acted before he had his little outburst."

Josie said, "Misty hasn't done anything to you. Tell her to pull over. Stop this now."

"No, she hasn't done anything to me. But you have."

"Harris," Josie tried. "He's only four. He's innocent. You have a son. Tell Misty to pull over and let Harris go at least."

"Do I have a son?" she said. "Is my son still alive? Or did you take him from me when you got him so upset that he thought jumping from a bridge was the only answer?"

"I didn't make him—"

"Misty," said Mary. "Remember what we talked about earlier when you were eating your brownies?"

Misty said, "Sure, Miss K."

"Good. Then it's time to be a bird."

The line went dead.

"Time to be a bird," Noah mumbled to himself. Then, "Good God, Josie. She's going to Red Hawk Lookout."

# CHAPTER FORTY-SIX

Josie's heart did a double tap. "Drive faster," she said.

"Call for backup," he told her.

Josie called dispatch while Noah drove. He didn't need any more directions to get to Red Hawk Lookout. All they had to do was follow Misty out of the residential area until it gave way to the single-lane, winding mountain road that led from Denton to the Alcott County seat of Bellewood. Roughly halfway between the two cities was an overlook, not much more than an extra-wide gravel shoulder on the side of the road at the apex of the mountain. It featured a small ledge that looked out onto a massive valley hundreds of feet below. Only a thigh-high metal barrier stood between visitors and the steep drop-off. A car could drive right through it if it was going fast enough, if it took the curve in the road just right without losing momentum.

Noah finally caught up to Misty's car and immediately started beeping the horn to get her attention. She sped up. Noah tried to pass her on the left, but Mary must have figured out what he was trying to do because a second later, Misty's car swerved into theirs. Metal crunched against metal. Noah pumped his brakes and jerked the wheel to disconnect. Misty drove on. It would be impossible to pass her, get in front of her, and slow or stop her, and Josie knew neither of them wanted to put Harris at risk. Although, she thought with a sinking heart, what Mary had in mind would kill him.

"Do you think she'll go through with it?" Noah asked, practically reading her mind. "Take herself out with those two? Go over a cliff?"

"I don't know," Josie said over a lump in her throat.

"Look!" Noah said. He pointed to the back of Misty's Chrysler, where one of the brake lights had dislodged. A tiny hand punched through the hole and started to wave. "What's he doing?"

"Exactly what I taught him," Josie said. He was so smart. Tears pricked her eyes. "I talked to him about how if a bad person ever tries to take him away in a car, he should try to signal someone from the road by dismantling the taillight and waving to get attention."

"Jesus, did that bitch put him in the trunk?" Noah said, pushing his car to get closer to Misty's.

"I don't think so," Josie said. "He cried out when they hit the mailboxes. I also taught him how to get out of his booster seat and pull down the backseats to get to the trunk. You know, in case of an emergency."

"Well, this is an emergency," Noah agreed. "I can't get around her. I'm not going to be able to stop her."

The road climbed and twisted. Noah kept gaining on Misty and continued to beep frantically. Little Harris pulled his hand inside the car. The lookout came into view.

"Noah!" Josie screamed.

Just as Misty's Chrysler hit the gravel of the overlook, her one remaining brake light blinked on. Still, she was going too fast. The car plunged through the aluminum barrier at the edge of the lookout. Josie braced herself to watch it go over the edge, but instead it teetered there.

Noah pulled up behind it, put his Corolla in park, and got out. Josie followed. The hood of Misty's car tipped precariously downward. They heard Harris scream from inside. Josie ran up to the side of it and put her hands on the trunk, trying to use her weight to counterbalance the car. "Harris!" she hollered. "We're here!"

She looked behind her but didn't see Noah. A few seconds later, he appeared from behind his car carrying a pair of bright orange ratchet straps. "What are you doing?" Josie said. "Help me get him out."

"The car will never stay on balance," Noah said. "We have to try to secure it somehow." His hands worked to unravel and unhook the straps and then connect them into one long strap. He looked around. "We can use my car," he said. "I have to move it closer."

Sweat poured down Josie's face as she held the back of the car in place. She realized they wouldn't be able to get the trunk open to retrieve Harris—not without the keys or Misty or Mary using the trunk release from the front seat. Banging against the trunk lid, Josie hollered, "Harris! Go to the backseat!" He must have heard her because a second later, the car wobbled beneath her hands. She looked up through the back window but didn't see any movement from the front seat. The wheels lifted from the ground as the vehicle continued to see-saw. Josie tried to apply enough pressure to keep it from heading nose-first into the canyon. Noah pulled his car nearly to Josie's back and got out again. Sliding beneath his Corolla, he slipped one end of the ratchet strap over one of his front tie rods. Then he shimmied over beneath the rear of Misty's Chrysler and did the same. Josie felt the strap take on some of the strain of keeping the Chrysler on the cliff.

Jumping up, Noah said, "Let's get Harris first."

Josie went to the back door and swung it open. The car wobbled, but held. Inside, curled into a fetal position in one corner of the backseat was Harris. Josie held out a hand to him. "Come on Harris. Take my hand. I'll get you out."

"What about Mommy?" he asked. "She's being bad. And Miss K. She's being really bad."

Josie looked to the front seat. Miss K's head slumped against the dash. Blood trickled from her hairline down the side of her face. Across from her, Misty sat stock still, hands still on the wheel. Waiting for instructions, Josie thought with a chill.

"Harris," Josie said. "Miss K is a bad person. She gave Mommy a medicine that made her sick and made her do bad things, that's all. I promise."

His lower lip quivered. "Can you make Mommy better?"

"Yes, just take my hand. We have to get you out first."

Tentatively, he scooted across the seat. When he got to the center, the car tipped abruptly toward the front again, throwing him up against the back of Misty's seat. All Josie could see of her friend was the back of her blonde head. Josie looked back toward Noah. His face was red with panic. "It's not going to hold," he said. "I have to try to get in and reverse it, see if that works."

But as he moved toward his own driver's side seat, both cars pitched forward. Afraid that they'd all go over, Josie quickly reached inside, stretching her upper body across the backseat and snatching the waistband of Harris's pants, pulling him swiftly toward her. He took advantage of the momentum and scrambled into her arms. Josie only had a second to squeeze him before putting him down on solid ground. "Go to the road," she told him. "But not into it, do you understand? Wait for me there. If you see a police car, wave your arms in the air and try to get them to pull over."

He nodded and took off running. Josie looked across the roof of the car to see Noah on the other side. "It didn't work," he said. "Her car is going to pull mine right over with it. Her car's heavier than mine."

"Can you reach her?" Josie asked. "Or her door at least?"

She didn't need to specify which "her." They both knew that they were going to try to get Misty out of the car before they tried getting Lyddy out.

Noah's head disappeared for what felt like an eternity but was probably only three seconds. "I think I can, but I need you to try to counterbalance."

"How?" Josie said.

He looked behind them where his vehicle's tires were making incremental marks in the gravel as it was being pulled forward. "Shit. I don't know," he said.

"I'll get into your car and hit reverse and just gun it."

"No," Noah said. "It's too precarious. It won't have enough purchase. I'm too close to the edge. If you try, you'll end up going off the edge with them. Can you get over to this side?"

Gingerly, Josie made her way to the trunk of Misty's car. She stepped over the ratchet strap separating the two vehicles, round to where Noah stood, one hand on Misty's door handle. "She's conscious," he said. "Misty! Misty! I need you to get out of the car."

Josie inched closer to Noah and grabbed onto his arm. He looked back at her. "I'm going to open the door just enough for you to pull her out. If I fling it open or it opens any more than that, both cars are going over, okay?"

"Yes," Josie said.

"Ready?"

Josie nodded.

As though he were performing a delicate operation, Noah slowly pulled on Misty's door handle. He slid the door open until the car began to teeter again ever so slightly. "That's as far as I can get it open," he said.

Josie looked up to see sweat pouring from his brow. She stepped past him and touched Misty's shoulder. "Misty," she said. "Get out of the car."

"Get out of the car," Misty repeated.

Josie stuck her hand out and Misty turned toward it, reaching for it. The car pitched forward again. Josie let out a scream. Noah's forearms were so tensed from holding the door exactly in place that his veins had popped out all over.

"Slowly," Josie told Misty. "Slowly get out of the car."

With infinite slowness, Misty turned her body until both feet were dangling from the open door. One of them was over open air where the cliff dropped off and the other was over the gravel ledge of the lookout. She stuck her hands out and Josie grabbed onto them. "I'm going to count to three," Josie said. "Then I'm going to pull you as hard as I can. I need you to throw yourself at me. Fast."

Misty nodded. Her pupils were huge, Josie noted, but she appeared to be obeying all of Josie's commands.

"Hurry," Noah grunted. "I can't hold onto this much longer."

Josie counted to three and then pulled as hard as she could, falling backward while Misty jumped from the car. She landed on top of Josie. Josie looked past her to see Noah standing on solid ground, one hand still on the doorframe. Then came a noise from inside the car. A primal scream. An animal raging. Through the windows, Josie could see Mary Lyddy's head rear up and her body flail as she tried to reach Noah through the open door.

"Noah, move!" Josie screamed, but it was too late. Noah vanished.

The sound of metal scraping against stone turned Josie's blood to ice. Pushing Misty off her, she scrambled to her feet. Misty's car was completely over the edge, the ratchet strap and Noah's vehicle the only thing keeping it from dropping. Josie looked behind her to see the back wheels of his car lift slightly from the ground. It was going to topple.

Josie reached down and pulled Misty to standing. "Run," she told her friend. "Go to the edge of the road but not into it. Find Harris and wait for the police there."

Misty took off in the same direction as Harris had. Josie inched closer to the cliff edge. "Noah?" she called.

She leaned over, and there he was, hanging by his hands from the open door of Misty's car. The muscles of his face were so tightly clenched, he looked like he was in great pain.

Mary hung half out the door, snarling and trying to reach him. Noah told her, "Stop moving or we're both going to die!"

"Noah," Josie screamed. She looked around, trying to figure out a way to get down to him. There was nothing. "Hold on," she told him. "I'll get a tree branch and extend it to you. You can grab it and I'll pull you up."

"Wait," came his strangled cry. "Josie, please."

Mary's feral howls receded. She had moved back to the other side of the vehicle. Josie could see her trying to push the passenger's side door open.

Josie kept her focus on Noah. "We don't have time," she shouted down to him.

"Please, Josie. Wait. I have to tell you something."

"No!" she screamed at him. "There's no time. I have to get you back up here."

Mary's frantic movements caused Misty's car to swing. On the ledge, Noah's vehicle lost a few inches of traction, slipping quickly, its front wheels sliding nearly over the edge of the cliff. The sudden movement jolted Misty's vehicle, and the door Noah held onto swung jerkily in the air. Involuntary screams ripped from both their throats. Josie felt hot tears on her cheeks.

"I was going to ask you to marry me," Noah yelled.

Josie thought she had heard him wrong. He was dangling from a car about to topple off a cliff, hundreds of feet above the ground, a serial killer only a few feet away from him. Had he lost his mind?

"I had a ring. Trinity helped me pick it out! I was going to propose. I want you to be my wife."

She could see the muscles in his arms bulging, fighting fatigue. "Ask me when I get you back up here!" she told him.

She turned to look for the nearest tree branch strong enough and long enough to get to him. His voice came once more. Two words.

"Would you—"

Then the back of his car lifted completely off the ground and with a moan, tumbled off the cliff.

# CHAPTER FORTY-SEVEN

Josie had no idea how much time passed before her sister arrived at the lookout, but it was dark. Someone had put a blanket over Josie's shoulders and seated her in the rear of an ambulance. She was pretty sure it was Sawyer. Many sets of eyes had stared into her face since Noah went off the cliff, looking at her with both pity and alarm. They asked a lot of questions. She answered none of them. All she could say was, "Noah went over the edge," again and again, as if saying it would help her mind process the horror of it. The reality of it. No, she thought dimly, she'd never accept it.

Arms wrapped around her, and she smelled Trinity's perfume. Trinity started talking. Josie heard some of it. Misty and Harris had been taken to the hospital in another ambulance. Both of them were fine, and it appeared that Misty would recover from her Devil's Breath experience with no lasting effects. Hudson Tinning had been recovered with serious injuries to his back. He would likely need surgery and a lot of physical therapy if he wanted to walk again. He had taken the news of his mother's demise with sadness but also some relief, someone related to Josie.

Josie let the facts wash over her, feeling no solace in the fact that Mary Lyddy had finally been stopped. The cost was too much for Josie to bear.

"…Mettner wanted to come in and talk to you but he's crying, Josie. Gretchen's here. You want to talk to her? No? Okay. Someone's going to drive to Rockview and get your grandmother. Mom and Dad and Pat are on their way…"

"Can I talk to her alone?" said a new voice.

Josie searched her brain until she realized it was Drake.

"Alone?" Trinity said. "She just lost the love of her life. She needs me right now."

"And she'll get you right back. I'm asking for five minutes."

Trinity bristled but then released Josie and exited the ambulance. Josie blinked the world into focus as Drake folded himself into the small area and sat down across from Josie. Everything was too bright.

"I can't leave," Josie said. "I can't leave him down there. I can't go home, but they're going to need this ambulance back."

"I know," Drake said.

"They won't be able to find him tonight. It's too dark. The drop is too far. But I can't leave him here."

"I know," Drake said. "I had an idea. Pat talked to a buddy of his on campus. They've got a small high-def drone with night vision. We can drop it into the canyon, get a look at the wreckage, locate Noah's…"

"Body," Josie choked.

Drake cleared his throat. "Yeah. Locate it. Then Mett and Sawyer and I will hike in through the bottom and carry him back out. Tonight. They can get Lyddy and the vehicles some other time. Chitwood already authorized it."

Josie closed her eyes. New tears spilled down her cheeks. "Thank you," she said.


She pulled the blanket tighter around her shoulders and walked out to the edge where everyone had gathered around Patrick's friend. In his hands, he held what looked like a combination tablet and game controller. On the tablet was a screen that glowed green. On either side of the screen, his fingers worked buttons and arrows. Josie didn't bother watching the screen. She didn't need to see it. Soon enough she'd be in the funeral home burying another man she loved. Thoughts of Hudson Tinning and his fall tore at her insides. She truly believed Hudson had been a victim and yet, why did he get to live and Noah didn't? It wasn't fair. Even as the thought entered her mind, Josie shut it down. Long before she had become a police officer, she had known—viscerally—that life wasn't fair. The bad ones didn't die. They lived and thrived, and if they didn't thrive, they squeaked through while decent people fell. That was how things worked. The job hadn't taught her that. It had just driven it home. Josie's entire personal life had been a study in unfairness. Railing at it—out loud or in her own mind—had never made a damn bit of difference.

She sincerely hoped none of them suggested therapy to her again after this. The first person who said it was getting punched directly in the throat.

Next to her, someone said, "He's not down there."

"That's ridiculous," said another voice. "He has to be."

"I'm telling you, he's not in the wreckage. I see a woman. That's it."

Someone whispered, "Could he be underneath?"

Josie felt sick. For some reason, she thought of their sweet dog, Trout. How long was he going to wait by the door for Noah to come home after this? How many days? Weeks? Would he wait months? He would forever be looking for Noah, and Noah's scent was in every corner of their home. There was no explaining to Trout that his "dad" was never coming back. For once, Josie felt zero guilt for their decision not to have children together.

"It's your drone," Patrick said. "Something's wrong with it."

"There is nothing wrong with this drone."

"Bring it back up," Drake said. "Check it over, make sure it's working properly."

There was a heavy sigh. "Fine."

Just when the whine of the drone came into range, the guy said, "Wait a minute. Hold on. What's this? Look at this."

Josie looked over to see Patrick, her parents, Drake, Trinity, Gretchen, Mettner, Chitwood, and even her grandmother, Lisette, leaning on her walker, crowd over the screen. The kid said, "Hey, give me some space!"

"What is that?" Mettner asked.

"Holy shit, it's an outcropping," Drake said. "Get closer. Can you tell if he's still alive or not?"

Every process in her body seemed to stop suddenly. Her breath. The movement of blood through her veins. The churning in her stomach. The pounding in her head. She dared not hope.

"No, not from this picture."

Patrick said, "Can you maybe land the drone on him? See if he moves?"

"I guess so."

Josie forced air into her lungs. Then she started walking away. She couldn't bear to lose Noah twice in one night.

She had taken three steps when a cheer went up from the group. "Holy shit!" her father said. "Josie! Josie! He's alive!"

Josie fell to her knees. Soft hands touched her back. Then her mother gathered her into her arms. "He's alive," Shannon whispered into Josie's hair. "He's alive."

Drake said, "Pat, you got any rock-climbing friends up at school?"

# CHAPTER FORTY-EIGHT

It was daylight by the time a crew made up of first responders, the fire company, and rock-climbing college students managed to get Noah off the rocky outcropping he'd caught himself on as the two vehicles fell. He'd taken a page out of Hudson Tinning's book and gotten lucky. The way the vehicles had tumbled, they hadn't crushed him, and he'd been able to grab onto a small ledge just as he started to fall, before his body gained momentum. He was badly scraped up, bruised, concussed, and suffering from a few minor fractures, but he was alive. At the hospital, Josie waited for the doctors to give her the okay to see him.

She went directly to his bed and climbed in beside him, pressing herself against him. With a sharp intake of breath, he maneuvered one arm around her and tried to pull her closer. She wanted to ask if she was hurting him, but she didn't care. He was there. He was alive. She found a patch of hospital gown on his chest and wept into it until she fell asleep.

A woman's voice woke her a few hours later. "Honey, you can't be in this bed with this man. He—"

Chitwood's voice boomed over the top of hers. "You leave that woman right where she is, you hear me?"

"Hear you? The whole damn hospital can hear you. Who do you think you are?"

"I'm the Chief of Police and those are my detectives."

"Well, I'm a nurse and that is my patient. Now if you'll excuse me—"

"No. I won't. You let them be. You can come back in… two hours and do all the checking you want. You got that?"

Josie heard indistinct mumbling and then footsteps receding. She blinked her eyes open to see a hazy Chitwood leaning over Noah's other side. There was some whispering. Noah saying a quiet thank you. Then Chitwood said, "No time like the present, son," and disappeared.

Josie reached up and wiped at her swollen eyes, blinking again until she regained her focus. She looked at Noah's face, unable to keep the smile from her own. She buried her nose in his chest again and inhaled. Then she said, "What was that about?"

Noah shifted gingerly, lifting his arm out from behind her back. "There's something I need to finish," he said. "I had this whole plan. Everyone was helping. Your sister, Drake, your parents, Pat, the Chief, Gretchen, Mett. They all covered for me while I put this together. I was going to take you out to the park, under the stars…"

"So that's what all that was about," Josie whispered.

"Plans are stupid," Noah said. "I should have just asked."

He nudged her gently. She lifted her head again and came face to face with a tiny box holding a huge engagement ring.

"Anyway, you may remember that I was trying to ask you, before I almost died, if you would be my wife. Josie Quinn, will you marry me?"

Josie grinned. She reached one hand up and touched his cheek, shimmied upward and kissed him softly on the mouth. Then she looked into his eyes. One word came to mind.

Home.

"Yes, Noah Fraley," she said. "I'll marry you."

# CHAPTER FORTY-NINE

Josie woke to the sun streaming through tall, arched windows, their heavy drapes left open. She opened her eyes and searched the ornately decorated room that looked as if it was about a hundred years old, save for modern conveniences like a television and forced air heat. The walls were a pale gold and the molding a dark heavy walnut that matched the huge bed cradling her body. It took a few seconds for her to remember where she was—where they were. Beside her, Noah slept soundly, his face slack, his breathing even. She turned on her side and traced his jaw with one finger. The diamond in her engagement ring sparkled in the sunlight. A prism effect caused dozens of tiny dots of light to twinkle above their heads.

It had been a month since Noah's fall. A month since they got engaged. Because Noah's elaborate plans to propose had been foiled, and because the Mary Lyddy case had traumatized them both in ways that Josie was still trying to process, their friends and family had purchased a weekend getaway for the two of them at a large, stately resort in the mountains of West Denton. It was called Harper's Peak. It used to be a large estate that had been converted into a resort. The views from just about any place on the property were breathtaking, especially now that the colorful fall foliage was in full effect.

But Josie and Noah had spent most of their time in their room. In bed. Noah was still nursing several injuries, but it hadn't stopped them from enjoying one another. For once, Josie didn't care what was happening at work or anywhere outside their room. All she cared about was being able to touch Noah and listen to him breathe.

With a contented sigh, she dropped her head onto his shoulder and rested her hand on his chest. Under her palm, his heart tapped out a steady rhythm. She closed her eyes, wishing they could hold onto this time forever. She hated that the weekend had to end. There would be more cases. More death. More people like Mary Lyddy who would have to be stopped somehow. Thoughts of the path of destruction Mary Lyddy had carved out of her life crowded Josie's mind, and she pushed them away. She didn't want to think about Mary Lyddy ever again, and now that the woman was dead, there was no need. There would be no trial, no need to testify against her, although the case would have been solid, especially considering that both blood samples from Dan Lamay and Clay Walsh had come back positive for Doug Merlos' synthetic Devil's Breath. The only small bit of good news to come out of all the tragedy that Mary had brought down onto the city was that Clay Walsh had survived. He would be hospitalized for months, Josie had heard, but one day he would return home to his daughter and granddaughters, and his reputation as a city hero would remain intact.

"Hey," Noah said, drawing her from her thoughts. "Stop that."

Josie lifted her head and looked into his hazel eyes. "Stop what?"

He gathered her into his arms, planting a kiss on her lips. "Thinking about things that aren't this."

"This?" she prodded as his hands slid beneath the covers and stroked the bare skin of her back.

"Us," he said. "Right now. We'll be back in the real world soon enough."

Josie laughed softly. "I know. I don't want to go back. I want to stay here forever."

He kissed her again. Josie felt an electrifying heat building between their warm bodies. "We can come back, you know," he whispered in her ear. "We could get married here."

"We should," Josie agreed before Noah's touch blotted out all conscious thought.

# A LETTER FROM LISA

Thank you so much for choosing to read *Breathe Your Last*. As always, it is a pleasure and a privilege to bring you this latest installment in the trials and tribulations of Josie and her team. If you're reading this, it means you didn't throw your e-reader or book across the room when Noah went off the cliff, and that you kept reading to get to the good stuff. For that, I am grateful! If you enjoyed the book and want to keep up to date with all my latest releases, just sign up at the following link. Your email address will never be shared, and you can unsubscribe at any time.

*www.bookouture.com/lisa-regan*

With each book, I have to take creative liberties with many things for purposes of plot and pacing. There is simply no other way to keep things moving along. Real investigations are often plodding and can take weeks or months or even years to complete. Since you're here for entertainment, I do my best to cut out the boring stuff and bring just the drama! I do a lot of research with each book, and I speak with a lot of different kinds of experts. Any mistakes, errors, or tweaks are entirely my own.

I absolutely love hearing from readers. You can get in touch with me through any of the social media outlets below, including my website and Goodreads page. Also, if you are up for it, I'd really appreciate it if you'd leave a review and perhaps recommend *Breathe Your Last* to other readers. Reviews and word-of-mouth recommendations go a long way in helping readers discover my books for the first time. As always, thank you so much for your support and your enthusiasm for this series. It means the world to me. I can't wait to hear from you, and I hope to see you next time!

Thanks,
Lisa Regan

 LisaReganCrimeAuthor

 @LisalRegan

 www.lisaregan.com

# ACKNOWLEDGMENTS

Lovely, amazing, devoted readers, you are simply the best! I cannot believe how your passion for this series grows with each and every book. It is truly a privilege to write these stories for you. I am so grateful for your enthusiasm and loyalty that I find it difficult to express it in words. Saying thank you doesn't seem like enough, but I'll keep saying it anyway. Thank you!

Thank you, as always, to my husband, Fred, who goes hours and sometimes days without my attention while I'm "in the book" and is somehow still my biggest supporter. I think you are now prepared to write your own book, my love, titled: *The Care and Feeding of the Author.* Thank you to my daughter, Morgan, for all your patience, good humor, and for giving up mom time so I can do this author thing. Thank you to my first readers: Dana Mason, Katie Mettner, Nancy S. Thompson, Maureen Downey, and Torese Hummel. Thank you to Cindy Doty. Thank you to my Entrada readers. Thank you to Matty Dalrymple and Jane Kelly for helping keep me focused and for being ready on a daily basis to help me with even the smallest writing issue. You ladies are a Godsend! Thank you to my grandmothers: Helen Conlen and Marilyn House; my parents: William Regan, Donna House, Joyce Regan, Rusty House and Julie House; my brothers and sisters-in-law: Sean and Cassie House, Kevin and Christine Brock and Andy Brock; as well as my lovely sisters: Ava McKittrick and Melissia McKittrick. Thank you as well to all of the usual suspects for your unwavering support and for always spreading the word—Debbie Tralies, Jean and Dennis Regan, Melisa Wolfson, Tracy Dauphin, Laura Aiello,

Ann Bresnan, Karen Powell, Amy and Starkey Quinn, Claire Pacell, Jeanne Cassidy, the Regans, the Conlens, the Houses, the McDowells, the Kays, the Funks, the Bowmans, and the Bottingers! I'd also like to thank all the fabulous bloggers and reviewers who read the first nine Josie Quinn books or who have picked up the series somewhere in the middle. I really appreciate your continued enthusiasm and passion for the series!

Thank you so very much to Sgt. Jason Jay for always being there at a second's notice to answer all of my crazy law enforcement questions without ever getting tired of me! I am so incredibly grateful for you. Thank you to Lee Lofland for putting me in touch with any expert I needed to help with research for this book. Thank you to Kevin Brock and Michelle Mordan for so patiently and thoroughly answering each and every one of my very detailed questions about EMTs, paramedics, and life-saving procedures. Thank you to Elizabeth Trostle for answering my many college swimming questions at all hours of the day and night, and for teaching me the word natatorium! Thank you as well to Geoff Symon for helping me work out the drowning scenario!

Thank you to Jenny Geras, Kathryn Taussig, Noelle Holten, Kim Nash, and the entire team at Bookouture for making this endeavor so smooth, so exciting and so damn much fun. Last but never, ever least, thank you to the incomparable Jessie Botterill for holding my hand during the writing of this entire book; for shuffling the schedule around so many times; and for talking me down whenever I went into a panic! I could not ever write a book without you now, and I would not want to! You are the most brilliant and patient editor in the world and also one of the most fabulous human beings I have the privilege to know!

Made in the USA
Coppell, TX
06 August 2021

60077397R00174